WHITTAKER'S WIFE

Why Lavinia Whittaker's husband, a millionaire, only left her a part share in a Rhodesian ranch was a mystery, for she had brought
him both companionship and glamour.

The partnership in the ranch is a strange
one. It is worked by Joe Latham, a shrewd,
intelligent settler, much liked by the neigh-
ouring ranchers. For Lavinia however, the
estate is merely a resort, a means to amuse
her friends at annual houseparties; inevit-
ably bitter animosities develop between
her and the Lathams. Then, ostensibly to
indulge her craving for danger, she organ-
ises a lion hunt—an especially perilous one
since the animals are hungry and desperate
after a long drought. But the apparent
motive is not the only one: Lavinia sees a
chance to recover some of the fortune
Jordan Whittaker withheld from her in his
will, and to do it by means of another
woman's husband—creatures who are as
much her natural prey as is big game. Fears
and hatreds accumulate and reach explosive
point as the hunting party brings a wounded
and murderous lion to bay.

HARRY BLOOM

Whittaker's Wife

COLLINS
ST JAMES'S PLACE, LONDON
1962

© Harry Bloom, 1962
Printed in Great Britain
Collins Clear-Type Press
London and Glasgow

To my wife Beryl, with love

" —————— and motives like
Stowaways
Are found too late."

W. H. Auden

BOOK ONE

I

I HURRIED to the hotel where we had agreed to meet, expecting to find him waiting and impatient to go. There were still six hours of driving ahead of us, nearly half of it bush-bashing the last twenty-five miles of meandering sand track from the main road to Malinda.

But there was a message for me at the hotel—" Gene: busy with auditors. This is taking longer than expected. Wait for me. Meantime—welcome home and hope you had a good trip. Dad." Unconsciously I turned the paper over, expecting to find something on the back. The message was so normal, even cheerful, and for my father it was almost effusive. It made me wonder if I had not read too much into my mother's letter, had not built up exaggerated ideas about the situation at home. I crumpled the note and tossed it away, then went out to the veranda, sat down and ordered a beer.

It was warm here, for I had left winter in Johannesburg. The air was full of birds, and from a nearby courtyard came the scent of blossoms and a hum of bees. I could see out over the town square; it looked curiously vivid and clear with mountain sunlight giving sharp definition to the buildings and intense blackness to the shadows. In the distance, a molten purple, were the Vumba Mountains, with motionless cloud over the country beyond. I had forgotten the feeling of this slow incandescence in the lungs during the time I spent in Johannesburg. Here in Rhodesia the air was warm and scented, and the familiar feel of it stirred up old responses and eased me a little out of my fears.

I waited on the veranda of the hotel, letting the time slip by and trying not to think too much. It was pleasant to feel my anxiety dissipate, to bask in an old mood and not look forward or back. My father would come eventually, and that would be enough time to hear the news.

It was late afternoon when I saw our battered yellow jeep come clattering along the street. It seemed to have aged badly since I saw it last. The window was cracked, there were numerous unrepaired bashes, a sweat of mud and oil covered the wheels, and it rode lop-sided, with the high, bulking ill-fitting tent giving it a spidery look. I went down to the pavement and waited for it to draw into the kerb.

" Sorry," my father said, reaching out to open the door. " Hope you found some way to pass the time." He seemed quite cheerful.

" I sat," I told him.

" Anyway, climb in." He looked at his watch. " We'll stop at the Bell to-night and crack the rest to-morrow." He was wearing his town suit and a clean white shirt that looked ill at ease against that deep sunburn. The jacket fitted badly on the shoulders and pinched under the arms. I knew he would shed it soon. His tie was already loosened and ready to be tugged off any moment. He revved the engine casually, causing the bonnet and a loose mud-guard to shudder.

" Climb in," he repeated, yawning and stretching his arms. " I want to make the Bell before sunset. I haven't booked."

I tossed my canvas hold-all into the back, at the same time noticing the groceries, cattle feed, fertiliser, and paper packets of cement he had bought in town; then settled into the hard seat. As we drove off I asked, " Was there something wrong with the accounts ? "

" No," he said. " What makes you ask ? "

" Taking so long. I thought something must be wrong."

" No. We checked and double checked everything—just to make sure."

" Is Christie coming out for the meetings ? "

" Yes—but I'll have to let him know the dates. He's drawn up a balance sheet and trading account—all duly audited. There'll be no arguments this time."

" Oh, yes, there will. She'll say you bribed Christie."

He smiled, then paid attention to the driving. His mood puzzled me. He seemed a little tired, but at the same time relaxed : yet withdrawn, as if keeping a brittle impatience just under the surface. I kept glancing at him without actually turning to face him. He was squinting through the dirty windshield, concentrating on getting out of the late afternoon traffic, the sun making a mottled pattern on his face. I was struck once again by his handsome looks. It was strange, he was my father, but whenever I saw him after an absence this was the first thing I noticed. Perhaps it was because he really was handsome—not just pleasant looking or good looking—but handsome in the way that made people turn round and remark on it. With the sun on him he looked darker than ever. He was so deeply tanned that he would have looked swarthy but for his intense grey eyes that somehow lightened his whole complexion. He had a beautifully shaped head that gave him great dignity, stiff crinkled black hair only beginning to speck with silver, and what I once heard described as "an actor's face"—lean, masculine, rather too well cut and a little immobile. Unlike the jeep, he hadn't aged a day since I saw him last. But that was another remarkable thing about him. Not even bilharzia could eat away his youthful appearance, and in both face and figure he looked much younger than a man in his mid-forties.

" When's *she* coming out ? " I asked.

" Monday week."

" A big crowd this time ? "

" About twenty."

" Twenty ? It will look like the Normandy landing."

" Yes, complete with Big Berthas. There's a pro-hunter coming out this trip. Fellow named Forsythe—heard of him ? "

" Don't think so. Who else ? "

" Kiki Pape, and Hoffman, of course. The Forster girls and

that golf man, Stanton. All the old regulars in fact. And a lot of new ones—among them some Americans or Canadians. Tourists, she said. So get busy on your statistics."

" How did you get the names ? "

" She sent out a list allocating the rooms."

We stopped to fill up at a petrol station ; when we moved off again he started asking me the usual questions about Medical School. I mentioned the swimming tour, and he said he was sorry I had passed it up, adding, " If you came back because of *that*, it was unnecessary. I've got everything under control." We discussed family matters—my young sister Peggy was staying with friends in Salisbury, my mother had gone to Dale to spend a few days with our neighbours the Seckers. Everything was fine at home. He had even managed to get a good price for some cattle he had expected to sacrifice on a poor market. I wanted to mention my mother's letter but it was obvious that there couldn't have been any change in the situation, or he would have told me. I began to think that I must have been wildly wrong imagining that there was some ominous crisis developing at Malinda.

But we stopped for a traffic light and, glancing down, I noticed his foot bobbing irritably on the pedal. And at the exact instant the light changed, he slammed down the lever and we catapulted dangerously through the intersection. Now I slewed round to look at him properly. He was out of the sun now, and the iodine colour in the corners of his eyes and the tight white lines that showed just under the skin around his mouth, told me a different story.

" Why has mother gone to the Seckers ? " I asked.

" She felt like a rest," he told me.

" Why ? Hasn't she been well ? "

" No, she's fine. Just felt like a rest. A change."

I began to give it my own meaning now. It was most unusual for her to leave the ranch unattended, merely to visit friends. She must have gone to the Seckers only because she was in a bad state of nerves or worry.

" Who's looking after the ranch ? " I asked.

" The ranch won't run away," he said irritably.

" You mean there's been nobody in charge for four days ? "

I could see him tense, before blurting out, " Is this a court-martial ? "

" Sorry," I said, feeling a sudden despair at this unexpected reaction. " I was worried about her, that's all."

He drove on for a few moments, then said calmly again, " She's all right. There's nothing to worry about. Everything's fine at home. Everything——"

" Are *you* all right ? " I asked sympathetically. " I mean—has it been hitting you up lately ? "

I thought he would continue to stare ahead and give some vague reply. But he turned to me and smiled. " Of course I'm all right. Perfect." And he playfully punched my arm.

It was impossible to pin anything down. In spite of the look in his eyes and the signs of irritability, he did seem in good spirits. But it was impossible to tell if he was well or ill under the skin, if mother was distracted with worry or just taking a holiday, if Malinda was carrying on as usual, or had been sold up under us. I just couldn't believe him, or anything about him, good or bad.

I tried to get on to a painless subject. " So she plans to get in some hunting this season ? " I asked.

" There won't be any hunting."

" But what about this Big White Simba Slayer she's bringing out ? "

" He'll have to play quoits on the veranda with the others. There are no animals to hunt. The drought has cleaned them out. And what the drought hasn't chased away, the wild dogs have. They're here again."

Of course, the drought. I had forgotten that. My mother had mentioned it in her letter. It had seemed to depress her abnormally—"sitting in the Retreat we can almost *hear* the drought like a storm raging outside," she had written, and I could understand that tense, oppressive feeling. Drought was a time of terror in the bush. The herds broke up and scattered, all wild life was in a panic and all nature out of balance.

Hunting in times like this was either a waste of time or too unpredictable to be pleasant.

"It's been a bad drought," my father said.

We drove on with those words ringing in my ears. The way he spoke had made them sound calamitous, and somehow they filled me with an anxious premonition about this bumping, clattering, jeep ride. What was I riding into?

We were in the outskirts of the town and he began driving in a ragged slapdash fashion, fretting to pass everything ahead of him, coming right up to the tail of the vehicle in front and hardly waiting for the road to clear before pulling out and darting away. When we reached the open road he pulled the hand throttle right out and we hurtled along at the jeep's maximum speed, bouncing and slithering on the crude road, roaring down straight patches, screeching around bends. The tent flapped as if in a hurricane and each separate part of the jeep set up its own din of clattering, slamming and shrieking. Conversation was impossible, and I sat through the maniac drive clutching the sides to avoid being thrown out.

After a few miles he stopped and we both got out. He rummaged among the things in the back and pulled out two bush shirts and two pairs of khaki pants, clean but terribly creased, and we changed into them at the roadside. I folded my blazer and slacks and packed them neatly on top of the box of groceries, but he just bundled up his suit and stuffed it irritably down behind the seat. We rode on and came to a good tarred road that ran through an agricultural development area. The country looked richly beautiful, with field lucerne in blazing blue blossom and deep-green tea bushes laid out in rows like trees on a toy farm. I started to remark on it, but I saw him sitting stiffly upright, gripping the wheel fiercely and staring straight ahead. His eyes were wide open and peering intensely, but he saw nothing of the road. He had the blind stare of one looking at his thoughts, not at objects in front of him. I saw it was hopeless trying to get through, so I sank back and let the countryside lurch past. I felt uneasy now, and for some peculiar reason I found that I was afraid to look at him. I knew his mood, but I had never seen him like this before. This was an inner hysteria. His tension communicated to me and for miles we went in bristling, pent-up antagonism, as if we had quarrelled violently.

Once he spoke. " You were a damn' fool to come home," he said in a harsh voice. " I didn't need you. You should have gone on that swimming tour."

" There'll be more tours."

" You were a fool, I tell you. I don't need you here. You shouldn't have taken notice of the women. They panic about nothing."

He seemed to be referring to something he imagined my mother had written me, but I couldn't understand what he meant by "the women." I thought he believed that Peggy had also written me about the ranch, and I wanted to ask what he meant. But I saw him glaring with feverish eyes through the windshield, shut off. It was puzzling, tantalising, like a fragment of a nightmare revealed by somebody babbling in his sleep.

Night fell as we were nearing the Bell Hotel. We were in a mountain pass taking the long, winding descent into the river valley, and darkness came down obliterating the whole countryside. We came round the shoulder of a mountain and saw the lights of the hotel, far out and far below, weak and twinkling, like the lights of a distant flotilla. Only then did sanity return to his driving. He eased up and we waltzed downhill, watching the lights rise and fall and change position according to the angle and course of the road, but growing ever more firmly embedded in the vast black velvet of the valley.

We came out of the mountain pass on to a flat road and a few minutes later plopped down on to the concrete floor of a bridge spanning the river near the hotel. Immediately the clatter and roar died out, the engine purred sweetly, and we glided gently between the steel girders to a rhythmic lilt of tyres. Just before we reached the other side he slumped back in his seat.

" Christ, I could do with a drink," he said.

I saw him smile to himself, and as I watched him he turned and smiled at me. I felt as if we had come to the end of a long tunnel.

As we climbed the curved driveway into the hotel, we heard Sibelius' Second Symphony come swelling out into the night, and we knew that Jimmy Cameron, the hotel owner, was at home. We found him in his office sitting in a leather arm-chair next to the radiogram, and he greeted us without turning it down. The room looked more like a den than an office. It was full of fishing and hunting paraphernalia, books on big game, botany, birds and entomology, stacks of gramophone records, shelves of silver cups. A whole zoo of stuffed heads glared glass-eyed down from the walls. The only objects to justify the sign "Office" on the door were a small desk holding a cash box and hotel register, and a board of room keys hanging on the wall under a case of butterflies.

" Una ! " Jimmy called out, turning a record catalogue face downwards on the arm of the chair. " G-guess who the wind's blown in."

From next door we heard Una's voice, but not what she said. It came through the hatch that joined the office and the bar, adding a husky contralto sound to the music. Una was Jimmy's wife.

" J-Joe and G-Gene Latham," Jimmy yelled out.

" Hell ! " we heard through the hatch.

" What's the trouble ? " I asked.

" P-packed out," Jimmy said, turning his long sad face in our direction, and bringing his peculiar cardboard-thin ears veering into focus on us. The sleeves of a blue cardigan were knotted at his neck so that the garment hung down his back. He wore shapeless brown corduroy pants and yellow rawhide boots. He looked tired, with the same taut vellum of fatigue stretched over his features that you could occasionally detect in my father. He too knew the scourge of tropical illness.

" P-packed out. The Old Hi-Hi-Hibernians are having their

annual fling to-night and a bunch of them are sleeping over. And a party of coppermining bods are d-due in later."

" Oh, just put a couple of beds down on the veranda," my father suggested. Jimmy had done that before when the place was full.

" D-don't like it, you know," Jimmy said, getting out of the chair. " M-mucks up the atmosphere." But he went outside and soon we heard him talking on the veranda to a bedroom boy, telling him in Fanagalo to go fetch two sleep things quick and fix it up there-there quick-quick, and fetch blanket stuff and whatchamacall and fig-fig-figalo nice-nice-quick. He came back dusting his hands and sat in the arm-chair again.

" B-been to Umtali ? " he asked.

" U-huh."

" Any sign of rain ? "

" Not a sausage. Plenty dust and muck, though."

" Tobacco and maize crops have had it," Jimmy said.

" I see that the notable, quotable, glamorous, amorous Mrs. Lavinia Whittaker is coming out for another bundu jazz-festival." I swung round to see Una at the door, her cheeks wobbling, her cigarette waggling, her dress rippling along her shoulders as she stood shaking a drink in a silver mixer.

" Correct," my father said. " We've been to Umtali to buy her a red carpet."

" How can you stand this hullabaloo every year ? "

" Don't mind it at all. Gives us a chance to see the fauna of the cities."

Incredibly he was in a good mood again. I could hardly believe that this was the morose fanatic I had sat next to for two hours in the jeep. I looked at him, mentally shrugged my shoulders and gave up trying to understand.

" Anyway, how do you know ? " my father asked.

" We know everything in this joint. Kind of bush tom-tom network. Beats me why you don't blow up that ghastly Big House of hers. That would put a stop to it."

Una finished shaking the drink and placed the mixer on the shelf of the hatch. She gave a shrill whistle and the barman's hand appeared and took it away. " Joe, what's going on down at Malinda ? " she asked. " I've been hearing rumours."

" What rumours ? "

" Oh—all kinds. What's going on between you and this Millionaire's Row call-girl you've picked for a partner ? "

" I didn't pick her—I inherited her."

" Well, you've got her. What's the difference ? What's going on down there ? " I noticed that Una looked at my father queerly while she spoke.

" Nothing's going on. Nothing new, if that's what you mean."

" Oh, come off it."

" We're having a dispute. A financial dispute," my father said, just too starchily. " That's all. Nothing to get excited about."

" Oh, you make me sick."

She actually was disgusted. She picked up a magazine and angrily flipped through the pages, then tossed it across the room.

" All right, all right," my father said. " If you must know she wants everything settled this time. Finally. The position has become impossible and she's not prepared to let it drag on another day."

" It was impossible from the start."

" Maybe, but that's what she says. So I've been in Umtali getting the accounts audited, so she can't come any of her stunts. In other words, we're all set for the last round."

" I d-don't get it," Jimmy said, reaching out and turning down the radiogram. " You k-keep having these settling jamborees every year come Michaelmas and n-nothing ever gets settled."

" How can it get settled when she says Joe's cheating her ? " Una snapped at him. " Use your head—if you had a partner and every time you showed him figures he yelled, ' Fraud ! Thief ! These figures are bogus—you've been housing guests in huts in the bushes and sticking to the proceeds ; you're

stealing the linen and cutlery and flogging it to an Indian '—
how far would *you* get with him ? "

" Then why d-don't they cut across the whole damn' thing
and t-take her to law ? " Jimmy asked in a bright voice.

" What ? And see her go into the witness-box and lie the
paint off the furniture ? " Una asked bitterly. " Watch her
wheedle and ogle the judge and dab crocodile tears from those
big baby-doll eyes ? And expect him to believe *them*, simple
country bumpkins, rather than *her*, the celebrated Mrs. Lavinia
Whittaker ? That smooth snake-charmer. Not a chance.
They'd be nuts to go to law."

" Just a suggestion," Jimmy said unruffled, and turning up
the music again.

" What's happening, Joe ? " Una asked intensely. She swung
round and snapped at Jimmy, " For God's sake Cameron, shut
off that racket." When Jimmy turned the music down she
repeated, " What's happening at Malinda ? The district is
buzzing with rumours."

" Then you know everything. If you believe rumours."

" Joe—— ? " she said, bunching her fists and glowering at
him like a prize fighter. " If you give me one more crack like
that, I'll let you have it, so help me."

" I've told you the position. We're going to settle the
argument once and for all. That's all I can tell you," my father
said, all prickly again.

Una fixed him with a long disbelieving look, then glanced
down at her watch. " I've got to take over from the barman
now," she said. " Come next door and I'll give you a drink.
I'd like to have a few words with you."

" About ? " my father asked suspiciously.

" Oh—things. I'll give you a drink and we can chat, then
you can go to our bedroom and clean up."

As we followed her out of the office Jimmy turned up the
music, celebrating our exit with a loud brass fanfare. On the
veranda Una said, " Got news for you. Your boy-friend's
coming out."

" Boy-friend ? "

" Yes, Conrad Webber."

My father stopped walking. " When ? "

" Next week. He's slipping over into Portuguese East to slaughter some elephant, then going on a week later for a court case in Livingstone. He wrote us for accommodation."

My father was thoughtful.

" Give him any message ? " Una asked.

" Mmm . . ." My father considered for a moment, then said, " No, I don't think so. Just my regards."

We followed her into the bar. She dismissed the barman and took his place behind the counter.

But she didn't start the conversation. Something was on her mind, and she poured the drinks with a frown on her face and darting quick flickering looks at each of us. She slid the drinks over then turned round and started pushing the bottles into a straight line on the shelf, poking at them with stiff finicky fingers, meantime staring at us in the mirror and screwing up her eyes to avoid the smoke drifting up from her dangling cigarette.

Suddenly she swung round. " Joe, is it true that you're getting out of Rhodesia ? "

" *What ?* "

" That's what I've heard—that you're doing a flit."

" If anybody says that again bring him to me. I'll knock his teeth down his throat."

" Look, Joe," Una said sympathetically, " I don't want to upset you, but I think you should know what's going on. An awful lot of clap-trap gets biffed about in this joint. For the most part I hardly listen. I don't get involved. But there's been a lot of this and I thought you should know."

" Well, I'm not clearing out. Somebody's jumping to conclusions."

" Well, that's what they're saying. Do you want to know what else ? "

" Go on."

" You're in trouble."

" Trouble ? *What* trouble ? "

" I don't know. All I've heard is that you're in trouble, or heading for trouble, or trouble's heading for you."

" Who told you this ? " my father asked, putting down his glass. It rattled as it touched the counter.

" It's going the rounds. I heard it first a couple of weeks ago from one of the tobacco boys. He was sounding off in here."

" What's his name ? "

" Dicky Cooper."

" Oh, *that* idiot."

" Okay, let's forget Dicky," Una said. " Last week a fellow named Jefferies was in here—I think you know him. Sort of hunched-up and Portuguese looking. Used to be foreman at Kotanga."

" I know him. Go on."

" Well, he'd just returned from Johannesburg where he'd seen the Rain Queen herself. Yep—in answer to an ad. She's been advertising for a man to run Malinda—honest, sober, hard-working and *single*. All the old guff. So Jefferies applied, and that's how he met her. What she told him is that the partnership is breaking up and that you're clearing out to save your neck. You're in some kind of a jam and she's giving you a chance to get out before the police . . ."

" The *what* ? "

" Yes, that's what she says. Now you know who's spreading the dirt about you. But I wouldn't take it too seriously. You know these boys, how they like to . . . chew . . ."

She stopped. My father was slowly swirling the liquor in his glass, not hearing a word.

" I know how you feel, Joe. It's a bloody shame when people start this kind of chatter behind your back. But I thought I ought to tell you."

She watched him for a moment, then turned round and in her embarrassment started jabbing the bottles all out of line again.

" Sorry."

" That's all right," my father said dully.

A few moments later he slid off the seat and paid for the

drinks, saying, " I don't know about any trouble. It's a lie. A bloody lie."

" I believe you," Una said, meaning it.

While we were cleaning up and changing our clothes in the Camerons' bedroom, I asked him, " What trouble *is* this ? Do you know anything about it ? "

He said, " Haven't the vaguest."

" You're not worried about it, are you ? "

" No—of course not."

" Why don't we tackle Jefferies and find out exactly what it's all about ? " I suggested.

" Waste of time. There's nothing, I tell you."

" Why don't . . ."

But the blind had rattled down again, and we were in different worlds. We went on in silence, and when I accidently dropped the soap into the tin dish, the clatter sounded deafening. Once, while I was washing at the handbasin and he sat combing his hair at the dressing-table, our eyes met in the two mirrors. His eyes looked as if he was going to tell me something, and I waited, watching him at the odd angle made by the two mirrors. But the message was stillborn. He looked away and went on carefully grooming his dark hair, running his hand behind the comb and pressing down the stiff, crinkled waves.

I tried to think about this estrangement between us. It was not so much silence that kept us apart now, but an antagonism that seemed to arise by a kind of spontaneous combustion when our two personalities were at a certain temperature and distance. Was it my fault?—my lack of sympathy or warmth, my youthful brashness, my habit of always probing, digging, backing him against the wall with questions. Or was it his ? His way of shutting himself in, cutting off communication. Did his attitude breed mine, or vice versa ? Why was it that certain subjects always brought the silence down—questions to him about my mother, any reference to the dispute that was not just idle comment or the kind of sarcastic jokes I had got into the habit of making—anything near to the bone ; and talk of

Lavinia of a certain kind—anything intimate, anything that sneered at or belittled her. Yet he didn't resent the kind of childish threats we were always making—pushing her off a cliff, putting cattle dip in her coffee—or Una's hatred of Lavinia. It was difficult to pin down. But I knew instinctively, though sometimes a moment too late, what I had to avoid saying.

When we finished changing we went into the dining-room for supper and sat near the Old Hibernians who were making a great noise around a horseshoe table. I tried a dozen times to talk to him without asking questions but found that unless I did so there was nothing to say. I said, " Jimmy and Una are as crazy as ever," and he agreed. I said, " We did the trip from Umtali in good time," and he said, " The jeep's beginning to pack up now." And the topic petered out there. He said, " A pity you dropped out of that swimming tour." And now it was my turn to clam up, for I had no inclination to discuss it. " Fancy Lavinia and Jefferies getting together," I said. " I wonder what they see in each other." And that was the wrong thing, and there followed five minutes of eating. I was glad when the Old Hibernians started the after-dinner speeches.

Afterwards we went outside and lay on the beds Jimmy had put up for us on the veranda. We were near the office, but hidden from the rest of the veranda by a folding bedroom screen. My father said, " I'll be glad when it's over, Gene— one way or the other. This thing's beginning to play hell with my nerves." That was the nearest he came to a confidence that day. He lay back with his hands behind his head and I bunched the pillow under me and stared at the distorted shadows of the swallows' nests on the corrugated iron roof, and listened, at a remove from the hotel voices, to the thousand small sounds of the bush.

I must have dozed, for the next thing I knew was the sound of men's voices coming up the steps to the office. There was a rich sure ring about the voices that told me they belonged to big men, big in stature and big in importance. Jimmy Cameron seemed to know them, for they began talking without introductions. Some of the voices sounded vaguely familiar. I heard one say that they had come down from the Copper Belt near the Congo border, and another that they were laying out a big new mine there. Engineers and geologists obviously— the copper "bods" Jimmy had spoken about earlier. They signed the register and were shown to their rooms, but after about fifteen minutes they came back and sat at a grass table a few yards on the other side of the screen. There was some desultory talk, and drinks were ordered : then I heard one say, " Your first trip out this way ? "

" Yes. I usually go the other way—Salisbury . . . Bulawayo . . . Beit Bridge—when I don't fly. Nice run this, though."

" Yes—very attractive. Pity they don't make more of it—I mean decent hotels and better roads."

" This place is all right."

" Oh, it's all right. I don't mean that. I mean it's a pity they don't pep it up from a tourist point. There's really damn' all to see in the Federation."

" Except the Falls."

" Yes, the Falls. But who wants to come thousands of miles just to see a lot of wet water bashing over some rocks. I don't mean scenery. I was in the States last year. You should see what those boys do with their natural beauty spots—super hotels, snappy holiday resorts, golf courses."

" Dude ranches ? "

" Well, in Texas and those places. But don't sneer, brother —those things bring in the dough. Here, where you've got everything—natural beauty, actual wild game, mountains—hell, there's a fortune waiting for someone with a little initiative. Take Kenya."

There was some business with the waiter—soda and ice being placed on the table and the clink of money on the tray, then another man said, " It's certainly attractive around here. I was out this way last year on a ranch. Took some movies, and you know how these things are, usually rather dis- appointing. But this place really came through. It's got something. Malinda, that's it. Out there somewhere, behind the mountains."

" Malinda ? Then you must know Winnie Whittaker ? "

" Winnie ? Of course I know her."

" Well, I'll be damned. I've also been out there—couple of years back. Well, there you are. Take this place of Winnie's. Wasted. Lost in the bundu. But introduce a little capital and imagination, build up that house into a high-class exclusive *small* hotel. I emphasise small because you want to keep the appearance of simple unspoilt surroundings. But high-class to get the better class of tourist. Hire a professional hunter—make hunting the gimmick."

A pause.

" I don't know."

" No ? Why not ? "

" Oh, I agree it's a beautiful place. But frankly what I found most beautiful about it was the geology."

" Really ? "

" Yes, malachite and azurite. Stacks of it."

" Well, I'll be damned."

" It was a bit of luck I discovered it. The formation there's rather deceptive. There's one of those old primitive mines there and at first sight it seems to be worked out. The lode was exhausted up to a rock wall, and they gave up at that point. But I did some poking around because I'd come across a similar thing in a survey near Mafulira some years ago. And it was what I thought. The rock wasn't solid at all, just a shell. And the lode going on under it. Pretty good stuff too. I took some samples—pretty high-grade stuff."

" Never happens to me finding a nice little copper mine tucked away in my backyard. Does Winnie know ? "

" Of course. I gave her the samples. She was surprised of course, but delighted."

" I can imagine."

" She kissed me."

" Lucky you."

" She said, ' Lennox, it's my birthday in three weeks and you've given me the grandest birthday present of my life.' "

" Well, good luck to her. Jordan Whittaker was a bastard to her in his will."

" Jordan was a bastard, period."

" He let her down badly. I hope this turns up right for her —she deserves it."

" Oh, it will."

" That reminds me of something else she said. ' Lennox, I'm now going to get out of the noose Jordan tried to throttle me with.' She was very excited. It will be interesting to see how that lode develops out."

" Anything been done about it ? "

" Not that I know of. Takes time to get these things organised."

" Yes."

There was a pause, then they went on to another subject. " As I was saying earlier, the Congo situation . . ."

I turned to look at my father. He was on his side, his head lying on his bent arm : like me, he had been listening to every syllable. Suddenly without looking at me he got up and began to dress. He seemed to be in a trance : his hands fluttered so badly he could hardly manage to lace his boots. He tucked his shirt untidily in his pants and still without a word to me stalked away down the veranda. I got up and followed him, saw him turn into the bar and reached there just as Una was handing him an old menu card. He slid on to the stool, turned the card on its clean side and started writing. He was not aware that I was looking over his shoulder. The message read, "Conrad—please come to Malinda. Please ! ! Joe." He folded the card, and wrote on the outside, " Conrad Webber, Q.C.— Urgent." He handed it to Una saying, " Give this to Conrad when he comes."

Una took it without saying a word.

" You might forget. This is important. You might forget, or lose it."

" I won't forget," Una said, pushing a hole in the card with her finger and skewering it over the neck of a bottle of Irish whisky on the shelf. " See—it'll stay right here until he comes."

2

WE WENT BACK TO BED but I did not sleep. Instead I tried to sort out the pieces of the unhappy past that had led up to these nerve-racking tensions to-night; and to the crisis that seemed to be heralded by my father's call for help to Conrad Webber. There had always been troubles at Malinda, not only the obvious ones stirred up by the bitter feud between Lavinia and my father, but deep, underlying troubles that lurked just out of sight and cast their spell over every aspect of our lives. I had always been aware of these obscure troubles without quite knowing what they were, just as one can detect the presence of submerged rocks and even their vague shape from the flow of the river above them. Their history went back to the time ten years before when my father gave up a good life in Johannesburg to come ranching on a lonely unhealthy site in the lowlands of south-castern Rhodesia. It had always puzzled me why our lives had taken that course, for my father was a construction engineer, not a farmer, and he held a big job with Jordan Whittaker—or, more exactly, with the Whittaker Organisation, as the powerful group of investment and mining companies under Jordan's control was called. I knew it was a big job because the Whittakers used to visit us and my father called them Jordan and Lavinia. I knew it too from the kind of house we lived in and the parties we gave.

Those were busy, important days for my father and whirling carefree days for Peggy and me. We seemed to spend our entire lives in the open air, playing games in the garden, swimming in our pool, watching my father on the golf course from the terrace of the country club, visiting somebody or other's enormous country estate, romping on the sands during glorious seaside holidays.

My father was a successful business executive then—well-dressed, cheerful, ambitious, fond of good cars, good times, good company—a clubman, a racegoer, a free spender of his money and talents. It was almost impossible to recognise in him the Joe Latham he became at Malinda. As he toiled in the hot sun and discovered the will to grapple with harsh conditions, he burnt off the city fat to reveal the clean honest man beneath. He gave up everything superfluous, luxurious, comfortable—things other men strove all their lives to acquire —and became a simple, taciturn, cattleman with muddy boots and khaki clothes reeking of the stockade. He became in fact as different from his former self and his former associates as our wild gaunt cattle were from the plump dairy breeds of the town.

It was not that we were rich in those days—not as Jordan and many of our visitors were. It was just that we lived well and that my father's job in the Organisation brought him into touch with the financial, mining and stock exchange people who made up the higher strata of Johannesburg society.

I remembered Lavinia at the time. She was a fairly frequent visitor, but my most vivid recollection was of a picture torn out of a newspaper and pinned up in the bar on the veranda, around the time that my father's friends were buzzing with talk about her marriage to Jordan. It showed her at the race-track in a voluminous fur that looped up behind her head and seemed to make a perfect match for the garland of flowers on the race-horse she was leading in. She was tall, poised, brisk, exquisitely sure of herself, as spirited as the snorting, wild-eyed aristocrat at her side. She had the striking photogenic loveliness of a beauty queen, but without the air of Cinderella surprise. Sophistication, professional glamour, these were the note.

There were two other people in the picture—the jockey, all boots, cap, crop and rippling silk, like a kitten dressed up for a children's tea-party—and Jordan Whittaker. Jordan walked on the other side of the horse, a distance away and not quite

in the same direction, and there was a queer uncomfortable
smirk on his dark oily old face. His striped trousers curled
inelegantly round his shins, giving an effect of bent spindly legs;
his boutonnière was broken and hung upside down in the tin-
foil. The picture was unkind to him in making him look older
and more shrunken than he was and in exaggerating the
stooping, crab-like walk. Clearly he did not belong in the
group and was obviously uneasy in the company of his
glamorous acquisitions—his horse, his jockey and his wife.
The name of the horse was Malinda, and there was all the
cruelty of victory in its face, as there was, one realised
suddenly, in hers.

Conrad Webber too—how strange that whenever there was
some crisis involving Malinda, he came on the scene. There
was an uncanny timing about this that sometimes made me
wonder whether his arrival did not create the crisis, just as his
appearance in a court case immediately made it important, tense
and exciting, and cleared the way for columns of reporting.
It was certainly a crisis that brought him into our lives.

For suddenly, like a room plunged in darkness that bright
Johannesburg era ended. It seemed to be on a particular
morning that the telephone stopped ringing, the cars stopped
turning into the driveway, the invitations disappeared from the
silver tray in the hall. I was never told the reason for this
chilling isolation. I was too young to be included in this adult
secret but there was no mistaking the trouble that settled on
our home like a witch-doctor's curse. It was unmentionable
but it was mentioned in a hundred looks and gestures, in
uneaten meals and ash-trays full of stubs, in doors being closed
on us during telephone conversations, and most of all in my
father moodily pottering about the garden instead of going to
work. I had to make what I could of chance clues and overheard remarks, and I gathered that it was something to do with
my father's work, something concerning stocks and shares, and
a court case that was being hushed up. But I never learnt more
than that.

Four months passed during which we saw nobody except

tradesmen and men with brief-cases who came to hold strictly private conferences behind the closed doors of the study. Then one day my father returned home with his arms full of presents. Crossing the lawn, he swooped Peggy up on to his shoulder, made joyful signs to my mother who was waiting for him on the stoep, ran up the steps and kissed her passionately. The crisis was over, but a week or so later a "For Sale" notice appeared on the front gate, and I began to hear talk of moving to Rhodesia.

Vaguely I knew that Conrad Webber was concerned in the trouble, and it was confirmed soon afterwards when my father took Peggy and me to meet him. I was both excited and terrified when we set out for town. Every schoolboy had heard of the terrible Conrad Webber, whose exploits in court were always making headlines, and whose picture, oddly enough, would turn up from time to time in wild life magazines. As I entered the room I was impressed by the highly polished desk with papers, ink-wells, silver boxes, a bowl of roses, and, intriguingly, a group of toy automobiles arranged in the position of a smash on a model of a street intersection, all standing precisely and ritually in their ordered places. And suddenly I was aware of the tense dandified little man, framed against a cliff of leather books, who tore us to pieces with his eyes for several minutes before speaking. I tried to look back into the fierce overpowering eyes, but my head swam and I felt as if blows were raining on me.

" How old are you ? " he asked at last.

" Ten," I managed to say, not hearing any sound in my voice.

" And you ? " he asked, looking suddenly at Peggy.

Peggy burst out crying and buried her face against my father's leg.

" Eight," my father answered for her, sounding as scared as we were.

" Pacify her," the great man said, making impatient patting-down movements with his hand. When my father had quietened her, Conrad started asking us questions, and for the next few hours, or so it seemed, he cross-examined us as if we were witnesses in a case. I knew later that we were just that, witnesses—or more precisely exhibits. All the time he questioned us he was tense, abrupt, direct. He never smiled or tried to put us at our ease. He just went on with questions that scoured into every corner and crevice of our lives like a jet-stream of water.

Finally he looked across at my father.

" I'm satisfied now," he said, and for the first time there was a spark of warmth in his eyes. " These kids will make it a lot easier for you, Joe. It's fortunate too that your wife was a school-teacher in her young days. That will take care of the educational aspect. I can only say that you're lucky." I remembered the remark not because of the implied compliment to us or the reference to my mother, but because he had called my father Joe.

My father mumbled something—" Thank you " or " I suppose so." He looked unhappy but after a moment he brightened up, and said, " I've been clearing up the details with Jordan. He's shown me the draft contract. We're buying four hundred acres in the Sabie Valley from some people named Secker. Old settlers in the district, I believe. That's just a start, of course. If the arrangement falls down they'll have the right to buy the land back at the same figure. That's in case we don't go through with it, but I can't see that happening. Jordan's too keen. Any difficulties in this land deal will be referred to . . ." Here he actually said a *referee*, and I wondered what on earth a man with short pants and a whistle could possibly have to do with this business.

" Sounds reasonable."

" I think so. Jordan's really keen. He's promised to buy more land as we go along, extra stock, all the equipment we need. And it's to be a *real* partnership—his capital and my work, the profits to be split equally. This is better than before. I'm going to be his *partner*, not just an employee whom he can hoof out at any time. I couldn't have *bought* myself into a deal like this."

It was a pleasure to see him so excited after the gloomy

months he had been through. But Conrad watched him without
a smile, and in the end his only comment was, " It will be a
long-term proposition, Joe. I hope it turns out the way you
want it to."

Then he came round the desk and placed his hands on my
arms. " Eugene—as you've heard you're going to settle in
Rhodesia. I know the part of the world you're going to. It's
lonely and wild, but very beautiful and it's real Africa. It's one
of the few parts of the old Africa left to-day. You'll find it a
hard life at first. You'll have no companions. You'll have to
find your own amusements. But I think in time you'll come
to like it so much you won't ever want to live anywhere else.
Good luck. I won't say good-bye, because I'll be dropping in
to see you from time to time. It's an old stamping ground of
mine."

As we walked out it dawned on me that the tiger whom we
had discussed at school and the ogre who started the interview
had declared himself our friend. It was incredible, especially
after the recent trouble and the way nearly everybody had
dropped us, but there was no mistaking the tone and meaning
of his words. I began thinking of the exciting new home
awaiting us—an elegant white ranch-house, rolling green
pastures filled with fat pedigree cattle, a pony of my own . . .

. . . Yes, everything went back to that puzzling switch in our
lives ten years ago. Everything started and spread out from
there. That was when Conrad came into the scene, when
Jordan planned the trick that nearly destroyed us in the
following years, when the course was set for the bitter snarling
broil over Malinda that was to develop between Lavinia and
my father.

That glamorous ranch I had pictured turned out to be a
wilderness. The cottage we had heard about was a ruin. The
first consignment of cattle that Jordan bought to start the
partnership were the cheapest and seediest he could pick up on
a third-rate auction. The soil was hard and stony, the climate
in summer viciously dank and unhealthy, the country wild,
silent and desolate. All we had was the glorious view of the

valley, spectacular sunsets, the music of the river rushing over
the rapids, a pool of hippo, baboons in the cliffs. Conrad was
right—it was beautiful, and the real Africa. But we set to work
and slowly, achingly, brought a ranch to life where nothing had
existed before—creating it purely out of soil, air and labour.

We had no help whatsoever from Jordan. It was all a ruse.
He never gave a penny of that extra capital, and we had to
scrimp and starve and scrounge and scrape for every loading
ramp, barn, windmill, water-pump, irrigation pipe ; for every
bag of fertiliser or cattle feed, for every head of extra stock and
for each use we made of stud facilities of other ranches.
Jordan's interest in Malinda had nothing to do with cattle-
raising, no concern whatever with making the ranch a success.
He wanted it for an obscure purpose of his own, and for that
it didn't have to make money, but merely to exist. It was a
partnership not between our work and Jordan's money as my
father had expected, but between our suffering and Jordan's
vindictiveness.

After eighteen months Jordan and Lavinia paid us a visit.
We thought it would be merely to see how the ranch was pro-
gressing. But Jordan hardly saw the cattle, the crops or the
numerous improvements. Everything annoyed him ; when
we showed him the new barn stocked with winter fodder
a bluefly buzzed around him and he got violently irritable.
" Why don't you get rid of these filthy things ? We'll all get
a disease ! " He had some idiotic theories about growing wheat
or tea, and insisted we use a cattle diet a man had told him
about. But that was as far as it went. He was not interested, let
alone impressed, by our work.

To our astonishment, instead of going home after a day or
two, they decided to stay on for a holiday. It was a holiday that
brought joy to nobody. Lavinia was miserable. She seemed to
loathe the place and dragged out the weary days reading on the
stoep or sunbathing on the rocks near the rapids. At meals she
made no effort to take part in the conversation. She was tense,
edgy, morose. Jordan fretted to be near a telephone, and com-

plained about the flies, the heat, and the stale newspapers with
their obsolete stock exchange news. He brightened up only
when playing a queer cat-and-mouse game with Lavinia that
set everybody's nerves on edge. He kept asking questions like,
" En*joy*ing yourself, dear ? " or " Having a *good* time ? " with
strangely misplaced emphasis that made it plain he was doing
it to torment her. Or he would ask, " What are your plans for
to-morrow ? "—knowing there could be no plans except read
a book or take a walk. In the evenings they would go for a
stroll along the river bank—the gabbling old man with wet red
lips and wet prune eyes, absurdly dressed in khaki shorts and
floppy sports shirt, with Lavinia holding his arm, taking short
steps to match his, and a look of screaming boredom on her
face.

Yet she never rebelled. Occasionally looks flared up between
them, but there was never an open quarrel. She was attentive
to him, tactful of their difference in age, appreciative of the few
things he did for her, and at times, it seemed, almost affectionate
—everything that could be expected of the wife of a much older
man. The change in Lavinia was extraordinary. I used to
puzzle about it for hours.

Jordan carried on the same kind of malicious game with my
father. He would say, " We miss you up there in the office,
Latham. The boys keep asking after you. Maybe we'll consider
bringing you back one of these days." Then he would wait,
watching keenly until my father responded with something
like, " It's nice to hear you say that—to tell you the truth, I
wouldn't mind going back "—then slice his throat, " How
can you think about going back at this stage ? We've got to
build up the ranch. That's the trouble with you young men—
no guts, no follow-through. In three or four years' time maybe,
but not now." When my father raised the question of extra
money Jordan asked him to make a list of requirements. He
did so, spending two nights consulting agricultural catalogues
writing exact descriptions, costing materials. Jordan stffued
the list into his pocket without even reading it, and that was
the last we heard of it.

They stayed ten days. It was astonishing, for there was not one moment of pleasure in that holiday. And they left only because Conrad arrived.

He came unexpectedly one morning while we were having breakfast. He greeted the Whittakers, calling Jordan "Jordan" and Lavinia " Mrs. Whittaker"—with a long straight look into her eyes that conveyed some secret innuendo. Jordan returned the greeting, but Lavinia said nothing. She lowered the coffee cup into the saucer with shaking fingers, and sat absolutely still. Suddenly she stood up, flung the napkin down on the table and stalked out of the room. Jordan followed her, and about ten minutes later they came out and told my mother that they thought they should be getting back to Johannesburg, and thanked her for a wonderful time.

They came again the next year, but that time it was a little different. There was the hunting which gave Lavinia a means of escape from Jordan, and also, I was certain, awakened her interest in Malinda. Jordan tried hunting only once. He stumbled over stones and roots, kept dropping his rifle, and stopped at all the wrong moments to light his cigar. He gave up, but Lavinia continued, although she too had made a bad start. She was enthusiastic but too excitable : if she remembered one thing she forgot another, or misunderstood signals or fired too soon. But towards the end of the holiday the hunting took, and by the following year she had stopped being a novice. She would find the spoor and judge the wind and snake up to the quarry and fire with a dead steady hand as if she had been doing it all her life. She became fanatically keen. She stayed in the bush until the last glimmer of sunlight and could hardly wait to start again at dawn next day. Sometimes she spent whole days at shooting practice. I would watch her from the stoep as she fired for hours at paper targets pinned to a tree— in tight black slacks and sweater that made her look bean-lean and agile against the background of trees—a mass of dark-red hair down to her shoulders, her body erect, feet planted apart, and a hard angry flash in her eyes as she squeezed the trigger.

Hunting opened her senses to the bush and so the germ of

her love for Malinda was planted. Yes, she too loved it—we all loved it in our queer and different ways. And the way the hunting took was the proof that Malinda had fastened its hold on her.

There was other proof in the way she began to look midway through that second visit—and for all the subsequent visits with Jordan : she stopped using make-up and took to wearing blue jeans and simple shirts, and it seemed as if all the city manner and breeding had been scraped off with the greasepaint. Her face looked entirely different without cosmetics— rather bony and gaunt, bald on the eyebrows, her eyes smaller and more limited in expression. As the days went by and her body tanned, it seemed to fill out subtly, the muscles grow taut, the fine but essentially decorative legs take on a sleek strength, her walk exchange its slightly stagey mannerisms for a firm, flowing grace.

But the strange cat-and-mouse game between her and Jordan still went on. It was an enigma that hung over that and all the holidays they took at Malinda.

Why did they take those holidays ? Every year they came to Malinda for a fortnight or three weeks of what looked like penance. The world's beaches and mountain-tops and spas and lakes were theirs for holidays. But they came to Malinda.

Jordan's miserliness kept Malinda just short of bankruptcy. Unless there was an emergency that threatened the existence of the ranch—such as a cattle epidemic that once wiped out a third of our stock—he refused to contribute his share. But he took his profits, to the last penny, only to spend them on senseless insulting extravagances like the wrought-iron bridge over the creek where he took his walks ; or the summerhouse, with stone fireplace and Dutch tiles on the cliff overlooking the river ; or the rosewood panelling in the two extra rooms we had built on to the Retreat for his visits ; and, finally, the Big House.

We had no warning that he was going to build the Big House. One year he complained about the "crowding" and mumbled something about making a change. A few months later we watched dumbfounded as a convoy of trucks loaded with building materials came crashing through the bush. A small village of tents and corrugated iron shanties to house the workmen grew up on the high humped land across the ravine. Arc-welders, concrete mixers, bandsaws, sent the first of the new sounds across the valley. We saw the house rise out of the hill, a freak monster that grew with no apparent limit to its size and shape. Week after week we watched helplessly from our stoep like victims of some huge unfunny practical joke, until the great misfit enterprise was complete.

Perhaps it was not really as big as we said. Perhaps, standing in one of the garden suburbs of Johannesburg or Salisbury flanked by other mansions of the rich it might have passed unnoticed. But here in the bush country where one's eyes grew accustomed to the low profile of ground-hugging vegetation, to humble huts and settlements that blended and disappeared among the rocks and trees, to the shy played-down hues—drab greens, dusty fawns, smudged greys and yellows—here, in these subdued surroundings, it shrieked. It shouldered itself out of the bush, jutted up against the sky and browbeat the whole countryside. Its bigness was not its only offence. Another was its whiteness, for the sun bounced off its walls and sprayed a tense glare from horizon to horizon. In the evenings when the sunset rays were reflected in the glass panels of the veranda it unsettled everything for miles around with its jittery winking St. Vitus dance. It was not only absurd and ugly, but disturbing in its meaning, for it was a symbol of the insensitive white man living in his little bubble of imported air in Africa.

Jordan rushed to get the Big House built in a single season, in spite of the rains that made a swampy mess of the last part of the operation. He must have had a premonition, for he died just as it was completed. There was to have been a big house-warming party, with celebrated people invited from all over Rhodesia and South Africa. But the invitations were cancelled by a notice in the newspaper, and instead of an invasion, we had one glorious season without the Whittakers. The house was never officially named. During the building everybody

called it, naturally, the big house, and when it was deprived
of a naming ceremony, they continued to do so, but with
capitals.

While the house stood shining new and unwanted, like a
bridal cake made for a cancelled wedding, Conrad came out on
one of his trips.

" Burn it," he said. " Now's the time."

I expected Lavinia's visits to stop after Jordan's death. She
had been so unhappy during those holidays with Jordan that
I was sure that she had come out only because she had to.
But to my surprise she not only continued to visit us, but came
out several times a year. There was an interlude, as extraordinary and mystifying as anything that happened at Malinda,
when she actually went out of her way to befriend us.

She came without friends on those visits. The chauffeur
would take her to the Big House to drop her luggage, then
drive her straight back to the Retreat. Looking superbly smart
she would step out of the station wagon, walk into the house,
and another dazzling break in our sober life would begin—
invariably with the unwrapping of presents.

She spent most of her time at the Retreat. In the mornings,
while my mother gave us school lessons in the outhouse she
had rigged up as a classroom, Lavinia would tidy the house, or
prepare elaborate meals with groceries and delicacies she had
brought out with her from Johannesburg.

Sometimes she would stroll across the fields and talk to my
father while he was working ; or she would saddle a horse and
go riding—disappearing with a jaunty burst of speed into the
bush. Our sleepy nags seemed to become electrified under her
and mustered up a spirit that we thought had been sapped out
by the heat and bush-weariness. In the afternoons she would
take us on walks along the river to the great red cliffs and
sprawling stranded waters of Monk's Castle, leading the way
with that brisk, sprightly stride of hers, stopping suddenly to
crouch and watch a bright-plumaged lourie or a herd of buck
in the distance, leaping from rock to rock across the river,

clambering up boulders—and I would think of those excruciating evening ambles she used to take with Jordan and the contrast between her misery then and the fun and excitement in her now.

In the evenings we would sit around the kerosene lamp in the dining-room talking late into the night. She would tell us anecdotes or give us descriptions of her trips abroad, of people she had met, the functions she had attended, with all the flair for amusing, scintillating conversation that had made her famous. Her wit and charm seemed to exist only for our entertainment. We saw then the Lavinia whom people idolised —generous, extravagant, concerned for her friends, alert, alive, endlessly fascinating.

Those eighteen months in which she gave us her friendship were our best years at Malinda. It was then that we managed, at last, to make the ranch pay. Lavinia honoured Jordan's broken promises—she was very sensible and practical about everything—and as a result we got more cattle, extra land, a second truck, the jeep ; we built new stockades for ailing calves, an irrigation system to flood some previously useless flat ground : we started raising crops of pineapple, avocado pear, banana : we built a silo, a new barn, and planted three new windmills about the property. Lavinia went even beyond the contract with Jordan—she refused to take out any of her profits, saying she preferred to leave the money for the farm to nourish on. I remembered my parents trying to persuade her to take some of the money due to her, and how, laughing and airily waving her hand, she said, " Don't *worry* about it. We'll work it all out one day." She used to apologise for not investing *more* money in Malinda. She explained that Jordan had put the assets of his estate out of her reach, leaving her only an allowance that depended on how much profit Malinda could show. I didn't remember exactly how she described it—the figure was to be a multiple or ratio of the Malinda profits or some such calculation. That and the half-share in the partnership itself was all she received. It was extraordinary—to whom else could he leave his huge fortune but to the glittering young wife who

added so much lustre to his public life ?—but we had no reason
to doubt what she told us, particularly as her generosity was
obvious in what she actually did for Malinda.

For the first time my father was without an overdraft at the
bank, and the feeling of financial security, of progress coming
at last, dispelled a hundred tensions and frustrations in him.
He did not work in the same panicky hurry, but nevertheless
managed to get more done. When his illness recurred, it
seemed much less harrowing and depressing. He did not feel
the need to make an impression, to shave and dress up, when
we visited the Seckers. From him, a new mood spread through
our family. Gone were those evenings when my parents sat at
a table strewn with invoices, bank statements, account books,
adding figures and trying to square the circle of Malinda's
finances. Instead we read, played cards, and went to bed to
sleep in peace.

And then that too ended—suddenly, inexplicably.

For about four months we did not see her. Then the summer
came and the heavy oppressive heat that once more shut us
off from the outside world.

And the following June she arrived in a new station wagon,
sitting in front next to a friend who was driving—a plump,
pink-faced man in a green Tyrolean hat—and slewed round
talking to the five or six smartly dressed passengers lounging
elegantly in the wide seats behind. As the car came down the
road past the Retreat, Peggy and I waved to her from the stoep,
but she ignored us and the fat blue vehicle went on, to stop on
the unkempt lawn of the Big House. From the stoep I watched
with a strange tense fluttering inside me, as the party climbed
out of the car and took the luggage into the house. Half an
hour later the old station wagon appeared, driven by her
chauffeur and filled with glum-looking African housemaids in
white uniforms, and two or three houseboys, and a couple of
dogs, and a bulky canvas-covered cargo of household supplies.
Next morning two more cars arrived and dropped passengers
on the lawn, and that afternoon one car went back with some

of the people who had come in the station wagon. In the evening a Land-Rover lurched past with more visitors. And all through the next three weeks visitors came and went, as if the Big House had become a hotel. It was the first of the house-parties.

Lavinia did not come near us. We would see her on the lawn among her friends, or occasionally taking them for drives or walks. Sometimes visitors would pass the Retreat, but we ignored them. My father was in a black sullen temper from the moment of her arrival and pointedly refused to have anything to do with these monsters who had overrun our ranch. She kept clear of the Retreat. And we, in turn, stayed away from the Big House. It was war, or the ominous watchful prelude to it.

On the fifth day she came to us while we were eating lunch. I saw her through the screen door, walking across the lawn with a brisk shoulder-swaggering movement that was like the gesture of a man dusting his hands before a fight. Behind her, stumbling and breathless, was a man in a blue silk beach suit, blue canvas shoes, and one of those peaked, plaited-grass Basuto hats ridiculously tied on by a ribbon under the chin. She came up the veranda steps, kicked open the door and stood holding it ajar with her back. She was in jodhpurs, and she pulled a piece of paper out of one pocket and a silver propelling pencil out of the other. Standing at the door, refusing to come in, she said, looking at nobody in particular, " I want you to produce your accounts and records for Mr. Hoffman. He's an auditor. It's about time you settled up with me. Have them ready the day after to-morrow." She turned to the man and asked, " Is the day after to-morrow all right, Frank ? " The man nodded uncomfortably. She looked at the slip of paper, ticked something off, then said, " Now—the geyser's been stuck since last night. Please attend to it this afternoon. Nobody's been able to have a bath. We can't live like this." She ticked that off too, and glancing at the list went on, " Oh, yes, that kitchen boy Amos has been playing up again. He came in drunk last night, and when I tried to talk to him, he gave me a mouthful. Will you please deal with him." Then, looking at my father with deadly venom she said, " It's come back to me that you're surly and rude to my guests. I won't have it. They're my guests, remember, and I expect you to behave yourself in their presence."

To my amazement, even that was on the list. She ticked it off, then she swung round and walked away, allowing the screen door to bang behind her. I watched her disappear over the rise, with Hoffman padding after her and nervously looking back at us over his shoulder. We sat, stunned, dumbfounded, as if a maniac had burst in and thrown acid into our faces. Then my father rose and went into the bathroom and a few moments later we heard the awful strangling sound of vomiting, which we knew from his bouts of bilharzia.

The accounts were produced for Hoffman who studied them and then threw up his hands, and said, " Impossible. I can't follow all this." My father tried to explain, but Hoffman seemed to find everything intensely difficult. The accounts were accurately, meticulously recorded, but they did not fit into any accepted accounting system, and that seemed to be an insuperable obstacle for Hoffman. Nothing could be settled that year.

Nor, for that matter, the following year. Or ever. The meetings when they sat down and tried to hammer out their differences got more and more complicated. They started with an attempt to ascertain just how much Lavinia had left in the partnership during the Friendship Years, as I called them, and how this contribution affected her share of profits. But the issues soon spread much farther afield.

The dispute grew uglier with every meeting, but it was always related, if tenuously, to a settlement of the ranch affairs. But the year before the whole tone changed. The quarrel became dirty, desperate and cut-throat. Instead of trying to buy us out, Lavinia did everything possible to kick us out. Her plan was to ruin us, even if it meant ruining Malinda in the process. There were so many acts of underhand sabotage, coming from so many unexpected directions, that we should not have been surprised if she had sent a man out to burn down the ranch buildings.

Now that puzzle was solved. I was grateful to the man on the veranda for giving us this vital piece of intelligence. Lavinia had learnt that there was a rich copper lode on the property, and she had made up her mind to grab it for herself. So the fight was no longer over a rather small and only moderately successful cattle ranch, but over a potential copper mine. The stakes had gone up immeasurably. And her methods and weapons had become proportionately more ruthless.

It was time for Conrad to pay us another visit.

I thought of him with affection and relief now. Of all the people we knew in Johannesburg, he was the only one who had stayed friendly with us. As promised he had visited us many times over the years, usually arriving unexpectedly in a truck that looked like a mechanical monster with all its gadgets and contraptions, and always accompanied by two African trackers absurdly named Cigarettes and Boots. At first we hated him. He was difficult and domineering, full of quirks and fads, critical of his food, his bed, the sanitation in our primitive outhouse. But in time we learnt how to deal with his crustiness—we simply ignored it. We found him quite unlike any man we had met before, in Johannesburg or elsewhere. There was a flint hardness about him, an unswerving honesty that did not derive from ready-made programmes of morals or ethics, but from his own deeply considered system of convictions. He was uniquely a product of Africa. His father had run a trading store in a remote corner of the Transvaal lowveld, so that his childhood in many ways resembled mine. He never lost his love of the wild country and he saw in the hard, sparse, cruel landscape of Africa a beauty that never dimmed in his eyes. The tough, solitary life in the bush was no hardship to him : it was a joy. Hardship was living in the city where, as he once put it, "people are pulped down into a grey sludge." It accounted for the striking contradiction in him—a barrister at the top of his profession who would suddenly grow bored with his practice and take long hunting trips into the bush—the source incidentally of all his other contradictions.

He was a puzzling man—in himself and in the role he played in our lives, but I was in no mood to think about that now. I felt only grateful that he was our friend, and that we could call on him in this new emergency.

I saw him now, a spruce compactly built little man full of self-assurance and vanity ; with silken sandy hair, a clipped ginger moustache and cool, fierce, pale-blue eyes that sometimes seemed to bore right through your skull ; a brisk decisive and very authoritative manner that made people take notice of him all the time, a bustling fussiness that kept everybody on the run. Age—about a year or two older than my father.

3

NEXT MORNING we left the hotel shortly before sunrise. I took the wheel and as we settled down for the long slog to Malinda I watched for the familiar landmarks and scenery. We were in the land of the baobabs, fat dropsical trees that gazed back into the headlamps like sleepy elephants lining the roadside. Grotesque shadows of freak mountains, huge naked granite spheres that looked as if they had bubbled up and hardened during the night gave a tormented look to the landscape. Occasionally a bus that had been travelling all night came hurtling toward us in a cloud of dust, a forest of bicycles tied on the roof, a crush of Africans behind the tiny, dim-lit windows. As the sun came up burning strongly even while slanting over the mountains, I saw the signs of awakening in thatched villages by the roadside—wood-fires glimmering behind trees, women coming out into the cold dawn air carrying pots or shaking blankets. Rhodesia—it was like seeing it on a postcard or travel brochure with everything self-consciously in character.

We did not speak. I had wanted to ask him what he thought of the mining man's talk about the copper on Malinda but he had gone straight back to sleep from the moment he flopped into the bucket seat. He was dead tired. I could tell from the sag in his face that he had slept badly, if at all, last night, but, anyway, this was a weariness that had been accumulating for days. He slumped in the seat next to me, his head jogging inertly with the rough motion of the jeep, his hands limply gripping the door handle and the side of the canvas cushion. I did not disturb him. The sleep would do him good. I thought he was in a better mood this morning—I could tell when we were dressing and getting ready to move off. He was just tired now. This was not the fever of gloom that had gripped him yesterday during the ride from Umtali.

I let my mind go blank and drove in a daze along the silent winding road to Malinda. There was so much I wanted to talk about and hear about, but I knew there would be no opportunity to do it during this trip. I had taken enough yesterday and I wasn't going back for another dose by pressing him again. I couldn't force him to confide in me, anyway. Best to let him sleep on. I simply drove straight through, not even stopping for breakfast at our usual spot at the river crossing. We turned off the main road and cut through the bush for the last slow, tortuous, meandering stretch to Malinda, and even then he didn't wake up. He must have been thoroughly exhausted. I plunged on, with thorn branches slapping into the windshield and screeching against the canvas tent—mile on mile over loose sand, sharp stones, exposed roots, dipping into catbacks, swerving to avoid fallen trees. Every spring was dry, the bush was grey and covered in dust, and I saw no game whatever.

As we dropped down into the familiar country around Malinda, he awoke at last. He yawned, stretched his arms, then slumped back and sat staring ahead with a stony expression.

" I'm sorry," he said after a while.

" That's all right."

" What time is it ? "

" Just on ten."

He looked at his watch, adjusted the minute hand, wound it, and sat back. " It's all Jordan's doing," he said a few minutes later.

" Yes, he seems to have taken care of everything," I said, idly, because I wasn't sure what he was trying to say.

" He's taken care of me all right," he said bitterly.

It reminded me of one of the remarks I had overheard on the veranda last night—Lavinia's words when shown the samples of copper ore—" Now I'm going to get out of the noose Jordan tried to throttle me with"—and for the rest of the way

I lost myself in speculation about the previous afternoon and night. What was this trouble Una had spoken about? Why was my father unwilling to get hold of Jefferies and track it down? Why had he taken Una's talk so badly? What had made him try to disguise his panic when he met me at Umtali? What was he hiding from me? Questions swirled in my mind. Yet when I asked him, " Is there anything behind this talk of Una's—about that trouble, I mean? " he answered, " No, it's just something Lavinia's cooking up. You're not worrying about it, are you? "

I had to say, " No, of course not." And I wondered again if I was not the victim of delusions, not working myself up into a state where I smelled mystery and disaster in every remark and gesture.

We rode on and for a while I took control of my imaginings. But before I knew it my thoughts were off again and I was saying to myself, " You're in trouble, or heading for trouble, or trouble's heading for you," over and over like a maniac jingle.

We came round a bend in the track and saw the Finger in the distance—a pale-grey rock tower with two vultures squatting on the top—and a few moments later the Big House sprawled out on the high ground beside the river, its long roof buckling and disintegrating in a mirage of heat. And then the whole of Malinda came into view—the whitewashed squares and diamonds of the stockades, the river twisting among the cliffs, the dark lush green of the tropical orchard, and finally the Retreat itself half-hidden in a grove of trees.

As we pulled into the yard I saw that the cattle were not grazing in the bushes as they normally did. Because of the drought they were living off fodder and keeping close to the river, and now they were hanging about the ranch buildings like unemployed men around a labour exchange.

I unpacked the things from the jeep, then drove it into the lands to look for Kamba the foreman. I found him in one of the fields ploughing back withered maize plants that had been killed in the drought. He greeted me with a wide white smile from his seat on the tractor. He was about thirty years old, but I had always thought him much older because he had been with us from our first days at Malinda. He was in white overalls with spanners, pliers, paint brushes and so on, sticking out of the slots, and he wore an old squashed police helmet at a jaunty angle—a bit of affectation that gave him an efficient look. " Who's this I see ? Beta ! " he shouted, shading his eyes to peer at me in mock non-recognition, and calling me by the nickname (it meant White Ant) that had been given me as a child. " We heard you weren't coming back this time ! "

" I changed my mind," I told him. " How have you been managing ? "

" The cattle are still here," he said, climbing down from the tractor. " They've been talking about you. They keep asking what's happened to Beta."

"Let's go and see them," I said, opening the door of the jeep. He climbed in and we moved off, driving to the stockade where we kept weak or ailing calves. There were more than the usual number, but we had more calves than ever that year and, anyway, there were bound to be some casualties in the drought. " One died two nights ago," he told me, with a mournful expression. " We tried to save it, but . . ." He shrugged. I told him not worry and that I thought he was doing fine. I put the jeep into gear and drove over to the barn : I had never seen so many beasts at Malinda. The place was overrun with them —but of course this was because they were concentrated in a small area. We looked at them from the jeep—they were thinner than usual and a bit lack-lustre, but seemed to be bearing up well. It was strange seeing them again—I could recognise their faces like relations. We bred a special type, crossing the stocky indigenous Sanga cattle which had natural immunity to the dry heat and local diseases, with huge long-boned Afrikanders for bulk and beef, occasionally feeding in a strain of aristocracy from the prize Santa Gertrudis bulls kept by the Kotanga ranch. It made for ugly humped wide-horned cattle, but with plenty of meat and a built-in resistance to the tick fever and foot-and-mouth disease which were prevalent in the area. This hybrid breed took well in the hot sandy bush country, going a little wild itself and roaming far afield, often to graze with the herds of antelope and zebra. We were lucky too, to be on the river, for the ranch had ample supplies of lush buffalo and urochlia grasses, and we were able to supplement with maize and lucerne grown by ourselves. We had a good herd now, after years of experiment—one exactly right for the conditions. It was impossible to believe that it had been bred from the woebegone specimens Jordan had bought to start the ranch.

" What do you know about copper mining ? " I asked Kamba as we drove on to look at a new irrigation scheme on the flat land below the rapids.

" My nephew works in the Copper Belt."

" What do *you* know ? I mean on the geological side. What would you do if you found stacks of azurite and malachite in a lode running under a granite shelf ? "

" I'd ask my nephew," he said, not even smiling, and certainly not letting me know that he saw I was pulling his leg.

" Close your eyes and try and imagine this place a copper mine," I told him.

He closed one eye.

" Now—from here to the Big House there's no bush, no crops—just a big hole deep as the river and four times as wide. That's to get the stuff out from the top instead of going down in tunnels like snakes and ant-eaters."

" Some hole," Kamba said in an unimpressed voice.

" Now clear away the Retreat—it's in the way. There you build a big corrugated iron factory—oh, much bigger than the Big House—where you refine out the copper. It stinks a bit and sends up black smoke that tastes like burning tyres. This is the reduction plant."

" I'm just a farmer," Kamba said.

" Then there's the train. Quite a small one but very busy. It runs all over Malinda pulling iron trucks full of the stuff that's been dug out of the hole. Do you like trains ? "

" No. For me, the bus."

" Then the slag heaps . . ."

" I think you'd better wait for my nephew. He'll be coming home in a few months. What's all this, Beta ? "

" Oh, just an idea."

We reached the newly irrigated land and got out to inspect it. The scheme was just starting and would need adjustment and experiment before it could work properly : I looked forward to helping on it for I liked this kind of work. I listened to Kamba telling me the details of the plan, pointing out the system of the furrows and showing how the water would be raised by a converted engine taken from an old truck.

When we got into the jeep again I started back to the house, but after a few yards I swung the wheel round and made for the hill-side beyond the Big House. It was just an impulse. I wanted to have another look at the old mine the man on the veranda had spoken about. I had no reason for going except that I could not get that conversation out of my mind, and was drawn by curiosity to see the spot of ground that had so dramatically altered the position at Malinda. We knew about the mine, of course. It was not the first time there had been talk of copper on Malinda. We had become aware of the old mine years ago when we kept digging up rusted pickaxes of curious shape, broken pottery with unusual designs in enamel, utensils and stone furniture. When drilling the foundations of the Big House, workmen had unearthed four human skeletons lying together and surrounded by digging tools—obviously the scene of some pit disaster now forgotten to human memory. All over Malinda there were relics.

Soon after coming to Malinda my father investigated this old mine. Although not a geologist he knew what to look for from his work in the Whittaker Organisation. He took a boxful of samples to be tested in Bulawayo and received an assayer's certificate proving that the ore was high grade. But when he examined the mine itself he found that the lode was worked out. It had gone down in a wide sloping stope that ended at a barrier of granite. The granite itself, a great rugged cluster of rock buried deep in the hill-side, was an emphatic "no" to any prospect of further excavation. Those ancient miners had extracted all the copper possible. The beautiful stones I had found as a child were merely some stray debris of the earlier operations.

Having satisfied himself that the lode was exhausted, he put the matter out of his mind. He wasn't even tempted to move in digging equipment and explore the mine farther. Other ranches had these old workings and we had heard of too many expensive disappointments resulting from wildcat treasure hunts.

But all this morning the idea had been lurking in my mind that my father might have made a mistake. True, he was an old mining man, but his experience was limited to the engineering and executive side, and if this were in fact a freak formation he could easily have been misled.

I could not help thinking that there must be something in the talk we heard last night. What we should do now was investigate the position in the light of this new theory—in other words, open up the old mine and see what it looked like from inside.

" Here's where it starts," I told Kamba when we reached the site.

We got out of the jeep and clambered up the hill-side to the vaguely discernable depression in the ground. The mine entrance had not only been buried by a centuries-old accumulation of earth, but even the signs of my father's digging of a few years back had been grown over with grass and weeds.

" Where what starts ? " Kamba asked as we stood with our hands on our hips looking at the empty spot.

" That copper mine."

He looked at me as if I had gone off my head, for there really was nothing to show that this was a mine, or anything else of the least interest. " All right, we've seen it," he said, tired of the joke. " Let's go back."

He turned to go down to the jeep, but I noticed something glinting in the ground a little above where we were standing.

D

I climbed up to look at it and as I got nearer saw that it had a blue sheen and recognised it as another of those azurite chips. I dug it out, wiped the dirt away, and then split it open with a penknife. It parted down the side, revealing a vivid sea-blue surface patterned with intersecting whorls like the design inside a watch-case. I threw the smaller section away and held the other up to catch the light of the sun. It flashed like a jewel ; I studied it, fascinated for a moment, then dropped it into the pocket of my bush shirt and went down to join Kamba.

On the way back he said, " I know those things. Lots of children in the village have got them."

As we drove home I found myself wondering why this talk of the mine had somehow taken on the aspect of bad news. We were on Malinda legally. We had rights and it was ridiculous to think that we could be scared off the ranch by a lot of loud threatening noises.

It was left to my mother to tell me the real nature of the crisis that I was prepared to dismiss so airily as a wildcat scare campaign of Lavinia's. When she did I found it easy to understand why my father had been in that mood of black dejection, and why she herself had sent the ominously disturbing letter that had made me drop the swimming tour and come back to Malinda.

When my father and I reached home my mother had not yet returned from Dale where she had spent the last few days with the Seckers. She came in only later that afternoon, and as she drove the Austin into the yard I could see immediately that something was amiss. With my father there was always an ambiguity, a doubt whether things were real or imagined because of the wild fluctuations of mood caused by his illness. But with her the signs of panic and pessimism were terrifying, because over the years her steadfastness had been the solid hub of our lives at Malinda.

She stepped out of the car wearing her grey costume and a silk shirt fastened with a cameo brooch ; her grey straw hat, with the artificial violets on the crown, was in her hand together

with her big leather handbag. The formal, slightly severe
clothes seemed to suggest the tone for serious news, although
that of course was accidental. Her hair was untidy, which was
unusual for her, and there was a jerky hurry about the way she
flung open the car door, gathered the things off the seat and
stepped out.

I went out to meet her, and while she didn't exactly fail to
notice me, it came near to that. She merely said, " Bring in
my suitcase, Gene," with a fluttering of her fingers toward the
car, and walked right past me. No greeting, no welcome home
—just this rather distracted command to fetch her luggage, as
if she had last seen me only a few hours before.

I took the suitcase inside and met her again as she was
coming out of the bedroom, closing the door quietly behind
her. " How is he ? " she asked. My father was inside sleeping
off the effect of the injection I had given him to hold down the
incipient fever.

" Tired," I said, " and generally in a bad way. It's one of
those again."

" I'm glad you travelled back with him. I would have hated
for him to do the trip alone." We spoke walking down the
passage toward the dining-room.

" What's happened ? " I asked, alarmed now and with a
return of the anxiety that had been pursuing me ever since I
had left Johannesburg. " What's going on ? I wish someone
would talk."

But she didn't answer. When we were in the dining-room
she stood looking at me with a strange lingering light in her
eyes, then kissed me. " This isn't going to be much of a
holiday for you, Gene," she said, holding me at arm's length
and looking at me again. " But I'm glad you came. We're
going to need you."

" Is something wrong ? " I asked.

She went over to the table and sat down. She waited a
moment then said in a level voice, " We're going to lose
Malinda, Gene."

It did not come as quite the surprise or shock I would have

expected. Too many events had been preparing me unconsciously for the news. I said, " Well ? "

" In fact, we've lost it already. Wait here—I'll show you
something."

She went out of the room and came back a few minutes later
with a long envelope. I sat at the table opposite her. She slid
it across and said, " Read that." I took it but did not open it.
" Read that, Gene," she said again. " You'll see what I mean."

I read it with my tongue sticking to the roof of my mouth,
my heart pounding. When I finished I sat holding it before me
and suddenly I had the wild impossible notion that I might have
missed something, that it didn't mean what I understood, that
somewhere among the thickets of tangled legal prose was a
qualification that reversed the plain meaning of the words. I
read it again, then dropped it on the table in disgust.

" Why didn't you tell me about this in your letter ? " I asked
curtly. For some reason I had become angry with *her*.

" I didn't know about it when I wrote you. Joe never
mentioned it to me. I found it when I was packing his clothes
to go to Umtali—at the bottom of a drawer. But I knew
something had happened. He's been in a terrible state ever
since it arrived—that's why I wrote like that, I suppose."

" Let me get this clear," I said, holding up the document
again. " This is a court order breaking up the partnership
because . . ." I looked down for the exact words.

" Because they don't hit it off," my mother said dryly. " The
whole thing now goes into the hands of a Liquidator who will
generally act as his name implies—liquidate everything."

" And they have the right to do that ? "

" Yes, I'm afraid so."

" But it's ridiculous," I said, feeling myself bursting with
irritation and annoyance. " Is that what Dad thinks ? "

" I don't know what he thinks. But he's probably taken
legal advice in Umtali, and learnt that this is the position. He
refuses to discuss it with me. I told him I'd found out and tried
to get him to sit down and make some plans. But the mention
of it only infuriates him."

" It doesn't make sense," I said, puzzled that she seemed to know so much about the legal position without ever having discussed it with my father. " How can she just go to Court and do this ? Don't *we* have any say ? "

" Let me explain. I went to Dale to get advice from the Seckers because I felt as you do—that the whole thing's preposterous. I took a copy of the document and Ruth drove in to the Bell Hotel and telephoned her attorney for an opinion. He went into it very thoroughly and we got his letter this morning. The position is that when partners are at loggerheads and there's no hope of a reconciliation, it's a ground for terminating the partnership."

" But *she's* caused all the trouble. This is simply a racket—a swindle."

" She says *we've* caused the trouble. That's not the point. There's no trust and co-operation any more and that's a ground for ending the partnership. We could file a reply of course. But we'd lose the case. All it would do is postpone the end for a month or two, but we'd have to get out anyway—and pay a lot of money in lawyer's fees into the bargain."

" So we're under two months' notice—just like that. After ten years building up the place, starting from scratch, working like mules—out we go."

" I'm afraid that's the position."

Somehow further talk seemed futile. There it was—a mound of hard cruel fact that no arguing could affect. I sat there with a kind of glaze over my mind, a stunned acceptance as if this were something we had earned and deserved, as if things had always been like this and always would be.

My mother stood up and went to the window. " Well, that's the news," she said. " Not a very pleasant home-coming, I'm afraid." I said nothing. I thought again of that conversation on the veranda of the hotel and of my fatuous hopes only a few hours earlier when I went to the site of the old mine with Kamba. I didn't even mention it to her. It was utterly pointless now.

" Let's have some tea," my mother said.

She went out and I walked around the room with the strange sensation of seeing it for the first time. Everything seemed to be brand new, or borrowed, or made of dust. I found myself seeing things in a glaring light, with peeled eyes, in an unreal atmosphere that nevertheless had the stark garish reality of a nightmare. Usually I came home and slipped into this room like an old set of clothes. There was a special kind of miracle in the prosaic fact that it was so normal and homely and civilised. It was hard to remember that this house stood all alone in the bush, that the view from the window was across a nineteen-mile wide valley with only one other white habitation in it. But now after ten minutes' conversation with my mother it had become derelict again, even though the walls still stood, and the furniture and pictures were in their usual places.

She came back carrying the tea-tray, and I saw that she had changed into her house clothes, tidied her hair and powdered her face. She wore a print frock and an apron and I could not help smiling to see her like this. She looked pretty, dainty, pert, a little schoolmarmish—this was how I liked to think of her, and somehow it gave an air of sanity even to this unbelievable situation.

" Did Peggy write to you ? " she asked as she poured the tea.

" Yes. From Salisbury—I got the news about the engagement, if that's what you mean."

" They'll be happy, she and Anthony," my mother said, and for the first time since I had seen her get out of the car, she smiled.

She asked me again to tell her about University. She was interested in the subjects I studied and as I spoke I felt myself calming down. Through the window I could see the wood-and-iron shack she had converted into a clinic, and I remembered the smell of iodine and permanganate of potash and the milky smell of African babies and the pain in an old induna's face when we set his broken arm, and the long twisted bandages that I washed and rolled up and stored away on the shelf : and

I understood again why I was studying to be a doctor and why, for me, some part of Malinda would never die.

The conversation drifted and led on eventually to the Seckers.

" How are things over at Dale ? " I asked, knowing now that my suspicions yesterday had been well founded.

" We-ell," she said, " Ruth's been a bit edgy. She's working too hard and this drought's getting everybody down. By the way, Bill's back. He went to Brazil this time—that's new territory for him—and he brought Ruth—well, guess ! "

I smiled but I didn't try to guess. It might have been anything from a set of diamond buttons to a helicopter, for Bill's home-coming presents to Ruth were preposterous. That crazy couple had been married since the beginning of time, but they still spoilt each other like moony newly-weds.

" A mink," my mother said, and my smile became a grin as I thought of the absurdity of anybody wearing a fur in this sticky climate, and at the idea of another expensive garment being crammed, unworn, into Ruth's bursting clothes cupboard.

Some time later I went out for a walk, and came across my father sitting in the summer-house that Jordan had built on the high land looking out over the river valley. He had bathed, shaved and changed, and looked rested now. I sat on the bench next to him and for the first few minutes we didn't speak. He must have guessed that my mother had told me the news for he seemed vaguely shamefaced, as if it were something to be blamed for, and eventually he referred to it himself.

He said, " Well, now you know the set-up. Wonderful, isn't it ? "

" Yes, I've seen the death notice," I said. We sat looking at the view. There simply didn't seem to be anything to talk about. There it was, hard and fast and final, and discussion was only a form of self-torment. I asked him casually if he had taken legal opinion in Umtali, and he answered nonchalantly that this was the reason for going there, adding that he had got the books audited to establish his claims with the Liquidator.

Liquidator—he said the word without emphasis as if he had been living with it for a long time.

It was a beautiful view and we sat there taking it in like tourists. There were eagles out in the valley and somewhere a jackal was howling and the setting sun was playing its old tricks on the slopes of the distant mountains.

Eventually I said, " I still don't get it. I just don't see how this is going to help her."

He gave a bitter laugh. " You don't ? It will help her all right. You can bet your life that she's already done a deal with this Liquidator. He'll get the ranch into his hands, then quietly sell it back to her—or to some stooge of hers. That's how these things are worked. Six months and she'll be back with plant and equipment to dig out that copper."

" What a dirty swindle ! "

" Yep," he said in an empty, tired voice. "And it was proved last night by something Una said. Why is she advertising for a man to run the place ? Because she's coming right back."

The ranch hands took it badly. Kamba kept asking me, " How is it possible that you're leaving Malinda ? " And whenever I tried to explain he got into an argument with me, as if we had deliberately engineered it to happen this way. The whole thing became immensely complicated, and obviously caused a great deal of talk in the village because on the second day I received a message to go and explain things to the headman.

I usually spent a lot of time in the village. It lay on the other side of the tall ridge on which the Finger stood, and out of sight from the Retreat. With its fresh straw roofs, its smooth walls decorated with geometrical patterns in different coloured ochres, its tiny gardens of pumpkin and millet, its maze of lanes marked out by trimmed reed fences, it had the clean hand-made look of new basketwork. One always thought that it had been built only the previous week, but it was old, older than the original Retreat, older than any man-made thing in the valley. Not even the two emaciated great-grandmothers who hobbled among the huts on thick wooden staves could say when it began. About forty families lived there under the chieftainship of a timid old induna who spent his time gossiping with the women and carving wooden animals that eventually found their way into the tourist curio trade. The village supplied us with ranch hands, milkmaids and herdsmen, but it was a floating population and floating labour for us, for most of the young men and women would go off for long spells of work in the towns.

" Beta," one of these returned sons would say, " so you've also been to town. How was it ? "—speaking in a way that made us both sound important.

" Not bad. But I like it better at Malinda. All the time I was there I was living there, I'd hear a sound in the night thinking it was those guinea fowl *chink-chinking* in a bush or the baboons getting into a fight on the cliff. I'd jump up in my bed, and what would it be ? "

" What, Beta ? "

" A tap dripping. The window rattling."

" So. But with me it is the other way round. Here when the baboons quarrel I think it's the bus starting up in the location. I've got money there," he'd say, taking out his Post Office savings book. Or he'd hand me a new watch or a coloured snapshot showing him in a city suit, to admire.

" Did you happen to meet my nephew Shadrak in Igoli ? " the village butcher would ask me. Igoli meant Johannesburg, being a corruption of the word gold. " He's working down at Ferrandi's Timber Yard."

" Where's that ? "

" In Newtown."

" No, I didn't come across him."

" Pity—he would have liked meeting you."

Children followed me wherever I went, for I always took a pocketful of sweets to hand out. Women would consult me about their babies' rashes or loss of appetite, and sometimes I would solemnly write out prescriptions which my mother would make up faithfully in the clinic. The witch-doctor

trying to prop up his pathetically unreliable hit-or-miss.
techniques, would try to wring a little aid from modern science.

" Beta, what's this stuff somebody was telling me about—
pencil something ? "

" Penicillin."

" That's right. Useful stuff, I hear."

" Yes, but leave it alone. You'll kill off the whole village.
Stick to your bones and herbs, old man."

" I wasn't thinking of that. I was thinking it might stop the
drought. . . ."

Here life went on in a low-keyed peaceful rhythm that made
our European anxieties seem far-fetched and distraught. We
had learnt much from the villagers—how to come to terms with
the bush, to sway to its moods, to accept nature as a fact and
a force in life, and not something to be resisted and twisted out
of recognition. They had learnt from us too—how to purify
water, how to treat ailments and infections in cattle, how to
rotate crops, how to prevent or treat enteritis in babies, and of
course, how to read and write. Who was in the greater debt ?
It was impossible to say, because we needed each other. There
were no politics on Malinda because the problems of politics
had either never arisen, or had been solved as soon as they
appeared. We had mutual respect and no phobias about skin
colour : we worked in a joint enterprise of building up a little
corner of Rhodesia.

The village was changing. There were alarm clocks in many
huts and people would come back from town with newspapers
and magazines, gramophones and even American pop records.
Many could drive a car, not even from having learnt it in town,
but from handling the vehicles on Malinda. They knew how
to use a tractor, or erect a windmill, or repair a truck. Like all
Africa the village was reaching into the future, but it was not
an agony to them as the changing order was to the whites.
There was the glow of birth and discovery—a dawning. They
were emerging clumsily, haltingly, out of the past of superstition, poverty and ignorance. And we? We were disappearing.

I found the old headman squatting outside his hut burning

markings on to a wooden giraffe with a heated poker. He greeted me without looking up, and spoke with his eyes on his work. It was a sign that he was embarrassed.

" Beta—what's this I hear—this trouble at Malinda ? "

He stuck the cooling poker into the fire, pulled out the red-hot one and continued scorching the pattern on to the giraffe gripped between his knees.

" We have to leave," I told him. " We're being chased off by the law."

" Does the law chase *you* people away from land ? I've never heard of that."

" But it's true, Mgali. Sometimes it happens that way."

" Who will give us medicine for our cattle ? And for our babies ? Who will teach our children to read ? Tell me one thing, Beta, are you throwing us back to the bush ? "

I tried to explain that everything was changing, that by next year there wouldn't be a ranch any more, but something much better—a copper mine ; that there would be a real school for the children, not that little shack with home-made desks; and several teachers, not just my mother. I said there'd be a proper hospital too, where pregnant mothers and ailing babies would be treated by a real doctor and nurses in white uniforms. As for the cattle—well, probably there wouldn't be any after a time, since cattle and copper mining don't go together, but it wouldn't matter because everybody would be working for regular wages. I tried to describe the tidy little brick township that would eventually replace the village. And thinking it might appeal to his fancy, I told him there would probably be an airstrip, if the mine grew big enough. I tried to paint it as attractively as I could ; but even while I spoke I realised how miserable it must have sounded to him.

He looked up at me for the first time, with weak, watery, old eyes and said, " I'm sorry. I see that you're not throwing us back to the bush. You're throwing us into the fire."

For ten days I loafed about Malinda with the feeling of living in a strange land. The stockades were full of new calves and we went through the routine of tending them, but wondering all the time "for whom?" The pineapples and avocadoes looked wonderful and the new orchard was a cool haven with its great shining tropical leaves, its intense greens and exotic blossoms. But it was as remote from us as a public park. I took a hand in the ranch work, something I used to look forward to with tingling keenness, but it was meaningless work. I spent long hours next to my father when we didn't speak a word because everything had been said. In the evenings we read and went to bed.

We were waiting.

Yet there was one more move in the game, conclusive and unbeatable—and it belonged to us. My father discovered it only a few days before Lavinia was due to arrive. One night he took down the tin box containing the ranch documents simply to acquaint himself with the situation before the meetings. Among them was the original contract under which Jordan bought the land for Malinda from the Seckers, but he read it and put it away without realising that there was a clause that allowed him to rescue himself and Malinda and end his troubles with Lavinia for all time.

It only struck him the next morning. We were repairing a loading ramp at the time, and he stood up suddenly, let the hammer slip from his hand, looked around in astonishment and said, "If I'm not the biggest, blindest, dumbest dope!" and started running back to the house.

I followed and inside he spread out the contract and showed me the clause. It seemed familiar. It started in a fugue of polysyllables about forfeiture penalties and what-not, but suddenly cleared its head and stated tersely that the seller had the right to buy back the land at the contract price if the partnership terminated. Just like that. The clear part seemed to have been added as an afterthought. I read on a few lines and saw that any disputes would be settled by—yes, there it was—a referee. This was one of the points my father had discussed with Conrad that time we visited him in his chambers in Johannesburg.

He was very excited. He had been sweating mildly from the work, but now his whole face was bathed in perspiration and he was trembling with impatience. He folded the contract, stuffed it into his pocket, jammed his shapeless khaki hat on his head and tugged it down over his moist forehead.

" Come on," he said, going to the door.

" Where are we going ? "

" To Dale."

We did the nine miles from Malinda to the Seckers' ranch without breaking any springs, slithering into boulders or getting bogged at river crossings, but it was miraculous. I had not seen him so happy since my return, indeed for many years. He was grinning and slapping his thighs, making a game of the driving, whistling loud tuneless snatches of songs, leaning back in his seat and roaring with laughter. His excitement was almost childish and at the same time just a touch insane. It reminded me of that ride from Umtali, for this was the reverse aspect of his mood then. Happy was an inadequate word. He was over-joyed, as brimful of exuberant delight as he had been of morose despondency on that previous ride.

At Dale we turned between the white gate posts, clanked over the cattle trap, and drove across the acre-sized yard towards the office at the far corner. With all its buildings— store-rooms, barns, dairies, repair shops, sawmills, silos, its petrol pumps, tractors, reapers and trucks—Dale looked more prosperous than ever. Coming from our pretty little postcard ranch at Malinda it was like entering a town.

Ruth Secker was waiting for us at the top of the little flight of wooden steps that led to the office. She had a pencil in one hand and a bunch of railway consignment notes in the other, and was wearing those heavy horn-rimmed glasses which she always used for paper work, but which were as incongruous on her as a pair of slippers on a kudu. She wore her usual ranch clothes—shapeless worn trousers turned up at the ends and splotched with stains of cattle dip, ink and iodine ; scuffed flat-heeled brown shoes, a threadbare khaki shirt with the sleeves rolled up on her plump, mottled arms, a faded scarf tied around her frizzy yellow hair.

" Whoa there, whoa ! " she said as my father pulled up with a skid. " What's the matter—Malinda burnt down ? "

" Ruth, I've got to talk to you."

" Come inside." She stood back and waved her hand toward the open door of the office, but my father peered out and saw that there were people working inside. " No, let's talk in the house," he suggested.

As we were walking toward the rambling brick and iron homestead with its wild cascade of bougainvillæa tumbling over the veranda, my father asked casually, " Bill around this morning ? "

Ruth put her hands to the side of her face. " Asleep."

" Hell ! "

It was past nine, but that was getting on for midday in these parts. I smiled—Bill must have been the only settler not actually laid up with broken bones or bad illness who was still lying in bed at that time of day.

" Please get him up," my father said urgently. " I need him in on this."

" Joe—what's the big secret ? "

" No secret. I'll tell you when we get inside."

When we entered the big gloomy sitting-room Ruth said, " Cool off in here while I go and rouse the lazy bastard." She left us and went down the long passage to the bedroom. On the way she passed the kitchen, and I heard her call out in Fanagalo, " Sheribo ! Kidneys, onions and eggs, and make fresh coffee. The master's getting up." The command was loud and authoritative but there was no exasperation in her voice, rather a fond pride at being able to do something for Bill. My father and I exchanged a smile. The way Ruth spoilt Bill was a joke all over the district. She really indulged him, let him take long holidays, buy himself new sports cars every year, go off to the races, in fact, live like a playboy while she did the work. It really was a joke—no ranch had a right to succeed with a man like Bill at the head, hitting it up, leaving all the responsibility to his wife. Yet look at Dale—one hundred and fifty thousand acres, equipment and installations enough for ten ranches, huge herds and pedigree stock that invariably walked off with the prizes at agricultural shows, a whole staff of clerks, managers, foremen, even a full-time veterinary. As we waited in the neglected sitting-room I thought of the irony that made Dale prosper in spite of itself, while Malinda had to fight grimly for every inch of progress.

Ruth returned and soon after Bill sauntered in, wearing a yellow silk dressing-gown and pigskin slippers. He was smoking a cigarette in a holder, gripping it in his teeth in the corner of his mouth while he shaved himself with a battery-run electric shaver. Bill Secker—a florid, broad-shouldered man with speckled blue eyes, thin sandy hair turning silver, ginger freckles spattered like tea leaves right up his high pink forehead —as pampered and nursed and expensive-looking as one of his own show bulls.

"Now, this is how it works," my father explained, after showing Bill and Ruth the decree and the clause in the contract. "You'll give notice that since the partnership is terminated you're exercising your right to take over the land at the contract price. Then you'll sell it back to me for the same figure. Simple. It's so bloody simple I could kick myself for not having spotted it earlier. Well—will you agree to this?"

"No trouble at all," Ruth said, and I had not the slightest doubt that this would be her answer. The Seckers were not only our closest neighbours but our closest friends, and had helped us on countless occasions during our ten years at Malinda.

A kitchen girl brought in Bill's breakfast on a tray and set it down at the far end of the table. As Bill started eating Ruth said, "In fact, there's no need for any money to pass. The amount involved is piddling, anyway—the land was worth nothing when that shrivelled-up old miser bought it—and I dare say you'll have no difficulty in paying your, excuse me, partner her half-share of the price."

" No," my father said. " It's quite ridiculously simple. Well, Bill, how do you feel ? Prepared to do the deal ? "

" Whatever Ruth says. She runs the show."

" I must mention one thing. There might be copper on the property," my father said to Bill, and went on to tell him what we had heard at the Bell Hotel.

" Every ranch has got a potential copper lode," Bill said, not letting that stand in the way. " It's a chance you take on every property deal. As far as I'm concerned, old man, I wouldn't stand in your way as to mineral rights."

" As far as I'm concerned," Ruth said in that excitable aggressive way of hers, " I'll do the deal, chance or no chance. You're entitled to keep any copper—or diamonds or uranium or any other claptrap you might find there. So far as I'm concerned I sold this land ten years ago, and I wouldn't dream of taking it back from you if you hadn't asked me to, even if I'd remembered that clause. And, anyway, we're not taking it back, just helping you get round a little corner, legally speaking."

" That's fair," Bill said.

" Anyway, if this copper proposition works out, I'll cut you in," my father told Bill. " It will be a square deal."

" Let's gather that one in when there's something on the stalk," Bill said, with a mouthful of grilled kidneys. He turned to Ruth, " Why did old Whittaker put that bit in ? After all, it says nothing about compensation for buildings and improvements—just reverses the deal. I don't remember the transaction very clearly. Why did he ask for that clause to be in ? "

" I wanted it in," Ruth said. " I thought we might want to expand over that side some day, so I asked for the right to buy the land back. That's all. He said all right, but only if the partnership broke up. I suggested the same price, and he just didn't argue. Didn't seem very interested. He took a fancy to that corner because it was "gorgeous"—that's the word he used—"gorgeous"—and I rather gathered that he was going to build a holiday shack there for himself and this partner, whoever it was. Not a ranch. I didn't know it was going to be developed and that *you* people were coming to live here. That's why it's swop for swop—the same land for the same price.

"Lucky for us it turned out that way," my father said, all smiles.

"Joe—you're a wizard. When did you think it up?"

My father looked at his watch. "About an hour and a half ago."

"Well, that's settled," Bill said, wiping his mouth on the napkin and standing up. "Good show, Joe. I'm taking a run into town to-day, so I'll leave you now. But good show. Any more little problems like that you want us to help you along with—well, you know the way over to Dale." He left us then, taking the top off the electric shaver and blowing the dust out of the blades as he walked out of the room.

"Shouldn't you put this in writing?" I suggested—not too happily because I disliked suggesting that we didn't trust Ruth. "You know—just to tie it up."

"Ruth's word is good enough for me," my father said

"No, Gene's right. Let's be business-like about it," Ruth said. She leaned back and reached for a wad of Dale notepaper from the sideboard drawer. She wrote two letters. The first, addressed to Malinda Ranch, stated that since the partnership was being dissolved she claimed the right in terms of the contract to buy back the property at the price therein stated. She chuckled over "therein". "See? I'm getting to be quite a lawyer. Running Dale gives me lots of practice." The second, addressed to Jeremy Joe Latham, Esq., stated simply that as and when she had bought the property from the partnership, she would sell it back to him for the same price. She signed both letters with a quick, business-like flourish and handed them over to my father. "Good luck," she said. "This calls for drinks."

She did that,—called for drinks in a loud ringing voice that echoed down the passage. When the tray of liquor and glasses was brought in, she poured strong double tots for each of us.

E

" Here's to the deal, Joe," she said, holding up her glass. " I'll be as glad as you to see the end of that Whittaker bitch."

We drank to the deal, to the future, to the end of the Whittaker bitch, to Malinda, to Dale, and to about half a dozen other splendid proposals. It was nearly an hour before we left for home. This time I drove, but I was too hazy to remember much of the trip back. I knew only that the country-side looked glorious, and that my father sat in a kind of daze beside me, a look of blissful happiness on his dark, handsome face.

4

THE CARS and station wagons arrived, the smart striped luggage was taken into the house, the shutters were banged open, visitors emerged on to the lawn in sun-glasses and holiday attire ; out came cameras and binoculars, up went sun umbrellas, on went the transistor radios to blare hit parade music across the ravine, and another annual bushveld gala was on its way.

But for once it failed to depress us. It was wonderful to know that this was the last house-party. We had never expected to see such a lucky end to this grotesque partnership between a hard-working cattleman and a city socialite, between the Retreat and the Big House, between a ranch and a holiday resort. We had only to wait a few more weeks before the party of the first part would say good-bye for ever to the party of the second part, and this blast of noise and colour emanating from the Big House was like a bright crackling bonfire celebrating the event.

But how we used to hate these invasions. " Guests " in lunatic hats and hilarious sportswear overran the property like a mob of seaside trippers. They made a lido of the flat rocks near the rapids, sunbathing on beach divans with white-coated servants trundling trays of drinks down from the house. They practised golf shots on the lawn, threw stones at the baboons, dandled the cute little bead-bedecked piccanins from the village, took movies of the hippo, chased giraffe in their cars. Some tried hunting with great fuss and heroics, but usually negligible results. They found the calves irresistible. They would step delicately, like storks, through the slush to stand and peer for

hours into the stockades. On first noticing us they stared as if
we were pigmies, obviously surprised to find other human
beings, even remote bush throw-backs, on Lavina's celebrated
game farm.

Later they would strike up conversation—leaning on the
fence and talking to our backs while we worked—what brand
of cattle were we breeding, how did we manage when we
needed a doctor, was the river free from crocodiles, what was
the distance across the valley, how high was the Finger, had
we ever shot a lion, wasn't it lonely living out here all by
ourselves—until we felt like braining them with the nearest
implement at hand.

It was always a shock to find them on Malinda. To us they
were fantastic and outlandish like the viridian dragonflies that
skimmed across the stagnant pools below the rapids or the
giant grasshoppers, vividly coloured like painted German toys,
that we sometimes saw in the tall grass. And their superior
tourist manner, their air of brash intrusion, their utterly secure
self-assurance always infuriated us.

But that year none of these things bothered us. We were
extremely good-natured about the holiday and the guests
thought us charming. When we got a message to come over
and mend the fuses we went immediately. We didn't mind
driving Mrs. So-and-So to the Bell Hotel to make a telephone
call. Or catching a monkey for one of the ladies, or taking
group photographs on the lawn, or shooting guinea fowl for
their table, or even standing around to give an authentic bush-
ranger touch to the proceedings. We were only too glad to
co-operate in making this the happiest of all the house-parties.

We didn't even mind the ranch workers being roped in for
domestic service at the Big House. This happened every year
as part of the general conscription of the entire village. Half
a dozen women would shell peas for dinner, a similar number
do laundry work or shine shoes. Vast quantities of firewood
were collected and piled up outside the kitchen door, cars were
polished several times a day, golf balls were retrieved by swarms
of small boys, floor cleaners nudging tins of polish along with

their heads were busy in every room. Even this senseless waste of labour now had its comic side.

On the second morning Lavinia drove over to the Retreat, saying as she stepped out of the station wagon, " I can only spare a few minutes now. I'm needed back in the house. We're all going off to the Bushman Caves."

It was a hurried visit—while she spoke to us she kept looking across the ravine at the crowd waiting on the steps of the Big House—and it was not about the partnership business. No, the most important thing at the moment was to arrange for the supply of vegetables, meat and milk to the Big House. My mother said she would provide them as before but would need a list of requirements every few days. Lavinia said, " That's sweet of you. I hope it won't inconvenience you." She was polite and subdued. I watched her all the time, with a feeling of faint amusement to see her so confident of her victory that she could afford to be nice to us all over again and to regard our departure from Malinda as less important than the supply of provisions to the Big House. In her mild manner there was just a hint that she was embarrassed—perhaps ashamed at what she had done. But I wasn't going to let myself be influenced by that.

As she was leaving she said, " I'm going to be busy for the next few days organising things and getting people into the swing of the holiday. But after that I'll be able to come over and . . ." she paused—" sort things out."

She left then, swung open the car door, slid in under the steering-wheel and with a bright smile drove off fast into the ravine to reappear a few minutes later in front of the Big House.

There was a party that night to which I was invited because some of the group had not yet arrived and there was a shortage of men. The same faces, accents, jokes ; the same smells of perfume and cigars ; the same buffet supper with drinks served from the bamboo bar in the corner. There were a few young people in the room, but I made no contact with them. They were smarting from sunburn and yawning from too much air and the trip to the Bushman Caves. It was the stage of the holiday when people were still becoming adjusted to the heat and surroundings, getting broiled in the sun, suffering aches, sprains, scratches, stiffness and headaches. The new-comers to Malinda still felt strange and kept to themselves. The odd thing was that I didn't even notice the girl, who was to make me soar on wings this holiday, although I spent nearly two hours in the same room with her : or if I did, it was too vaguely because my antagonism shut off my interest in the crowd. The truth was as I had to admit later, that she must have merged so naturally with them.

I saw them as a crowd, a flock of birds, noticing only those who had been at Malinda before. " Kiki " Pape was there, of course ; she was a kind of regimental mascot of all these holidays. Kiki, the spy, fixer, stooge and stand-in for Lavinia. No party was complete without Kiki perched on the veranda wall swinging that tiny doll-like foot ; or standing glass in hand, feet planted apart, rump sticking out, body tilted at a fixed angle as if held in position by thumbscrews at her hips— a stance adopted in advance to keep her firmly anchored to the floor as she got drunk : or, wearing a Chinese straw hat and an artist's smock that smothered her like a collapsed tent, painting landscapes on the lawn. Kiki with the lank platinum hair hanging straight down the back of her curiously flat head, the delicate china figurine complexion in which age showed not as wrinkles but as minute cracks, the enormous pale-blue eyes of such child-like innocence that they were the most out-rageous lie of all about her—for Kiki was a seasoned old adventuress, the motive of a once sensational murder in which her baronet lover shot away a large section of her husband, Lord Somebody-or-Other, with a shotgun in a bungalow in the Bahamas. After the case, which kept her stunningly photogenic face in the world's newspapers for six months, she reverted to the name of a former husband, lived for a while on the Riviera, drifted steadily south to Cairo, Nairobi and finally Johannesburg ; here she was living out her remaining years with the spectacular dash of a gentleman tramp. Kiki, the elegant drunk, the sugary liar, the human trash-can always at hand to receive Lavinia's cast-offs—clothes, handbags, dogs, men.

And Hoffman, naturally. Frank Hoffman—Lavinia's accountant, business adviser, flatterer and foot warmer—and the resident comedian. We knew him well, of course, the tubby perspiring figure, the gingery hair glistening with lotion, the shrewd freckled face with the glowing massaged look, the foppish holiday dress—mauve shantung lounging pyjamas, canvas shoes, or dove-grey slacks and country club blazers with thick embroidered badges on the pockets. To see Hoffman stand at the top of the veranda steps within half an hour of arrival and gaze with deep content over the valley was to witness the ceremonial inauguration of the house-parties, just as the sight of the first pair of Egyptian geese promenading along the sand beside the river announced the arrival of spring. He was the wit of every party. He could top anybody's jokes, and his own were untoppable and unstoppable. With the Big House crowd he gave the impression of being an amusing ass, but we knew from the meetings that he was wily as a jackal.

The Forster girls were there for the second time. Tall, horsey, lanky twenty-five-year-old twins, they had graduated during the year from heiresses to millionairesses, for their grandfather had finally died and bequeathed them half the fishing and cigarette industry. They looked exactly alike and seemed to have suntan everywhere. They wore each other's off-shoulder dresses and clanky jewellery and had the identical rangy way of sitting, or leaning over the table so that their breasts skimmed the sugar. Although spinsters they did not lack for sex, for it was no secret that they were promiscuous with any reasonably pleasant celebrities. Indeed, it was impossible to conceal any secrets about those big, bare, uninhibited girls.

I recognised Charlie "Chips" Stanton, both from his previous visit and from his photograph in the newspapers. A golf professional, he seemed to have grass growing out of his ears and tiny red flags in his eyes. He was purple and stank of drink

from yards away. Ed Scobie the stockbroker was there again,
for ever tearing open telegrams. In ten days he managed to
receive more mail and telegrams, despite difficulties of delivery,
than we had done in ten years at Malinda.

But the rest were the usual Big House crowd—fashionable,
colourful, yet faceless, like their striped luggage. Only one man
did not quite fit into the pattern. I met him about half-way
through the evening. He sauntered up to me, and said, " Hear
you live around these parts ? Well, glad to know you, pal.
I'm an old Africa buff myself." He shook my hand with a great
abrasive palm, while the other fished in the inside pocket of
his dinner-suit. It pulled out a business card which he handed
to me. The card gave the name of a sporting goods firm in
Durban with, in the corner, " Managing Director Ronnie
Forsythe." Ronnie, just like that. A friendly type. He was a
tall, heavy, lazy-moving man in his late twenties with a black
beard that smudged over, rather than grew on, his pudgy
youthful face. His eyes interested me. They were small,
shrewd, wide-awake, humorous and ruthless. I had seen eyes
like that before, especially in South African men who came
from farms. He said, " Thought I'd get in a little huntin' and
shootin' this trip, but seems to me the bush jes' ain't willing
to co-*ar*perate." He spoke in a queer way, with an American
accent but not quite the way Americans do it. It was more
American than the real thing, rather the way the sheriff talks
in cowboy serials. Wise guy, tough guy, Slim Sam and Honest
Al, all mixed up and phoney as hell.

" You American ? " I asked, glancing down at the card with
its Durban address.

" Nope. S'African."

After that I could detect the South African accent on which
the Wild West speech had been grafted—the dropped syllables,
the flat vowels. Yet there was something likeable about him.
He was handsome in a tough masculine way, despite the rather
soft look about his features. And his casual affability was
disarming. As he talked on I found the reason for the accent.
" Yup, I'm what folks call a Big White Hunter—but don't get

me wrong. I don't go for that tusk-and-claw stuff. No, sir, that's dead. I operate the modern way—Bwana Moneybags, that's me. You see, I've got this shop and I've got my clients, and true I've done plenny hunting in my time. But where I get my dough is helping out the movie and TV companies. Sell them the stuff they need for these safari epics—rifles, tents, camp kitchens and all that jazz, then buy it back when the shooting's over. And sell it again to the next outfit."

" Smart rackct," I said, meaning racket. But he took it as a compliment and went on, " Then I help out in the pictures— sometimes getting my name in the credits, like 'wild life adviser' and 'consultant anthropologist.' And tell you some- thing—I'm a movie actor. I mean, I play bit parts in the pictures like local game warden or native commissioner, and I'm the guy that actually bumps off the lion when it looks like the big man's doing it. Standing next to the camera . . . pow ! " He raised his elbows and shot an imaginary lion with an imaginary gun. "You remember that picture where Ava Gardner . . ."

He was different from all the other men in the room, and a new type for thc Big House. All he shared with the others was the lady-killer look, but somehow it was rather frank and brash, and not really unpleasant. The accent of course, had rubbed off on to him during all that film work. At any rate, that could have been the explanation. But there was something so ridiculously bogus about it that I began to wonder if I could believe a single word he told me. I wondered too, how he ever got into this house-party.

" Pal, you and me must have a proper pow-wow some time. Maybe we can have a look over the district together. Ain't never been aroun' these parts afore," he said, lapsing heavily into his adopted dialect. " So long, keed." He slapped me on the arm, then walked away giving me a wide, breezy salute. I saw him go up to a girl, take the glass from between her fingers, pull her out of the chair, and cha-cha expertly around the room, talking all the time.

I was intrigued by Lavinia that night. She was in great

form, very spirited, very much in command. She had a volatile gaiety that I had not seen in her for years. It was the old Lavinia again—sparkling and excited, as if she had thrown off a burden that had oppressed her ever since those far-off Johannesburg days. Her vivacity held me mesmerised, as it did the group of people with whom she managed to carry on half a dozen separate yet simultaneous conversations. " Eddie, they're saying terrible things about you in town—was that really a bear squeeze ? I don't care anyway, you were a darling to remember me, and I'll hang on to those shares until you say when. . . . No, thanks, Charles, I've given it up, I threw my clubs into the lake at Kensington last year, and that's that. . . . Angela, you look a sight : I simply can't understand how a girl like you, worth your weight in de Beers share certificates can go around looking like an Arab. And that goes for you, too, Pamela. Everything I say to Angela goes for Pamela, and vice versa. . . . No, I won't take it up again. Charles wants to improve my grip—or is it my rhythm, Charles ?—anyway, thank you, but I've really given up. Try Kiki, she's losing her grip. . . . Thanks, soda and a pinch of lemon. Eddie, I only hope they hold up and not make us lose our pants as we did in that Rooiplaats swindle. Well, if you say so—yes, that's just right. Oh, yes, and a little cold chicken salad. . . . Oh, you and your stories, I don't believe a word you say, Baxter, you just make these things up to stun people. What's that, Frank ? . . . Oh, listen to this everybody—this is gorgeous ! "

Once or twice she brought me into the conversation. " Ask Gene, he knows all about nature and wild life." And something about the servants getting drunk and making too much noise in the kitchen—rather like a director tossing some minor business to a small-part actor—and was off again with some patter about a restaurant or a sea cruise.

It was not that she was merely keyed up. The word that best described her was *elated*, and somehow that made her mood vaguely ominous and threatening. Yet there was an under-current of uncertainty, or anxiety. One could not detect it in her voice, her talk or her expression. It showed in her hands.

Over the years I had come to observe that her nervousness always came out in her hands, even when, as now, she gave all the appearance of being in a vivacious mood. All the time she was talking, her fingers were contradicting her, threshing and twisting her rings round and round and betraying her tensions.

There was a blurred outline to her mood, a suggestion of echoes of another underneath, that was emphasised by the portrait of herself that hung on the wall behind her. It had been painted about eight years earlier when Jordan was still alive and she was at the height of her beauty and success. I knew the picture well and each time I saw it, it seemed to give me a little more insight into Lavinia, for it was a many-sided interpretation. It was modern but not modernistic—deft, informal, clever, a shrewd amusing commentary on the sitter rather than a true likeness. It gave the quick instantaneous impression, but at the same time explored deep, and then lightly tossed off the discovery as a joke. It said : those frank laughing sea-green eyes are not quite what they appear. Look a little deeper and you'll see the eyes of a wanton. Also of a trapped animal that would smash anything to get what it wanted. Observe that hungry, acquisitive gleam. That fine aristocratic nose ? Beautiful—but it's a little too alert, too sensitive. That sniff is dangerous. That intriguing humorous smile on the fine expressive mouth is not as friendly as you think. See the smile behind the smile. Find out what she's smiling about before being captivated. And as for the astonishing effect of perfect features set in a fine elegant face, the high intelligent forehead, the graceful slim neck—be careful. It's all too perfect—as deliberate, cunning and functional as a jungle flower whose beauty is a snare for insects.

She had changed, but not very greatly since the picture was painted. Her hair was not so red now. It had lightened to a golden colour and its new short style suited her better. She looked older of course, but not less attractive. Her face was a little thinner, the lines more pronounced at the corners of her mouth, her figure had lost something of its litheness, but there was still the same poise and dash and disdain about her, and the same power to captivate people with charm and glamour.

As I watched her, the older and subtly changed version of the portrait behind her, I felt a sudden access of pity for her. Despite all her advantages and assets, her life was sliding into the same sort of failure as Kiki's. She had married a millionaire and dazzled a city. Once everybody clamoured to attend her parties. To be on her guest list was not only a mark of social distinction, but a guarantee of business or professional success. For a word in the right place, a secret divulged, an introduction at the Whittaker home could lead to an important job, a big contract or a scoop on the stock exchange. She had been the darling of the gossip columnists, the star of the women's pages. If she dropped a remark on hats or cats or canapes, it was quoted as the wisdom of a society oracle. The newspapers were always showing pictures of her at cocktail parties, opening nights, mayoral receptions. Or it might be tossing a bottle of champagne at the steel girders of a new gold mine headgear, or laying the foundation stone of a new skyscraper, for Jordan had used her as royalty is used, to give prestige to his business undertakings.

But now all that was over. Even the miserable legacy Jordan had left her was about to disappear. Something had gone wrong and with all her beauty, intelligence, flair and influential friendships, she was coming face to face with total ruin.

The picture was an irony now. It showed her riding the crest —a tossed shoulder, a cocked eyebrow, an expression that laughed at the world, and said, " To hell with you." But the defiance had misfired.

" Frank thinks we ought to make a film record of this holiday—oh, not one of those boring ' that's-me-when-I-fell-in-the-water ' things, but a real slick job. He probably wants to flog it on television. Hairdressers ? They've all got a castration complex. Put a pair of scissors in their hands and they scalp you. Kiki ! How about steak *tartare* ? . . ."

While she talked I watched her hands. The writhing fingers

kept up their own commentary, a silent supplement of her words, and suddenly like a message in deaf-mute language, they seemed to spin out a sentence. "Now I'm going to get rid of the noose that Jordan tried to throttle me with." Then I understood. In fighting for Malinda she was fighting for her life.

5

THERE WAS A MEETING between my father and Lavinia and Hoffman a few days later. I didn't go because there seemed no point in it. Nor did Mr. Christie come out from Umtali. But apparently my father infuriated Lavinia and Hoffman by his new tactics—sitting unruffled and unperturbed, suggesting nothing, saying the minimum, refusing to be provoked. He was playing the waiting game. He had merely to sit tight until the time set in the decree expired. Then he wouldn't even have to deal with Lavinia. He would simply send Ruth's letter to the Liquidator and that would be the end of the Hundred Years' War. For these tactics he didn't need Christie. He certainly didn't need me. The meetings were merely a formality now.

And waiting and feeling that the long struggle was over produced a sense of anti-climax, so that when I met Marjorie and found a sudden new excitement in my life, I was more than ready to forget Malinda and its troubles.

We met, appropriately, at the Finger, that ubiquitous landmark which seemed to have a way of busying itself with everything that went on in the valley.

The Finger was a geological freak of balancing stones standing near the stump-nosed end of a ridge which poked out into the valley. Originally one towering stone mass, erosion had thinned it down and severed it in two places, leaving a tall coffin-shaped slab standing up-ended on two granite boulders, each as big as a hut. The shape and especially the joints had made the name inevitable. The balance was so delicate that it gave the illusion of swaying in the wind, and during a storm when we gazed at it from the window of the Retreat it seemed to bend its arthritic knuckles and beckon us in agitation.

It was more than just a landmark. It seemed to serve some obscure and ancient purpose in the valley. On dull days when the air was ominous with rain and the dry silent lightning streaked through the veins of the sky, the wild turkeys, whom we only saw in such weather, would flap lazily towards it and rest there a while before resuming their slow brooding inspection of the valley. On fine days it seemed to point joyously at the sky as if saying, " What remarkable weather ! " In drought the vultures would use it as a lookout, clawing for footholds on the rounded top, snarling at each other with an obscene dribble of red tongues, rustling their corpse-dry wings, harrumping their bald, bony hag's shoulders.

It told us of death, for a fire burned there when there was a funeral in the nearby village ; of birth and initiation, for the appropriate ceremonies were held on the flat rock apron surrounding it ; of the coming of visitors, for the grey top would catch the reflection of windscreens from a distant point on the road long before the sound of an engine could be heard. It helped us know the size and depth of the valley, for surveyors used it as a beacon. It even told us the time, for before we came to Malinda some people had laid a half-circle of white stones around it turning it into a huge Druidical sundial. There was something almost sentient about the Finger and it seemed to play a part in everything that happened in the valley.

That morning it rose grey and sullen against the hard blue sky, a dour proclamation of the continuing drought. The top was streaked with the excrement of vultures but the big birds were not there. I saw them far out in the valley, tiny black rags gliding so slowly that they seemed motionless. As I walked the sun caught the stone from a new angle, changing its dry porous look to a kind of glassy translucence with only the edges strongly visible. It was in an equivocal mood. I tried to find some message in this apparent smile on the face of the Finger. Looking for signs and omens in the Finger was an old game of ours.

I was wearing torn old hunting clothes and carrying my rifle because I had been down to the village to investigate another leopard scare. I came back along the ridge which was the shortest way back to Malinda, although it involved a steep climb down the side. I reached the Finger, passed it along the narrow ledge skirting the base rock, and saw her as I emerged from the shadow.

She was a distance ahead, at the edge of the ridge, dwarfed by the immense landscape. I stopped. I felt a strange sensation, almost a shock. Her white dress fluttered in the wind, making a startling contrast to the drab grey surroundings, and there was a sense of danger in the menacing rocks and the vast emptiness of sky and valley behind her. I caught the glint of binoculars in her hand and saw that she was looking out across the valley. I walked on cautiously, stalking her almost, as if she were an intruder. I was puzzled. This was well off the map for the Big House crowd; it was a difficult climb unless one knew the routes. Besides, she was alone. I thought she might be a visitor on her way through to Dale, but this was unlikely. The road was several miles away.

As I came closer and made out the firm shape of her back in the tight-waisted sleeveless frock, the jet black hair, the golden skin, I felt an absurd jolt of excitement.

She waited for me to come right up then lowered the binoculars.

" Hallo," she said casually. " What's all that commotion out there ? "

" Vultures meeting for luncheon."

" You mean a *kill* ? "

I tried to place the accent and decided tentatively that it was American. " Not necessarily. Probably an impala or giraffe dying of exhaustion." She gave me a quick look that suggested I was trying to be smart. I explained, " They're all sick out there. It's the drought. It could be the dogs, of course."

" Dogs ? "

" Wild dogs."

" Oh, wolves."

I laughed. " No, pretty little dogs with soulful eyes. . . ." Another quick look. " They're just like ordinary dogs, rather . . ." I found the word—" cute. But they're the worst killers of all. Those vultures are kidding themselves."

She was smiling now. " Why ? " she asked, still looking through the binoculars.

" Because the dogs don't leave anything for the vultures. They've got healthy appetites."

" I see."

She went on looking at the tiny black specks circling slowly in the sky. She *was* from the Big House. Whether I recognised her vaguely or knew it from her manner I could tell that she was one of Lavinia's crowd. She was old for me but young for the Big House—about twenty-three. She was not pretty but not ugly either. She stated her own case for attractiveness with personality and a kind of calculated sex-charged allure. The great thing about her was her body—tall, taut, with supple lines, a small waist, beautiful limbs. There was an instinctive grace about her that reminded me of the style of athletes and gymnasts—people trained to control every twist and inflection of their bodies. And there was something else that took me a moment to define. She had that special air of people who are thoroughly used to being looked at. Men—it came to me in a flash. She was one of those used to having men around her— men to bring out the sparkle.

" Here—you look," she said, handing me the binoculars. I focused them but could see nothing in the dense bush. Then I knew that she was studying me. She was sizing me up—very deliberately—and with a private smile that brushed all over me. I dropped my hand with the binoculars to my side, and just stood looking out over the valley. She went on eating me up with those dark-grey eyes until out of embarrassment I turned to her and said, " There's a place a little farther back where you can get a much better view than this. Around there, just under the Finger. You can see all the way to the border and also take in Dale. On clear days . . ." I stopped, feeling I was talking too much.

" Wonderful. Let's go there."

I led the way thinking "what the hell's this?" then defensively

F

slipped into my old role of guide around Malinda. I helped her over rocks and crevices and each time I took her hand I felt its silken strength. " The rest of the crowd have gone to the Bell Hotel. Everybody suddenly wanted to mail letters and call their homes : it became another junket. So I slipped out of it. And started walking "—she was a little breathless—"and found a path and just kept walking. Then I saw the Finger looming over me and I had to get up. I just kept on going. No oxygen masks, no Sherpas—just me. And I made it." She kept talking and I said "really" and "very good" and other gummed-up remarks. But I found myself listening to the dark tones in her voice—which had the same sinuous quality as her movements —rather than to what she said.

I led her to the scooped-out rock shelter near the edge of the cliff that I had made my secret hideaway in the remote age of my boyhood. There were still some of the things I had brought up there—bird traps, drawing pencils, a home-made telescope, a water carafe, even some books and magazines. I found an old zebra skin wrapped in a newspaper, crackled it open and spread it on the floor for her to sit on.

" You look like a mountain brigand," she said, laughing. "Why are you going around armed to-day ? "

" There was talk of a cat on the prowl near the village. So I went to investigate."

" Cat ? "

" Leopard. But it was just another scare. I saw the spoor. It was a hyena, not a cat. They both make the same kind of print except that the hyena's has got a slit in front made by that long dragging claw. Their pads look the same and they're about the same size. . . ."

" *Oh, shut up*," I yelled to myself, feeling how utterly boring and deadly this boy scout prattle must have sounded.

" Go on," she said, smiling.

" I've told you. It was a false alarm."

" Genc—I'm glad we've caught up with each other at last. I've been looking for an excuse for days "—she said it just like that—*wham* between the eyes. " But you're always in the distance and you keep disappearing. You're so elusive. Where do you get to?"

"Oh, I work around the place," I said vaguely, not sure whether she was having a game with me, or thought of me as a kid who couldn't possibly get false notions from a frank approach like that. "And to tell you the truth, I don't go to the Big House more than I have to."

"Yes, I've been hearing about that: this is Horse Collar Gulch, right down to the feuds. Anyway, here we are. . . ." She looked up at me and smiled—a warm, lovely smile that dazzled right into my eyeballs. I looked away, really scared now. I was sure she was leading me on, waiting for me to take encouragement and make some stupid move—then slap me back into place.

Embarrassed, I pulled the rifle between my knees and started emptying the magazine, catching the cartridges in my hand as they flipped out. She watched me with a smile, a rather plump, cat-like smile.

"You seem so at home with that gun."

"Is that so?"

"Yes. Do you shoot a lot?"

"Not more than I have to."

"I see . . ."

I felt awful. I was so stiff-lipped and tongue-tied, I was clubbing the conversation to death. Try as I did, I could not think of a thing to say.

She smiled again. "This *is* a wonderful view. How far . . ."

"Nineteen point six three miles."

"Thanks, now answer the next question I'm thinking of."

"One hundred and two feet from base to tip. The upper section is sixty-one feet high, tapering from a base width of twenty feet. The top is the highest point in the area, just on twelve hundred feet above sea level."

"Thank you. Obviously everybody asks these questions. One more . . ."

"Go ahead."

This was better. Words were coming out of me without sounding like waterlogged birds.

" Malinda—what does that mean ? "

" Mean ? "

" Yes—isn't it some kind of native name ? "

" No. It's the name of a racehorse. We were named for a nag that used to get its name in the papers about ten years ago. It doesn't mean anything, so far as I know—except perhaps Dirty Deal."

" Malinda. It's a nice name."

She was leaning forward, caressing her ankles with her lean sunburnt hands, her head tilted sideways so that she looked out over the valley. The silver bracelets fell over her wrists and reflected tiny flashes on the sheen of her bare legs. I felt my eyes tracing the shape of her arms, breasts, waist, and the long flowing curve of her thighs. I wrenched them away and went on talking with my throat dry.

" It belonged to the Whittakers. It was their favourite race-horse and when the ranch was started it was called Malinda. So we're very honoured. It's like a decoration."

" You sound bitter."

" Not really. Not any more. As it happened, everything turned out for the best. But for a long time we had to fight like hell just to keep going here. And then, even when we got things right financially there was that feud."

" Was? "

" Yes. It's all over now. . . ."

I checked myself. This was going too far. I had no right to be discussing my father's business with a stranger. Yes, a stranger—I had to remind myself that I had only just met her. And that she was from the Big House, and one of Lavinia's friends.

" It's a long story," I said. " I'll tell you about it sometime."

As I said it I realised that there was nothing to encourage me to think we should ever meet again. This delusion was getting out of hand.

" That is, if you want to hear about it," I added.

" I'd love to." She paused, then looked straight at me and said, " I'm bored to death with this holiday already. I've been trying to find an excuse to get back to Johannesburg. But maybe things will start looking up now."

" Let's hope they do." It did not seem quite the right thing to say, so I went on, " I thought everybody has a wow of a time at those house parties."

" What? With *that* crowd? Do you know Frank Hoffman "?

" I know him," I said finding nothing pleasant in the reminder.

" He's a raconteur—with accents and actions, everything. I hate listening to jokes. And Kiki Pape ? She sings."

" When she's sober."

" When she's drunk too. Oh, all that drinking and those flat parties and musical beds."

" Musical *whats* ? "

" Musical chairs but with beds. I mean all that angling about who takes who to bed. I didn't come all this way into the Tarzan country for that. This holiday's been a flop so far as I'm concerned." She stopped and peered out over the valley, her thoughts out there with the vultures for a while. " Oh, I guess I know what it is. It's that partner Lavinia's teamed me with. I spent one day with him and the next three running away from him. That red sports car . . ."

" Oh, Alfa Romeo ? " I said, for we never bothered to sort them out but just called them after their cars, their clothes, their hair-dos.

" Peter Wickam," she said, slightly confused. " You know that he's the best accountant in the universe. Oh, he's devastating."

" Now *you* sound bitter," I said, laughing.

" No—it's just that he's put a damper on my holiday. He's such a youth."

" I see," I said, nodding my head in keen agreement, but feeling suddenly a little sick. Peter Wickam must have been every day of twenty-nine.

" I mean he's so immature."

" You can see that," I said. I thought I had better put a stop to this nonsense right away, so I told her, "*I'm* only nineteen, you know."

She laughed, looking at me with that queer little cat-smile, her eyes glimmering with some joke. She just looked at me, while I waited, feeling like a man who has scuttled the canoe in which he was crossing a river.

" Age has nothing to do with it," she said at last. " He's inane and boring, and you—well, you don't make me conscious of age. Yours or mine. Toting that rifle and hunting leopards . . . sorry, cats and dogs, and knowing your way around these parts."

Again I wasn't sure whether she was fooling or not. I decided, on balance, that she probably was not, even though I didn't quite follow what she was trying to say. It sounded nice anyway.

" Will you take me hunting one day ? I'd like to learn."

" Of course," I said, while a thought at the back of my mind was struggling for recognition. Suddenly I remembered the last time I had taught hunting to a beautiful city girl. It was many years ago, and the girl was Lavinia.

" Things are looking up," Marjorie said brightly.

" How did you get roped into this thing in the first place ? " I asked.

" A ballet tour."

It made no sense and after puzzling over it for a moment I asked the question that had been waiting to be let in ever since I met her. " Where exactly *do* you come from ? "

" Canada. Montreal."

" And you have wolves out there ? "

" Don't make fun of me. I came out to Africa on this tour. I'm just a dancer—not a ballerina, just one of the corps. Not specially good. In fact, I gave it up about two years ago and switched to—well, lots of things—theatre direction, journalism, modelling. But a friend of mine was getting up this tour and he invited me to join. So I'm back in tights and tutus again. My stage name is Nina Borasina—corny, isn't it ? My dancing teacher gave it to me when I was fourteen and it's stuck. You've only got to say Nina Borasina and I go into action." She did, just to show me, executing a very professional Dying Swan with her long fluid arms and fluttering fingers.

" Off stage . . ."

" Let me guess," I said.

" Right." She folded her hands and laid them on her lap, raised her chin and presented her profile, as if posing for a photograph. I decided that there was probably some French in her, that she came from a well-to-do family, had attended the best schools, and carried a name which if not Russian was at any rate exotic and distinguished.

" Madeleine de Fresnaye," I guessed, combining the names of a florist shop in Johannesburg and a smart avenue in Cape Town.

She burst out laughing. " Marjorie Harris," she said. " Plain Marge and Harris as in Tweed. A bit dead for the ballet, I agree. But right for the grocery. My father's a grocer in Montreal, a quiet, neat little man who lives above the store. My mother used to help in the business but she died a few years ago. I don't know how on earth they happened to have *me*."

Somehow I felt enormously better after that.

" I met Lavinia in Johannesburg," she went on. " At an after show party. She took us up in a big way in Johannesburg —she was wonderful to us. She invited the whole company to come to Malinda. But the tour was over and the others wanted to get back home, so I was the only one who accepted. With the results I've described—chained by the ankle to a clammy boy with a draughty sports car. And now look at me—a fugitive from the Big House—talking to the resident brigand in his mountain hideout."

The afternoon was ending. A haze of dust and heat was settling over the valley and the sun was coming down behind it, dull red and swollen, sending a purple carpet creeping over the huge floor of treetops below us. I helped her to her feet and with the smell of dusk in our lungs we started walking back to the Big House. I led her down by a track used by baboons and bush-buck and we reached the bottom as a magnificent sunset was flaming across the sky.

I took her back by a short cut and as we pushed our way through the tall buffalo grass on the last flat half-mile to the Big House she was gay, playful and talkative—so different from me with my dark churning misgivings. The difference in our moods made her seem completely unattainable. I made up my mind that as soon as we said good-bye at the Big House I would forget about her, the afternoon, and everything that it seemed to promise.

But resolutions were powerless against what happened as we entered the gates. Somebody came out in a car, driving too fast and lighting up late. He saw us suddenly just as we leapt to different sides of the path, swerved towards Marjorie, pulled away just in time, then came straight at me and stopped as I jumped on the bumper. It was Scobie and a woman. " Sorry, fella," he said, leaning out. " You all right ? "

" Okay," I said, and he put the car into gear and drove away.

I went over to Marjorie. She was standing with her arms rigid at her sides staring at the bouncing tail light. " Pig," she said, then took my arm ; her hand was trembling, and without thinking I put my arm around her waist. We walked a few yards and then suddenly we were kissing. I had no idea how it happened. We turned to each other, our lips met and we were kissing violently, passionately. She was still trembling when we started, but the kiss must have been her way of spending the tension, for she gradually relaxed and I felt her body soften, her lips grow warm. We went on kissing and then stopped for no more reason than we started. Neither of us spoke. We walked holding hands and as we came near the veranda steps she squeezed my hand and whispered, " Go home now, but come over to-night. I'll see you then."

Back in the Retreat I bathed, changed my clothes and ate dinner, trying to avoid looking at the Big House. But I listened to every sound for sounds carry freakishly far in the bush. I heard the voices, the clink of glasses and squirt of soda siphons from the veranda, and after a while the tinkling melody played on the dinner gong by a servant walking about the grounds. I heard the voices go into the house and become a muffled drone of table conversation. Dinner went on and on, and I waited in an agony of impatience, picturing each interminably drawn-out course of the meal. At last I heard voices in the front room and somebody thumping the piano; I got into the jeep and drove across.

Marjorie had changed into an evening-dress, very sleek and glittering and sensuously skimming the smooth contours of her body. Her hair was heaped into a shimmering black crown that gave her a tall commanding elegance. Her make-up was subdued but dramatic—a shell-pink mouth expertly shaped, a touch of greenish-blue eye-shadow, a gleam of lacquer on her long eyelashes and of moisture on her eyebrows—all set against the cool smooth skin. When I came in she was standing next to the window talking to two men, a glass of liquor in one hand, a cigarette held shoulder-high and dangling downwards in the other. She did not see me at first. She went on talking and I stood across the room waiting. Then she caught sight of me, her eyes narrowed, a word formed on her lips and a message flashed in her eyes, neither of which I understood. But she did not come over. She went on talking, sipped her drink, elegantly smoked her cigarette, danced with one of the men, sat down, ate a sandwich, danced again, looked at herself in the mirror of her evening-bag, without once glancing in my direction.

I decided to go home and was at the door when she sauntered past and murmured, " Dance with me." We didn't really dance, just held each other loosely and walked around the room while she whispered in my ear, " We'd better not make this too obvious. I'm in disgrace for running away to-day. Don't go, I'll tell you about it later." After a few minutes we stopped the pretence and simply left each other in the middle of the floor. I waited, but again nothing happened. I watched her being glamorous and alluring to all the men that came her way, charming to the women, dancing superbly but aloofly, without effort or enthusiasm—smoothly carrying out a decorative function—drinking liquor in a practised off-hand way, doing all the deft, pleasant, acceptable things. I knew then why I had not noticed her at that first party. She fitted perfectly into this milieu. She was, in fact, another Lavinia, even if a quieter, smoother and younger version.

I decided to go home and went over to say good night to Lavinia. As I was going out I saw Marjorie say something hurriedly to the man next to her, put down her glass and come after me. She caught up with me on the veranda. " I'm sorry," she said, reaching out and giving my hand a sisterly squeeze. " This has been a shambles. I'll explain some time. I shouldn't have asked you to come. It was a mistake."

I said, " You don't have to apologise. And there's nothing to explain. Good night. . . ." And I stopped there, not knowing whether to call her Marjorie or Miss Harris or Nina or Mademoiselle Borasina or just Bitch.

On the way home I realised that I was glad I had come to the party and that it had turned out this way. I knew where I stood.

The next day I wanted to keep as far as possible from the Big House so I found work to do on the other side of the ranch. We were putting in an irrigation scheme on some newly cleared land, and I spent the time trying out drainage furrows, testing water pressure and flooding off small experimental plots. I enjoyed the muddy, sloshing work and managed not to think of Marjorie for most of the time. I told myself, flatly, that we belonged on different sides of the ravine and that had a nice finality about it and ruled out regrets and hurt feelings.

When I came home late in the afternoon I found Kiki Pape waiting on the veranda, wearing skimpy shorts and a blouse that tied in a knot between her breasts. " I'd just about given you up," she said. She crossed her small shapely legs to show them off to advantage, and looked up at me with those huge glimmering blue eyes. " As you know, the crowd's bigger than ever this year," she said, " and there are some who've never been out here before. It's quite a problem keeping them amused."

" I'm sure," I said in a flat voice to show how desperately sorry I felt for them.

" Some of them have suggested hunting and actually it's rather a good idea. You know, a hunt with beaters like we've had before. There should be enough guns at the Big House, but perhaps if we're short you could help out."

I laughed. " And you'd like me to organise it for you ? "

" That's what I was about to suggest."

I said, " O.K., leave it to me," thinking it would be a nice touch to have one of these futile shoots to round off the silly season. " Hunting" was hardly the word for these gun-toting picnics which were simply an excuse for novices to get out into the bush and let off some old ammunition at imaginary game. Usually the only things that got hurt were the trees.

I arranged it for the following afternoon. I collected about forty youngsters from our own and nearby villages, equipped them with tin cans, rattles, cow-horns, anything to keep up a sustained racket, took them by truck to a point about three miles from the Big House, and deployed them in a wide semi-circle. The guests I bedded down comfortably at vantage points behind rocks and thickets, each near a game path and so placed that he would not shoot another guest's head off unless he went berserk. I explained about the rifles, told them which way the game was likely to come and advised them simply to aim at a certain spot and fire if anything came past. Forsythe turned out for this charade armed with an elephant gun, a double-bore shotgun, two bandoliers slung crossways over his chest, a horn-handled hunting-knife, a snake-bite outfit, and jammed over his eyes was a woman's hat covered in silk ribbons and imitation fruit. Big joke. He chose a place carefully and flopped on to the grass with a clank of ironware. " Say, bud," he yelled to me, " got a proposition—let's go partners in the ivory."

Most of the women stayed out of it as they usually did in the end. The "danger" of even these tame expeditions out-weighed their initial enthusiasm. Lavinia did not come for reasons of her own. But I was surprised to see Marjorie in the party. She carried one of the old rifles that had been gathering dust in the Big House, and was dressed in a borrowed khaki shirt and trousers that fitted her like a sleeping-bag.

I treated her as one of the crowd. I was the guide again, the local game warden. I found a tree stump for her to sit on, placed her hands round the rifle and showed her how to aim and fire. I called her Miss Harris and patted her into position. I pointed to a gap in the bushes and said, " If anything comes it will be through there. So keep your eyes on that spot. But don't fire too soon. Wait until it's in line with that tree "—I pointed to an acacia about twenty feet in front of her—" *then fire*. Straight ahead. Like this."

" And if it charges me ? "

" Keep steady. Don't panic. Hold your ground and when it comes up poke its eye out with your finger."

" Oh, shut up."

" Now get comfortable. Don't sit bunched up like this. Relax. Don't stick your legs out in front of you. You'll be thrown off balance when you fire. Remember a gun kicks. Allow for it."

She was very serious. It was the first time she had held a rifle and she wasn't likely to fire it—but she was as tense and alert as if she were keeping half a dozen lion at bay behind the acacia tree.

" Right," I said. " If you want any help, call me. I'll be stationed at the top of the path behind that thick bush."

As I stood up her eyes followed me. I could tell she wanted to say something but I did not give her the opportunity. She had said everything possible that night at the Big House. I was not annoyed with her. I understood exactly what had happened. And I wasn't going to lay myself open to being duped again.

When everybody was settled and the bush pulsated with people, like children jammed in cupboards in a party game of hide-and-seek, we signalled to Chiwambo our chief herdsman who was standing on the high ground above the falls. He dropped a white flag to start the distant yelling, banging and

halooing of the beaters. I parted the branches to look at
Marjorie. She was sitting exactly as I had left her, the rifle
across her knees pointing at the acacia tree, her eyes fixed
unblinkingly on the space between the bushes. From where
she sat, isolated in a little enclave in the tree, the bush must
have looked alarmingly wild and deserted.

I heard the noise swell in volume as the beaters came through
a defile in the hills and I could sense a commotion in the bushes
away over beyond the ridge. I looked at Marjorie again and
saw her still sitting very tense and erect. Then I realised that
she was scared. Not merely keyed-up as I had thought earlier,
but actually scared. It seemed ridiculous—how could anybody
be taken in by this tame impersonation of a hunt? To me it
was like a scene from *Swan Lake*. Something urged me to play
a prank on her. I found a chunk of snapped-off log and pitched
it over the bushes to crash among the loose twigs just behind
the spot she was watching so intensely.

She swung the rifle round and fired—a wild soaring shot that
whiffled through the leaves overhead. The weapon fell out of
her hand and she stood up, staring anxiously at the place where
the log had landed. Then, when nothing moved and nothing
happened, she began backing nervously into the bushes,
watching the spot with bulging eyes and feeling behind her
with her hand. After a few seconds she stopped, then raised
herself on her toes and peered in my direction. I could see from
her face that she was debating whether to call me. But she
decided against it and with a puzzled look she went back to the
log, picked up the rifle and sat down.

I waited for her to get settled, then groped around and found
a heavy stone. I held it for a moment, then when she happened
to glance down at her rifle I sent the stone hurtling into the
trunk of a tree about ten feet behind her. The tree was rotted
and the side fell away in a smoke of greeny fungus, and a
porcupine that had been hiding inside came scuttling out in a
queer, wobbling, panicky gallop and ran right across her feet.

She screamed and pulled her feet up under her, then stood
up on the log and called " Gene ! " not too loudly, because she

must have realised that this was a ridiculous way to behave while hunting, but nevertheless, urgently. I could have let it end there, but I was playing her on my home ground now, as she had played me on hers the other night, and I wanted to score all the points. I took off my bush-jacket and sent it whirling over the bushes, with its pockets weighted by hunting and fishing bric-à-brac, to plop down in front of her. Then I strolled over and casually asked, " Bag anything ? "

" Oh, go to hell. You make me sick."

" You did fine. You really know how to work that thing. I mean you pointed it away from you and everything."

" What kind of infantile joke is this ? Go back and leave me alone." Her dark-grey eyes blazed fury at me, but after a moment the look chilled and became scorn. " Here—get dressed," she said, tossing the bush-jacket to me. " And take that idiotic grin off your face."

I buttoned it back on and took the grin off my face. She watched me coldly, then picked up the rifle and took up her position again. I turned to go but she said, " I'd rather you stayed with me."

I hesitated and she said, " Please don't go. In fact, I think you can take me home. I've had enough of this."

There was only one way home—down the game track covered by an assortment of museum-piece firearms poised to blaze away at the first thing that moved into sight. I said, " You'll get swotted by your friends and get blood all over this pretty outfit. Wait—it will be over in about fifteen minutes."

" Thank God for that. I must have been mad to come. But, please, Gene, stay with me until this idiotic business is over." I sat down next to her on the stump. She was still trembling and did not speak or look at me. I took the rifle out of her hand and propped it against the log. " With those keen little fingers of yours you're liable to kill a couple of beaters," I told her. She gave me a reproachful look but said nothing.

The beaters had reached our part of the bush now. As they approached flocks of birds lifted in wild whirling panic out of the trees, and all the queer and nondescript things of the undergrowth came scurrying past—rodents, snakes, bush pigs, porcupine, rock-rabbits, jackals, lizards. The shooting started, rapid, excited and wasteful. I climbed an anthill to get a view over the bushes and signalled the beaters to hold back. When the ammunition was used up I waved my arms in the all-clear sign. Another historic hunt was over. I rejoined Marjorie and called the party together. The bag was spectacular—two hares and a baby zebra that had somehow got caught up in the stampede. The few game animals who were left in the bush that year had decided against playing this one, not because they were alerted by the preparations but because they had been scared out of the neighbourhood by all the hubbub when the house-party arrived.

On the way back to the house Marjorie said, " I *did* make a fool of myself, didn't I ? But I was scared, and it was a dirty trick. You had no right to do it to me."

" No worse than what you did to me the other night."

" I see . . . revenge."

A few minutes later she said, " I was in trouble that night at the Big House. Didn't you see it ? Lavinia was watching me all the time. She was annoyed because I slipped out of that trip. She didn't really *say* anything. She asked me where I'd got to, and I told her I had a headache and stayed home and read a book. But I don't think she believed me because she started acting very cool towards me."

" Maybe she doesn't like her friends running out on her. Her friends are her possessions, like the cattle of the Induna in the village. And you've all been chosen for special reasons."

" And what's *my* reason ? "

That was easy to answer. Lavinia surrounded herself with glamorous people to create an atmosphere that kept her own glamour alive. I could quite see how she would get excited over a whole ballet company. But I told Marjorie, " You're a Canadian and they're rather rare in this part of the world. You provide a new kind of interest for her."

" Maybe," she said. " Anyway, I didn't want to quarrel with her. I'd been away all day and if she'd seen me——"

" Fraternising with the enemy ? "

" No, not that exactly. She quite likes you. At any rate, she doesn't *dislike* you. But she wouldn't have been pleased. I could feel it."

I let it go at that. We had dawdled behind the rest of the party, whom I could see strung out along a footpath a few hundred yards ahead. From their voices they seemed to have enjoyed themselves. Nobody had complained and I counted the afternoon a success.

" That wasn't a real hunt, you know," I told Marjorie. " If you want to see the real thing I could take you out one day."

" No, thanks. My hunting days are over. I'm hanging up my powder horn or whatever you do."

I was carrying both rifles and I stopped to distribute the weight more evenly on my shoulder. As we walked on, I asked, " What made you come, anyway ? "

She gave me a look that said, " Don't ask fool questions." A few moments later I felt her arm twine into mine.

After that I saw Marjorie nearly every day. We tried to keep our association out of Lavinia's sight, and for that reason I stayed away from the Big House as much as possible. When I did go, we acted out a charade of being polite strangers to each other. We would meet at the giant wild fig tree in the ravine and I would take her to pretty and interesting places all over the district. Each time we met she had some new escape story —I was sure they couldn't have fooled anybody after the first few days. But we started that way and we kept up the pretence. Possibly it did avoid trouble or interference. At any rate, Marjorie didn't mention any further objections from Lavinia and I didn't ask her about it.

We spent hours together in the sun. I drove her across the valley to picnic on the slopes of the mountain with the mauve haze of the Indian Ocean in the distance. We went to Turgeni Drift with its white sandbanks and flat rippling water emptying into the Sabie River, where she sunbathed while I fished from the rocks. We rode on horseback to Monk's Castle and studied the rock paintings in caves in the red cliffs. I took her several times into the village where she met Mgali and the local personalities and on the way back would break her tongue trying out the clicks and kisses of the local dialect.

We sat among the reeds and saw the noisy, colourful, bazaar life of the river birds. We watched the lonely swooping flight of eagles, hawks and buzzards from our rock shelter under the Finger. We poked into the huge mud nests of termites and studied the soft, blind white slugs that were gnawing away half of Rhodesia. She loved to sit on the river bank among the twisted roots of the fever trees and watch the baboons in the cliff opposite living out their round of baby raising, house-keeping, gossiping, committee meeting, play-acting—showing off to us in a coughing, stuttering language that came so near to making recognisable sentences—and she gave them all French names because of their excitable disposition—Apollinaire, Angélique, Marcelle, Ferdinand, Pierre. I taught her how to identify bird calls, how to judge the weather by wind direction, sky colour, the flight of birds. I showed her how to pick up a spoor and even got her to try her hand at bringing down guinea fowl with a shotgun.

As the days passed we began to feel that we were the only people in the valley. A tender, affectionate relationship grew up between us which I refused to call love only because I dared not trust myself to use the word. So much was new, so much was old and waiting to die. I had never been in love before, not even deceptively. In Johannesburg I had been out with girls my "right" age, college students, friends' sisters and so on. They bored me silly and I bored them comatose. When I thought of love it was of one vast cliché—something to do with engagement rings, wedding cakes, dates, fighting off rivals, petting in cars, using hair tonic, making a show on the tennis court—a catalogue of ritual behaviour as formal as a square dance. Experimentally, fumbling, I became involved with a hospital probationer and slept with her to our mutual dissatisfaction. The affair dissolved and formed into another with her best friend, a music student, to whom I made love

G

on a divan covered by a Khelim carpet with gramophone records strewn around us. But none of this touched me.

I was totally unprepared for the upheaval that Marjorie caused in me—for a love affair with a beautiful dancer pirated from the Big House.

We did not make love, although I believed it would have been possible. We were affectionate and shared many intimacies but it never quite came to that. I had even seen her naked—sunbathing on a rock island that rose like a fat rowing boat in the middle of the river at Monk's Castle. We had arrived there at midday on horseback and had stripped off our clothes and swum in the river to cool off. There was nobody within miles of us, the bush was engulfed in a deep primeval silence, the sun beat in hot shimmering waves off the red cliffs—and it was perfectly natural to shed our sticky clothing and plunge into the water. She lay on the black basalt rock just below me, her breasts slumped into different shapes, her belly flat between the smoothly rounded pelvic bones, a yellow necklace and her red finger- and toe-nails making a vivid contrast to the pale sepia tinge of her body, and she told me in a sleepy nonchalant voice about the time she won a big sum of money at the races.

Perhaps there was an equilibrium between us that I was reluctant to disturb. Or perhaps I was afraid.

For about a week my father was away from Malinda. At first he had planned to do nothing about the copper until Lavinia went back home, but he changed his mind and left suddenly for Salisbury to get expert advice. Bill Secker was going up for the races, so they left together. His intention was to consult with officials of the Chamber of Mines, to study geological maps of the area and generally to try and get a more accurate assessment of the position.

With my father away the dispute receded farther than ever from my thoughts. It was almost as though he had taken it with him in the attaché-case full of rock specimens that he held between his knees as they drove off in Bill's big grey Jag.

When my father returned he was cautious about his talks in

Salisbury, but nevertheless optimistic. He said, "We won't know for certain until we've had a magnetometric survey—that's all I can tell you." But he could not help giving me a big wink that told me he had picked up some good news in Salisbury.

There was a note waiting for him from Hoffman, asking for a meeting to be held the next morning. The question of compensation had to be discussed and they wanted to get a clear answer from my father about his arrangements for leaving. The note depressed me because I had made plans for the following day. I was going to drive Marjorie out to Kotanga Estates to see the magnificent Santa Gertrudis stud bulls and show her over the biggest and best equipped ranch in the country. I felt that perhaps I ought to stay behind and attend the meeting. I had missed the last one and I felt guilty to be showing so little interest in ranch affairs. Not that I could help. My father had his plans and strategy worked out, and all I could do was serve tea, empty ash-trays and generally act as ball-boy. But in my father's absence I had been on one long glorious spree and his return had sobered me. I went to bed thinking it would be better to call off the date with Marjorie and attend the meeting.

Next morning I awoke early, loathing the idea of wasting another minute on those dreary and now futile, accountancy sessions. I sat in the jeep, with the engine running, wondering what to do. And then I saw Marjorie come out of the Big House and walk across the lawn to the gates where I had arranged to pick her up. She was wearing slacks and a sweater, but it was the bright-coloured beach bag hanging from her shoulder that decided me. I couldn't explain why, except that it seemed to exemplify all the hours of sunshine and laughter we had spent together. Joining Lavinia, Hoffman and my father in a wrangle over figures and legalities suddenly became an utterly senseless alternative to spending the day with Marjorie. I put the jeep into gear and drove over.

6

LATE the same afternoon Conrad arrived. Marjorie and I had just got back when he came speeding past in that famous safari truck with three trackers crouching in the back like hunting dogs. I was so startled I nearly ran the jeep off the road. So much had changed in the past few weeks that I had almost forgotten the desperate message my father had left for him that night at the Bell Hotel. But now, like a demon out of a nightmare, here he was, ten days late, but hurtling along as if he hadn't a minute to lose.

He went right past the Retreat where he usually stayed on his visits, bumped down into the ravine with the tail of the truck flying, whooshed up the other side, swung in between the gates of the Big House, and then to our amazement, cut straight across the lawn to pull up inches short of where Lavinia and her friends were drinking sundowners under a garden umbrella. It was a piece of cheek that left us breathless, a beautiful gesture that demonstrated exactly where he stood in the dispute—and somehow all the more touching now that the dispute was settled in our favour.

I said, " I'm not going to miss *this*," and told Marjorie that this was one night I intended to spend at the Big House whatever anybody thought. We drove on, stopped the jeep in the ravine, and clambered hurriedly up the bank to the Big House.

When we got there Conrad was carrying a long brown canvas bag into the house, Lavinia was looking flushed and outraged, and the rest were standing around stunned and incredulous as if a robber had ridden up and sprayed machine-gun bullets at their feet. I heard afterwards what happened. He had told Lavinia flatly that he was staying at the Big House and asked to be put in the big front room. When she said it was taken he politely but firmly requested the couple who occupied it to move out. They did.

I left Marjorie and followed him into the house. He dropped the luggage in the room, then stalked down the passage to the kitchen and gave the staff instructions on how he wanted his food prepared. He spoke passable Shona and immediately won nine allies. He left orders to give dinner to his trackers, fill the water storage tanks in his truck, spray out his room with insecticide, and then came back into the lounge. Some people were sitting around, but his entrance stopped the conversation. He looked around and saw the open windows. It was a hot afternoon with a faint breeze stirring the lace curtains. He crossed the room and closed the windows, slamming them down briskly and turning the clamps to lock them. He had a quirky dislike of fresh air at sunset hour. The worst time for mosquitoes. He sat in the chair, crossed his freckled gingery knees, patted the tips of his fingers together and looked around the room as if waiting for an appointment. Nervously one or two people tried to make conversation. He disagreed with everything they said, even the most innocuous remarks. The weather was *not* pleasant—there was no such thing. Yes, he *had* been hunting but why did they want to know where? Soon his hard gritty aggressiveness restored the silence. He looked at me, gave a curt nod of recognition, then got up and went into the room he had commandeered. I waited, everybody waited, but he stayed in the room. An urgent silence fell over the house as if some life-or-death surgery were being performed behind the pale-green doors.

It was pure histrionics, of course. I knew Conrad. It was an old custom of his to rattle people before a showdown. Wind them first, then knock them out. It was one of the tricks that made him the best criminal lawyer south of the equator. His wholesale onslaught against everybody within distance showed that he had come prepared not only to take on Lavinia but the whole population of the Big House. I thought it very amusing, this wasted chivalry on our behalf, and I wondered how anybody was going to set about telling him that he was charging into a battle that was over.

He had arrived in hunting clothes—but hunting clothes as only Conrad could wear them : a pale-blue linen shirt with a red flannel kerchief knotted at his neck, stylish khaki shorts, fawn hand-knitted hose with red tabs tucked under the folds, hand-wrought safari boots of dark supple cowhide laced at the sides, a stiff-brimmed terai creased with three deep dents, a grouse feather in the leather band. The beautiful boots gleamed, the wide hat was pure swagger, the clothes fitted to perfection and sparkled as if just from the laundry. He had an air of cocky elegance that made him look like a model advertising a swank brand of watch or whisky.

His startling manner of arrival, his high-handed piracy of the best room, his interference in the house routine, his brutal rudeness to Lavinia's guests jerked up the tension all over the ranch. But he was like that—he had a knack of creating tensions and sharpening conflicts. There was a new mood from the moment he arrived. Lavinia's reaction was extraordinary. She seemed to be shocked, utterly bewildered and completely lost for a way to handle the situation.

He did not come out of his room and Marjorie went inside to take a bath. I walked across the lawn to the truck which was still standing up against the sun umbrella with folding chairs scattered all around. I greeted the trackers Cigarettes and Boots, and stared for a moment at the third tracker—a boy about my own age—then recognised him as Cigarettes' son who had come out on a trip a few years earlier. I asked where they had come from. Cigarettes said they had been hunting in Portuguese East Africa, had gone on to Livingstone where Conrad " spoke to the King," then back again to Portuguese East for more hunting, and had only reached the Bell Hotel last night. That explained the delay. We spoke a makeshift language of signs, Fanagalo, Shangaan, Shona and kitchen English. We could not hold a conversation, but we could

understand each other. He told me that Matchbox—the name
of his son came back to me—had joined them on the trip
because he wanted to learn hunting. He had worked for a while
on the gold mines, but didn't like it and now that his contract
was up he was learning his father's trade. I asked him if he still
worked as a witch-doctor. He smiled and patted the skin pouch
containing powders and bones and magician's garb that he
wore on a thong around his waist. " Yes," he said, saying yes
in English. " There's not enough in hunting." We talked a
little while longer, then as Conrad still obstinately refused to
come out of the room I went back to the Retreat, deciding to
return to the Big House after dinner.

When I got back an hour or so later I saw that Conrad was
not the only unusual visitor at the Big House. Ruth was there
too—probably for the first time in her life. I was surprised not
only to see her but to notice that she had dressed up for the visit
—in a patterned silk dress that fitted badly, silk stockings and
tight shoes. She had even done up her hair, in a disintegrating
coil pinned to the top of her head and a straggling fringe, moist-
ened with some preparation, across her forehead. She was
almost unrecognisable in these clothes, after the old ranch
sling-me-ons I was used to seeing her wear.

Bill was there too. This was not so remarkable, for he often
came over to the Big House to chat to the visitors. It could
be boring at Dale and Bill was a sociable type. But he was
wearing a black suit, very narrow and tailored, a white shirt,
silk tie, gold cuff-links—and *that* was peculiar. I had never seen
him in anything but a tweed sports coat with leather patches
on the elbows, grey riding breeches and leather leggings—a
habit that was like a trade mark on him, for he was fond of
presenting himself as the Squire of the district.

Conrad and Ruth in the Big House. Bill dressed like the best
man at a debutante's wedding. But the biggest surprise of all
was seeing my father there. I hadn't noticed him at first. He
was perched on a low riempie stool in the corner, with people
standing in the way. He had seen me before I saw him—I could
tell from the way he acted when eventually I did notice him.

He looked at me only when he could not avoid it, then took a long, slow drink from the tumbler of whisky in his hand as a diversion. I had not seen him at dinner, but thought he had some work to do and would come in later. And all the time he was here at the Big House.

I thought at first that the Seckers and my father must have come over at Conrad's invitation. That would be right in character for Conrad—taking over Lavinia's party and making it his own. But that didn't seem to be the case for none of them were near Conrad, or seemed interested in him. There was no apparent reason for this strange muster of guests. Nothing unusual was happening. Ruth was sitting in an arm-chair all by herself, looking alternately bored and intensely interested. Conrad was listening to some talk of Ronnie Forsythe's, standing with his head averted and obviously finding him insufferable. Lavinia was sitting near the piano, very subdued and preoccupied, with Scobie, Hoffman and one or two others gathered around her like rooks and bishops protecting a harassed queen. Bill was hanging around the drinks. My father was just hanging around. All the windows were open, although rain was threatening and the night was cool and the women were clutching scarves and stoles around their goose-fleshed arms.

Nothing was happening and it didn't seem as if anything was going to happen. It was, in spite of everything, just another social evening, and for me, forced to play the non-recognition game with Marjorie, both a strain and a bore. It was so uneventful that I was half-asleep when the action started. Somebody asked Forsythe a question, and he must have said something astounding for a crowd started to collect around him. That was all it needed, an audience, to set him going on a series of safari anecdotes.

He stood with his ankles crossed, his elbow resting on the mantel behind him, and sounded off about some spine-chilling exploit on location when he and a cameraman dug a hole in the ground, persuaded a lion to charge them, dived into the pit at the last second and got some of the greatest lion close-ups in movie history—yes, sir, then turned round and swotted the cat while it stood there wondering where its dinner had disappeared to. After that we started getting the lions in his life— big ones, hungry ones, cute ones, clever ones, the one he trailed for fourteen days before nailing against a cliff in Tanganyika, the one that used to visit his camp at night to lick the dregs out of the beer cans, and so on until, very casually, he tossed in the news about our own lion. He said, " By the way, there's a couple of leos right here in the vicinity. Yep, heard them tootling myself—last night. Out thataway." He pointed to the third window with his gold signet ring flashing in the light. " Can't say I liked the sound of them. Crazy mixed-up characters they seemed to me."

The effect was extraordinary. Somebody said, " Go on, you're kidding ? " and before Forsythe could reply a man started roaring and another yowling and others joined in and the thing built up with all kinds of yelps and growls and jungle calls and people crawling on the floor, baring their teeth and snarling and others fending them off with chairs, and wit and wisecracks flying everywhere. Then some people lifted their glasses and started singing, " The Lions of Malinda" to the tune of " Waltzing Matilda," the same words over and over, and Chips Stanton banged it out on the piano and everybody sang the new theme song, swinging their glasses and raising them to the ceiling, like Heidelberg students. And then, just when the nonsense was ending there was Lavinia's wild overwrought voice, " Let's go and *shoot* them. Let's go and *shoot* them."

I saw Conrad swing round and stare at her from across the room. Then his eyes became crafty and I saw him sizing her up, measuring the distance for an attack. " Oh, no, you won't. Not if I've got anything to do with it," he said in a rasping voice that stopped the hubbub cold.

There was a quivering, jangling silence before the mine went up.

" Oh, you're a bloody raving genius, Conrad Webber," Lavinia screamed. " Who asked for your opinion ? And what are you doing in my house, anyway ? Who asked you to come here ? Keep your filthy prying paws out of my affairs and if I want to go hunting I'll go and to hell with you."

" Not if I can help it," Conrad said, not even minutely ruffled by her outburst.

" Well, you *can't* help it. Now, will you please shut up and leave me alone."

" I've got every right to restrain you. You'd be a menace with a gun," Conrad said, using that exquisitely crisp diction which I knew he saved for only the big league arguments.

This was preposterous. I saw Lavinia tense with rage, and thought she would rush across the room and claw the smug conceit out of his face. But at the last moment she controlled herself. She had realised that he was deliberately baiting her and that she was reacting exactly as he intended her to. When she spoke again her voice was quieter, but scathing and contemptuous.

" Not nearly such a menace as you are without one," she said.

It drew a polite round of applause.

" I have the same right to restrain you as I have to restrain an irresponsible lunatic," Conrad said in the same silken voice. He was playing it to the limit now. It seemed impossible for anybody to remain calm after a taunt like that, but Lavinia had seen his trick just in time.

" Exactly what have you got in mind, Conrad ? " she asked with a cunning gleam in her eyes. " Please say that again—I want to get your exact words. Unless I'm mistaken you seem to be implying something pretty filthy and disgusting—even for you. . . ."

It was extraordinary. With Lavinia beginning to rally, eyes were lighting up in excitement all around the room.

" Now, please repeat what you just said."

Conrad did not repeat it. He gave her a steady icy glare right into her eyes, then changed his pace.

" It's no time for hunting, and you know it," he said sternly and very steadily.

" I don't have to get permission from you, Conrad Webber."

And so it went on, with Lavinia twisting and insisting in that eye-gouging way of hers, attacking Conrad with talented sarcasm, playing all the time to her local audience of socialite women and country-club men. Conrad parrying her attacks with lawyer's skill, trading taunt for taunt, provoking and belittling her. " What is it you want—another bedside rug ? You don't have to *prove* that you've got more brains than a verminous half-starved lion. I'm prepared to accept that. Leave it alone. If you're so keen to kill something, why don't you hunt a nice peaceful impala ? At least you could eat it."

But there was a mettle and ruthlessness about Lavinia that I had never before seen in her when faced by Conrad. She was blindly determined to win. And Conrad, sensing that the tide was running against him made the mistake of appealing to *his* friends for support. He turned to Bill Secker and said, " Explain it, Bill. Try and talk her out of this ridiculous idea."

It was a disaster. Bill looked all around the room with his big freckled face screwed up in discomfort, then suddenly squared up to Conrad and said, " Tell us your objection, old man. I still don't see your objection. There's nothing *to* it so far as I can see and, frankly, I can't see what all the palaver's about." This from Bill who knew the district and the conditions as well as we did, and who, to my knowledge, would never bother to trudge after a lion when it was possible to poison or trap it. I saw Conrad fix him with a long murderous look, then turn away. And Lavinia, timing it beautifully said, " Just a minute, Bill's got the floor. You live here, Bill ; give us your honest opinion. Should we or shouldn't we ? "

" Sure," Bill said, winking, raising his glass and speaking in that cosy drawing-room croak of his, " Sure, let's go and pot the bastards. Let's have some fun with these characters."

Then, to my dumbfounded amazement, Ruth stood up out of her chair and said in a queer, tight, worked-up voice, " Yes, it's a bloody good idea. I'm ready any time to go and bump off any stinking pigs that come marauding into the district. Let's go." Ruth !—who loathed Lavinia and all she stood for and who always opposed her on any issue, automatically and on principle.

There was still a chance of avoiding it if my father had stood by Conrad. Few people would have disregarded Joe Latham's advice on the method of hunting in the Rhodesian bushveld. Furthermore, it was he who had taught Lavinia hunting and even she would have found it hard to go against his opinion. But when Conrad turned to him he pretended not to hear and then, shrugging his shoulders and with a dead glaze of evasion in his eyes, he said, " I don't know . . . I mean it makes no difference to me. If they all want to go so badly, well, why not ? "

Just why she was so determined to go after these pathetic prizes was hard to say. It might have been that she wanted to provide her guests with some genuine bushveld adventure after the veranda quoits and tame walks and afternoon teas they had amused themselves with during the previous two weeks. Or that she wanted to get even with Conrad for arriving in that offensive manner and insulting her guests. Or perhaps to make it clear to everybody that at Malinda *she* made the decisions, that if she wanted to hunt lion on her vacation nobody was going to stop her. Or perhaps it was just obstinacy—having got into this argument in front of her friends, she was determined not to back down.

It could have been any of these. But whatever the reason, not one person in that room was prepared to help Conrad stop a hunt which nobody in his sane mind could have supported— except me, and I was not asked for an opinion. Everywhere eyes were saying " Congratulations, Winnie. That's the girl. You fixed him all right." It had taken guts to stand up to Conrad and the whole room was brimming with admiration at the way she had bounced him into place. It had also taken several inexplicable switches of loyalty, but nobody seemed to be thinking about that.

Lavinia herself was happy and relaxed now. Her confidence was back, her temper gone, and she had the same kind of triumph in her face that I remembered in an ancient newspaper picture showing her leading in a victorious race-horse named Malinda.

Conrad took his defeat without changing a muscle in his face or a note in his acid, brittle voice. " Very well, we'll assemble at five a.m. to-morrow," he announced.

" We ? " Lavinia asked, turning round sharply.

" Yes. I'm coming with you. I'll supply the trackers—I have them with me here—and since I know the area, I shall lead the hunt."

I expected another explosion over this, but Lavinia did not object. She had won the argument with Conrad, and that was all that seemed to matter. With her brightest, most glittering smile she said, "You're a good sport, Conrad. But five ? That's gruesomely early. Can't we make it eight ? "

" Not if we want to shoot lion. Six, if you like, but no later. Even that's cutting it thin."

" Very well, let's make it six."

This called for another round of drinks, for everybody felt more comfortable having Conrad as a friend than as an enemy. Besides all of them expected to be included in the hunt. But with a crowd that size crashing through the bush the lion would keep about five miles ahead and disappear over the hills. And it could be dangerous. It *was* the wrong time for hunting. None of the ordinary rules applied during a drought like this, and if by chance we did stumble on the lion (or they on us) there would be no way of guaranteeing the safety of so large a group.

So we set about limiting the party to those with hunting experience—Lavinia, Conrad, Bill and Ruth Secker, the movie idol Ronnie Forsythe, my father, myself and the three trackers with the ridiculous names. Even that was too big—three guns and two trackers were about as much as a lion-hunting party could carry comfortably—and I expected Conrad to divide the group into two parties next morning.

There were groans of disappointment but Lavinia seemed ready for this. She said, " Don't worry. I was going to suggest anyway that everybody goes on a picnic to-morrow.

We can all leave together and ride out to the base camp where the hunters can separate from the picnickers ; then we can all come together again at the end of the day." She sounded very enthusiastic, and rather like a Sunday school teacher organising the kids for a game of oranges and lemons. " I'll have the food hampers prepared to-night. Now I want everybody to come, everybody, please. Frank Hoffman wants to take some moving pictures and he'd like everybody to be included. And I want to give the servants a day off."

Conrad stood up and said, " This is for the members of the hunting party. Will you please see that your rifles are delivered to me at least half an hour before we set out. I'll be waiting in my truck outside the front door. No cameras, please." This seemed to be meant for Forsythe. " And we won't wait for anybody after six o'clock." This was definitely meant for Lavinia. He looked slowly around the room, seeing nobody in particular, but spraying pure disgust from his frozen blue eyes ; then turned and stumped off to his bedroom.

Afterwards, when my father had gone home in the jeep, and the lounge was beginning to empty, I sat in the swinging seat on the veranda and waited for Marjorie. It was raining now, the first time in more than five months, except for a light shower the previous night. This was a good rain, heavy and soaking, and the thudding on the roof and the gurgling in the drains was the sweetest music I could wish to hear. A few more storms like this and the drought would be over. The bush itself would recover quickly ; it would suck up the water greedily and within a few days be green and flowering again. The animals would not be so lucky.

Marjorie came out with a coat slung over her shoulders and sat next to me on the wide seat.

" That was quite a show," she said.

" The best so far."

" Does this kind of slanging go on every time you want to have a hunt ? "

I tried to explain. " No, it's just that Conrad and Lavinia are always flying off at each other." Trying to gather the facts in one bunch in my fingers, each fact the end of a a skein of events that tangled back through the years, I told her what I could. I said that Conrad and Lavinia had known each other for a long time, that there was something between them I could not understand, that he was the only man I knew who could unsettle and fluster her, and that I had become convinced that she was afraid of him ; but that he had a way of confusing her so that she never seemed to know whether to fight back or run away. Consequently this was not so much a fight over the hunt as a trial of strength. " And therefore an important win for Lavinia," I added. " It's the first time she has turned the tables on him."

" What do *you* feel about it, Gene ? " she asked.

I said I thought they were crazy not to listen to Conrad who was easily the best hunter there, except maybe Forsythe who sounded fabulous from his description of himself. As for me —well, I didn't like it—with the conditions like that, and the whole thing got up like a game of charades. But I'd go if necessary. To me killing a lion was only another kind of ranch work like felling a tree or fixing the dam wall, a nuisance you had to attend to ; not something you ran out to meet. I tried to make it sound tough and nonchalant, a line that sometimes went over with Marjorie. But this time it didn't impress her.

" I think everybody in that room—including you—was scared, and wanted to go just for that reason. If it's just like felling a tree, why all that fuss and argument ? And why didn't they listen to Conrad, anyway ? "

I simply did not know the answer to that. " I suppose he got everybody's back up by being so aggressive," I suggested.

We said nothing for a while.

" What a waste," she said, nestling her head on my shoulder.

" What is ? "

" That picnic."

" Oh, that ? " I was thinking the same thing about the hunt. How did *I* come to be dragged into it ?

" And with only four days left," she said. " What am I going to do all day ? "

"Work on your tan. Bird watch."

" Oh, hell."

It was then that I decided to slip out of the hunt if possible. The party was too big anyway. I was sure Conrad would be only too glad to drop me if I asked him.

" I think I'll be joining you on the picnic," I told her. She gave a little shudder because of the cold, then moved up closer.

" I still don't get it," she said, after a while, speaking in that sharp, slightly aggressive voice that I knew meant something was troubling her. " You've hunted lion before. You're all hunters. What's so wrong about going after them ? "

I tried to explain, without making it sound too woolly and poetic. But it was getting late, and as we sat in the seat swinging gently back and forth, the scent of her hair began making nonsense of my serious talk about animals and the equilibrium of nature and moods and fevers of the bush.

Many things were said during the argument that had nothing to do with hunting, but some very pertinent things were left unsaid. Conrad's remark, " This is no time for hunting," concealed a whole intricate description of conditions in the bush. That year the bush was sick. Drought and a plague of wild dogs had caused a widespread collapse of the system and organisation of wild life. Antelope and zebra broke up their herds and spread far south in search of water. With the water-holes dry they were forced to drink at the rivers, something that was abhorrent to their instincts because of their fear of crocodiles. Because of this the crocodiles flourished and we knew that for years to come the rivers would be full of these gluttonous reptiles, that the fish population would diminish, that several breeds of birds would disappear. Hyenas and vultures were gorged and failed to eat carcasses clean, and as a result giant ants swarmed everywhere and a foul stench hung over the whole countryside. Out of the dry, scorched grass came snakes, scorpions, tarantulas, rats, porcupines and tortoises, roaming everywhere in search of food, stealing from chicken runs, invading granneries, infesting huts and barns.

Worse perhaps than the drought were the wild dogs. That year, their arrival coincided with the drought, but the dogs were a plague, like locusts, that appeared every five years or so. I could never explain this cycle, why the packs would suddenly grow to great numbers, and then, when they seemed to have the bush at their mercy, suddenly disappear. But their coming was a time of dementia in the bush, a relapse into a recurring mental fever.

These were not gaunt, slavering, loping creatures like the wolves in story books. They were just dogs. True, they were filthy and full of vermin, but you felt that if you caught one, cleaned it up and brushed its fur, it would make a nice present for a child. These bush pirates had a deceptively mild appearance. They were only a little bigger than terriers, with pretty black, tan and cream colouring, cuddly round the ears like a panda, and great appealing black eyes.

But they hunted with particular cruelty and ferocity. They flouted the laws of stalking, scenting and concealment—the fair hunting code observed by all other animals—and roamed in noisy, excited packs. When they came upon a grazing herd they routed it with hysterical yelping and yapping, and they brought down their quarry by the hideous method of gnawing at the hamstrings while the animal ran. And with the victim lying crippled and in terror they ate it alive, devouring everything, hide, eyes, unpassed dung, even chewing the hooves and horns to a pulpy mess. When they finished there was only a saliva wet skeleton left for the vultures wheeling overhead and the hyenas lurking in the bushes.

The dogs concentrated their warfare on the antelope, harassing them day and night and creating a reign of terror that had repercussions throughout the bush. The antelope could cope with the lazy and not too inhumane killing by lion and leopard. It was almost as though there were a pact to let them kill off a certain ratio of the herd in return for the safe conduct of the rest, much as primitive tribes make human sacrifices to appease the gods. But they could not deal with the ravenous and unpredictable dogs. Their instincts became confused, they took fright at harmless things, a bird flapping out of a tree, a piece of mica glinting on a hill-side. They suffered diarrhoea from unsettled browsing, from being constantly put to flight, from losing their normal pastures. They sought safety in places they were ill-equipped to inhabit, rock ledges, caves and bare stony hill-tops.

Their courting code broke down. Normally, in the beginning of spring, the rams and ewes separate and roam in two herds, to come together later in a great festival of love-making. But fear of the wild dogs made them loath to leave each other ; the separation was harried and nervous, the rutting disturbed, and that year there was a great reduction in the number of young. Everything was confused, and the herds suddenly broke up and scattered, making a long migration southward in search of water. And the carnivora—lion, leopard, hyena—helpless at the loss of their food supply, followed them in an angry, vicious temper and so joined them in exile.

For one terrible season the scavenger dogs became kings of the bush, and the lion whose place they had usurped became mean delinquent and savage. Lion are great family folk. They like to indulge their children as fond human parents do, but in times like this the cubs had pinched little purse mouths, gaunt staring eyes and were constantly listless and irritable. The lion took to doing grotesque things to get food—killing giraffe, for instance, a feat requiring incredible stamina and savagery, for despite its frail, delicate appearance, a giraffe has immense strength. And sometimes he went to the other extreme and humiliated himself by chasing hares and rodents. He too was berserk and we could not depend on him to behave predictably if we tried to hunt him.

BOOK TWO

7

WE WALKED along the game track that followed the cliffs high above the river. The wet ground soaked our boots and the ends of our pants, and we walked in step, one behind the other, squelching rhythmically in the thin mud. My fathers' khaki hunting-hat with the leopard-skin hat band was pushed to the back of his head ; his cartridge belt was fastened over his bush-shirt, his telescopic sight in its cylindrical leather case hung at his hip, and he carried his rifle in his characteristic manner, gripping it by the muzzle and balancing it back to front on his shoulder. He had the heavy Winchester .458 that he had brought with him when he first came out to Malinda. It was designed for shooting elephant and rhino rather than lion, but it was his favourite weapon and he used it for all heavy game. I had the more graceful and soft-spoken Greener that Conrad had given me for my fifteenth birthday. My ammunition was in my shirt pocket, with a reserve supply in the tattered ruck-sack I carried on my back, together with a waterproof blanket and a clattering assortment of hunting and fishing odds and ends. We walked into the dawn with the night air cool on our faces and the taste of coffee and toothpaste in our mouths.

I looked about me and tried to judge the weather. A rill of pink light was forming along the edge of the mountains, indicating a strong rising sun. A brisk wind was blowing to the west pulling clouds across the sky and leaving ragged holes through which we saw the stars, now weak and fading. The birds were busy. Guinea fowl and wild turkeys, packed thickly on the branches of a baobab, made the whole tree shudder with their early morning stirring. Down by the river weavers were whirring out of the reeds in quick excited swarms, like gusts of coloured wind. Wood pigeons and coucals were piping duets from island to island, spanning the water with parabolas of pure flute sound. A pair of hadidhas, disturbed by our walking, took off from a beach in theatrical alarm, harking and honking raucously as they skimmed downstream with their feet drawing trails on the water.

The bright sunrise and the excitement of the birds meant a hot day, the scurrying clouds meant a brisk wind to aid stalking, and with the wet ground making spoor-finding easy, conditions were perfect for hunting. My father, even now, was walking with that soft spongy movement in his legs that was his gait when on the trail. The hunt was an absurdity, and still hours away, but whenever he had his rifle in his hand, and his cartridge belt on, he walked like that. It was a habit, a kind of training, and he slipped into it unconsciously.

"Do you think we'll see these cat to-day?" I asked him.

"Possibly. They were on the prowl last night. Did you hear them?" He spoke without turning his head but pitching up his voice so that I could hear him from behind. I *had* heard them, some time in the early hours during a pause in the rain. They were far away, but I had heard them distinctly. They sounded unhappy; they did not roar as lion do when fed and contented, nor growl with that resonant purr of self-assurance, but were snapping and snarling and quarrelling among themselves. Their night prowl had yielded them nothing and they were hungry and ill-tempered. I knew exactly what their spoor would look like when we found it later—short, restless steps in meandering half-circles, abrupt stops and endless criss-crossing, so different from the straight, confident stride of the lion that has killed and feasted.

"Sounded bitter, I thought." I raised my voice against the hollow metallic sound of the cascades that, by some accoustical effect of the cliffs and water, reached us with sudden volume. "COULD YOU MAKE OUT WHERE THEY WERE?"

"OTHER SIDE OF TURGENI DRIFT," he shouted, shifting the rifle into a more comfortable position on his shoulder. "PROBABLY MAKING FOR CRAMPTON FALLS."

I agreed. That was more or less where I had placed them. They would naturally make for the Rezandi Valley so as to follow antelope forced to the river by the drying up of the water-holes. Crampton Falls would suit me fine, I thought, Marjorie had not seen it yet and I had actually thought of taking her there on one of her remaining days. Crampton Falls would look good after the rain—a tall feathery waterfall dropping by stages into a deep chasm that roared and hissed like a steam boiler, a tropical rain forest with huge ferns, twisting lianas, mahogany trees with orchids in the branches, Samango monkeys, parakeets, giant butterflies—a hothouse exuberance not to be found anywhere else in these parts.

"I'd rather sit this one out," I said. "I hope the old pigs take it into their heads to moon off the other way. Back to Wilkie's Pass—and I wouldn't bust myself trying to catch them. In fact, I'm all in favour of leaving them to the Wilkie's Pass people."

He walked on.

"What's the big idea of this hunt?" I asked him. "I mean why's Lavinia so keen on it?"

He didn't answer and I tried again. "What got into her last night? And everybody, for that matter. Why's everybody so hell-bent on chasing these half-starved cat?"

He said nothing and walked on in silence. I saw that he was ignoring my questions and I watched him, puzzled, and thinking about his strange actions last night.

The track led to a point where the cliff hung out over the river, and from there we could look straight down into the pool that had been scoured out of the rocks at the foot of the cascades. I peered over the edge; the pool was a black oily swirl still obscured in darkness. I listened, and for a moment heard only the threshing water of the cascades. Then a grunt and a greasy slithering on the rocks told me that our fat obnoxious neighbours were home. I kicked a stone over the side ... waited ... heard the sharp, walled-in blast as the stone hit the water, and I knew from a blubbery sucking turmoil that I had annoyed the colony of hippo out of their green underwater sleep.

My father watched me, then walked on, but I waited, struck by the way the first dawn sunlight was creeping around the stone lookout tower of the Retreat. The wet thatched roof made an intense black patch in the gloom, but the tower was beginning to light up like a pink minaret. As I stood there I saw the lantern lift off the kitchen table, pass the dining-room window, float into the bedroom and go out. It meant that my mother was returning to bed for a few hours' sleep before leaving for the Anglican Mission, the country store and other places where she had things to do in the district. This was her routine every Friday. The Retreat would be empty to-day.

So would the Big House, I realised. A nice peaceful day for Malinda.

I caught up with my father and fell into step behind him. His rope-soled canvas boots made deep clear imprints in the mud, but I trod them out automatically with my hobnails, for our stride matched exactly. As we squelched in step with each other I found myself thinking of the hunting party. Conrad, being leader, would of course take number one gun. Although he hated this hunt and had come into it only to ensure that it was done properly, he would organise everything down to the last detail; plot the route, determine the guns to use, check ammunition, inspect clothes for conspicuous colours, ration food, allot places in the line, decide when to rest, when to resume, when to change places, run everything to a stop-watch time-table, and generally fuss, nag and worry until you felt like shooting him in the back. Conrad did not hunt for sport and certainly not for pleasure. Nor for the mundane necessity of protecting crops and cattle. Hunting had a totally different meaning for him, and his motive could only be understood in terms of that code of warfare and survival, conflict and surrender that governed all wild life. Animals met him in silent rendezvous deep in the bush to provide the climactic encounter that satisfied a lust. Hence every hunt became surrounded with the glamour and excitement of a secret affair with an exotic woman. Hunting was love, in the same way that in the world of animals and primitive peoples conquest is love. Conrad was one of those who carried within him the mysterious heredity of ancient times when man fought animals to control the world. So for him it was the fulfilment of an obscure rite, the satisfaction of a vestigial instinct ; and also a striving after an unattainable standard of physical perfection and style. Whatever it was it was not an amusement or pastime. It had taken me years to fathom the complicated motives that made a man like Conrad become passionately devoted to killing animals, and even when I understood, I had never felt remotely the same way about it myself. But I was always glad of his insistence on discipline, planning and precaution. Hunting mishaps did occur, and could nearly always be traced to one cause—carelessness.

Bill Secker would be useful in the line. Big, lazy, casual, he had neither the concentration nor the stamina of Conrad, but at the right moment he would tighten up and shoot straight and fast. He was used to hunting. At Dale he always wore a shotgun in his armpit like a third arm, and although killing eight hundred pounds of uneatable meat had no particular appeal for him and he preferred disposing of a lion by other methods than following it for miles in the hot sun to give it a bullet, he still got pleasure out of doing it well. He knew the district like the skin of his hand. That was a big asset. It was always important to know what lay behind that hill, if there was a water-hole concealed in that thicket, if that dark spot ahead was a shadow or a cave. It told you what the quarry was likely to do and what it was possible for you to do—knowledge that was worth more than the most expensive, precision engineered weapons. Bill would be valuable ; Conrad would probably put him second in the line.

My father—more serious and less impulsive than Bill, a better shot, and more intelligent in working out a situation : he was also less tight and more flexible than Conrad, but he was beginning to forfeit skill to age and lack of interest. His reactions were becoming slower, his alertness losing its edge. For all that he was still reliable and resourceful. He hunted without enthusiasm, but with the steady efficiency of one who has mastered a craft. Probably third.

Me—rusty ? Clean out of it, or failing that, last.

Ronnie Forsythe—an enigma. That big hunter talk to boost himself up, that film-world aura he drew around him, the phoney wild-west slang, the smart-aleck cracks and the whole cheap, corny effect of him, left one doubting if he had ever seen a wild animal outside a zoo. But I had noticed the three very formidable guns he brought with him—a heavy calibre elephant gun, a medium-bore carbine for thin-skinned game, and a double-barrelled shotgun—expensive and obviously much used. You don't buy toys like these just to impress the girls. Moreover, although his talk was annoying, there was a strain of accuracy and expertness running through it. I had waited for him to say something absurd or inaccurate for the pleasure of correcting him, but I never once caught him out. It was impossible to know what to make of him. It would be interesting to see where Conrad put him in the line, for it would indicate his assessment of him.

The ladies : Ruth Secker—tough as a bushman on the spoor, quick, confident, cool and with the capacity to work up sufficient hatred to blot out a whole lion family if necessary. She handled a gun like a man, as she did most things, riding a horse, branding a steer, driving a truck, running a business or repairing a windmill. To her lion were not beautiful or dignified or regal. They were cattle pests. Lion cubs were not cuddly and lovable. They were potential kidnappers and murderers. Ruth could hold any position in the line, but Conrad would probably put her behind my father.

Lavinia : the big problem. I could never understand her hunting temperament. A hunt is an X-ray—it shows up hidden flaws of personality, unsuspected traits and weaknesses, and also buried reserves of skill and character. In the early days she had started badly, but had picked up unusually quickly when she put her mind to it. Her style was quite different from Ruth's. She was efficient, but in a feminine way, feline rather than tomboyish. Nevertheless, she became expert and reliable and hunted with something of Conrad's tense, fanatical pleasure. But when she mastered it, she lost interest. During those early holidays when we went out on routine early morning hunts for the kitchen, she preferred to stay at home. We saw then that it had been a craze, like bridge or speedboating. Later, she took it up once more. We thought she would have to start all over again, but to our surprise she seemed to have lost nothing by resting from it. She was relaxed, confident, cool-headed, and we were able to hunt without having to think of her. At her best she could be a great asset, at her worst a handicap and a nuisance. But she hadn't done any serious hunting since the house-parties started four years ago.

I doubted if her skill would revive unimpaired this time. Much had happened since then, her way of life had changed, and if it affected only such things as her ability to walk distances or withstand the heat, it could make all the difference. And then, her hysterical behaviour last night was a warning that she might no longer have the nerves for it.

No, I would not know where to put Lavinia in the line. Even at her best, her erratic temperament made it hard to decide, but now it was pure guesswork and risky at that. The best place for her, I told myself, was right out of the hunt.

I thought too of the trackers, Cigarettes and Boots. I knew their methods and capabilities well, for Conrad always picked them up on their farm in the northern Transvaal when taking hunting trips up-country, and I had often hunted with them at Malinda. They were skilled, seasoned veterans. Cigarettes had been hiring himself out as a tracker at fifteen shillings a month and bonuses on kills for twenty years, and lately turning to account the bush-wisdom he had accumulated over that time, he carried on a side-line as a witch-doctor. He was a superb

tracker with swift instincts and an uncanny understanding of
the bush. It was hard to judge his age—he looked anything
from thirty-five to sixty-five. Age left too many marks on his
face, which was handsome, grave and wise, but none on his
body which had the beauty and grace of a youth.

Boots I knew too. Square, taciturn, cunning, he was probably
as good a tracker as Cigarettes, but there was a style and
delicacy about Cigarettes's work that made one think, unfairly,
that he was the better of the two. Boots was brains, Cigarettes
instinct, and they complemented each other perfectly. To
have Cigarettes and Boots in a hunting party was a privilege,
not only because their skill made for greater safety, but for the
joy of watching artists at work.

I thought of Matchbox too. When I saw him last he was a
thin gawky boy with thick knobs of knees and elbows. But he
had grown up so fast I could hardly recognise him. He was tall
and muscular with bulging biceps ; but he had great clumsy
hands and feet and an uncertain inexperienced manner about
him. I thought I saw something of his father's grace in the
good shape of his head and a nice way of twisting his torso
and relaxing his shoulders, but he needed to trim down—the
grace was there, but still dormant.

As a hunting party it was patchy and too large. But there
were some good shots in it, and first-class trackers, so I had no
doubt that it would be able to handle any hunting contingency.
I knew that Conrad would not give the hunt more than a day
—that would be the limit of his concession to Lavinia—which
meant that there was a strong chance of not seeing any lion at
all. Of course one could never tell—I had known people chase
the cat for weeks without getting a glimpse of it, and then kill
three or four in one morning.

I decided that Conrad would have to divide the party in two.
I wondered how he would sort us out and what order he would
put us in, and felt sure that there would be a solution that left
me out of it altogether.

The track climbed to a high point on the cliff from where we

could see the river as it flattened out and made a wide sweep
around a bald granite hill before fingering out across the valley.
The water had a flat, chill reflection and the broken river strips
stretching into the distance looked like dull gleams of steel.
We saw smoke rising from the huts at Dale, but not Dale itself,
for the valley was covered with a pale clinging mist. Dale was
nine miles away, but still less than half-way across that ocean
of mopani, azalea, wattle and thornbush. The sun was lighting
the eastern hills, sending great smoking sunbeams slanting into
the valley, but the hills on the other side of that vast perimeter
were still in darkness, so that from where we stood we seemed
to see both sides of the world at once.

I had grown up with that view, but it never failed to stir me.
I knew the valley in all its phases—brooding and cold as now,
or lit by the sun and shimmering with myriad colours that
subtly changed with every mood of the sky, or exhausted in
the late afternoon heat and set on fire by some mad masterpiece
of a sunset.

All around us were the sounds of early morning—the cold
thresh of water in the cascades, distant animal noises—a jackal
howling good night to the moon, the sudden *yawp* of a startled
wildcat; the splash of kingfishers plummetting into the river
from overhanging branches, the urgent air rush of wild duck
on their first morning flight, the swishing wingstride of a
bataleur eagle taking off for the sky—light, slight sounds that
filled the morning with silver embroidery. And the deeper,
more purposeful human sounds—the flinty ring of wood-
chopping coming from kraals and settlements all across the
valley; the wild yodelling, echoing its own echoes, that
aroused the village for another day. And the silence that was
louder than the sounds—and the sharp tang of woodsmoke,
resin and cattle. It was a joy to be here on a morning like this,
and I understood all over again why I missed Malinda so
intensely while I was at Medical School.

But suddenly, like a stone smashing through a window, there
came a blast of jazz from the Big House. It was noise without
tune, for it came with blown-up electronic strength, a mangled

roar of brass ripping across the ravine. It lasted a few seconds, then the volume was turned down, the music brought into focus, but the jittery blare went on loud enough to obliterate every other sound in the bush. Then that too ended, in the middle of a note, as if the playing arm had been violently knocked off the record.

Mists rose out of the ravine and wreathed and wisped in front of the house. The farther wing came into view and as we approached the light went on in Lavinia's room, at first dull pink behind the drawn curtains, but suddenly the curtains were wrenched open and the light streamed out of the french doors on to the lawn. Dimly in the distance I saw the deep blue of the carpet, the yellow smudge of the silk settee and the confused colours of the oil-painting above the writing-bureau. For no particular reason we stopped. As we watched I felt cold and uneasy. There was something uncanny, something sobering about that bold light high on the hill plunging out into the mist.

" She'll be on time," I said.

" She wouldn't miss it for anything," my father said. " You saw her last night."

" Yes, I've never seen her like that—so what's the word ?—determined."

" Vicious."

I swung round to look at him. He held my look for a moment, then turned away.

On an impulse half playful, I fixed my telescope into the slot on my rifle and kneeled and took careful aim into the room. Magnified by the lenses, different objects came into view, crystal bottles on the dressing-table, a gold evening sandal lying on its side next to the bed, a pair of ornamented spectacles and a magazine on a bedside table ; and things reflected in the dressing-table mirror—the door into the bathroom, a row of clothes in Cellophane covers hanging in the open wardrobe. I saw her place something in a drawer, then walk across the room. As she did so, I followed her in the sight of the rifle.

" Well ? Say the word." I curled my finger around the trigger.

A smile flickered on his face but disappeared almost immediately. He watched me without speaking.

" I'm ready," I said. " Just say the word. It will be quick and easy."

" Oh, chuck it," he said, but his voice and face were expressionless.

As she moved about the room I kept the sights on her, a detail of arm and shoulder magnified in the brass circle and quadrisected by the neat hairline cross. I noticed that she had a quilted dressing-robe wrapped loosely around her and was standing in fluffy blue bedroom slippers. A slight shift of aim, and now the rim circled her hip with her hand resting on it, a cigarette burning between her fingers.

" Just one shot. Conrad will defend me. He gets everybody off."

" Don't be an idiot."

I moved the aim away from the lighted bedroom to the front of the house. " Let me take a crack at those veranda windows. I've always wanted to do that. It will make a nice sound."

" Let's go," he said.

But he waited, watching me keenly, and I knew he was getting pleasure out of this joke although he would not admit it.

I brought the rifle to bear on the room again, and saw her pick up a towel and disappear into the steam-filled bathroom. Then as I changed aim the telescope accidently found the clothes laid out on the bed. I could see the fawn suéde jacket with leather buttons and white stitching, the neat white jodhpurs.

I studied the clothes she had laid out to wear, then moved the telescope and noticed an odd thing. Puzzled, I let the magnified circle travel along the red satin bolster at the head of the bed, then back across the flat and still undisturbed counterpane.

" She's going to be a lame Lena to-day," I told my father.
" You'll probably have to carry her home."

" Why ? "

" She didn't go to bed last night."

" Nonsense."

" Want to have a look ? "

" No. Let's get moving. Conrad will be waiting."

We followed the track down into the fog and darkness that
filled the ravine and so once more back into the night. We let
the slope propel us and jogged downhill with our gear clanking
until we reached the road at the bottom. It was a narrow dirt
road that twisted past boulders and trees, but had been firmed
down and broadened by the traffic to and from the Big House.
We reached it at the Retreat side of the ravine and about three-
quarters of a mile from the Big House. The heavy mist kept
forming into fine spray that beat into our faces. I stopped to
roll up the ends of my trousers, unpacked the waterproof
blanket and clipped it over my shoulders, covering the rucksack too. My father put on his creased mackintosh and took out
a flashlight.

As we walked on he asked, " Are you sure she didn't go to
bed last night ? "

" It *looked* like it. Why ? "

" I was just wondering."

But he said nothing further, and I walked beside him
with the flashlight stabbing into the opaque mist in front of
us.

" Why ? " I asked.

" Seems peculiar, that's all. I was wondering if it might have
something to do with what happened yesterday."

" Yesterday ? " He could be infuriating when he was like
this.

" Yes, at the meeting."

" Sorry I missed it, but I'd promised to show Marjorie over
the Kotanga outfit, and—well, you know——"

" I know."

It petered out there and we walked gingerly along the muddy road. I hated probing him. I decided to wait for him to tell me what had happened, if he wanted to.

After a while he said, " They know about the deal with the Seckers," in a voice, that had a tremor of nervousness.

" You mean you *told* them ? "

" No. They found out. Or rather snooped it out. Anyway, they know."

Now I understood why he was upset this morning. But as I thought about it I came to the conclusion that his fears were groundless. The whole thing was tied up, in writing, and as legal as a judge's wig. Even without the letters from Ruth it was safe as a rock ; we had the Seckers' word—and their friendship—to rely on, things which were worth a whole truck-load of documents. So they knew ? Too bad.

" What happened ? " I asked, merely out of curiosity.

" Well . . . it started in the same old way. Figures and prattle to arrive at a basis of compensation. I showed them the balance sheets, and just sat back. Hoffman said, ' Interesting,' then pushed it back to me and said, 'That will be helpful to the Liquidator.' Next he wanted to know when we were getting out. I said I wouldn't discuss it until I'd got counsel's opinion. And so on and so on. It was going along beautifully."

" I'm sorry I've missed *these* sessions," I said. " I've always been there when we were getting the flack."

" Then, just as the meeting was ending, one of the herdboys came to the door with his wrist bleeding. He'd caught it on the timber saw. I took him out to the clinic and then Agnes came and took over. I couldn't have been away more than ten minutes. But when I got back I saw that they'd been at my papers. They were in a cardboard folder I'd left on the table. The folder hadn't moved, but when I opened it I saw Ruth's letter on top of the file—*open*. It had been at the bottom and folded when I went out. They must have heard me coming and slipped it back quickly."

" You're not worried about it, are you ? "

" Well——"

" The whole deal's watertight. There's nothing they can do about it."

" I suppose you're right. It's just that I didn't want them to know, that's all. They're as tricky as a treeful of monkeys."

" But you've got it all tied up. I wouldn't worry about it. Did they say anything ? "

" Not a word. Just sat there looking sick."

" Are you sure they saw ? "

" They saw all right. You only had to look at them to tell. And it was obvious from the way they just collected their things and ended the meeting, without another word."

" I wish I'd seen their faces. I'm really sorry I didn't come yesterday."

" It wouldn't have happened if you'd come," he said.

There was a rebuke in his voice that made me wince. Yes, I should have been there, even if this particular incident hadn't resulted in any harm. I had no right to be leaving everything to him.

" I can't see that it makes any difference," I said defensively. " They had to find out some time. Now everybody knows where they stand. And you can stop going through the farce of having these meetings."

As we walked on I began collecting the rest of the arguments to show that there was no cause for worry. She would be leaving for Johannesburg in a few days' time—what difference could a few days make ? The air was cleared now, and we could start making plans for the next stage. They would stop pestering us now, and so on. I saw that not only had no harm been done, but that it was lucky I hadn't been there yesterday to prevent it happening.

" She asked for it," he said tensely as we stepped over a rivulet that was running across the road. " If she'd played clean with me I wouldn't have done it this way."

I was pleased to see that he was thinking about it in the same way I was. I was pleased too that he had spoken about it and given me the opportunity to dispel his worry. It was that bloody illness of his, I told myself. It was always getting him into depressions over trifling or imagined difficulties. Now I felt that he would shake off his mood and give himself a few hours of fun in the bush. He hadn't done any real hunting for a long time—hunting that wasn't just routine—and with Conrad, Ruth and Bill in the party, he'd be able to relax and amuse himself for once. He needed some of that again.

8

I MUST HAVE BEEN half-blind that morning. Not only to the landslide taking place in the Malinda situation, but to obvious physical manifestations of it that stared me in the eyes.

As we walked to meet Conrad I was too busy enjoying the morning, instilling my own cheerfulness into my father, and mulling over the usual hunting preoccupations with spoor, places in the line, the weather, rifles, trackers, to see that this might be a hunt in no way like any that I imagined. Although I realised that there was something peculiar in the way it had started last night, I still believed that I was on my way to play the good old-fashioned game of men armed with rifles tracking down and destroying an animal. I had been in all kinds of hunts, in all kinds of parties, and the object had always been to kill some unfortunate beast in order to eat it or hang its head over the fireplace. I was too unsuspecting—or diverted by other matters—to see that this might have something to do with the discovery of promising quantities of vivid green malachite and beautiful blue azurite in that hill on the other side of the Big House, or that it linked with those farcial accountancy sessions. My mind just wasn't thinking in that direction.

I was not even aware of the feverish gossip going on in the road in front of me. Usually my eyes studied the ground as I walked, if only idly and from habit, but this morning although they picked up the message they failed to get it past the silly fog of complacency that filled my mind. It was only when I saw my father standing with one hand on his hip pointing the light at the track marks in the mud that I realised that something was amiss.

" The Seckers," he said, indicating two identical sets of tyre marks plaiting in and out of each other. " This is the Firestone Heavy Duty tyre I bought for them in Umtali about two months ago." He indicated the newest and sharpest of the tyre tracks. I looked at the pattern of broad arrows bitten deep into the mud by the Seckers' Land-Rover and saw that they pointed in opposite directions—one to the Big House, the other away from it.

" That's all right—one trip there and another back when they came home." But I realised as soon as I spoke that this could not be right. It had not started raining when the Seckers came to the Big House. " No . . . that can't be," I said.

" They might have gone back for something," my father suggested.

" Then it must have been very late. *I* didn't see them, and I was the last to leave the Big House."

" Hmmm . . . how did you get home ? " he asked.

" By this." I pointed to the single thin line of embroidery in the mud made by the bicycle I had borrowed from the kitchen.

" I see," he said, walking on.

If the Seckers had gone back for something, they must have left again, I told myself. In that case there would be a third set of tracks. I examined the muddy road carefully now and saw suddenly that there was not only a third, but a fourth, a fifth and a sixth set. It was difficult to distinguish them for they crossed and obliterated each other, but after studying the road for a while I was able to unravel them like lengths of tangled tape. I noticed that there were other tracks too—apart from those of our own jeep—and these also went in two directions. There must have been a lot of traffic here last night after I had left the Big House and after the rain had started.

I drew my father's attention to the multiplicity of tracks.

" What do you make of it ? " I asked.

" I don't know," he answered with a worried frown.

" What were the Seckers doing up and down this road in the early hours of the morning ? "

" I don't know. I wish I did."

" And these other tracks—whose are they ? What was going on last night ? " I was alert and alive to it now, my mind searching keenly for an answer.

Cars often drove around the Big House at night but not in the rain. And none had gone out while I was there.

" Come—Conrad's waiting," my father said, standing a few yards in front of me and impatiently waving the flashlight. I caught up with him, and as we walked on my eyes threaded among the confused tangle of tracks until, realising that the problem was beyond me, I gave up trying to solve it.

But I noticed that my father stared intently at the road in front of him. There was a look of anger in his face, but a troubled leaden expression in his eyes.

We came round a bend in the road, and made out the vague form of a truck parked on a grass verge at right angles to the road. Conrad's truck. My father shot a quick look at me. It echoed my own surprise, for I remembered that Conrad, on leaving the room last night, had asked the hunting party to meet him outside the Big House.

This was peculiar, but I was beginning to feel that there were more odd happenings this morning than I could cope with. As we approached the truck took shape—the giant fog lamps, the winch on the roof, the bulging water and petrol storage tanks, the wire mesh sides, the numerous contraptions that made it look like a mechanical dragon grinning at us through the mist. The light was on inside and Conrad was standing up in the back. One of the trackers, with a tarpaulin over his head was on the ground below handing things up to him.

I could see merely from his stiff silhouette that Conrad was in his ripest, most blistering temper. It didn't surprise me. This hunt was an impudence, an insult. In this exquisite, dedicated business of killing animals one was entitled at least to choose one's own times, companions and conditions. And —perhaps this stung him most—his coming was the price of his defeat by Lavinia.

" *Hold that bloody gun properly!* "

The tracker was Matchbox. He was passing up a rifle in a brown chamois sheath holding it by the strap so that it swung loosely in his shaking hand. The terrified boy looked confusedly at the rifle, then changed his hold, gripping the chamois fabric as if picking up a kitten by the skin of its neck.

"HOLD IT PROPERLY ! "

Matchbox made a funny little juggling throw with the rifle, almost dropped it, caught it again, changed his grip and poked it at Conrad, muzzle first.

"DON'T POINT THE BLOODY THING AT ME ! " Conrad roared. " *Haven't you learnt how to hold a gun yet ?* "

He stood—hands belligerently on his hips, bristling, glaring —until the boy got it right. Then, " Give it to me," twiddling his fingers impatiently. " That's better, thanks." And he took the rifle and prised open the press studs of the sheath.

" Hallo, Conrad," I said brightly.

He stopped to gimlet me with his eyes, then slid the sheath off the rifle. Very deliberately he examined it. He held it flat on his outstretched hands, bounced it gently, then opened it and peered through the barrel. Next he wiped away a dab of grease with his finger, clicked the gun closed, sprung it open again, tested the mechanism, closed it with a tap under the barrel, slipped it back into its sheath and placed it in the built-in gun rack behind him. Then only did he notice us.

" What the hell was the matter with you last night ? " he whipped out at my father.

" Why . . . what do you mean ? " my father said, startled at the venom in his voice.

I saw Matchbox giggle and hide his mouth with his hand, relieved to have the stinging anger diverted on to somebody else.

" I mean," Conrad said, dropping the words on my father like blobs of scalding fat, " why didn't you support me ? You saw what was happening. Why didn't you try to stop it ? "

" I thought you put the position plainly enough. What more could *I* say ? "

" You live in the district."

" I know. But so do the Seckers. Why didn't——? "

" You live in the district. You could have helped me. Your opinion——"

" Might have swung her round ? That's a joke."

" No, not her. But you might have stopped the others. That would have put an end to it."

My father looked around helplessly. " I don't know what you're talking about," he said, making a futile gesture with his hands. " I mean what's wrong with knocking off some cat that have strayed into the district ? We do it all the time."

But Conrad just glared at him and the silence had the effect of making his words patter away into banality. " I don't know why you're making such a song and dance about it," my father said. " What's wong with it ? "

" What's *wrong* with it ? You know damn' well what's wrong with it. This is the most stupid, dangerous, insane idea I've ever heard of."

I interrupted, " Maybe it's not the best time, but we've hunted before when the bush was all mixed up, and so what ? We're not novices. What if the cat aren't in their most cheerful mood ? We've got four useful guns in the party. Five, counting Forsythe."

Conrad ignored me and somehow my words too died futilely around him.

" What I can't understand," Conrad said, " is how you came to agree to this idiotic suggestion."

" I didn't agree."

" Well, it looked damn' like it. You might have stopped it if you'd put in a little effort."

I saw my father take a deep breath and control his temper. " Look here, Conrad, let's get this straight. I didn't agree. I merely fell in with it when it was obvious that they were all going anyway. Besides, the Seckers carried more weight with that crowd than I did. And so did you. If they wouldn't take notice of you . . ."

But he wasn't listening. While my father tried to repeat his excuse, Conrad took a rifle out of the rack, raised it to his shoulder and carefully aimed at the top of a nearby tree. My father, finding himself talking to the air stopped in the middle of his sentence. I saw Matchbox stifle a fresh attack of giggling and duck out of sight behind the truck. I felt miserable, embarrassed both by my father's futile attempts to defend himself, and Conrad's talking to him like a magistrate dressing down a pickpocket.

It was more than I could bear and I started to walk away. But after I had gone a few yards Conrad called out after me, " Gene, while we're waiting would you check the water and oil in the truck."

I didn't answer but nevertheless went to the front of the truck to do what he asked. I found the water can empty so I took it back along the road to fill at a spring we had passed earlier. I was furious. I walked hitting the can against my leg, bristling at the degrading scene I had just witnessed.

But after a while my anger subsided and I began to wonder if Conrad's outburst might not have some other reason than pique at my father for not supporting him, or bad temper at being dragged into a hunt he didn't want. I took a grip on myself and tried to look steadily at the whole situation. *Something* had happened at the Big House last night after I left Marjorie. People had been coming and going all night and Lavinia herself hadn't gone to bed. This *must* have had some connection with that earlier set-to between Lavinia and Conrad. There was something odd about that, echoes I couldn't quite catch, an atmosphere of hidden pressures at work, of things pent up and things implied but not said. Was it all rigged after all ? Those stories of Forsythe's leading up to the news about the lion in the district—was all that staged ? Was he working in collaboration with Lavinia ? To what purpose ?

There was something very odd about the hunt—that was clear now. Too many peculiar things were happening to ignore this conclusion. I began to revise my opinion that Conrad's opposition was due to the conditions in the bush ; that might be one factor but it was not all that important, and would not normally make him so violently bitter about it. What then was troubling him? Did he really think somebody was planning to use the hunt for a little quiet homicide? That hoary old gag! I dismissed it at once for half a dozen reasons that I didn't even bother to separate in my mind. There must be something else, and to find out what it could be, I looked to my own instinctive mistrust at what was happening. We weren't going after these cat because they were troubling us, or because there was a real need to kill them, but to settle an argument or prove a point— I wasn't sure which. This brought in motives and considerations which were extraneous to hunting. It blurred the issues, and since hunting was an affair of guns and ammunition, it was a real cause for uneasiness. Conrad, being a hunter, would see that and react immediately in this way. The hunt had too many ramifications to be comfortable, and Conrad who was a stickler for planning, would hate to run a hunt so pestered by shadowy and slippery intrigues. As for that motor traffic to and from the Big House, I could not tell yet what that meant. I couldn't even say if it had anything to do with the hunt. All I could do at this stage was accept that something peculiar was going on, that the situation was obscurely dangerous, and make up my mind to keep my eyes and cars open for developments. Only one thing seemed to be clear—my chances of slipping out of the hunt were fast dwindling.

I returned to the truck, filled the radiator and poured in the thick lubricant from a bottle I found in the driving cabin. While I did so I heard Conrad and my father talking at the other side of the truck. I could not hear what they said, but their voices were low and droning, and I thought with relief that they must have stopped quarrelling.

I went round to join them expecting to find a more relaxed and friendly atmosphere. But immediately I sensed the tension in the air. My father was sitting on a tree stump staring disconsolately at the ground between his feet, his hands dangling lifelessly between his knees. Conrad had come out of the truck and was standing in front of him, counting cartridges that he had tipped from a box into his hand, not speaking but his anger showing in the cold stare in his eyes, and the hard throbbing muscles in the corners of his jaw.

The change in my father was incredible. The blood had drained out of his face, leaving it parchment dry and a sick greyish colour. His eyes were flat and lifeless. His whole body was limp, inert, as if he had been drugged. I stared at him, frightened and anxious, but he gave no sign that he noticed me.

I felt a sudden overwhelming anger and I swung round to Conrad. "Why don't you leave him alone?" I burst out. "Can't you see the man's ill?"

Conrad raised his eyes from the cartridges in his hand, slid them in my direction and back, but he did not speak.

"Why do you pick on him?" I shouted. "Why don't you save your smart cracks for the Seckers. They're responsible for this, not him. Yes, why don't you blame the Seckers?" I spoke bitterly and heatedly, without realising that I had never before dared to address Conrad in this fashion.

As I spoke he seemed to stiffen, but he did not look at me. He paused, for just an instant, then went on counting the cartridges, very slowly and deliberately. I saw my father raise his head and a look leave his eyes and curl past me to Conrad, but Conrad did not respond. At last he poured the cartridges back into the carton and carefully rolled them into position with his finger. Then he turned to me.

"Her ladyship is up," he said dryly, jerking his head in the direction of the Big House from where, subconsciously, I had been hearing sounds of activity. "It looks as if the hunt is *on.*"

"I . . ." I wanted to pursue my question about the Seckers, but something that was neither a look nor a gesture, but a tug in the triangle of tension between us warned me not to. I looked away and as I did so I felt Conrad's eyes draw after me in a quick but deep scrutiny, then shift and rest infinitesimally, in a flick of ice-cold lightning, on my father. The look was gone in an instant but it speared us and I had the sensation of short-circuiting time such as one feels when recovering from a stun. I saw him climb back into the truck and stand waggling his fingers at Matchbox to get on with loading the equipment. The ceremony that we had interrupted by our arrival started again—Matchbox nervously passing up the rifles and Conrad inspecting them with fanatic care, peeling each one out of its case, manipulating the bolt, testing the trigger, the safety catch, squinting into the barrel, flipping the sights up and down, blowing on them and sliding them on their grooves, and finally holding the gun flat on his outstretched hands, weighing it, considering it, communing with it. I watched in silence. He was deeply absorbed, for he had a fetish about guns. When he was through with the guns from the Big House he signalled for ours. I passed up my father's heavy Winchester and my own Greener, and we saw him go through the whole procedure again. I watched for what seemed like hours before he finally aimed and fired my unloaded Greener at a distant tree. At the click he came out of his trance.

" Somebody had better go and hurry them up," he said, placing the Greener in the gun rack. He looked at his watch, raising it off his wrist to catch the light. " Hmmm." He glanced from me to my father who was still sitting on the stump, making a single immovable grey shape with it. As if choosing between us, he said, " Joe, go up there and tell them I'm waiting down in the ravine. We can assemble here. Don't let them waste time with breakfast and dolling themselves up. We've got to start at six. Chase them up and get everybody down here as soon as possible."

Without saying anything, my father got up and started walking along the road to the Big House. Conrad watched him go, standing with his foot on the ledge of the truck and following him with a strange thoughtful light in his eyes ; then he turned round, opened the mirror door of the small enamel cabinet fixed to the wall, and took out his shaving things.

I too watched my father as he left for the Big House. He walked like an automaton, mindlessly, lifelessly. There was an emptiness about him that made it seem as if the current had been switched off inside him, or his personality had fled his body. What was it ? The slack way he walked ? The way his shoulders bent? It was nothing perceptible. There was a deceptive light in the air that morning, a freak effect of sunshine melting into the grey steaming mist that gave body to shadows and hallucinations and made fantasies of solid objects. It made me see him in a strange new way, in a kind of multiple vision that recreated him simultaneously in several different stages of his life—much younger, in Johannesburg, when he was debonair and careless and well-to-do, with laughter in his eyes and roguish curly hair and a love of puns and sports and games in the garden; and when we first came to Rhodesia and he worked like a team of mules to get Malinda established, sweating the city softness out of him until he became hard and lean and spare of talk but aglow with a new-found pride in physical toil; and when we nursed him through the first attack of bilharzia and he emerged apparently fit and well, but with something gone out of him, like a violin ruined by an invisible crack after a fall. And I was seeing him older too, older than now, old as a mountain, with the years and disappointments heaped on his back like a prospector's load.

When I recalled the scene later, the stiff black figure melting into the grey mist, poignant and harsh as the mood of an etching, I found new and better words to describe it. It was that of a man walking with ink on his feet, taking the graph line of his life to the last point before it ran off the page. I was watching a man marked down, although at the time I did not know it as anything so explicit, but only as an anguished surge of pity for him.

" I'm putting her ladyship first," Conrad said, applying lather to his face with a stumpy shaving-brush. " You next. Then Ruth Secker. After that myself, then your father, with this actor fellow Forsythe bringing up the rear."

My first impulse was to laugh. " I see. In other words you expect the cat to creep up on us from behind. Tell me, are we hunting them, or are they hunting us?"

He ignored the comedy. Speaking in a crisp no-nonsense voice he went on, " And don't change your place. I want you

there, second in line, behind Lavinia. We're going to stay in
one party. No dividing up, under any circumstances."

" No ? " I said, becoming slowly convinced that he had lost
his senses.

" No. Now it seems to me that the best place to start from
is Crampton Falls. Agreed ? "

" Agreed," I said mechanically.

" Very well. Then we'll start off in the river bed below the
Falls, follow it down to Isinga's Tomb and if we haven't found
the spoor by then, cut across country to Iniswayo Hill. There's
dense bush there and Iniswayo's a favourite haunt for lion. So
that, for the time being, is the route. Don't shoot——"

" Why no dividing up ? " I interrupted, not keeping pace
with these brisk instructions. " Surely this party's too big ?
What if there are several lion ? As I think there are. And if
there's a wounding—aren't you going to leave the weak shots
behind ? " And before he could answer I asked the question
that suddenly leapt into my mind. "And what about Bill
Secker ? Where are you putting him ? "

"No dividing up," he said. "And Bill Secker's not coming."
He swirled the shaving-brush in the water and went on, "Don't
shoot at wild dogs—or any other animals for that matter.
We're after lion."

" Shouldn't you save this until the others get here ? " I
asked. " You'll only have to tell them all over again."

" I want you to know the arrangements in good time. I'm
going to need your co-operation to-day. There are two important things—the order and not to talk about it. *I'll* tell
them when the time comes. One more thing—stay close to
Ruth Secker to-day. All day. Don't let her out of your sight.
I don't mean only during the hunt. I'd like you to ride out to
Crampton Falls with her. She'll have her Land-Rover—you
might drive it for her."

" But why ? " I protested, seeing the hope disappearing of
spending even this part of the day with Marjorie.

" To keep her company," he said, infuriatingly. " That's
all—for the time being." He went on shaving, pulling the

skin flat on his chin and scraping away with one of those old-fashioned strop razors.

Watching him, I realised that he had not come down to the ravine a short time ahead of us, as I had believed earlier. He had slept here in the truck. The bed was already raised and clamped back to the wall, but behind him I saw the neat pile of foam rubber mattresses and khaki blankets waiting to be put away in the locker. There were other signs—the bottles of pills, tumbler of water and spectacles lying on the little flap table near the bed, the canvas blinds clipped over the wire mesh in the section nearest the driving cabin. The truck had a lived-in look. I wondered what could have made him drive down here and sleep in the truck when he had gone to all that trouble to get himself the best room in the house. And in the rain too.

Then I saw the saucer full of cigarette butts. It stood on the far corner of the shelf that held his books—a heap of twisted broken stubs that had been smoked nervously and stabbed out half-way down. Conrad did not smoke, but it was not the cigarette ends themselves that interested me. It was the fact that they were stained with lipstick.

Well! Conrad Webber, Q.C., having a little adolescent fun in the bush! I had never thought of Conrad in this light before. I tried to puzzle out who the visitor could be. For there was not one woman in the Big House on whom he would waste ten minutes' conversation, let alone take to bed.

I stood there gaping at the squirming mess in the saucer and only turned away because Conrad was looking at me. He watched me with the razor poised in the air, a mixture of intrigue and amusement on his face. But he said nothing. I thought he would be furious that I had found out, but he just gave me that ambiguous look and went on scraping off the lather.

I began to feel uncomfortable and wished that the people in the Big House would hurry up and get down here. I could hear them now—voices and that gramophone again, and the *thwick* of somebody practising golf shots on the lawn. And from far out in the valley I heard the soft putter, occasionally magnified into a muffled drone, of a vehicle coming in our direction.

" That's Ruth," I said.

Conrad looked at his watch and nodded. He seemed satisfied that Ruth would get here on time. He finished his shaving and started to busy himself tidying up the truck, clicking doors closed and strapping things into place.

" What's the matter with Bill to-day ? " I shouted into the truck.

" Can't make it," Conrad said over his shoulder.

" Sick ? "

" No."

" Oh, I see. Business in town."

" You could call it that," he said, coming back to the end of the truck.

That was one mystery solved and it encouraged me to try again. Although I hadn't the nerve to ask who had visited him last night there were lots of other things I was curious about. That highly amusing hunting order, for instance. But I knew I would have to play it carefully. Conrad was in a tricky mood this morning, one wrong move and I would find myself thrown to the floor by some verbal judo.

" We'll be using dogs, of course," I said. This was purely a diversionary tactic, for I knew that to him with his artistic notions about hunting, dogs were a vulgarity.

" No," he said, screwing the top on to the Thermos.

I waited for a more positive reaction, but there was none.

" These are half-starved killers. Why are we being so delicate with them ? "

" No dogs," he said flatly.

I ventured a little nearer. " This man Forsythe—seems you don't rate him too highly. Putting him last."

" I'm putting myself fourth."

" I don't follow that either. But Forsythe last ? After all, he's a visitor. He won't get in a shot."

" There's no special protocol for visitors," Conrad said loftily. " He might be the world's best hunter, or just an actor." Nobody could say "just an actor" quite like Conrad, with just that measure of Olympian disdain.

"Those guns of his look pretty useful," I said, jerking my head towards Forsythe's sheathed rifles in the rack. "Specially that elephant flattener. Looks used too. Going by the notches . . ."

"He owns a gun shop," Conrad interrupted.

I hadn't thought of that. It seemed to prove conclusively that Forsythe was a fraud, so I slipped him out of the discussion. I decided that it was time to play the big cards and I gathered them together under my thumb.

"Isn't Ruth well to-day ? "

"Ruth's well."

"I mean—why have I got to look after her ? And why have you put her third ? Behind Lavinia—and *me* ? "

"Because I'm making you the ham in a sandwich," he said, in one of his rare essays into wit. He waited, holding his hands on his hips in an attitude that said, "Next question ? " I saw I was getting nowhere but I was in it now, and decided to carry on.

"I don't understand about Lavinia," I said. "How can you put her up front ? She hasn't done any serious hunting in years, and then you saw how jumpy she was last night. And what's more . . . she . . ." I was just going on to say that she hadn't slept in her bed last night when the saucer of cigarette ends seemed to loom up and dance in front of my eyes, and a wild impossible notion came into my mind. I dismissed it at once as absurd but I let the sentence dribble out. "I mean . . ." I said lamely, "first. In front of yourself, my dad, Ruth."

"This is her hunt," he said. "She's entitled to first shot."

"I don't get it. You're letting her take first crack when she's almost certain to foozle it."

"It's her hunt and she wants to show everybody what a keen shot she is. She's trying to cut a figure. Let her."

"Okay, now what about me ? You've put me second. If you're depending on me to make up for the weakness in front, you've definitely got the wrong man. I've been writing exams and smoking too much, my wind's gone and I think my eye-sight's packing up. In fact, I'm quite prepared to stand down if you think the party too big." But while I spoke I knew it was a lost cause. I saw it from the faint derisive smile on his face and also from the hollow unconvincing sound of my own words.

" Sorry, Gene, not a hope. I need you to-day."

He waited a moment then turned to attend to things inside the truck. I saw him pottering about, placing the blankets and mattresses inside the locker, hanging up a lamp. Unconcerned, he moved over to the bookcase, picked up the saucer of cigarette ends, came to the end of the truck to tip them out.

" Ruth Secker," he said, tapping the saucer to get rid of some sticky tobacco débris. " She paid me a visit last night."

I didn't know why he said that. I hadn't asked him. Maybe he thought he owed me an explanation. But I wanted to hit him. If he meant it as a joke, it had a misfit sourness that I found disgusting. If he was really trying to cover up some amorous adventure it was so futile and clumsy, that I felt insulted to think he could hope to mislead me by it. Ruth Secker! Plain, frowsy, kindly, wonderful Ruth. In all Rhodesia there was nobody less likely to go in for this kind of fooling around in the bushes. Why did he have to say Ruth ? If I had any faint lingering doubt that it might be her it was dispelled when I saw the lipstick-messed cigarette ends lying on the ground. Ruth never wore lipstick, or any cosmetics.

I had had enough of him and wanted to leave and find some other place to wait until the hunt started. But I decided to ask him the one question that I had tried to lead up to earlier. I was not interested in finesse or tactics. I asked him bluntly, " What happened here last night to upset my dad like that ? "

I didn't expect any reply but he leaned forward with his elbow resting on his knee and said, " Gene, there's a very tense situation here at Malinda. I wish I could tell you more. Unfortunately I'm bound to secrecy. What I know has been given to me in professional confidence."

" Professional ? "

" In my capacity as a lawyer. I'm mentioning this because possibly you think I'm being unnecessarily suspicious making these "—he paused for the word—"arrangements."

I said nothing. I saw that he was playing it tight, but at last he seemed to be giving some serious attention to my concern.

He went on, " There have been some unhappy developments, but I'm trying to stop things getting any worse. I'd better make one thing clear to you now. I have not made these arrangements because I suspect anybody of harbouring improper motives or illegal intentions. It's simply that this is the kind of situation that could easily lose its innocent character."

I would have preferred him to say outright, " Nobody's planning anything but Lavinia might be tempted to knock off your father or vice versa." He chose to speak as if making a cautious evasive statement to the Press, but I was grateful nevertheless. It put things in perspective. He added grimly, " I know about these things. I've dealt with them in court. They're never planned."

I nodded. I understood and accepted it and told myself that this was the best attitude to adopt. It put a stop to morbid speculations. It was a relief to be able to take up a settled point of view and stop bothering myself with hare-brained notions that belonged only in detective fiction.

I looked at my watch. Five forty-five.

There was a lot of noise up at the Big House now. I wondered what was holding them up. It seemed strange that Lavinia had not come down to discuss plans with Conrad. Was she simply leaving everything to him ?

I heard the Land-Rover, louder now. The engine had a new note, hollow and echoing and slightly boosted up, which meant that it was coming through the boulder-strewn stretch near Monk's Castle, about four miles away. She would make it on time, provided the river crossing just outside Malinda wasn't too high after the rain.

The mist was disappearing and I could see patches of blue

sky overhead. I unclipped the waterproof, slipped out of the rucksack and sat down on a log alongside Matchbox. He stared at me, then his face broke into a wide white grin. I grinned back but we said nothing. He thrust his thick wooden feet in front of him and stretched his muscular arms so vigorously that his shirt burst open at the chest. Then his whole body slumped and he went into a doze.

A whizzing of wheels and an angry churning roar—that was the Land-Rover, out of Monk's Castle, but having difficulties in the mud. The sound levelled out and became rhythmic as the wheels found hard ground again.

I sat back and waited. In a few minutes Ruth would be here and the crowd would come streaming down from the Big House, and we'd set off for Crampton Falls. I wondered what I was going to tell Marjorie. I thought of last night again, of the way she and I had sat on the swinging settee afterwards and made love. What was there about last night ? Something happened that seemed to mark a new point . . . the tender way she kissed me, and things she did with my hands and an eagerness that both delighted and terrified me. I felt sick at the thought of playing watchdog to Ruth and bothering with the tedious business of guns and animals while she spent equally boring hours with the picnic party.

Now I heard the Land-Rover climb out of the river bed, chug up the hill-side and with a walled-in muffled note start its descent into the ravine. I saw Conrad come out and peer along the road, and possibly because of his attentive attitude, I did the same.

The high box-like vehicle came out of the mist, slithering a little on the wet road. But instead of pulling up next to the truck it went right past, back into the mist, up to the Big House. I saw Ruth at the wheel. Without turning her head, she greeted us with a casual absent-minded wave of her hand, and drove straight on. I heard the Land-Rover roar up the last curving climb to the Big House, slow down to enter the gate, grind along the driveway and switch off.

But just at that instant another car engine jerked into life at the Big House. The horn sounded, angrily, violently; it was Lavinia's station wagon. It took off fast with a swish of tyres and as it crunched around the driveway there was a flash from the windshield in the sky above us. I thought it was coming down to join us. But at the gate it turned off the other way, on to the meandering sand road that stretched across the valley. I listened, dumbfounded, as the sound of the engine faded into the distance.

I felt, suddenly, utterly foolish. The whole thing was a hoax. Lavinia had never intended to go hunting after all. All she had wanted was to make a fool of Conrad. The ridiculous ideas that had formed in my mind . . . all that suspicion and secrecy and cunning of Conrad's . . . I hardly dared look at him.

When I did look, there was no thunder, no fury in his face —only mild surprise. I took a deep breath of relief and told myself that he too was glad the hunt was off. He gave me a musing look, but after a moment his expression became serious and he slowly, slowly shook his head. Turning to the rack behind him, he took out Lavinia's Martini-Henry carbine, but after holding it for a moment replaced it without removing the sheath. Instead he took out my father's Winchester, briskly stripped off the cover, and lugged it up heavily to rest the butt on the ledge of the truck. That gun he studied again.

After about five minutes Ronnie Forsythe drove down in his battered old Chrysler, fitted like Conrad's truck with gadget and contraptions for safari work, though not nearly so elaborately. When I saw him I realised it was not a hoax, unless Lavinia had hoaxed her friends as well. He was dressed in hunting clothes—or rags. He had on a huge grimy safari jacket torn under both armpits, with half the buttons missing and the pockets bulging with what seemed like bits of brick and scrap iron. His hat, in spite of the swagger note of the leopard-skin band, was drooping, ancient, ragged and weather-battered. This was authentic hunting attire for the bushveld. He too had expected to go after the lion.

He leaned out of the window. " Ma Whittaker regrets but do you mind sticking around for a bit ? She's got some business to attend to out there in the bundu." He waved his arm in a huge vague gesture over the valley behind the Big House.

" Where's she gone ? " I asked, for that road went miles and miles through the bush, passing nothing except occasional African huts and villages, and led nowhere except to the border of Portuguese East Africa.

" Out thataway," he said, pointing.

" But where ? "

" Didn't say, Chief."

" And she wants us to wait ? "

" That's the message. Wait for her to come back, which should be . . . let me see . . ." He looked at his watch. " Around next Monday."

" No kidding—how long will she be away ? "

" Around two or three hours, pardner."

" And that dumb dame really seriously expects us to sit around here waiting till she gets back ? She must be crazy."

" Thank you," Conrad said curtly, before Forsythe could answer or produce a wisecrack. " We'll wait."

" Okay ? "

Forsythe turned the big ramshackle Chrysler around and drove back to the Big House.

Conrad watched the car lurching along the road. When it disappeared he yawned, stretched his arms, then turned and lowered the folding bed to the floor of the truck. He pulled a rubber foam mattress out of the locker, threw it on to the bed and lay down with his feet crossed and his hands behind his head. Then he turned over on his side and went back to sleep. It seemed a good idea, and I walked round to the front of the truck, climbed into the cabin, and, following Conrad's example, stretched out on the seat.

BOOK THREE

9

I AWOKE about an hour later feeling confused about my whereabouts and forgetful of the fact that there was a hunt ahead of me. I yawned and stretched my arms, then revolved my shoulder to get rid of the stiffness that had settled in from the twisted position in which I had been sleeping. Slowly, still a little stupefied, I stuffed the waterproof into the rucksack, slipped the straps over my shoulders then climbed down out of the cabin. The mist was clearing, melting away in ragged sheets ; the sun was still too low to be visible, but I could see the strong blue of the sky and feel the heat seeping down into the ravine. Conrad would still be asleep, I told myself ; no point in hanging around here. I decided to go and find Marjorie.

But when I passed the back of the truck I saw him inside writing at the little flap table next to his bed. He looked very perky and business-like—his sandy hair freshly groomed, his spectacles, which had lenses only half-way up, perched firmly on his jutting bony nose, his back erect and alert, his pen writing swiftly in a foolscap-sized note-book. Everything looked neat and shipshape in this efficiently designed, space-saving, equipment-packed safari truck, and Conrad himself might have been a district engineer at work in his travelling office. Seeing him like this reminded me both of the hunt and of how remote and theoretical it had become now that Lavinia had gone off on that trip. It would be hours before we reached

Crampton Falls, and by then there would be little hope of finding the spoor. Spoor is not just the paw-prints of animals neatly pressed into the ground to guide you like road signs, but clues, hints and indications of every kind—broken twigs, dislodged pebbles, the carcasses of animals slain in the night, a heap of dung, sand soaked with urine, a torn spider-web, a trail of ants, the flight of birds, distant cries, sudden silences, the telltale collateral spoor of hyena, wild dog and vulture—the whole documentary of signs, marks and circumstantial evidence that tells of an animal's activities. It is sharp and crisp—and hence most revealing—at sunrise when the events of the night are still within recall. The bush lives at a heightened pitch and at a different tenor at night. Then, the battle for life and survival is waged in tense silent frenzy. In the day the bush drowses. It lives on two levels, and the darker, submerged but more significant one is best revealed by the light skim of signs that remains when the sun rises. Later, heat and wind dry it out, dust and the traffic of other animals blur and destroy it. Hunting late makes both for failure and increased hazard. The spoor is the framework, the compass of action, and to wander aimlessly in search of dangerous game, or follow a confusing spoor, may make a hunt either boring and pointless or nervewracking because of its uncertainty and lack of shape.

If we were serious about chasing those cat we should have camped at the Falls and started at dawn. Or even have gone after them with lanterns during the night. Yet here we were sitting around and frittering away any chance of success we might have had. It was absurd—but then everything about this hunt was absurd.

I rested my elbows on the raised ledge of the truck, and waited for Conrad to notice me. He went on working. He was busy, brisk—this must be something important. I saw him come to the end of a page, read it back, make some insertions and corrections, turn over the leaf, write—oh, yes, this was important. Everything he did was important. His memoirs? A petition to the Appeal Court? An article for the *Encyclopædia Britannica*? It could have been any of these.

At last he placed the fountain-pen in the middle of the book, looked up, then down, wrinkling his forehead to peer at me through the empty part of his glasses.

" Gene," he said, " unless I'm mistaken you seem to be getting involved with the Big House crowd this year."

It took me completely unawares. " Well . . ." I said defensively, puzzling furiously to find out how he knew, " that is—well, not exactly."

" Tell me if I'm mistaken," he said in a not unfriendly tone.

" No, you're not mistaken," I said, wishing he would leave the subject alone. " But it's not like that. It's not what you think."

" Gene—take my advice. Leave that crowd alone. They're not for you."

" I can look after myself. I'm not a child."

" In these things you are. I understand of course that you would miss companions of your own age out here. But don't get involved with *them*—I know them, believe me ; you can get into deep trouble with people like that."

I appreciated his tact in saying "them" and "that crowd" instead of "her." I had intended to tell him about Marjorie, but later—when he'd had a chance to meet her properly, to see her *away* from the Big House, and appreciate her real qualities. But it was the wrong time to discuss it now.

I slipped out of it. " Don't worry, I'm not getting involved with that *crowd*," I said, taking unfair advantage of his consideration in speaking obliquely.

Sensing my embarrassment he said, " I'm sorry I raised the matter—I can see you'd rather not talk about it. Perhaps later —if you're in the mood."

He picked up his pen again, sat tapping it against his teeth for a moment, then asked me, " This man Forsythe—how old would you say he is ? "

" About twenty-seven," I told him.

I saw him turn back a few pages in the note-book and make a note in the margin.

" Have you any idea how he came to be included in the house-party ? " he asked, turning to me again with his hand on his hip.

Growing curious, I told him, " Invited so far as I know. He was on the list Lavinia sent out here before she arrived."

He made another note. " You've spoken to him, I suppose?"

" Oh, yes."

" Tell me your opinion of him."

Not quite sure what he wanted, or even how to describe Forsythe in a few words, I said, " He's a kind of camp-fire comedian—as you must have seen last night."

" I don't mean that. What do you know about his background ? "

" Only what he's told me himself." I patted the facts together and prepared to give him Ronnie Forsythe, abridged. " He's a big game man—a pro. But not one of those Slow Joe vermin killers or ivory baggers. He's in it for big stakes—Bwana Moneybags, he calls himself."

Conrad's eyebrows raised—*really?*—but he did not comment.

I went on, " Runs a sporting goods shop, which is really a blind for a racket he operates on visiting film and television people. Sells them equipment, buys it back for peanuts, and flogs it again to the next outfit. Neat. Then, does bit parts in the pictures, shoots the odd lion from behind the camera, and sells himself jobs like ' Resident Animal Psychologist' and ' Professor of Snakeology.' Speaks like Buffalo Bill in the Quaker Breakfast Cereal programme, has done more to open up Africa than any man since Livingstone, and has a keen line with the girls. That's about all I know."

" A man of initiative," Conrad said, serious and joking in about equal measure. He turned back the pages again and made some quick jottings which obviously didn't cover all I told him. This *was* puzzling.

" Apparently you don't believe all this about him ? " Conrad said, looking at me again through empty glasses with an owl-like expression.

" I didn't say that."

"Nobody said you did." The court-room manner was creeping into it now. "But it's obvious from the way you deride him. Why do you mistrust him?"

"I don't know if I *do* mistrust him. I can't make up my mind. It's the way he talks—that Howdy Pardner claptrap—and the way he tries to bowl everybody over with his heroism, and of course all that film talk. . . ."

"And that you *don't* believe?"

"I wouldn't go that far. It might be true. But he's so gee-whiz keen to drag in Ava Gardner and people, and make out he's the original Jungle Man—well, it sounds kind of phoney. But I'm sure of one thing—he knows animals and the bush, and he's no stooge on safari."

"Have you any idea how he shoots?" Conrad asked, after a pause.

"All I know is that he shoots a good line."

"That's important in his kind of business," Conrad answered, square as a tin of biscuits. He wrote something that he thought of himself, then looked up and asked, "And her Ladyship—when, to your knowledge, did she last do any shooting at Malinda?"

"Serious shooting?"

"Serious or otherwise."

"Last year she potted a couple of bush-buck from the road near Dale. Serious . . ."

"How *was* her shooting?"

"I didn't see her in action, of course, but I saw the buck. Not bad—one bullet each. Serious shooting? Let me see. About four years ago. She hasn't touched any real hunting since the house-parties started. I wouldn't trust her to-day—her nerves, I mean, and then on top of everything she—well, she'll be a bit of a drag to-day. I can see one hell of a mess-up if we're unlucky enough to corner those pigs."

Without commenting, he wrote a long paragraph in the note-book.

"Preparing a dossier?" I asked him.

"No, just my log-book." He held up the black plastic cover

to show me. It said "Journal" on the label. " I keep a record of every hunt."

That was true. What he did with these records—whether he stored them in a bank vault, or kept them for fireside reading on lonely evenings—I could not say, but he did document every hunt in which he participated. From the look of things this was going to be quite a record.

" Tell me about Ruth Secker," he asked, flattening down a new page.

" Top of the class," I said. " You can rely on her."

" Do you think she'd ever lose her nerve in a hunt ? "

" Ruth ? Never. She's steadier than nine out of ten of the men hunters I know. She'd nail every lion in the country if she had the chance—she hates them."

" And your father ? " he asked, interrupting.

" Well . . ."

He waited, while I thought of the best way of putting it.

" Well, he's still pretty useful. Efficient, reliable, never panics. But I don't like the look of him to-day. Couldn't we leave him at home ? "

" He's set on coming—*I* couldn't talk him out of it." He sat staring through the wire mesh for a moment, then went on briskly, " When did he last shoot a lion ? "

" Last July," I said. " Two in fact, near the river at Turgeni. He brought them to bay in the burnt-out kraal, then let them have it. It was beautiful—bang-bang—one shot almost, and they just toppled over. They'd killed two of our bullocks . . ."

He was writing this down fast, almost word for word.

" Now one last question. How has his health been lately ? "

" Fine—recently. He was down when I first came back from Johannesburg, but later he had some good news and pepped up wonderfully. I'd never seen him looking better. It's only to-day. It frightens me. I wish we could leave him out."

" Perhaps we'll think of a way," Conrad said. He looked at me with the hint of a smile in his eyes, then very pointedly screwed the top on the fountain-pen, closed the book and removed his glasses. " I won't ask about you," he said.

" You'd only give me a string of tales and excuses." He stood up and reached above his head to slide the book into its place above the cabinet.

" Isn't this whole thing a bit crazy ? " I asked. " Starting out near midday or later. That's what it'll be—a couple of hours before she comes back, two and a half hours getting out to Crampton. And that's provided we get across at Turgeni and don't have to look for a crossing higher up. And provided there's no trouble on the road with the cars. To me it seems crazy."

" Utterly crazy," Conrad said.

" Then why are we hanging around ? Why don't we go home and tell her to sweat this out by herself ? "

He came to the end of the truck. " Gene, I don't know where she's gone or why she's gone," he said, speaking with his foot resting on the ledge and his elbow on his knee, " but I'm quite certain that when she comes back she'll go on this hunt. So . . ." He shrugged.

" Even if we start in the afternoon ? When there's no spoor left and we simply drift around like a bunch of Girl Guides gathering mushrooms ? I don't like that kind of hunting."

" Nor do I. But she'll go, and that means all the others will go. You saw what happened last night. And that means . . ."

" *We'll* go."

" Exactly." He paused. " Anyway, there'll be nothing to worry about if you do as I tell you. I'm relying on you to-day. Simply carry out my instructions, and everything will become clear to you as the day develops."

" Just what *is* going on ? " I asked. " Do you really think there might be some funny business out there to-day ? "

" I'm guarding against possibilities, that's all," he told me. " The police station is a long way off and very much out of mind when you're hunting in the bush. Normal safeguards tend to break down."

Suddenly he stiffened and a hard look came into his eyes. " That's the position, young man," he said, in a different voice, loud and officious. " You'll stay where I put you. You'll come

on the hunt, and I'm afraid that for one day you'll just have
to give up the idea of dancing around that lady friend of
yours."

I boggled at him. Incredibly he seemed to be taking a rise
out of me.

" Talking about me, Mr. Webber ? "

I swung round to see Marjorie. She had come up from
behind me, her approach hidden by bushes although visible to
Conrad from his position in the truck. I smiled to see her, but
an instant later, when I noticed her clothes, the smile froze on
my face. She was wearing tight-fitting purple jeans, a floppy
snow-white sweater with a wide collar and lapels rolled open
to show a green silk shirt underneath, a flimsy hand-painted
scarf on her hair, green knitted gloves, soft black pumps—
clothes that not only made her look like the latest sex-bomb
from the Cannes Film Festival, but which were about as useful
on a muddy day in the bush as an evening-gown in a coal mine.
With dismay I realised that this apparition must ruin whatever
good standing I had with Conrad.

Yet when I turned to him he was smiling. A rather aloof,
but genuinely amused smile. Not a flicker of mirth had
crossed his face since his arrival yesterday, and now, of all
things, it was the sight of Marjorie that brought on his amusement. I felt myself prickle. This was going to be even worse
than I had imagined.

Oddly, Marjorie didn't seem to notice how he was looking at
her. She walked past me with the lilting artificial carriage of
a mannequin. As she passed, I tried to grab her hand and
pull her back, but I missed, and she went on to stand in front
of Conrad below the truck. Conrad did not move ; he just
stood watching her, with that beautiful chocolate-brown
hunting-boot resting on the ledge and his eyes swarming all
over her in a way that somehow managed to avoid the provoca-
tion of her figure and concentrate on the abomination of her
clothing. I came up and stood behind her.

" Do you expect to shoot those cats to-day ? " she asked
brightly, and the sentence, apart from the word "cats" which

she had borrowed from me and then misused, sounded quite awful.

Conrad's smile became a grin. I felt Marjorie stiffen.

" It talks," Conrad said to me, indicating Marjorie with a jerk of his head.

I whispered in her ear, "Ignore him."

" You're damned impertinent," she burst out, and I felt a leaden gloom come over me. " You're just a conceited, puffed-up . . ." But her flustered anger choked off the words. She turned to me and said, " Oh, let's get away from this—this egomaniac."

" A good idea," Conrad said, giving her one brief up-and-down survey with those mean eyes. " Far away."

" Oh, chuck it," I said, loathing him.

Marjorie swung to face him. " I don't know why you make a point of being rude to everybody, Mr. Webber, but if you don't mind, please don't pick on me."

" Then keep out of range," Conrad snapped. He looked at her a moment longer, his face serious now, then turned and started strapping something down on the floor of the truck.

We were dismissed. I stood looking at the small arrogant back wondering if I had really lived through these few minutes. I was stunned, incredulous. I felt a whirl of conflicting reactions —disgust with Conrad and a suddenly discovered impatience with this kind of unpredictable nonsense—anger with Marjorie for coming here dressed like a freak and provoking the incident. My first impulse was to tell her to go back to the Big House and let me to have it out with Conrad in private. But there was something in his attitude as he crouched tugging at the straps on the floor—a kind of stubborn unrepentance and self-righteousness—that made me finally side with Marjorie. I put my arm around her shoulder and led her away.

We walked along the road silent for a while, and came to the long sloping path that climbed out of the ravine. I let her go ahead and walked leadenly. I was miserable and ashamed. I felt it was my fault ; I was responsible because it was through me she had been exposed to Conrad's ridicule. I felt embarrassed too because of all the flattering things I had told her about him. I hated him almost as much for letting me down as for his boorishness towards Marjorie. He was in the wrong, in every way, yet when I started to talk, I found myself driven to make excuses for him, inept, far-fetched excuses.

" You shouldn't have taken him seriously. He only did it to insult you."

It sounded idiotic. She glanced at me over her shoulder, said nothing and walked on. I told her, a bit desperately now, that this insulting business was a gimmick to arouse people because that way he got to know them better. It didn't necessarily follow that he disliked them. Sometimes just the opposite. It was a court-room trick. . . .

" I think he's a horror. An opinionated, mean-tempered old fool," she flung at me over her shoulder.

" You've started on the wrong foot, that's all. He's not so bad once you get to know him. There are some pretty good things about him."

" That means exactly nothing," she said. " You can say that about *anybody*—even murderers and psychopaths. There's always somebody around who's prepared to like them because they happen to know them."

I couldn't argue against that, but I didn't want to let her end it on this note. I went on to explain that it was merely his particular approach, that to him all people were witnesses, in a sense, and that when he treated them like this it was no more a sign of dislike than if they were real witnesses in a case. It was simply his way of getting people to reveal themselves to him, a bit unorthodox perhaps, but Conrad did things his own special way. " You can't judge him like ordinary people," I concluded.

" Why not ? " Marjorie asked sharply. " Who does he think he is—God ? Anyway, let's forget him. I'm tired of talking about him."

She waited for me and we ambled hand-in-hand up the sloping path. She did seem tired, but it was a relief to see that she was not unduly upset by the incident. She was taking it far better than I was. We came out of the shadow that enveloped the ravine, up into the sunlight that slanted across a ridge above us. At the top I clambered over a ledge and pulled her up after me, and we walked on aimlessly.

I could not forget him. This was not a passing flare-up. It struck deep at a relationship that had been of the greatest importance to me during my years at Malinda. It worried me that Marjorie had become an issue between us. He disapproved of her, and of me for getting involved with her, and the exhibition this morning was a deliberate attempt to exploit his influence over me to break up the affair.

I saw that, but it didn't help. He meant much to me. He was a friend of our whole family, but of us all he seemed to like me the best. I think it was because the one lack in his life was a son. Over the years he had taught me much and influenced me more than I ever realised. If my mother gave me my education, it was he who gave me the outlook, the ideas and ethics that helped me to mature early. I copied him in many ways. I too began to look at things critically, to suspect the ready-made idea, to seek the hard grain of integrity and honesty. His taste was for the lean, the hard, the elegantly simple, the austere style and the clean uncluttered life. This in time became my own catalogue of values. Possibly he had set out to mould me in this way, but if so he did it with affection, and this was a high compliment because there were few people he warmed to.

How could I get him to see the real Marjorie? The Marjorie I knew—not this creature from the Big House. He had judged too quickly, and on a wrong assumption.

" Oh, come on in. Here I am," Marjorie was saying, clicking her fingers in front of my eyes. "I said, 'Why are you so busy defending him?'"

" Him? I'm not defending him. I was trying to explain him, that's all."

" Why are you so grouchy? "

" Am I? I'm sorry."

" Oh, come on—it's a beautiful day." She took my hands

and shook them up and down like a blanket, as if trying to shake the despondency out of me. I pulled her to me and we walked arm-in-arm.

Suddenly we both started humming the same tune. "Explain *that*," she said, and full of playfulness she propelled me into a kind of tango. Then suddenly her steps went ragged; she tottered helplessly and without warning flopped into my arms. Now she was a drunk and I was steering her home. I stopped to bend a branch out of our way, holding her upright with my hand in her armpit, and then limply we turned to each other and kissed. Her lips were wet and cold and her breath fluttering in my face smelled faintly of the sherry she had drunk at the buffet the night before. She was all langour, her breath rhythmic and gentle, her eyelids closed and quivering, and she let herself lie in my arms in that extraordinary way that made her seem completely weightless. I slid my hand under the garments and felt her ribs, fragile and fluid as the bones of a bird, and the warm weight of her breast as it squashed into my fingers. I stroked the skin of her back, thin and slippery as a snake's skin, and ran my fingers up and down her back, sliding over the nodules of her spine.

We kissed that way, dazedly, as if we had found each other in our sleep, then she opened her eyes and looked around, and holding her hand behind my head she crushed a kiss with tense violence on to my mouth. She stopped, looked around again, then nudged her body closer and slid her moist lips back and forth across mine, her tongue burrowing like a lizard, then made a trail of wet kisses right around my face and back to my mouth. We kissed, with a fervour mounting and denying itself, until denial, as it had to, prevailed, and the tenseness ebbed; and she stood with her face buried in my shoulder holding her slender flowing fingers this way and that before my mouth, to be kissed in whimsical tribute to our disappointed passion.

Suddenly the air was full of bright, hard missiles of noise, for the bush birds seemed to reach a crescendo of excitement over the coming hot day. Our birds, which sing like clocks and toys, were sending up massed fireworks of sound—porcelain-pure flute noises, crazily precise scraps of the chromatic scale, private island-to-island calls, music box nursery snatches, trills, shrills, screeches, whirrs, whizzes and whistles. And from the distance came the crowing of cocks and the lowing of cattle, which were not bird and animal sounds at all, but sounds associated with kitchens, and rumpled beds and buckets slopping fresh water at the well—the sounds of man. The sun was well above the hills now, huge and blood red, but rapidly burning down to its proper size ; and as we watched, suddenly, before our eyes, the butterflies were born, all in one white, dew-drenched moment.

" Where are we walking to ? " Marjorie asked.

" Nowhere—anywhere," I said, not caring if we were walking on the moon or under the sea, for I wanted to be only where she was.

" Let's go to the Finger," she said excitedly, and took my hand and began leading me across a field. The grey, tapering stone looked jubilant—washed clean and glittering in the sun-light, as if covered with crystals. " What is it saying to-day ? " Marjorie asked.

" Dance—the drought's over."

I laughed and squeezed her close to me. What a wonderful idea to be going to the Finger this morning ! With Marjorie's holiday nearly over it was already becoming invested with a tense flavour of nostalgia for me. Now it seemed to call us, saying by its dazzling whiteness, " Hurry . . . hurry." And as we approached it seemed to beat time like a metronome, lifting and passing on another message that rose out of the green bush. For riding lightly on the breeze was a strange sound, a soft, rhythmic pounding, like a heart-beat, against a background of faint but frenzied whirring.

She threaded her arm through mine and walked with her head resting on my shoulder. The scent of her hair stirred me, and her warmth communicated itself to me—yet I felt an uneasi-ness, a panic almost. I knew at that moment, by the secret tension passing between our bodies, that we were drawing together in a new tenderness, that our love was driving towards

L

fulfilment. But I did not want the time to come; I preferred the present moment and wished it would stay with us for ever. It was perfect like this. I felt that we had reached a balance of miraculous delicacy, that our happiness hung on a hair, and I sensed devastation in the new, urgent demands our bodies were making on us.

We came to a cattle gate with iron rollers fixed lengthwise over a pit in the ground—a device to let vehicles through but keep the cattle from crossing. I jumped over and turned to help her across. But she declined my hand and instead started to walk gingerly on the slippery rollers. Half-way over she held her arms out and balanced unsteadily, saying, " I've never quite believed in these things before. But now I've proved it—they work." She revolved the rollers with her feet, then leapt. I caught her and we walked on, laughing.

The tense mood left us, and after a few moments she began talking about the "happenings" at the Big House last night. At first I misunderstood her, thinking she was referring to the argument between Conrad and Lavinia.

" Yes, quite a slugging match," I said.

" I don't mean that. I mean after you went home. *Phew!* I'm glad I'm not going hunting to-day. I'm conked out. If I saw a lion now I'd simply lie down and let him eat me."

" Tell me about last night," I said, tugging at the fingers of her gloves and pulling them off. It was getting too warm for gloves. As I stuffed them into my pocket she said. " Well, to begin with, she's locked me out of my room. That was this morning, of course, when she was having a cadenza about that picnic. Fighting with everybody, including Forsythe. Especially Forsythe. And then I don't think she went to bed at all last night. Everyone seemed to be on the prowl. And outside it sounded like a motor rally."

" Just a minute. Ju-ust a minute," I said, holding down her gesticulating hand.

She stopped and took a deep breath.

" Start at the beginning," I said. " And try to organise it a bit."

She tried again, speaking more slowly. " Well, I went to bed soon after you left, and a little while later, I'm not sure just when, somebody walked past my window shouting something —that's why I woke up—and then a car started and drove off with the engine roaring. In a big, big hurry as if it were really going places. But after about a minute it stopped. Just like that—*pfft*. Silence. I waited for it to start again, or something to happen, footsteps or somebody coming back for help. But nothing. It just waited out there in the rain a few hundred yards from the house. I thought, 'that's funny,' but didn't bother too much about it and tried to go back to sleep. But I had a headache now, so I went to the bathroom to get some water to take a tablet, and who enters the picture bang on cue but old Saddle-sores. Yes, your lovable, cuddly, boyhood chum, Conrad. He came out of his room carrying that long brown bag and shining a flashlight. . . ."

" Did he see you ? "

" Oh, yes. He swung round and shone the flash on me."

" Maybe that's why he was so fierce with you," I suggested.

" Maybe," she said. " But he didn't seem very put out. All he said was, "Sorry," as if he'd expected to see somebody else, and then went out of the front door. Well, the same thing."

" How do you mean the same thing ? "

" I mean he started his truck, drove it a little way down the road and stopped. Just stopped. That made two of them out there waiting in the rain. It was eerie——"

" That fits in," I said. " Conrad brought his truck into the ravine and slept in it last night. What's more, he had a cutie to keep him warm."

" Him ? That old buffalo ? I don't believe it."

" I wouldn't have believed it myself, but I saw the evidence. She left a spoor like a lame elephant with white paint on its feet. Go on, this is getting interesting."

" So I waited for those two cars to do something, start up again or shots go off—it was getting like a Hitchcock film— but nothing happened and I dropped off to sleep. But a little while later I was awake again. This time it was car lights flashing into my room. There was a car turning round on the lawn outside Lavinia's bedroom, and powerful lights were zipping all over the walls and ceiling of my room. Oh, more and more like that. This kind of thing was going on all night. Do you want to hear it all ? "

" Yes, please go on."

" What does it mean ? Does it make any sense to you ? "

" Not yet. I think it will later. There's something phoney going on around here, but everybody's clammed up. Just tell me everything and maybe it will add up to something."

" Okay," she said, rubbing her hands in a let's-get-down-to-business gesture. " Well, this car stops, somebody gets out and goes into Lavinia's room. I hear voices—Lavinia's ' Hurry—what held you up ? ' and the man's ' I couldn't help it,' something like that, then swish, the curtains are drawn, and silence descends heavily."

" Seems Conrad wasn't the only one in a romantic mood last night."

" No, it didn't look like that. Because fifteen or twenty minutes later they came out again and drove away. Fast, screeching tyres . . ."

" Both of them ? "

" Yes, going like dervishes, zooming . . ."

" Just a minute. You didn't see them ? "

" No, heard them."

" Then how do you know they *both* went ? "

" Because both doors slammed in the car. This time . . ."

" I think you're a genius," I said, genuinely impressed. " You're an absolute marvel."

" Just because I thought of something you wouldn't have thought of makes me a genius ? "

" Go on, they both left—Lavinia and this man . . ."

" Yes . . . and travelling fast. Then suddenly it's a race. Now there's another car out there, and they're chasing one another out in the valley. I could hear them both, the two kinds of engines, one deep and throaty and the other more fussy, going hell for leather out into the valley. On and on, hitting it up until they were out of earshot. Then I went back to sleep."

" You certainly had a night. I don't know how you managed to wake up this morning."

" Oh, that's not the end of it. Some time later, I think it was a long time, I can't be sure, because an alarm clock went off somewhere—well, there was a car again, out there somewhere, in the ravine, I think—not a car, really, but a sort of truck. Let me say this again . . ."

" No, it's all right. I've got it."

" This car, or whatever it was . . ."

" Land-Rover ? "

" Could be.

" I mean a kind of heavy-duty diesel thing they use on the farms out here. They're called Land-Rovers. Kind of big jeep."

" Could be. Anyway, it circled around for a while, stopping, starting, stopping—sort of looking for something—then finally made up its mind and stopped. That was a long stop ; nothing happened until Lavinia came back. She went into her room and this visitor went away . . ."

" Alone ? "

" Yes."

" One door ? "

" You're learning. Next thing, who goes to Lavinia's room but this Ronnie Forsythe character."

" Forsythe ? Are you sure ? "

" Positive."

" How did you know it was him ? "

" Because he stuck his head in my window, and said, " Hi, Marge, why aren't you asleep ? "

" Damn' smart of you to work it out."

" Oh, shut up. Then I actually went back to sleep again. I'm a good sleep snatcher, so I got in about twelve seconds' sleep, and next thing there's Lavinia waking everybody up, hustling them to get dressed and ready for that picnic. I just rolled over and went back to sleep, but she came in and practically dressed me herself, pushed me out and locked the door. She was impossible, yanking everybody out of bed—in a filthy temper—even Mrs. Taylor, poor thing. Her stomach's upset or something, but Lavinia insisted she comes. Tell me, why's she making such a production of this picnic ? "

" I'm damned if I know."

" Then, while we're all waiting, she gets into this fight with Forsythe. I couldn't hear it all, it was in the back of the house somewhere, but she threw a real Callas with him. Next thing she stalks through the house, gets into her car and zoom— disappears into the blue—leaving us all sitting. Seems to me, Gene, there's more to hunting lion than meets the eye."

" Yes, it's quite a sport."

We had reached the bottom of the ridge now, and as we climbed to the top along the narrow track that wound among grey jagged rocks I heard her voice going round in my head. I tried to go over what she had said, and to fit it in with what I already knew.

IO

ON TOP, we crossed to the other side of the ridge and walked along the cliff edge until we came to the rock shelter. A change had come over the shelter since the day I first brought Marjorie there. Things that had no business in a boy's hide-away had found their way in—scented suntan lotion, sun-glasses, a gay beach hat, chiffon scarf, a hand mirror, some canvas cushions, a plaid travelling rug, a copy of McCalls magazine, a tin of Nescafé, bottle of sugar, cups, spoons.

Marjorie slipped out of the heavy white sweater, left it in the shelter and went out on to the little rock platform that jutted over the cliff. I dropped the rucksack and followed her, and we stood looking out across the vast floor of tree-tops that stretched away to the film-thin overlapping mauves of the mountains on the far side of the valley. The whole valley had revived in the night's storm—the trees fresh and glistening as if in the first flush of spring, the air washed clean of dust and so sparkling clear that it made objects up to twenty miles away visible with crystalline sharpness. Directly below us, reduced to toy scale, was the pentagon of tidy cultivated land that made up Malinda—the patchwork of different-hued fields, the white frames of the stockades, the barns, storehouses and sheds. The Retreat with its squat tower and black thatch roof looked from that angle like an old-fashioned locomotive chugging among the trees. From here the Big House was out of sight, hidden by the ridge, but we could see down into the ravine. It was still wrapped in shadow with shreds of mist clinging to the steep winding road, but the part around Conrad's truck was clear. I saw that Ruth had returned from the Big House now ; the

Land-Rover had stopped near the truck and Conrad was standing in the road talking through the window. As we watched, the vehicle started to move, backing up the road and manœuvering into position on a verge ; as it moved, Conrad walked alongside holding the door handle and continuing the conversation.

The game track my father and I had taken on the way to meet Conrad was a red pencil mark outlining the top of the cliff, beyond which, and partly visible from that height, were the river, the cascades and the hippo pool. Some hippo had come out of the river on to the muddy beach which gave access to their private right of way, leading right across the ranch to their old-established pasture on the Dale side of the boundary.

In a different direction was the village with its straw roofs, neat walls and maze of lanes : it hid shyly among the rocks and trees, merging with rather than emerging from its surroundings. Usually at this time of morning it sounded to a racket of hammering, chopping, pounding, singing and children's cries, but now it was wrapped in an eerie silence. It crouched among the trees like a frightened animal, but as an animal will always give itself away by some sign—a twitch of its tail or a white spot in its marking—so the village announced itself by the soft monotonous drum-beat and the background sound of whirring gourds.

" What's that queer noise ? " Marjorie asked.

" Oh, some witch-doctor junk," I told her. " Probably Cigarettes."

" Cigarettes ? "

" One of Conrad's trackers."

" What a name to saddle a person with," Marjorie said.

" Nobody saddled him. He chose it himself."

" Tell me about this witch-doctor junk."

" Oh, it's just some hocus-pocus he carries on before the hunt. Cigarettes is a professional witch doctor—sort of bush colleague of mine. Usually, before he goes hunting, he holds a kind of seance—conjuring and coloured fire and fortune-telling, that stuff—and that gives him a head start on the lion."

"Cigarettes . . ."

Suddenly she gripped my arm. "It's fabulous. . . . Oh, Gene ! " The sun had come out from behind a cloud and the whole countryside began sparkling with coloured lights. "Let's wait here a while. I've never seen it like this." She held my arm then suddenly clenched it tight as an eagle flew past. It flew only a few feet out from the edge of the cliff, about level with our knees, so close we could almost reach out and catch it. We could see the expression on its face, the worried eyes, the harassed crest feathers, the grim mouth. It gave us an unsurprised look and went on like an earnest little messenger boy trudging uphill on a bicycle.

Then suddenly it exploded. A blast of wind funnelling up against the cliff snatched it out of the air and tossed it into the sky a hundred feet above our heads. There for a moment it came to rest, pinned back by a countervailing wind, frantically clawing the air and beating its wings in a midget paroxysm of fury. Standing on stiff, helpless legs, its cruel beak turned to profile, its butcher's talons splayed out like black iron hooks, its wings stretched to the limit, its crest feathers in angry disarray, it looked exactly like one of those mythical eagles on flags and coins. Then suddenly it found a space in the wind, a narrow layer of quiescent air, and lowering its head and tucking in its legs, slid into it and sailed away. We saw it row across the valley with smooth powerful strokes, maintaining the same position in the landscape, but growing steadily smaller until it disappeared.

"Don't tell me," Marjorie said, peering after it with her hand shading her eyes. "It's a bataleur eagle."

"Dead right," I said. She had pronounced it battler, but I didn't correct her. It was good enough.

"Do you know what my favourites are—makirikiri and blouborstintinkies." She meant her favourite names not favourite birds. She made a shambles of the Afrikaans names, but I wouldn't have changed it for anything. I gave her a hug.

We spread out the rug, arranged the cushions and made ourselves comfortable. She sat with her back to the wall, but after a few moments she yawned and stretched, with a rubbery cat-like twist of her arms, sprawled out her legs and lay with her head on my lap.

I took her hair and pressed it back behind her ears, and for a moment she looked ridiculously like one of those ventriloquist's dummies—the wax gloss, the flat eyebrows, the long gleaming eyelashes, the head suddenly too light and small and comically boyish. The whole thing an affair of paint, glue and wood. I imagined I had only to squeeze a rubber bulb to cause the wide canvas mouth to open and pop out some startling wise-crack. I pressed on her chin, opening her lips against her teeth and said, " I'n Gilly the kid next door, and I cane to gorrow an ungrella."

" What's that ? " she asked in a sleepy voice.

" Nothing." I closed her mouth, smothering it with my hand, and let her hair fall back in place. Suddenly the hollow mannequin look was gone, and the dramatic beauty, symmetry and colour contrasts were back.

" You're very pretty," I told her.

" Pretty ? Not really. I'm damn' ugly but all tricked up."

" Well, glamorous, then."

" Hmmm . . . aren't you going to argue with me ? "

" Okay, you're very pretty."

I wanted to tell her that I didn't know what she looked like because she came all to pieces whenever I tried to think of her. She was too close, or took up too much room in my mind, and consequently I found it impossible to get her into focus. All I did was carry around a whole jumble of impressions—the sound of her voice, the way her elbow kinked back when she stretched her arm, the tiny hole in her ear, the fact that she swam well and rode a horse badly. Odd miscellaneous things like that.

We fell silent and in a new mood I asked, " Do you know where you'll be this time next week ? "

" Nearly home, I guess." She rolled over and looked up at me with great slumbrous eyes. " Crazy, isn't it ? "

" Yes, ridiculous." Crazy, fantastic, ridiculous that she could be here now and next week on the other side of the planet, separated from me by the whole width of the earth. " I can't believe the time's passed so quickly. Four days and you'll be gone. And to-day might be chucked away because of that . . ." I didn't say "hunt" because I was beginning to get sick of the word. " Because of Lavinia."

" Oh, God, Lavinia," she said. She changed her position again, lying with her arms along my legs and her head resting on her hands. " Do you know what she said to me while she was hustling me out of my room this morning ? ' Marge, honey, don't try any rough stuff with that boy. He's a nice kid—don't maul him.' I could have kicked her. What an insulting thing to say."

" How did you get talking about *me* ? " I asked, surprised not only that I had come into their conversation, but that Lavinia could have found anything pleasant to say about me.

" She just came out with it. She knows I've been seeing you. I've been a prominent absentee from the Big House, and I dare say this was her way of mentioning it. But it was a dirty thing to say. That woman flummoxes me. What *is* there about her, Gene ? I used to think she had everything—looks, intelligence, personality, position. She completely wowed me at first. But now I'm not so sure. I keep feeling there's something odd about her—this behaviour of hers this morning for instance. And that high-tension gaiety. One gets the feeling there's something out of gear somewhere. What's her story, Gene ? How does she come to be tied up to a cattle ranch ? "

" Because she was tied up to Jordan Whittaker. He had a queer streak of humour in him and he fixed it that way. He was a mean, morbid misanthrope, as my mother used to say."

" The old, old story—Beauty and the Loaded Beast. Well, lots of people do it."

" But this time it came unstuck—all the way. She was miserable with him. I remember the first time she visited us.

Everybody had been talking about her and I'd seen her pictures in the papers, but when she came I couldn't believe that this was the famous Mrs. Lavinia Whittaker. She looked like a young girl, but overdressed and covered in make-up inches thick. Jordan and my dad sat on the terrace talking Stock Exchange and taking no notice of her. She just sat with her legs crossed —I remember that : long, long legs very stagily crossed—and looked straight ahead with that plastered stiff face, and a kind of goo on her eyes that made them look wide and furry like a donkey's. I never heard her voice. She didn't say one word. She didn't seem like his wife at all—rather his niece whom he'd collared for a round of boring visits."

" She's made up a lot of ground since then. Do you think he married her out of school ? "

" No, the talk was that he met her in a night club in London. She was a show girl. Everybody was very sarcastic—how she used to stand there draped in a pink light, wearing a simply cut Grecian urn : how Jordan proposed to her in a letter dictated to his secretary, and how she arrived in Johannesburg by return mail. How it was love at first sight—of the Whittaker Organisation, and so on. But of course they fell all over her when they met her. We had a party at our house and you should have seen the football scrum around her. That time she was the Lavinia *we* know—dynamic, very confident. That's how she had looked in the newspaper pictures, and that's why I was so surprised the first time I saw her. It was just from close up, when she was alone with Jordan, you caught this picture of boredom and misery—of everything out of tune. I saw the same thing when they came to visit us here at Malinda—it was a torture for her. Jordan kept taunting and nagging her. She never once hit back."

" Lavinia ? That's hard to believe."

" But it's true. She took it like a browbeaten little hen. They never quarrelled. She just let him walk all over her. Then he died and she changed completely. She was so happy— laughing and full of excitement and nonsense, like a child almost. We were good friends for a while and we saw her

often ; she was on top of the world. But she got nothing from
Jordan, or just about nothing. Instead of walking into a cool
couple of millions, all she wound up with was this half-share
in Malinda. And an income worked out according to how
much profit is made here. A multiple or something. She told
us about it once but I've forgotten the details. That's all.
After making her work for it like that he failed to come across
in his will."

" The cad," Marjorie said with feeling.

" So if she wants to go to the races or have her teeth filled
or buy a new car, she must first find out if enough calves have
been born on a small Rhodesian ranch. The popular, fashionable
Winnie Whittaker—it must be sheer gall for her. No wonder
she and my father have been clawing each other to death all
these years. If ever anything was guaranteed to turn two
people into enemies and make each other's life a hell, it's this."

" Do you think Jordan planned it that way ? " Marjorie
asked.

" Maybe."

" What's your theory, Gene ? " she asked, slumping on to
her back again.

" Theory ? "

" About this hunt. Is somebody going to settle a vendetta
or something ? Isn't that what's supposed to happen when a
bunch of high-spirited characters like this get together in a
hunt ? "

" In the who-dun-its, yes."

" You don't take the possibility seriously ? "

" No, not really. It's not so easy to bump off a troublesome
old acquaintance in full view of experienced hunters who know
the score. Especially when they're on the alert for something
to happen. This stunt can't work—it takes too much explaining. What do you tell the judge—sorry, but I could have sworn
old so-and-so was a kudu—when you hunt in line, and fire
in turn, and automatically observe safety rules, and have
trackers to guide you ? It's an old gag, that's all. Whenever
you go hunting some comedian in the party is sure to come

out with a joke of that kind. But it's the most obvious and incriminating way of doing it, if you're planning a little homicide. Better to do it in the kitchen when the servants are off—no witnesses, more chance to make up a story."

" Who'd do it to who, anyway ? " Marjorie asked.

" That's the point. Suppose Lavinia has rigged up the whole affair to get rid of my father ? What if he says no, I don't feel like hunting to-day ? If he decides not to keep the date to get knocked off ? It just doesn't work. And after all that business last night, only a lunatic would think it possible to talk his way out of it. No, there's something queer about this hunt—what it is I can't say yet—but I'm sure it's not *that*."

" But you don't like it ? "

" No, I've told you so."

" What's on your mind, Gene ? Tell me."

" It's just that people have got yanked into this hunt for reasons that have nothing to do with swotting those pigs out there, and that makes me nervous. And walking in the bush, miles from anywhere, with loaded rifles in their hands. . . ."

" And all this beautiful Sicilian hatred in the air . . ."

" Exactly—anything might happen. But I think Conrad's got everything under control and I'm not worrying."

" Gene," she said brightly, after a few moments, " it's just struck me. Maybe somebody's planning to bump *you* off."

" Could be," I said. " Now, let's talk about something else." Her head was lying on my lap again, and I was playing with her hair. What I really meant was, " Let's not talk at all for a while."

II

Stretched thin over slightly bulging eyes, her eyelids
seemed almost transparent in the strong sunlight. A tiny
filigree of veins showed up like the fine grain in marble and
somehow it gave me a thrill to see such a minute detail of her
body. It was as though I was being let into an intensely
personal secret. The long black lashes gleamed like a beetle's
wing, the deft arcs of eyebrows gave a clean symmetry to the
high forehead. Her face had a slightly strained look, as if
yearning for the sun, but her body was completely relaxed.
She could relax beautifully, her body finding a languid rhythm
in repose. She lay with her arms flopped out at her sides, yet
in an instinctively graceful attitude. The swell of her breasts
gave way in a smooth descent to her flat, firm belly and the
subtle geometry of curves and convex triangles in her groin.
In the tight jeans her thighs looked plump and voluptuous.
Her knees were raised, one crossed over the other, in a lazy
haphazard attitude that looked as if it would collapse at a
touch. This was the way animals relaxed, sending different
muscles to sleep in turn, like switching off the lights in a house.

I felt her hand slip up inside my bush-jacket and flutter across
my chest. "Hard but not bulky," she said in a drowsy voice.
"And so smooth. You've got a nice body. I like a man to
look like this, taut and young . . ."

The gently scratching fingers felt like an insect on my skin.
My whole body tingled and I felt a dull thumping under my
ribs. Why did I have to leap at her touch, in this panicky
fashion? It terrified me, but I did nothing to stop her. I did
not even move, but tried futilely to ignore the intense prickling
exhilaration that ran through me like an electric shock.

" Not an ounce too much," she went on, opening the bush-jacket. " A nice colour too, tanned but not that lotion tan. It's pure gold and the tan goes inches deep. There's something very sexy about you, Gene. Those green carnivorous eyes . . ."

She seemed to be babbling. Her voice sounded drowsy and there was a lazy carnality astir in her. Through the partly open shirt I could see the rounded flesh of her breasts, and now I undid the shirt buttons. She wore a flimsy brassière, merely two shallow cups that gave support from below, and at a touch the breasts fell out. They were warm, nubile, with a life of their own that made them nestle into my hands. She did not object. In fact, she didn't seem to notice, for she went on talking.

" I just hate the idea of going home." she said.

I said nothing, not wanting to think about it.

" You'll write to me ? " she said.

" Write ? Yes, if you like."

She must have detected my doubt for she said, " Don't you want to ? Must we simply snuff this thing out next Tuesday ? "

Tuesday—the word started doing antics, stretching out and convulsing, bunching up, melting, shimmering, dissolving into a meaningless echo. Tuesday—a guillotine that would slice the present from the future and make the future one long search for the hallucination of these few weeks.

" Do you want it to end like that ? " She flicked her fingers.

" No," I said, but not sure what I wanted.

" We *must* keep in touch with each other, Gene."

Write ! Keep in touch ! What did touch mean in that crass phrase ? Touch, which to me meant the contact of flesh, the flow of warmth from body to body. How would that be delivered by mail ? How could I squeeze all this turmoil through the nib of a pen ? How dull and sterile was this ceremony of "keeping in touch" ?

" I'll write you beautiful letters," she was saying. " Long letters, fat as magazines, and I'll tell you everything that happens to me, every little thing, so you'll know exactly what I'm doing and thinking and where I'll be. I'll send you books and phonograph records and theatre programmes and newspaper clippings, and all sorts of presents, on your birthday, and just any old time. And we can talk to each other too, sometimes."

" How ? "

" By telephone, stupid."

How desperate it sounded.

" A good idea," I said, not wanting to tell her that I would find it unbearable to hear her voice coming from the other side of the world.

" Gene—hold me."

She raised herself in my arms and kissed me with her breasts crushed against my chest. She held my head with both hands and kissed me tensely ; her mouth was wet, slack and avid, and her flesh smelled warm and musty with sunshine. I slid my hand over the contours of her body into the join of her legs, pressing into the moist yielding heat of her.

" Just kiss me, Gene, that's all."

" Please . . ."

" No, Gene, not here. Please . . ."

She moved away from my hand, but did not let go completely and held it tightly clenched between her thighs. As we kissed I felt her shudder in a pent-up spasm of emotion, then suddenly she wrenched herself away and struggled violently out of my embrace.

" What's the matter ? "

" Not here, Gene. I'm sorry, I can't explain."

My hands fell to my side like lead weights : I moved away and sat staring, with the sound of a waterfall thundering in my ears. She slid up next to me and placed her hand on my forearm. " I'm sorry, Gene. I couldn't. There's something wrong with this place. Don't be angry."

" Thanks," I said, brushing her hand off my arm and standing up.

I did up my bush-jacket and went into the shelter for the rucksack. When I came out I found her sitting as I had left her, a little dazed and unhappy. She gave me a rueful look, then started tugging her rumpled loosened clothes into place. I went back for her sweater. " Here," I said, tossing it to her.

She stood up and pulled it on, then said, " You must think I'm an awful bitch."

" Come—let's go down to the village."

" Do you hate me ? "

" No. Come, it's down this way."

To get to the village we had to pass under the Finger. I led the way to the narrow track around the base rock, walking ahead and leaving Marjorie to follow as best she could. But as I reached the shadow of the rock I stopped and waited for her. I felt a sudden cold shock that not only dispelled my anger towards Marjorie, but filled me with a sudden wondering admiration for her intuition. For I knew suddenly that we could not have made love then. We were not alone.

I shivered as we walked into the cold gloom. There was a sharp dank smell of moss and weeds, mixed with the sour flesh smell of an animal's lair and an unpleasant *sound* of putrefaction—a keen high-pitched whine of hyper-active insects. I walked cautiously, alert and looking all around me. As we came out of the shadow into the widening track on the other side of the Finger I stopped and held out my hand to keep Marjorie back. I waited, then moved forward again and peered around the rock. I saw nothing, but hearing sounds ahead I kicked my boot with a flinty screech on the rock floor. A moment later a great humped vulture pulled itself out of a cave a few yards away. It flapped lazily away, turning once to look back. Its face was covered in blood. It flew in a straight line for about two hundred yards, then suddenly banked steeply and swooped in towards the cave. I thought it was coming straight towards us, but at the last moment it changed course and veered off into a wide gliding flight around the Finger. It went on, round and round, sailing swiftly in perfect circles as if whirled on a string.

I picked up a heavy stone and sent it crashing into the cave. As I expected a second vulture appeared, pulling itself out backwards and tearing its feathers as it struggled to extricate its clumsy loose-hinged wings from the jagged rock. It broke free and flew away carrying a strip of dripping red flesh in its beak.

I saw it choking and hiccoughing as it tried to swallow the morsel in flight; then suddenly the morsel slid down the bald scraggy throat, causing the big foul bird to make a sudden spurt forward in the air. It flew out but came back again, and waited for its companion to come sailing round. It joined it on the next circuit, and the two huge scavengers flew side by side, making about half a dozen flights around the Finger, until, as if to plan, they stopped and hovered over the cave. I picked up stones and hurled them fast, hearing them thud several times on the huge leather bodies before the birds turned and flew away. They went reluctantly, mewing complaints and looking back balefully. They flew low over the valley for about a quarter of a mile, then started a wide spiral flight that I knew would take them high in the sky, but still directly above the cave, to wait there until we had gone.

All around us were the signs of a crime. Blood was sprayed in tiny squirted drops on the rock next to us, red splotches and spats covered the wall and floor making a trail to a sticky pool of darkening blood outside the cave. The pool was alive, seething with a viridian green and vivid bronze scum, intense as enamel, for it was covered with a festering agitation of flies and beetles. The blood had been stepped in again and again, and neat, clear red prints had been impressed all over the rock floor. I recognised those marks and knew the signature—a leopard. Tufts of fur, shreds of flesh, snapped twigs, a broken claw, and the widespread spattering of the blood itself, spoke of the ferocity of the struggle. Beyond the rock I saw a dark patch of urine-soaked ground : I went over, pressed my finger into it and smelled the peculiar sharp acid-sweet odour—yes—a leopard. Then I saw the hand. Not a paw, but a hand wrenched off above the wrist, lying with its fingers curled under a bush. Not a human hand either, but one with the long oblong palm, stubby fingers and short, jointless, toe-like thumb of a baboon. A hand—a cousin. I kicked it away into the bush, then looked back hoping Marjorie had not seen it. But I saw her staring horrified into the cave. I reached her in three strides and peered inside. I saw the mutilated grey baboon in the gloom, lying on his back, his fur matted with blood, his left arm torn off, a gaping hole in his side. But the long-snouted good-natured face, with the black mane that made him resemble a musician, looked at peace—despite his wounds and the flies that clustered on his mouth and eyes. His remaining hand rested in a kind of photographer's pose on his chest, the short bent circus-clown legs were crossed at the ankles, the penis drooped sideways over the scrotum, just as if he were sleeping peacefully.

" Oh, God, it's him," Marjorie said.

It was Apollinaire. Only the day before yesterday we had watched him from the river bank as he sat on the ledge outside his cave, lecturing a group of baboons who squatted at his feet. It was a proper lecture, with exhortations, declarations, fist-thumping, sky-pointing and handwringing, and we had come near to understanding what he said. He was the grandfather or sultan or kabaka of the colony of baboons who lived in the cliff facing the Retreat for as long as we had lived at Malinda. Like neighbours across the street we had watched the children grow up, seen families form and dissolve, heard their dirges at a death, the excitement at a birth, seen them go off on long, inexplicable holidays and come hobbling back with curious-looking luggage and new babies clinging upside down to the hair on their mothers' chests. Often they sat studying us too, talking about us, and sometimes they came over at night to borrow things—sneaking into the kitchen and taking honey or packets of jelly and on one occasion an egg-beater.

Apollinaire was the biggest baboon in the whole cliff, a great dictator, a temperamental tyrant, who could be terrifying or charming or pernickety, and whose moods set the tone for the whole colony. He would sit on the shelf outside his cave, as if on a bench on the stoep, and make the women wait on him, fetch him things, pick dirt out of his fur, clean his feet. He punished the children, played practical jokes, laid down the law. He was a great talker and a wonderful actor and I knew his hoarse stutter as well as the voice of anyone in our house.

Now he was dead. Killed here, not dragged to the lair as usually happened when a leopard slayed. His end had come here, at the foot of the Finger, where from immemorial times, birth, death, initiation, marriage, all the occasions of human life, had been celebrated. What brought him to the Finger last night? What made him leave his sleeping family and come alone to this haunted spot? Nothing I knew of animals or of baboons in particular, could suggest an answer. Perhaps in some dim glimmering way, the Finger had a meaning for him as it had for us, and there was an answer that had nothing to do with the search for food, the provision of shelter, the protection of the young—the usual economics to which we ascribed all animal behaviour. Something had brought him here—to die—at the foot of a cenotaph already erected and waiting.

" Hell! I feel quite sick," Marjorie said. And she meant it literally for a little stifled yelp rose in her throat.

" Let's go," I said.

We started walking away, but after a few yards I heard something that horrified me. It came from the dark shadow above the great rounded boulder—a scrape and a yawn with a kind of squeak in it, a sound so slight, so brief, that Marjorie did not hear it. But it froze my blood. Leading Marjorie by the hand, I walked fast but cautiously until we reached the nearest bushes, then ran, pulling her after me. We went faster and faster, skeltering down the slope until we reached the mud wall surrounding the village. We stopped there and she doubled up, panting.

" What's the matter? " she asked, trying to regain her breath.

" I couldn't take the stench," I told her.

I did not tell her that all the while we had been talking and making love and scaring away the vultures and mourning poor Apollinaire, a leopard had been watching us from the rock above our heads. But she had known it, in her own way.

Nor did I tell her about the queer dismay that came over me at the thought of a killer leopard taking up residence at the Finger.

12

INSIDE THE VILLAGE the huts were deserted, but we followed the drum sound to Mgali's kraal where I knew everybody would be watching the witch-doctor at work. As we threaded along the narrow twisting alleys, I looked over low mud walls into empty yards—at flattened earth so fantastically clean and swept that it looked like a synthetic plastic surface : at domestic paraphernalia—worn grey millstones, gourds, baskets, clay pots, sweat-darkened wooden pestles leaning in mortars of hollowed logs, heaps of white, yellow, and brown corn on wooden platters, long-handled axes and tidy piles of firewood, hides pinned out to dry, hand-wrought kitchen implements, assagais, rawhide shields—earthen things made by hands for hands, arranged in the mood of a stone-age still life.

We found the crowd in the big kraal and stood and watched from the side. Cigarettes, crouched before a fire of wood embers, was in the witch-doctor's garb which he always carried, packed incredibly small, in a pouch on his waist—a cape of monkey tails over his shoulders, a pair of duiker horns fixed on a band of python skin around his head, armlets and anklets of dried pods that rattled at the least movement, a girdle of cowrie shells, another of rock-rabbit skulls. He wore his medicines around his neck, in scooped-out claws and small antelope horns, a blown-up lizard bladder threaded between each ; over each nipple was a small round shaving-mirror suspended from a thong tied around his chest. His eyelids, which drooped heavily in a thick drugged way, were painted with violet ointment ; a single white line ran from the top of his forehead to the tip of his nose.

Behind him, with an impassive face and webbed-over, expressionless eyes, stood one of the villagers beating the drum, mechanically, trance-like. Squatted next to him was Boots, whirling a calabash gourd filled with pebbles, jerking it with a quick tireless motion of his wrist. Standing in a wide circle a distance away, as if held back by unlucky or bewitched ground, were the silent, fascinated villagers.

Cigarettes was an old man, but hunting and a spare life had preserved his figure and he was superbly built. But now, dressed in that dangling, rattling get-up of bits and pieces, in his hunched, shrunken position, and the kind of shivering fevered tension he created around himself, he looked as thin as a stick. He was squatting, small and active as a monkey, his heels touching his haunches, his knees shoulder-high like a grasshopper's, his body swinging as if balanced on a pivot. From a skin pouch he spilled a collection of charms on to the ground—smoothed vertebra bones, yellow claws, lucky beans, a monkey's testicles, a military button, coloured pebbles. He peered at the pattern, shading his eyes and muttering without indicating what it told him, scooped the objects up and replaced them in the pouch. He repeated the procedure two or three times. Then, swaying and chanting, he poured powder from a gourd into his hand and flung it into the fire. A blue flame whooshed up, reflecting green on his sweating chocolate skin.

Now he reached for his own calabash gourd and whisked it in circles, and the whirring took on a suddenly deeper and more intense note. Then—how he did this I never knew—on his rigid left hand there suddenly appeared a little black cup with the black horn of a baby impala standing upright in it. His body swayed back and forth, his head obeyed a mechanical horizontal motion of its own, his right hand whirled the gourd, but his left hand with the cup and impala horn standing on it remained rock still. He did not look at the horn; he peered with burning pin-point eyes into the fire, and a weird jumble of words that sounded vaguely like Shangaan but which defied recognition, fluttered out of his lips. The horn pointed straight up in the cup, like a speedometer needle, while the gourd begged and pleaded for it to lie down. For several minutes the contest of horn and gourd went on to the steady persistent whirring and drumming and the hypnotic machine-like body movements.

Suddenly the horn fell over and lay against the side of the cup. Both gourds came to a stop, the drum slowed to the beat of a dying heart, the witch-doctor's body became still. Slowly, achingly slowly, he turned his head and looked at the subjugated horn, holding the impressive, heavy-lidded gaze for a moment after seeing it. Then all at once the expression exploded, the eyes opened wide in amazement, the mouth fell agape, and a huge grin broke over his face.

I let out a long breath of relief.

But I noticed that no expressions changed in the faces of the crowd, and the measured, almost expiring, beat of the drum continued. I turned, and with them, waited.

Then as we looked, the horn stood up again. Aghast, incredulous, Cigarettes shook the cup, tilted it, bounced it on his palm, and in a frenzy of rage spat at it. Nothing would make it lie down again. It was back from the dead, back on its feet, but now with a supernatural contempt for gravity and all earthly laws. He tried again but the horn continued to defy him, and finally, as if stung by a scorpion, he swept it off his hand. As the cup and horn rolled into the sand, he turned away in loathing. He sat absolutely still, his body in a curious shrunken collapse—until an intense feverish shuddering seized him and then an attack of violent hiccoughing. For a full minute he crouched in a paroxysm of shuddering and obscene belching until his human soul was wrung, shaken and exploded out of his body, and he sagged with his hands hanging lifelessly between his knees, a limp cold ash of a man. I looked into his eyes—they were gone. His breathing was gone. Nothing seemed to remain inside the miserable assortment of rags and rubbish that clothed him.

Slowly he came back. He moved an arm, tentatively, splayed his fingers stiffly, bent them, wagged his head to shake the

stupor out of his eyes, took a deep, deep breath. Like a Japanese
paper flower expanding in water, he filled back into himself.
Mechanically he poured the powder into his hand, tossed it
into the fire—a burst of blue flame. He fumbled for the pouch
containing the charms, shifted his feet . . .

He saw us then—I knew it from the sudden live gleam in his
eyes ; his hands stopped and a muscle twitched in his face.
He looked away, but turned back suddenly and gave us a long
curling glance over his shoulder. As he did so, the eyes of the
crowd were drawn on to us, and by some wierd act of trans-
ference we seemed to become magic and ugly and terrible. It
was as though, with that long look, his genie had taken a short
swift flight out of his eyes and landed inside us. Suddenly we
felt intensely white and extraordinary. My clothes felt freakish,
my many-pocketed bush shirt the quilted uniform of some
nonsensical expedition, my hard brown boots the heavy lead
boots of a deep-sea diver. Marjorie was fantastic—her lipstick
a red gash far wierder than the white stripe on Cigarettes's
forehead, her white face more ghostly than the chalked mask
faces of boys in initiation schools, her unkinked hair a monstrous
wig, her pale hands like peeled roots, her scarlet fingernails an
array of enamelled hooks. In her purple slacks, a skin glued
to a skin, she looked more naked than the bare-breasted women
suckling babies around me, her floppy white sweater and flimsy
silk shirt was the most flamboyant, impractical blanket ever
pulled over a woman's back. I looked around at the slow, heavy
faces, the rich chocolate skins, the deep withdrawn eyes, the
muscular shoulders and arms, the unglamorous breasts, the
wisps of calico wound into skirts, the hard thick-soled feet, and
wondered at the outlandish she-thing I had brought with me.

When I turned to Cigarettes again, he was yawning and
stretching his arms, finishing the movement by snatching the
horns off his temples. He stood up and started changing into
his hunting clothes that had been lying in a heap beside him.
The cup and horn lay where he had thrown them—toys now,
a little wooden cylinder that children use for throwing dice
in cardboard games and a silly little antelope horn with a

rounded lump of tar stuck underneath to keep it balanced upright. The spell was over.

He packed up his collection of props and came over to us. Speaking our makeshift language, he asked me what was happening about the hunt. I told him that we were waiting for the Big Missus to come back, and that he had better go down to the ravine in case Conrad wanted him. He left and followed Boots who was making for the gate, walking in the opposite direction to the crowd now streaming back to their huts. Now he was just another villager, talking and laughing and greeting his friends. He had on those knee-length khaki shorts that had started off by being full length, but in a lifetime of wear had frayed away from the bottom. The ragged, uneven pants, the old army tunic, devoid of buttons and patched with animal skins reminded me, as on so many previous occasions, of a marooned sailor—of a man who maintained himself by hunting, fishing and the produce of his hands, but who owned an island. He walked with an easy confident swing, his wonderfully shaped calves tensing with every step, his shoulders relaxed, his head upright, his eyes alert, his senses tuned to every sight, sound and smell in his surroundings. Walking was a thing of importance to him—an art. It was *his* art, and every step was a proclamation of his dominion over the bush. I knew that walk well. Often I had followed him as he picked up the spoor for Conrad, and the rhythm of it sometimes came into my dreams.

Cigarettes! What a name to saddle a person with! Boots— Matchbox! Cheap, ridiculous, contemptuous names—names of trifles, rubbish, discarded things. Yet they were titles of an aristocracy. Trackers gave themselves these disparaging names to mark them apart from the city-bred hunters and their servants they worked for. True, it amused the Bwanas and spared their feelings when relying on the sure skill and instinct of the trackers to save the hunt and possibly themselves. It amused the trackers too, to give a little of themselves away, to play simple, in order to bring out the foolishness of their white masters. They could afford to give much away, for in combining the intelligence of man with the instincts of animals, they became the princes, priests and poets of the bush. It was right that they should have these trashy names : they asserted their mastery by concealing it, by the device of camouflage. And camouflage is one of nature's laws.

We let Cigarettes and Boots go ahead along the track, then turned off and followed a little used track into the ravine in order to avoid passing the Finger. I felt uneasy. I could not get Cigarettes or the mutilated baboon out of my mind and I was pestered by superstitious notions that there must be some connection between them : that they were omens casting an eerie shadow over the crisis at Malinda. I had often seen Cigarettes carry out these rites before a hunt, but he had never been like this—so transported, so frenzied, so sub-human. He seemed to suck the crisis out of the air, to process it in some manner inside his shrunken exhausted body, and give it back in a new monstrous form. Against all my judgment and reasoning I had to admit that I had been moved.

I walked away filled with uneasiness not simply at the ominous message that seemed to hang in the air, but at my inability to explain what I had seen. Yet when I saw him walking in the distance, so calm now, the sane, efficient tracker, I found myself wanting to laugh it off. How could I, a medical student, a man pledged to scientific inquiry and rational attitudes, make any concession to this nonsense ? How could I allow my intelligence to be affronted by the idea that there might be something in this hysterical mumbo-jumbo ?

Marjorie must have been going through the same conflict. " Did you believe in this ? " she asked, waving her arm back in the direction of the village. " I mean, was it a stunt of some kind, or the real thing ? "

" It's the real thing to him," I told her. " But not to me."

" So you don't believe in it ? "

" That's an irrelevant question. He believed in it—and that's the point."

I was groping to find an explanation that would not ridicule

Cigarettes—that, I felt, would be crass and uncharitable—but at the same time allow room for my modern rational attitudes. This matter went down to the very root of the differences between African and European cultures. Usually one was pitted against the other in a contest of usefulness and intelligibility. I had been inclined to approach it that way myself, but now I felt the stirrings of other ideas that had been planted in my mind years ago, when I was still a child, and much more susceptible to the ceremonies I used to witness in the village.

" I wish you'd explain it to me—that little thing in the cup," Marjorie said. " That standing up and falling down again. What did it mean ? " There was something too sharp in her voice. She too was disturbed, and irritated at not being able to understand. But confronted with the question, forced to take up a stand, I reacted in a peculiar way. I found myself skating round the issue by talking sarcastically and facilely.

" It means anything you—or he—want it to. If that horn thing's supposed to be the lion, the answer's obvious. The old cat gets bowled over but refuses to lie down. That means a lot of unpleasant work all round. If it's supposed to be the hunter —or himself—well . . ."

" Well ? "

" The same thing. Somebody's going to get hurt. Your scarf's falling off. Let me tie it on properly for you."

" No ! " She snatched it from her hair. " Gene, please don't be so high-hat and superior about this. *I* thought it very impressive. A man can't go through all that—what's the word ? —emotional expenditure, without it meaning something very important to him."

" It does mean something very important to him."

" Then tell me."

" It means he's gone through a deep spiritual or religious experience—that's important."

" For the hunt ? "

" Yes, especially for the hunt. His mood, his confidence, even his belief in this fortune-telling are important factors. Just as important as the weather, the spoor and so on."

" Fortune-telling ? "

" Yes, it's a kind of conjuring trick. All you do is move your thumb very slightly and the thing balances any way you want it to. I can do it myself—I'll show you one day. And those little bones, pebbles and thingummies he tosses in front of him . . ."

" Yes ? "

" He looks at the pattern . . ."

" And that gives the positions and details and so on ? "

" No, not quite, but it could." How could I explain this ? She seemed to think it all went according to a book of rules, like canasta. " No. All it tells him is ' good ' or ' bad, ' in a general way."

" I see. And what was it—good or bad ? "

I hesitated before answering. There was an answer, but it was complicated, and, anyway, it jibbed with concepts of mine that I didn't feel like throwing out at the moment.

" That's hard to say," I told her. " He doesn't let on what the bones tell him. You go by his reactions. The way he sort of clucked made me think 'bad.' Only you never know which side he's clucking for—us or the lion."

" Gene—SHUT UP. What's got into you ? Why are you so prejudiced ? I thought you'd have more sympathy."

" Oh, sympathy," I said. I thought she had had enough of the discussion and I walked on without speaking, but she squeezed my arm in an agitated way and said, " Gene, I *must* know. I'll never get it out of my mind. Just try and be sensible and explain it to me."

" Okay," I said, knowing I was going to have a hard time keeping my tongue from babbling in the way it had been doing. " Right. Let's start with fundamentals. First, this is only symbolic, and not symbolic in our terms but in his. Does that make sense ? "

" I think so. You're trying to say that we're trying to give it a meaning that wouldn't be valid for him."

" Exactly—in terms of our own background and civilisation. Now, this really falls under comparative religion. Most people

call this stuff voodoo—implying that it's primitive and evil and
thousands of light years behind our enlightened religion. But
it's not behind or in front—it's on another track altogether.
To us God creates the world like a clock, winds it up, sets the
hands, gets the thing ticking, then goes off to attend to other
business. That's because we're mechanics and gadgeteers—
that's the outlook of our civilisation : practical, functional.
With Africans it's different. There are no machines. The sun
is the clock—literally ; ask an African the time and he looks
into the sky, then holds out his arm to show how much day
is left. With them God is creating life all the time—all movement, nature, growth, disaster is not just the work of God, but
God himself. Am I making it clear ? "

"Yes, I think so. Go on."

"Well, this explains why there's this strong fertility angle in
African religions. And the wild dancing and hypnotism and
frenzy—orgiastic, in other words. Now we're getting near to
Cigarettes. This show this morning was just that. A witch-
doctor doesn't make literature out of religion. He lives it, fuses
himself with the universe—trees, animals, insects. That's why
they have these animal masks, or that spooky make-up like
Cigarettes was wearing this morning. They don't preach or
make precepts—that's the utility angle—our angle. What they
do is express the feeling of their religion through their bodies,
the more violently and physically the better. This is getting
to be a lecture."

"That's what I asked for—not that scoffing you were giving
me earlier," Marjorie said.

"You wanted the explanation, and I'm giving it. But that
doesn't make *me* a convert," I said, feeling the other side of
the dilemma coming to the fore, and going on the defensive
again.

"Don't start that now," Marjorie said. "Tell me what this
meant this morning."

"Meant ? "

"Yes, why does he do it before a hunt ? What's there about
a hunt ? "

" That's when he comes closest to nature—to animals and the bush. By closest I don't mean just proximity. I mean action too—he takes a part in the drama of nature. He climbs right into the bosom of the universe, as it were. . . ."

" *Olé!* "

" Well, it's hard to explain it in two-letter words. Anyway, as I was saying, hunting is one of the most religious experiences there is. So naturally he goes through the performance before setting out. In a way it *is* fortune telling, and those things are tricks. But they don't alter the position really. He comes out of it convinced that he knows, in a vague way, how the hunt is going to turn out. And he's been asking not for precise advance information, but for the help and guidance of the tribal spirits. So you see, it's a bit silly wanting to know if he's found out whether there'll be one lion or four, or if they'll jump or creep along the ground or get hit in the nose or tail. That's just our European way of looking at things—we expect some plain no-nonsense information in order to make proper plans. Plans—that's what we live by. Plans, clocks, schedules—as if we control nature. He looks at it the opposite way. Nature controls him, sort of swirls him around. Okay ? "

Marjorie walked on thoughtfully. " I don't know," she said after a while.

" Don't know what ? "

" It worries me. It happened—it was real. I'm going to have nightmares over it. It seems you can't dismiss it either by making jokes about it or pigeon-holing it like an anthropologist. How do you *feel* about it ? "

" I feel it ties up with other things that are happening here. It's serious." I was not joking. I knew that he was both responding to and influencing events and that he would introduce a wayward, tenuous element that we would have no power to control. This was not being superstitious but allowing that superstition might help shape events. This summed it up, but it still left me uneasy.

Marjorie said suddenly, " It was horrible. I'm all queezy inside. That—and Apollinaire too—it was awful. Everything's so violent and ugly this morning. Why don't we get into the jeep and go away for the day ? "

It sounded a wonderful idea, but I knew that it was impossible for me not to go on that hunt. I too was involved. In what manner I could not say exactly, but I knew that I was being pulled in by subtle and intangible forces. The crisis had thrown its net over everybody.

As we walked I saw the Finger looming up against the sky, white and dazzling as if covered in frost, and I was struck by the contrast between its jubilant air and the sombre happenings relentlessly piling up as the morning progressed. I thought of the sleek silent killer lurking in the shadow of the rock, and of our favourite baboon lying there, ripped to death while on some inexplicable nocturnal expedition. And suddenly it struck me that I had been giving the wrong meaning to the Finger's glistening excitement. It was not celebrating the end of drought and distress in the valley, but the arrival of a conqueror. It was like the fresh paint and gleaming clean windows of a house taken over by a new owner. Omens ! Everything was conspiring to undermine my belief in a rational, ordered world.

13

WE FOUND the hidden game track and followed it downhill past clusters of wattle trees in vivid yellow blossom. We crossed dozens of new rivulets born in the night's storm. About half-way down we came to a group of native huts that had been abandoned a few years before because of a fire. Three of the five huts were burnt out and rain and erosion had worn down the smoke-scarred walls to almost ground level. But two had survived with no more damage than a few holes burnt in the thatch. We stopped and looked at the geometric pattern in different ochres that was still clear on one of the walls. The bush was dense all around us—we could not see down into the ravine nor up to the ridge—and in that isolated clearing the huts looked like the ruins of a forgotten city.

I told Marjorie about the fire but all she said was, " It's so deserted and silent." She was in a confused mood, pensive, distant, but inwardly taut and nervous. As we walked on she held my arm with both hands, as if needing something to cling to, and I could feel a stirring in her, an animalism that came to me through the tenser surface of her misgiving. I too felt the stirring of tension beneath the crust of restraint. There had been too many climaxes that morning ; now, with their impact diminishing, I was left with the residue of brittle nervous excitement. Fragments of the morning hung about me like a disjointed reverie—our love-making on the rock high above the valley, the background of exotic birds and wild glorious views—disturbed by the stench and hum of enamel-bright insects feasting, jarred by the black ritual in the village. Tenderness and beauty, violence and savagery ; the morning

had a note of discord that found expression in our own mood.
As we walked I sensed an atmosphere that at times comes over
the whole bush like a shudder or a shadow—a feeling of utter
desolation as if one's heart has stopped.

We came to a stream that normally we should have crossed
with one easy leap, but we found the banks collapsed and an
impassable gulf before us. We turned back to find another way
down into the ravine, and now Marjorie walked heavily, pulling
on my arm as if this were a fresh calamity.

As we came in sight of the abandoned huts again I heard a
sound in the bush ahead of me, a swish of leaves, a tiny crackle
of twigs. I dropped on one knee and pulled Marjorie down
with me, then moved over to take cover behind a bush.
Suddenly an impala sailed across the track in front of us,
followed a split second later by two more so close together
and in such like attitudes that they seemed to be one figure,
then another, and finally after a few seconds, another. They
leapt high, holding a stiff ships' figurehead pose, formal and
stylised as a moving frieze, their black-tan-white markings
clear as new printing, their thin curved horns enclosing
equations of blue sky and green foliage. They landed with a
jerk of their striped tails and a crash of twigs and then the tiny
hoofs thudded away into the bush.

" Oh, aren't they wonderful ? " Marjorie cried out.

" Yes," I said, thinking how pleasant it was to be seeing
impala again.

" Oh, what lovely perfect things."

Something in her voice made me turn to her. She was staring
into the bushes, following the lost sound of the hoofs with a
strangely rapt expression : suddenly her eyes blurred with tears.
She shot a look at me then turned in embarrassment. But a
moment later she swung round and buried her face on my
shoulder. I tried to comfort her. " What's the matter ? " I
asked. She didn't answer. " Why are you upset ? " She didn't
speak, but just stood tense and still while I held her in my arms.
But I knew she was crying from the tear that splashed on to
my hand. This was a private sadness. I had no part in it, could

not even soothe her. I held her with the anxious feeling of being totally estranged from her, and waited for the distress to pass.

At last she looked up. " I feel such a fool," she said, giving a bleak smile and reaching into my pocket for a handkerchief. " They were so beautiful "—she blew her nose, dabbed her eyes, stuffed the handkerchief back—" that's why. Seeing them like that, so unexpectedly . . . they looked so beautiful . . . it just caught me here." Her hand went to her throat. " But it was damn' silly of me. I'm sorry."

As we walked on she said in a suddenly bright voice, " Anyway, I feel better now." Somehow I too felt better, as if she had wept for both of us.

Near the huts was an old baobab tree, its bark sagging like melted candle wax. " Aren't these the craziest trees ? " she said, gay now. " They don't look like real trees at all, but like those drawings kids make in nursery school." It was an apt description of these comical trees with their grotesquely fat trunks and drooping bark and hectic untidy tangle of branches. I told her that Africans call the baobab "the tree that grows upside down," and pointed up to show how the smooth writhing branches looked like roots. But she didn't look up. Instead she turned to me with a quaintly stiff and solemn expression. " Are my eyelashes all down my cheeks ? " she asked. I wiped away some black smudge with my finger.

I placed my hands on her shoulders and pressed them back against the tree, meantime looking deep into her eyes. She stared back but then she caught her breath and looked sharply away. I held her chin in my fingers and turned her face back. There was a strange defiant fire in her eyes—wild, aroused, hostile. It reminded me of the sharp manic alarm in the eyes of does in the rutting season. I pressed her hair against her temples, meantime peering all over the immobile silent face. I drew one hand lightly down her cheek, across her throat, to rest on her prickling nipple. Without moving her eyes, she brought up her hand and held it over the tips of my fingers. Then something stirred, a tightening of her shoulders, a tremor in her eyes, and my senses scattered; one moment I was floating in the air and the next I was plunging—dizzy, desperate.

" Gene ! "

" *Please!* "

" Gene, please don't. *Gene!* "

I pressed her against the shining green trunk with the old baobab becoming my accomplice and holding her for me. But he lost his grip and we slithered down the green slippery skin to lie on the great sleazy boot he held out to catch us. I sat up and gripped on to a root that hooped out of the side like an exposed water pipe. She rose to her knees and kneeled facing me with both hands flat on her thighs. " You're so wild," she said. " Do you want to kill me ? "

I looked away feeling miserable and embarrassed, but she leaned over to me and whispered, " Not like this." And as the clamour inside me died down, " And not here."

We saw the empty hut at the same moment.

Inside I scooped up leaves and twigs from the floor, shaped them into a bed as I did when camping, and spread the waterproof, blanket side up, over them. For a pillow I wrapped the bush-shirt around a log, first removing the things from the pockets, among them the fragment of azurite I had found on my first day home. I sat down to undo my clumsy hobnailed boots while she undressed quickly, eagerly, kicking off her shoes, shedding her sweater, shirt and brassière, wriggling out of her jeans. Then she stood laughing, with her thumbs in the top of ridiculously flimsy mauve chiffon pants. " Hurry, don't take all day," she said, laughing and teasing, and as I stood up and removed my trousers she peeled off the comically useless pants, rolling them down her thighs with her flat palms and dropping them on to the heap of clothing on the floor.

We stood facing each other in the hot twilight of the hut, our bodies tinted and metallic, like lizards, in the greenish gloom. We looked at each other across the hut, then she held out her arms, and we embraced. For a while we did not speak or even kiss, but just stood with our bodies pressed together. Then she leaned back and looked into my eyes.

" I'm going to say it now," she said, running her fingers through my hair. " I love you. I mean it—I love you. Oh, I know it doesn't make sense—me, old enough to be your mother. . . ."

" Hardly."

" Well, old enough. But I do, and it's wonderful, and I refuse to think how ridiculous it is. I love you, Gene. I adore you." She kissed me, reaching up to place a comical little peck on my nose; I felt her warm silken flesh caress my whole body as she rose on her toes. " There." She held her finger on the spot where she had kissed me. " You're sweet and kind, and you've got ruthless eyes. Sometimes I think you're going to eat me up like a snake. Oh, I love you." She hugged me tightly, then leaned back and looked into my eyes again; then she started kissing me all over my face—experimentally, gaily, teasingly—and dropping sentences between the kisses. " I've never been in love like this before . . . and to think it's . . . with a schoolboy . . . you're such a *schoolboy* . . . but you're adorable . . . and I'm never going to forget you . . . never . . . my schoolboy lover."

She did not ask me if I loved her. I would have said yes, if she had, but I could not bring myself to say it without a question. Besides, she suddenly stopped the play and took my hand, and led me to the bed. For a while we lay together in silence, then she said, " Oh, God, I don't know how I'm ever going to leave here," with such vehemence that her whole body tensed.

" Let's not think about it," I said into her hair.

We started to make love casually, almost accidentally. A shift in position, a shrug, and we shared the first whispered secrecies of our mated bodies. We lay calm for a while, my instinct held in check by some subtle restraint from her body. She closed her eyes, and in the greenish light her face seemed to take on a new kind of beauty. She seemed to be years younger—a child almost—with all the contrived and sophisticated effects suddenly gone from her. Yet I was aware of the deliberate craft in her body that held me in an equilibrium of calm and exhilaration, and tamed my precipitate impulse to rush blindly on and destroy our pleasure.

The rhythm came into our bodies and we swept out on a tide, a single oblivious creature adrift in an ocean of sensual pleasure. In ways I little understood she aided and guided me on the blind journey, her body becoming both the instrument and the master of mine, responding and persuading, answering and cajoling with infinite subtleties of mood and movement. I watched her breasts rise and fall with the mounting pace of her breathing, felt her hands play on my back, tracing tingling patterns with her nails, or kneading a shoulder muscle with her tense fingers. I pressed her shoulders to the ground, at the same time feeling the hard, whip-like resistance of her writhing body. Now the expression on her face changed, the child gave way to the eager, triumphant female ; her eyes were two thin slits of moist glee, her mouth was hot and avid. She gripped my arms and pulled me to her and we joined in a fierce savage kiss, intense, cruel, violent, imparted with all the pent-up force of our locked bodies. Now we were no longer together but each swept headlong in the heedless drive of sexual passion. The surge rose higher, vaster, mounting to a giant shudder, a wracked seizure. At the climactic moment I found a new strength, a total potency that brought the teetering agony crashing down. She cried out, a cry of pain and release from the depth of her body, then went limp. A few seconds later my own frenzy burst, my eyes blinded, my vigour exploded, and we lay together in the throbbing, descending peace of the aftermath.

Slowly we came back to our surroundings, to the derelict hut with its mud walls and blackened timbers and the shaft of dusty sunlight pouring through the hole in the thatch. We lay dazed and spent like a fitful sea creature washed up on to the sand in a storm.

" Not bad," Marjorie said in a bright new voice that seemed to belong to a stranger. I did not answer and we lay side by side in the gloom staring at the light that filled the small oval doorway, and hearing the now overwhelming sound of insects in the bush outside. I felt a strange desolation, as if the whole world had become a wilderness.

" How clever of you to wait for me," Marjorie said, perky as a sparrow. I found the difference between her mood and mine disturbing. " I can see you're good at this," she went on, holding her foot up to the light and then, in an oddly detached way, twisting it into a ballet step. " Your schooldays are over. I've got nothing to teach you." She accompanied the remark with some vaguely appropriate choreography, gliding the long slim leg into a pose, melting it down and flowing into another. As she did so she studied her leg very objectively, as if it were a piece of equipment rather than a part of her body.

The posturing was having an odd effect on me, but nevertheless I said, " Thank you, Professor."

" Thank *you*. Thank you for having me, as well-bred little girls say."

I tried to smile. I wanted more than anything in the world to be gay and lighthearted, to continue in the strain of teasing banter that was the usual note between us. But a deep change of mood had come over me. I tried to define the mixture of feelings that lay in the pit of my stomach like the lees in a glass. I felt elated yet empty, triumphant yet depressed, and underlying all the other feelings, apprehensive. There was more in this than I had anticipated : a whole new depth to our relationship had suddenly appeared. This was not going to be a passing experience : a fever for Marjorie had been planted in me. How could I ever go back to my dull student life after this ?

" Are you sad, Gene ? " she asked, sitting up and hugging her arms around her knees.

I nodded.

" Don't be sad. Maybe it's better like this—short, intense and doomed. Maybe that's why it's so special and successful. The other way . . ." The sentence died out.

" I wish it were the other way."

" No, then it would have to face the truth. And that would kill it. This way there's no time to think about the truth." She reached for the cigarettes, lit two and gave one to me. " But it's been wonderful. And especially to-day. It's not often that it comes off like this."

I did not want to think about it and for a while we lay and watched the smoke of our cigarettes drift listlessly in the still air of the hut. I was happy as well as sad, happy to be in love, happy to have cast off my boyhood at last, happy above all to have had this beautiful experienced woman as my lover. But I was desolate at the idea of losing her, at the thought that in four days' time she would leave for ever, while I remained behind among the deserted monuments of our love affair. I had the panicky fear that I would never find another girl like her, that I would never again fulfil myself in love as I had just done.

" I'm not sorry it happened," Marjorie said. " I don't regret any part of it. I don't mean it's just been fun. This has really meant something to me. I'll never look at a man in quite the same way again. I found something here "—she let out a slow trail of smoke—" at Malinda."

The smoke of our cigarettes joined in a spiral, curled slowly up to the roof and disintegrated in a gust of wind that came through the hole in the thatch. Malinda! Of course. Only here could it have happened. Only at Malinda where one was drugged by the seclusion and silence and the scented air, where fact and fantasy impersonated each other and truth disappeared in a wisp of laughing gas. Anywhere else it would have had no more substance than the smoke dissolving about our heads.

" I never imagined it would come to this," she said. " I started it because I wanted someone to talk to, to save myself from what looked like a screamingly boring holiday. Then I thought it would be fun to lead you on a bit. You were so young and fresh—and, well, a challenge, I suppose. And now look at me—up to my neck in it."

" Maybe you should have just stuck around with Peter Wickham. And kept to the beaten track instead of climbing up to the Finger."

" Remember that day? I was standing up there looking through the binoculars and you sort of crept up on me."

" I remember. It was fifteen years ago, but I remember."

" I *knew* you would turn up. I just knew it, and it's a funny thing, when you get hunches like that and they come true everything that happens afterwards seems completely inevitable. It had to be the Finger, of course. What was its message that day ? "

" Batten your hatches. Hurricane ahead."

" Maybe I should have listened. Maybe we both should have."

" You were very nice," I told her. " Very much the Smart Lady, but you were friendly, and I liked that. You had a queer kind of accent, but it's gone now, or maybe I don't notice it any more. And you kept on asking me questions. How far are the mountains ? How high is the Finger ? I thought you'd ask me how much it weighs."

" I wasn't interested in the information really. You were so gummed up, I was trying to make conversation. I'll always remember you that morning—with your rifle across your knees in that cave—like Wildcat Kelly on the run from the law "

" I was scared of you."

She laughed. " And now ? "

" I'm not sure. I think I still am but in a different way."

She did not take it up. She became serious for a moment, smoking reflectively, a little gauntly. " I'd seen you before that, of course," she went on, blowing out a thin stream of smoke. " When you came to the Big House to help organise things. And at that party on the second night. Do you know what I liked about you ? The way you spoke up to Lavinia. She wanted you to go and tell the servants not to make such a racket in the kitchen, and you told her, ' They've been drinking the left-overs from your party. Don't start with them now. They'll go home soon.' "

" You must have been surprised that I spoke English, or any recognisable language and didn't just make guttural noises."

" Of course not—don't be silly. It wasn't so much what you said as the way you spoke to her—sharp, sarcastic, looking straight into her eyes. You were so cool and contemptuous. I dare say you've picked that up from Conrad. Anyway, it was effective. Everybody had been fussing and flattering her, and *you* come along, the local farm boy, and sass her like that."

" I'm not one of her fans."

" Maybe not. But it was a nice change. For some odd reason —don't ask me why—I liked it. You thought the rest of us dirt, of course. We could see it all over your face."

" I didn't notice the rest of you."

" Not even me ? I was looking at you all the time."

" I didn't notice. I wasn't looking, that's all. I dislike everybody who comes to the Big House, on principle. So I don't look at them. That's why, I suppose."

She looked at me in an amused way, then went on, " And then I saw you early one morning from my bedroom window. You were wading across the river with your boots hanging round your neck and some dead birds mixed up with the boots, and holding your rifle up over your head. You were so alive and so sure of yourself sloshing across that river—so full of animal tension ; this straw hair of yours was blowing about in the wind, and somehow—how should I put it ?—you seemed so expert and quick. You looked just right out there—I can't explain. Then, soon after, Peter Wickham came to take me to the Bushman Caves. His hair was plastered with brilliantine, he wore a foulard and a sports blazer and suède shoes. And that did it. It's a funny thing—he's a good ten years older than you, but I think of him as an immature, inane youth. And you——"

" As a solid, square, family man."

" No, but as a developed person. Somebody responsible and sane, and—well, male."

" It would have been the other way round in town."

She didn't disagree with that. She sat thoughtfully for a moment, then went on, " Then I met you. At first I wasn't sure about you. I even thought of dropping the whole idea. Remember that night at the Big House ? Then you played that dirty trick on me during the hunt and I adored it. After that we started meeting every day, riding horseback, swimming at Monk's Castle, walking and talking. And suddenly I found I was having a wonderful time. And looking forward to seeing you each day, until—well, it ended like this."

She leant over to reach for her clothes, and sat holding them on her lap. Until she did that I had forgotten we were naked. " Well, the party's over," she said, starting to dress.

Maybe she didn't mean what I thought she did. Maybe I was twisting her words to mean the same thing that was in my mind. It might have been my own feeling rather than hers that this was the furthest it could go and therefore the end. But I had a sudden distaste for talking about it. My mood changed, so rapidly and completely that it appalled me, and I began saying things out of an irrational impulse to destroy, now and for all time, this impossible agonising affair. She was dressing, pulling on her pants. They were truly indecent pants—a flippant shred of chiffon made somehow more suggestive than ever by the poodle dog embroidered in black sequins on the side.

" Why do you wear those things? "

" What do you mean ? "

" I mean for whose benefit ? Who sees you in them ? "

" Nobody. Oh, you wouldn't understand—they make me feel good."

" But why ? "

" They just do. You wouldn't understand. It's a woman's thing."

She looked down and laughed. " I like things like this, that's all. Who knows ? I might have an accident and land up in hospital. . . . No, it's not that. I like to have nice things next to my skin, that's all."

" But this can-can stuff ? "

" Does it give you ideas, Mr. Latham ? " she asked, her tone suddenly sharp.

" Yes." I wanted to tell her that garments like this could only have one purpose—to tease and excite visitors to her bedroom—that they were an advertisement for promiscuity, that wearing such things only went with a mania for exhibitionism. An absurdly illogical jealousy was aroused in me, for I knew that she must have had lovers before me. Indeed, the special meaning that this love affair had for me, depended on this fact. I said, " It makes me wonder how many men you've had."

" Hundreds," she said. " I keep their names in a little black book. I'm a slut—didn't you know ? Just ring the bell and ask for Marge." She raised one shoulder, placed her hand archly on her thigh, and did a mincing imitation of a whore's strut. " I'm like a bus—anyone can climb on if he's got the fare. Oh, but you needn't worry. College boys can ride free— in the off season."

It was unbelievably harsh and cutting. I could hardly believe that I had unleashed this vicious torrent. Although I had provoked it I was astounded at the mood of sadistic destructiveness that had now taken such a complete hold over her.

" Have you never been with a call-girl before ? "

" Oh, shut up ! " I shouted.

" Did you think I was a virgin? Did you really think that?" she asked in a tone of mocking disbelief. I said nothing. She stopped making those twitchy shoulder movements and stood watching me with her hand on her hip waiting for the reply.

" No, of course not," I said glumly, reaching for my clothes.

" No, and neither are you. You've also had a few bites at the cake. Your *affaires*." She said the word with the hint of a French accent, and in a tone of scorn that made me feel that I had been caught in some particularly sordid adventure.

" That's different," I said irritably.

" Different—oh, sure. It's always different where you yourself are concerned. Because you're a man, I suppose ? Is that the line ? "

" Oh, give it a rest."

We finished dressing in bristling silence. I did not look at her. I rolled up the waterproof and packed it in the rucksack, while she leaned against the centre pole, pulling on a new cigarette, and looking at me with narrow exploring eyes through the smoke drifting lazily before her face. I pulled violently to tighten the straps of the rucksack, then stood up and kicked the leaves back over the floor, doing it a little too thoroughly, spitefully, to leave no trace of our bed of love.

" Gene," she said, leaning against the pole, and speaking in a level voice that was not unkind, " it preys on your mind, doesn't it ? How many lovers I've had."

" I never said that."

" But it does. I can see that. Well, I'll tell you . . ."

" You don't have to."

" I think we'd better get the record straight. It's not as many as you think. In fact, considering that I'm twenty-four and not exactly repulsive, and have been in theatre since I was sixteen, it's been pretty tame. Right, here it comes : *four—including* you. Does that stagger you ? "

" No . . . I don't know."

" The first was a plain straightforward seduction. I was seventeen, and on a ballet tour in London. It happened at an after-show party—upstairs on a bed as big as a garage. I never saw the man again. I never even knew his name."

" Let's go back," I said. " We've got a hunt on to-day."

" Lavinia's not back. We haven't heard her car. Light me another cigarette."

I did so. She pulled on it, then said, " Let's not go yet. Come sit down here."

She sat on the ground and patted the space next to her.

I hesitated, and she said, " I want to tell you something, Gene."

" I don't really want a case history—I get the general idea."

" Okay. But sit down."

I sprawled on the ground in front of her. She seemed worried and nervous now, and unable to find the words she wanted. She gave me an unhappy smile, then said, " You're going to hate me for this."

I did not answer. Her tone and sudden air of distress alerted me for what was coming, and I even intuitively knew it before she said it.

" I'm married, Gene."

" I see," I said, hoping for a wild bleak moment that it was a joke. But she was serious all right. " Yes—for eighteen months now. And I can't even say unhappily."

I should have exploded with anger, raged and used my arms. Instead I felt only a cold, cutting scorn for her, an icy distaste. " Thanks for telling me," I said. " Especially now. Has all this been a gag of some kind ? "

" No. I meant everything I said, every single word and syllable of it." She was looking away but suddenly she jerked her head towards me. " It's probably the first time in my life I've ever been completely honest with somebody. Oh, Gene." She sat looking at me, misery and tenderness brewing in the moist film that had come over her eyes.

" You couldn't hold it for another four days ? You had to deal this one out too ? "

" I couldn't leave here and not tell you. I just couldn't. Oh, Gene, please try to understand. I said I love you. I meant it. Not telling you makes the whole thing dishonest—a dirty trick on you. It would ruin everything."

" Of course, telling me does it a world of good."

She did not answer. She sat with her arms around her legs and her head resting sideways on her elbow. There was something pathetic and appealing about her distress, but I was hating her now, and was not going to let myself be swayed again.

" All right, let's have it," I said. " You've started now. Let's have the full story."

" What do you mean ? " she asked, with eyes full of misery.

" Let's have the whole case history. What about number two ? You skipped him. You *wanted* to tell me—now go on."

" Gene, don't."

" I see, so the honesty campaign's over ? "

" He was a man I lived with for five years," she said glumly.

" *He* sounds interesting. What was he—a stockbroker ? "

" Oh, shut up, you big oaf," she said, suddenly angry and blazing at me through tear-filled eyes. " I'm not your wife. I'm not your fiancée. And don't try that Conrad Webber stunt on me. What's it to you if I've had a love affair ? I was engaged to him, if you must know. It didn't come off, that's all. Is the

idea that I was supposed to save myself up for you ? Oh, grow
up. Yes, I was his mistress. We were going to get married,
but it didn't come off. As for my husband—now what would
you like to know ? His age ? Fifteen years older than me.
Profession ? Doctor. Seems I have a weakness for doctors."

" I'm not a doctor."

"Well, you're a tadpole doctor. A cute little embryonic
doctor. Same thing. He's a specialist—cardiac diseases. Nice
looking too, but of course not athletic. He couldn't shoot and
skin and eat a hyena. Doctors don't have that kind of background where I come from."

I was looking away, trying not to hear the sharp bitter voice,
trying to shield myself from the words that were ripping at me
like claws. Her husband—the words boomed in my mind with
a kind of multiple echo. Her husband—some poor hard-
working hack whom she was ready to dupe for a farm boy. For
me. I wanted to laugh.

" Is he good at it too ? " I asked over my shoulder.

" You make me sick."

" And this ballet-in-bed act. I bet that fetches him."

" Gene, SHUT UP ! "

I was lying with my back to her, waiting for another tirade.
But suddenly she was on the ground next to me, tugging to
find a way to put her arms around me, kissing me wildly and
desperately. " Oh, please don't talk like this. I can't stand it.
Please . . . please . . . look at me. Don't be like this. I should
have told you in the beginning. But it didn't seem to matter
then . . . I didn't know what was going to happen. And
later—later it was too late. I was scared of losing you. I
was going to—a hundred times—but each time I funked it.
I was a coward. Please, don't be cold. I can't stand that.
Please, Gene, kiss me. Just once. For the last time."

I kissed her, then pulled myself away. " It's all right, you
don't have to explain," I said. I said it in a kindly way.
" Really, you don't. It's me—I'm just plain stupid."

I saw the things that had been emptied from my pockets
lying in a heap on the ground. I went over to get them. She

followed and knelt next to me, picking up the objects and dropping them one by one into the pockets of my bush-jacket.

" String. Scotch tape. Penknife. What a lot of silly junk you carry around. Fish-hooks, cartridges ; What's this ? "

" Azurite."

I was not sure how I felt about her now. There was something tender and sad in her eyes that made me want her desperately. We were kneeling on the grass floor, facing each other, our hands hanging at our sides and I looked all over her groping to find some new definition of her that would fit her into this new context. She raised her hands a little, let them drop. I leaned forward and embraced her, then pulled her head on to my chest and kissed her hair. I wanted to make love to her all over again, to put time back and fix it in a slot so that it would never move on. I wanted her gay comical affection back again. I wanted my love for her again, and even my wild vain hopes which I had always known were fantasies bred in the distorting surroundings of Malinda. And I wanted, simply, to hear once more her voice that seemed, in that silence, to have vanished for ever.

I knew of no words that could express what I felt at that moment. I said, " I love you, Marjorie," because the much-exploited phrase happened to form on my tongue, but I didn't honestly mean it for my love was bleeding to death inside me.

She said nothing, but hugged me gratefully.

" Come—let's go back," I said, standing up.

We came out of the low door of the hut and stood up in the blinding light. I led the way through the bush on to a track that would take us down to the road at a point near Conrad's truck. We did not talk. The bush was quiet now except for the furore of insects. It had awakened noisily with the dawn, but had gone back into a drowsy half-sleep in the heat. Now it was the frenzied, microscopic day of the insects. A whine came out of the grass, a hum filled the air. We passed bushes *zing-zinging* with crickets like empty telephone boxes ringing with wrong numbers. Great bronze beetles hurtled past us like projectiles, huge fat moths with thick velvet wings flitted past slowly, precariously airborne because of their weight. Huge milky-opaque spider-webs hung on the bushes like pillow-cases, the rain-water collected in bulging sacs and pouches like a precious secretion. The hot sun had already steamed the wet off the trees, but the rain smell remained, sharp, ammoniac, evidence of the chemical ferment starting up once more in the earth. The hot breath of resumed putrefaction came out of the bush, the life-giving stench of sodden leaves, rotting wood, decomposing dung. Great muddy mushrooms cracked up through the earth between the roots of trees : glistening yellow blobs of resin burst out of branches attracting swarms of dragonflies and wasps that hovered tempted, but afraid to touch the sticky mess. Fluttering everywhere, like leaflets dropped from an aeroplane were tiny white butterflies.

We reached the road and began walking downhill in the direction of Conrad's truck. We said nothing. The air prickled between us and I was conscious of the tense traffic of our unspoken thoughts. She took my arm, clinging to me as if afraid that she would lose me for ever if she once let go of the physical grip. One hand was clasped on my elbow, the other rested on top of it, but clenched into a distorted fist. I saw that she was carrying something in her hand.

I thought again of the extraordinary turn that our love-making had taken. There seemed to be a wall of years between the time we made love and the present moment. Our love had seemed so intense, so important, so secure. But I had deluded myself. I had been bemused and dazzled by having such a lovely creature as my lover. I had been misled by the triumph of stealing this handsome prize from the Big House, of proving my superiority to the smooth supercilious men of the Big House who for years had made me feel like one of the zoological attractions of Malinda : of nailing up the flag of my manhood. Flattery and pride had combined with my love for her to make me blind to the realities. She was wrong for me. We were wrong for each other.

I wondered again why she had chosen that particular moment

to tell me she was married—right after we had made love for the first time. It seemed incredible—a fatal blow not only to our affair, but to all the things we had built up between us, all the things I had thought of her, all the good times we had spent together. I would never be able to look back on these in the same light again. Why had she reacted with such sudden violence, giving it that sadistic twist ? And why had she been so full of remorse afterwards ? I saw the answer. Like me, her instinct had been to smash up the whole thing before it became too dangerous. To destroy it before it destroyed us. The affair was doomed, as she had said. It was the surgeon's knife employed in a merciful killing.

I had complained because we had only four days to go, but I realised now that we had left our love behind, dead, in the derelict hut. The leopard had moved in on us too.

I opened her hand. In the sunlight the stone scintillated azure blue—intense as the breast of a peacock. She looked at it in surprise, forgetting that she had kept it in her hand instead of returning it to my pocket.

" What did you say this was ? " she asked.

" Azurite," I told her, closing her fingers over the chipped geological sample. " Copper ore. Keep it—a souvenir of Malinda."

14

WE CAME round a bend in the road and found everybody sitting about waiting for Lavinia. One of the station wagons had been driven down from the Big House and a number of people were inside—I saw Hoffman and Kiki and that honeymoon couple whose name I never found out, and a few others. The back door was open and Jackson, the Big House cook whom Lavinia had brought out from Johannesburg, was arranging the picnic equipment and baskets of food covered with white napkins. He sparkled in a starched white suit and a chef's hat perched at a jaunty angle. Ronnie Forsythe's derelict Chrysler was there, parked near the truck. And a little distance up the road was the Land-Rover with Ruth Secker sitting inside.

Marjorie said, "I can't let people see me like this. I'm going back to the house to change." She left me and went through the bush to the Big House.

As I walked on I saw my father sprawled out on the bank at the side of the road. His feet were crossed and his hands were clamped behind his head : his belt with the cartridge pouches and the attached telescopic sight were on the ground at his side, his stiff-brimmed hat with the leopard-skin band lay on his stomach. But he wasn't sleeping, for he kept turning his head, and with it his elbows, as he slowly peered up and down the road. He was alone up there on the bank— obviously he didn't want to be bothered talking to anybody— and he was the only one who seemed to be anxious about the delay. The three trackers, who sat a little way above him on the bank, were a complete contrast. They squatted in line, all facing the same way and in the identical pose—arms held straight out over their knees, hands dangling, heads tilted back looking into the distance with half-shut eyes—three hunting machines set for a fixed quantity of stupor.

Conrad was sitting on the step of the truck talking to Forsythe who was sprawled out on the ground below him, while one or two of the picnic crowd stood around listening. It surprised me to see Conrad and Forsythe together—and actually friendly. They were engrossed in conversation and didn't seem to notice me as I came up. They looked rather comical—Conrad like a little dandy game ranger and Forsythe like a big sloppy bull moose that he had captured and tamed. Conrad, drawing a pattern on the ground with a twig, was talking about the Watussi, the tallest people on earth. " Lords of Africa," he called them, who had slaves even to carry their spears. Strange too that they lived so near to the pigmies. Was it diet ? Or a matter of sunshine ? " Africa's one big circus," Forsythe said. He knew all about the Watussi *and* the pigmies and added a few facts that Conrad didn't know. They talked like old soldiers recounting campaign adventures. I saw that they had found a common interest and that it had dispelled Conrad's earlier antagonism to Forsythe.

" Hi, Gene," Forsythe said, giving me a breezy salute. " You and Marge been giving the place a once-over ? Wanna buy it or something ? " He had keen eyes : he must have noticed us on the road before we separated. He really looked a mess in that broken-down hunting outfit. The jacket was sweat-soaked and torn under both arms, revealing the dense hair in his armpits, the khaki shorts were dirty and tattered and held up precariously by an old tie, the faded knitted stockings were pulled unevenly over his fat calves, the scuffed and mud-stained rawhide boots were laced only half-way up and gaped open around his ankles. Yet it was reassuring to see him like this. Nobody except a tough old veteran who had lost his awe for the bush would come hunting in this tramp's outfit.

He said, " Yeah, about the pigmies—funny thing. They're getting taller every year. Eating better and getting cured of hookworm and other diseases. Soon there won't be any left because they're growing out of being pigmies."

As he spoke he pulled out a leather cigarette case, clicked it open, waved it in front of me and the others standing around, all without interrupting a sentence or taking his eyes off Conrad.

"Thanks," I said, helping myself to a squat Turkish cigarette. He gave the case a jerk with his thumbnail to flip his own cigarette into his mouth. Still without looking at us, he fished for his lighter, sprung it open, and lit all the cigarettes. He was like that—cool, impudent. In spite of myself I could not help liking him.

I looked at my watch. Half past nine and still no sign of Lavinia. She had held us up for more than three hours ; there was not the slightest hope of starting the hunt before afternoon. It was obvious now why Conrad was taking the delay so mildly. The more time wasted, the less chance of finding the spoor, and the less time spent on this farcical outing. Probably he'd go through the actions for an hour or two, then call the whole thing off and come home.

Or possibly it would be cancelled altogether now. When eventually she did come back it should not be difficult to convince Lavinia how pointless it was.

Ruth Secker made me uneasy. Sitting alone in the Land-Rover she gave an air of quarrelling to the group. I kept turning to look at her, impelled by a curiosity that had been aroused by all the times she had been mentioned that morning. I could not see her properly. The windscreen was dirty and there was a dark shadow inside the vehicle, but I kept seeing her cigarette glow and fade behind the glass. She was smoking tensely, and every few seconds her hand came out to flick the ash nervously out of the window. She seemed to be reading something : a square, greenish shape was moving about in front of her, a magazine perhaps. I could tell that something was wrong. These signs of agitation were enough, but even without them I would have known, simply from the fact that she kept all to herself in the car. Normally Ruth would have been the first out, bustling, organising, or simply talking to everybody about the hunt.

I wondered why Conrad was not sitting with her. It was strange to see him so calm when she was so upset. They were good friends, and I expected him to stay with her, to comfort her if that was what she needed—or at any rate, to be with her and distract her from her mood. I knew from seeing him walk alongside the Land-Rover while we were up at the Finger that he had already talked to her. But there seemed to be more than mere neglect of her in his lack of attention. It was as though they knew something together, or had talked it out so that there was nothing to be gained from further discussion.

I was about to go to her myself when I saw her lean forward into a patch of sunlight and look at her face in the rear-view mirror. I saw her clearly then. She pulled down the flesh under her eyes then drew her eyelids out at the corners, as one does when very tired. Her face was tense, and from where I stood, very white, as if dowsed with powder. She pulled her hair back tight against her skull and looked at herself, then patted it up and fluffed it out. I had seen my sister Peggy do that when experimenting with hair styles, but this was different. There was something mocking and self-disparaging about the way she did it. Suddenly she pulled back into the shadow and raised the magazine. She had seen me looking at her.

I looked away, but as I did so my eyes hesitated briefly on the Land-Rover. I noticed the thick viscous mud clotted under the fenders and splotched all over the bodywork. I saw, too, the greyish pack of dead moths and insects squashed on to the radiator grid. Until then I had suspected that Ruth had a part in the all-night motor rally that Marjorie had told me about. This confirmed it. As I looked away something else clicked almost subliminally in my mind ; the canvas sides with plastic windows which fixed on with thumb-clips, were clean. Creased, as if unpacked after being stored away for a long time, but free of mud.

It told me that Ruth had been in a hurry last night, in so much hurry that she hadn't time to put up the side canvasses when driving through the storm. The insects trapped and annihilated against the radiator spoke of fast travelling. And the whole vehicle had the look of having travelled far as well as fast.

I was trying to work it out, to piece it together with what Marjorie had told me, and with the puzzle of the tracks we had seen on our way to meet Conrad, when I noticed the Land-Rover move silently down the road to us. It glided without power, and it seemed without steering too, but after a moment the gears engaged and the engine took. By the time it reached us the engine was being churned into a roar by impatient pummelling on the accelerator.

Ruth stopped the car and leaned out of the window. " I'm going back to Dale," she told Conrad. Her voice sounded frantic—I had never heard it like that. There was a white, tight look about her mouth : her eyes were distraught and a little mad. She looked as if she had been through a desperate illness. I actually had a fright seeing her—I gasped and my heart pounded.

" I'll be back," she said in a rasping overwrought voice.

" What's the matter ? " Conrad asked, getting up. He looked serious.

" Nothing's the matter. I want to go back for something. I'll be gone about half an hour."

" If Lavinia . . ."

" To hell with Lavinia. Let her wait for *me*. I've waited long enough for her. Oh, for God's sake, Conrad, do I have to get your permission to go back to my own house ? "

" All right. But don't be too long."

She started to move off, but after a few yards she pulled up sharply, skidding the car into an angle across the road. " Gene, I'd like you to come with me."

I agreed to go and went round to the door.

She thought for a moment, then pointed her chin at Forsythe. " And you ? Would you like to join us, young man ? " It was a command, and Forsythe got up fixing his belt on his collapsing trousers.

Conrad was looking at her strangely.

" I feel like male company. That's all right, isn't it ? Do I need permission for that too ? " Startled by her hysteria, I opened the far side door and got in. As I did so I heard her say, " That's right—they'll be witnesses. I don't care a damn."

" Ruth ! "—that was Conrad.

Forsythe was in now and as she engaged the clutch she leaned out of the window. " Yes, let's have witnesses. Let's get it properly sewn up." And she fluttered her fingers and screamed " Good-bye" as if she were drunk.

" Ruth ! "

But we were moving off, gathering speed, and I didn't hear what Conrad shouted.

We were sitting all in front, myself in the middle, and nobody spoke. I felt a twittery nervousness. Her taut, suicidal excitement unsettled me, but it was more than just an atmosphere between us. It seemed to disturb the whole landscape of personal relations around me. I tried to work out what the trouble could be. It had something to do with Bill. The fact that he was not coming on the hunt told me that. For a moment I decided that they had had a tiff. But I rejected it. This was something different. This was no ordinary domestic quarrel.

Forsythe said, " Useful jobs, these Land-Rovers. We used them on a Kalahari expedition last year. Tough. . . ."

Nobody was listening. Ruth's eyes were narrowed to thin slits and she was gazing out through the windscreen with a glazed, numbed expression. The bush track was humped and uneven, and she drove badly, the flesh shaking under her chin and her hands wobbling on the shuddering steering-wheel. I looked at her trying to get a clue to what was troubling her— at her neglected hands with their incongruous gold rings with dirty diamonds, at her untidy mop of gretchen-yellow hair, the delicate complexion burnt by the sun to a blotched pink, the small, slightly hooked fleshy nose, the wide mouth that even now kept something of the sweet look in the corners— who could want to harm *her* ?

". . . But this was a scientific bunch, one of those Carnegie Grant outfits. Not much glam there, with those eggheads, but those boys were allergic to getting out front of their own cameras, so they had me doing it—you know, walking over the sand dunes, finding a skull, turning it over in my hands, sunset and fade-out. . . ."

Ruth—much the same had happened to her as had happened to my father. She too had become a simple cattle man—and I say "man" because it was hard to say cattle woman, particularly where Ruth was concerned. The sun had burnt her down leaving not merely the core of a person, but a new person— tough, seasoned to hardship and the weather, skilled at dealing with cattle and the valley, but guileless and vulnerable when faced with slick nimble city folk. Yet with a difference. With my father there was always a hankering for the past, a lurking regret that he had taken up this life, while Ruth found and fulfilled herself at Dale, found real happiness according to her recipe.

Living near to the Seckers—being next-door neighbours, if that term could be applied to families living ten miles apart, borrowing from each other (anything from a tractor to an onion) in short, being their friends, taught us to see each other in terms of true values. And to us, Ruth was the most glamorous person we knew. We saw glamour in her achievement and character and hardly noticed how she dressed or did her hair.

Everybody knew the story of Dale. Dale was one of the most prosperous ranches in Rhodesia and the story was one which used to be chewed over for hours in hotel bars, cattle shows, or wherever settlers got together. It made them feel good to talk about Dale. It encouraged them to believe that it was not such a harebrained idea trying to wring a living out of that hostile valley. Dale did for them what the discovery of a big diamond on a nearby claim did for out-of-luck diggers—it kept them trying.

In fact, Bill Secker started Dale in much the same slap-happy trust-your-luck spirit of a diamond digger. He had been a

trooper in the B.S.A. Police but he gave that up to start ranching with a few dozen head of cattle, a corrugated-iron shack,
and about a thousand acres bought with money he had
scrimped from his wages, or somehow got his hands on while
patrolling in the Sabie Valley. He was the first to ranch in that
area (Dale started in the 1930s), and he went there mainly
because he could get the land for next to nothing. But luck, or
success, nearly by-passed him. He was too lazy, he drank too
much, and the loneliness used to send him berserk. So he was
always getting into his ramshackle truck and driving half-way
across Southern Rhodesia to drop in on friends for a few days'
holiday. He would treat himself to drinking week-ends at the
Bell Hotel, or take trips into Umtali on any trivial excuse—to
buy a bag of fertiliser, to place a bet on a horse, or simply to
read the newspaper. It would be wrong to say that he let the
ranch go to ruin ; it hardly started to be a ranch, and it was
a wonder that any animals survived. He had lots of encouragement for this ruinous way of life. He was big, cheerful and
irresponsible—a blond, twinkle-eyed gadabout—and there
was always a good time for everybody when he was around.
People always begged him to stay longer, invited him to come
again, and so made the loneliness of Dale more unbearable than
ever. Everybody liked Bill immensely, but nobody expected
him to last in the cattle business.

But fate was saving something up for him—a huge slab of
good luck that came in the disguised form of a motor accident.
One night, while drunk at the wheel, he crashed his truck into
a tree on the strip road outside Melsetter. When a car came
past two hours later he was still unconscious, and he was rushed
to hospital with both legs broken, most of his ribs cracked, and
a fractured skull. His life was in the balance and he was saved
by a series of emergency operations. And he struck his fortune
not only without conscious effort on his part, but as the result
of the hazy maunderings of his fuddled mind while coming
round from an anæsthetic. For he started making indecent
proposals to the nurse who was wiping the dribble from his
chin, a strapping flaxen-haired girl named Ruth Thompson.

He kept up the same line of suggestive talk when he was conscious and when convalescent he pursued Ruth all over the hospital in his wheel-chair. They were married three months after the accident, with Bill still in the wheel-chair.

Ruth brought many things to Dale—routine, thrift, organisation, book-keeping, discipline, and most important of all hardworking hands and a business head. Dale began to flourish like a neglected garden taken over by a horticulturist. The herds were improved and enlarged, extra land was bought and the fences spread farther and farther out into the vacant bush ; trucks were added to trucks, barns, stockades, cattle stations and loading ramps grew up like frontier posts right across the valley, until Dale became one of the name-places of Southern Rhodesia, a ranch of a hundred and fifty thousand acres. And it was all Ruth's doing, for as the enterprise grew Bill did less and less work, and became simply a gorgeous pampered mascot.

People used to remark how extraordinary it was that two such similar women as Ruth and my mother should have come to live next to each other in all that vast, empty area. But of course, they weren't similar at all. My mother made a triumph of housekeeping, or better, home-making, in grimly unpromising circumstances. One thought of her in her neat apron baking a cake in a log fire exactly as if she were in a modern electrified kitchen, or sewing curtains on the treadle machine, or teaching in her improvised school. Cattle were things she put up with, rather like leopards crossing the lawn when she hung out the washing.

Ruth's house was a mess—a dark-brown confusion of cracked rawhide furniture, dreary animal-skin rugs ruckled up and kicked into the corners, broken celluloid lampshades, cabinets stuffed full of brokers' notes, old cash books, stock sales catalogues, grimy farming magazines. The sideboard in the diningroom was covered with bottles of cattle medicine. The only wall adornment in the living-room was a huge flapping calendar, advertising tractors and windmills. Ruth had a bricklayer's hand at cookery, and when she tried to decorate the house for visitors she stuck flowers in the vases like trussed-up bunches of

asparagus. But she could deliver a calf and take charge of the
bellowing, panicky confusion of a cattle dip, and keep the farm
hands under firm but fair control, and handle a gun like a man
and shoot a marauding lion as casually as spraying flit on a bluefly. And she had a keen money sense and a flair for administra-
tion that enabled her to run Dale like an up-to-date business.

When we came out to Malinda, Dale was already a great
ranch. And Bill was a big name in the district. At Dale he
always looked the country squire, in tweed sports coats with
a shotgun tucked under his arm and a pair of red-eyed trigger-
tense pointers sniffing at his feet.

But he spent a lot of time away from Dale. The urge to get
up and go that once nearly caused his ruin could now be
indulged on a lavish scale and instead of tearing all over the
district in a rattling truck, he flew the airlines to Europe and
America, though with still no more purpose or point than
formerly. While he travelled Ruth looked after the ranch,
though in later years she also began taking trips, leaving the
ranch in charge of a manager. She always came back ahead of
Bill after what seemed a mere few days of absence. She would
kick off the new shoes she had bought on her travels, get out
of some tight, expensive-looking costume that seemed to
suffocate her, change into her old slacks and leather jacket, and
go sloshing in the mud of the cattle stockades. We used to
wonder what she ever did in London, Paris or New York.

It was a strange marriage. They were childless, and seemed
to be not so much married to each other as joined in a kind of
tripartite union with Dale. Yet they were very fond of each
other. Bill always came back with extravagant and completely,
unsuitable presents for Ruth—perfume which she never used
gowns she never wore, fancy lingerie, jewellery. Sometimes
she wore some of the jewellery—perhaps to show her apprecia-
tion—at the cattle dip, or while slopping about in the barn in
rubber boots preparing the cattle mix.

And Ruth had a great mother-bear affection for her overgrown cub of a husband. She gave him complete licence for
his playboy life, and it seemed to lend zest to her own life to

do this. If he fell ill, even with a mild dose of 'flu, she would put him to bed and nurse him like a crisis case in her old hospital. The quickest and most ridiculously easy way to win her affection was to say something complimentary about Bill.

In our early days at Malinda, when things went hard for us, we relied heavily on the Seckers. They helped us with transport, fodder, veterinary services, and sometimes we seemed almost to be living on them. They never minded, and only got annoyed with us when, out of diffidence, we failed to ask them favours. They relied on us too, for certain things—family evenings, domestic interest, Christmas and children's parties, and so on. We shared many things, and here the catalogue was long—the valley itself, its vagaries and moods, a love of the wild country, a common outlook on Africa and a friendliness for the African people that was rare among settlers, a hatred of the Big House, amusement and contempt for the queer, clumsy, bright-clad strangers who every year alighted as if from a flying saucer, to spend holidays amongst us; a disgust for old Jordan Whittaker and the trick he played on us. As for Lavinia, we shared the fervent wish that she would catch pneumonia fatally, or get bitten by a puff-adder, or fall over a cliff.

Forsythe was speaking. ". . . makes me laugh, this yak about the character of animals. Take cat—it's Kenya I'm talking about—used to be if they heard a truck coming, they beat it quick as hell over the horizon. That's because a truck was an enemy. Kinda tin animal that spat out things that made holes in their sides. But not to-day . . ."

He had been talking all the way from the burnt-out kraal, not the least put out by our failure to comment or answer; I didn't mind. Since we didn't have to listen, it wasn't really irritating. It just sounded vaguely silly—or trivial—with Ruth in that disastrous mood. I heard him go on.

"Not to-day, not since everybody picked up this S.P.C.A. bug and started hunting with cameras. Now they throw meat from the trucks and the cat come from miles around to pose for their pictures. They only gotta hear a truck in the distance and they come pouring outa the trees. It's that Pavlov stunt—

remember? And tell you something—they're even learning how to pose properly like movie actresses. Look proud, growl for the lady, side face, please—because those that oblige have all their food problems solved. And they're some there that trade on their good looks, make the big time, just because they happen to be photogenic. Just like Ava Gardner and people . . ."

There he was again.

" Animal character? The proud lion, the slinky hyena, the gentle giraffe—that's stuff outa kids' nursery books. All depends on how they're treated . . . just like people."

I wondered why we were going to Dale. And why she wanted us to come with her. And what she meant by "witnesses." We were nearing Dale now and I was anxious; I was sure something unpleasant was going to happen there. She had not spoken a word during the drive.

I found myself thinking about last night again. Strangely, everything seemed to go back to that. I began to see things in a different light now, with a different emphasis. Details began to emerge, small things that had been swallowed up in the talk and noise and forgotten in the later argument about the hunt.

The high-strung excitement in Bill's voice, and the way he sweated and fidgeted. And that fancy suit, with white shirt and silk tie, instead of his invariable sports coat. And Lavinia's silence and moodiness in the early part of the evening, and the way Kiki kept talking, as if to orders, covering up the silences and diverting the conversation with inane chatter. Ruth sitting in that arm-chair, her legs crossed, her finger-tips touching, pretending to look interested but not hearing a word anybody said; and trying to pass messages with her eyes to Bill, and the general air of edgy frustration about her. And of course, *her* clothes and idiotic hair-do. The strange mixture of embarrassment and cosy assurance with which Bill threw in his weight with Lavinia—not saying, " Well, no, I wouldn't advise it. Not for a couple of weeks. Conrad's right," with his thumbs stuck in his armpits and his usual authoritative this-is-*my*-line-of-country manner; but raising his glass and croaking, " Sure, let's go and pot the bastards." Ruth, almost leaping out of the chair, and saying in a queer tense voice, " Yes, it's a bloody good idea. I'm ready any time to go and bump off any stinking pigs that come marauding into the district." And the particular vehemence of her remark.

Yes, one thing was beginning to crystallise out of the confused events of last night and to-day. Whatever it was that troubled Ruth so deeply—and I could still only guess at it—it was the same thing that caused my father's black mood this morning, and his peculiar behaviour last night at the Big House.

Yet at Dale nothing happened. Just before we reached there, Ruth speeded up as if anxious not to waste seconds, and we clanked violently over the cattle gate at the entrance of the ranch buildings. But then she pulled up slowly with a sense of dawning disappointment, and sat looking from a distance at the whitewashed buildings and sheds and farmyard litter of Dale. Her eyes went first to the low, rambling house with purple bougainvillæa scrambling over the roof and tumbling thickly between the white pillars of the stoep. The windows and fly-screen doors were shut and there was a vacant gloom behind the glass panes that told one the house was deserted. Her eyes lingered on the house, then a hard look came into them and she wrenched them away to make a quick but careful survey of the whole square acre of the yard. They stayed momentarily on the trucks, tractors and threshers drawn up in a row outside the repair shop, and she moved her head a little as if trying to peer behind them. Then she made a slow sweep around the perimeter, taking in the barns, stables, store-rooms, the saw-mill, dairy, petrol pumps and garage, the smithy, windmill, horse troughs, power room, even the trees with lime-washed trunks, and the piles of logs and the stacks of milk cans. But she was not taking an inventory. She was looking for something. And I saw that she knew, from the moment we arrived, that it was not there.

At last her gaze came full circle and she started the car again. She turned it around and started back for Malinda, driving with her shoulders slumped, her hands hooked loosely, tiredly, over the steering-wheel, her feet resting disconsolately on the pedals. It was impossible to say whether her purpose in coming to Dale had failed in that something she expected was not there ; or whether it had succeeded in that she hadn't wanted it to be there.

We had been at Dale only the briefest time—enough to take one sweeping look over the house and around the yard—and now we were on our way back. But I felt as if we had visited the scene of a railway accident or mine disaster. Now, not even Forsythe spoke. After a while Ruth said, " Sorry I troubled you, boys. You must think I'm a hysterical old woman."

About two miles from Malinda we heard a car behind us. For several minutes we could not see it ; the track twisted sharply every few yards and bushes and trees closed in behind us to obscure the view. But it caught up with us just before we made the steep climb down into the ravine. It was Lavinia. She came right up behind us and blew the horn to pass. Ruth looked at her in the rear-view mirror with hard eyes but an expressionless face—and refused to give way.

Lavinia was driving and there was a man next to her, an African whom I recognised. She wore butterfly-shaped sunglasses and a yellow bandana on her hair. She had on the corn-coloured suède jacket without lapels that I had seen on her bed earlier, with a fluffy mist of pale-green chiffon in the triangle below her throat. She was dangerously close to us for the narrow corkscrew road was slippery with mud and she could have skidded into us and sent both vehicles slithering over the edge. Whether she did it to disconcert us, or simply because there was always a showy, impetuous touch to her actions, I could not say. Ruth drove on unperturbed, as if she hadn't noticed her at all. As Lavinia negotiated the steep descent behind us, hovering at times almost above our heads, I caught glimpses of her, variously angled and fragmented by chromium and glass—the red gash of lipstick, the high white forehead, a fleeting view of her profile, the blur of red nails, the gold flash of her watch ; and not only refracted details, but whole expressions that detached themselves and hung, like phrases, outside the car—the quick glittering smile, the sudden pout as she swung sharply to avoid hitting the bank. At one point the road made a sharp double bend and simultaneously she passed over us and we under her, and for a few moments I lost her from view. With the dazzle, not so much of colour or facial details, but of her personality still in my eyes, I looked at Ruth, at the plain trusting face, the dowdy clothes. Ruth wounded and in the throes of some bitter private torment. My mind made a sudden leap of association and I thought of the scene at the Finger, and the participants in it—the velvet plunderer from other parts and the grey friendly neighbour suddenly set on and ripped to death.

Ruth turned the Land-Rover off the road and stopped on a patch of grass about twenty-five yards away from Conrad. Lavinia, on a sudden impulse, swung in alongside us, then reversed and turned the station wagon to face the other way— an announcement to all present that the hunt was on, for that was the way out to Crampton Falls.

She got out, took the dark glasses off her eyes, removed the bandana from her hair, and looked first at us, then at the crowd gathered around the other station wagon, and finally at Conrad and my father. She greeted nobody; her expression did not change. She stood toying with the sun-glasses, one hand on her hip with the yellow bandana trailing from her fingers, and challenged us all. It was deliberate, as premeditated as a line in a play. Her look said, " Here I am. Think what you like. To hell with you."

Every gesture, every nuance of stance or facial expression, every detail of her clothes, heightened the effect. Her tall slim figure that had no right to look so young, that had successfully handled the raids of time, said, " I can handle this." The insolence of one gauntly raised shoulder said, " I'm ready for you." She mocked us with the tilt of her head, her tossed hair, the thin faintly smiling line of her mouth. The tailored jodhpurs and elegant suède jacket gave her the swagger and authority of one whose clothes had been deliberately designed for that moment.

She turned to us again, ignoring Ruth, barely noticing me. Her look found Forsythe ; they exchanged some dialogue with their eyes, then she turned and nodded her head to the man in the car. He got out and they both started walking over to Conrad.

We followed.

I knew the man well. He lived about thirty miles away near the African reserve in a kraal perched on a ledge half-way up the side of a mountain. We called him Mac, which was a nickname with a long history behind it, but one that had nothing to do with Scotland, for he was a pure Zulu. His real name was Mtetwa, but when he was a young man he served in the Merchant Marine where nobody could manage the spliced consonants, the long flat vowel and chopped-off end of the Zulu name. So it was changed to Mac Tweetwee. Then the aviary sound was dropped and he became Mac.

Of course it was to pick up Mac that she had made the trip this morning, but I tried desperately to think what the purpose could be. Mac walked behind her in a grey alpaca suit, its numerous creases evidence that it had been hurriedly unpacked from the wooden box where he kept his clothes. He walked awkwardly in new rubber-soled brown shoes that seemed too tight, and he kept glancing at us over his shoulder, with frowns and shrugs, as if he were as mystified as we were.

He was a reliable gun bearer and moderately good tracker, and occasionally in the past he had come with us on hunting trips. But Conrad had a team of expert trackers so it couldn't have been for his hunting talents that she wanted him. Certainly she couldn't have wanted him badly enough to take a sixty-mile trip through the bush and an hour's walk up a mountainside. I would have thought his coming had nothing at all to do with the hunt, if it were not for the fact that she was taking him to Conrad.

Lavinia also knew Mac well because at one time he had worked as a chauffeur for the Whittakers. I remembered him

from those far-off Johannesburg days when he used to bring
the Whittakers to visit us. While they were being entertained
inside the house, Peggy and I would sit in the car and listen to
Mac. He would lounge in the glassed-in front section with his
dark-blue helmet pushed to the back of his head and his tunic
unbuttoned and tell fabulous lies to impress us. His accent
amazed us as much as his stories : it had a cockney flavour,
rather like that of comedians in British films ; it was the first
time we had ever heard an African talk that way. He used to
tell us incredible yarns about his work in the ships, and then
encouraged by our amusement tell us how he had "joined" the
Whittaker Organisation as an assistant in the gold refinery plant
at one of the mines ; had later gone into the hotel trade to rise
eventually to head chef in a big Durban hotel ; how the
Whittakers had spent a holiday there and were so impressed by
his cooking that they took him back to be their chauffeur. He
was a natural comic and these absurd tales would keep us in
shrieks of laughter.

He seemed to weave in and out of our lives, for soon after
we came to Malinda he "retired" as he called it, and came to
live near us in the district. He retired with a determination that
we thought amazing, for he not only stopped doing work of
any kind, but resolutely cut himself off from all contact with
Europeans, never going to town, having no truck with White
settlers, or even with the Native Commissioner unless it was
absolutely unavoidable. Those hunting trips with us were rare
exceptions, and he only came because we knew him from former
days and that gave us a pull over him. He packed away his
wrist-watch, fountain-pens, framed photographs, dressing-
table trinkets, all his clothes, shoes and hats in a big wooden
box covered with wall-paper, and went about in skins, blankets
and bead ornaments like a primitive induna. In time he acquired
five wives, eighteen children, a good small herd of cows and
oxen and about twenty acres—all the time maintaining his
kingly indolence, for he hired labourers to tend his land and
animals. He refused to speak English, or even to answer to it ;
he spoke only Shona, the local dialect, but now with a Zulu

instead of a cockney accent. However, some relics of his past remained. In his large round hut, which was bigger than any I had seen, there was a huge jangling brass bed mounted on castors. He slept alone in this and I believed he used to ride it around the hut, for it always stood in a different position. Hanging from a nail on the centre pole was an American cookery book, covered with oilcloth and fattened with pasted-in recipes clipped from magazines. This he would often read, squatting half-naked outside his hut, chuckling and grinning as if an unusual ingredient were a witticism, a new sauce a clever pun.

An enigmatic, amusing, and in some ways unhappy character whom we often discussed at home, and whose story we often exploited for the amusement of visitors.

Now he, too, was here. He made me uneasy. His own nervousness, the spectacular way Lavinia produced him, made me feel once again that there was so much more to the situation than I knew about. But after a moment I felt it was right to include him in the day. There was an air of reunion about this hunt. It was as though the cast of a long-forgotten play had kept a date made years before at one of those sentimental fare-well parties. And the play was about the old trouble in Johannesburg when my father left the Whittaker Organisation and came cattle ranching in Rhodesia. It was the first time since then that my father, Lavinia, Conrad, Ruth Secker and now Mac, all of whom played some part in the old crisis, had ever assembled.

Yes, Mac completed it. Completed something.

As we approached, the group around the station wagon started walking over to Conrad. I saw that the whole Big House crowd was there, with binoculars, cameras, beach bags and sun umbrellas for the picnic. I noticed Marjorie among them—in a linen skirt now, and a khaki shirt and flat, useful shoes that made her look suddenly squat and a little dumpy. As I came up she caught my eye then looked down without turning her head, at Conrad ; it was a warning to expect some-thing. While she did this Conrad stood up, but he did not look at Lavinia. He watched Mac, his eyes swarming all over him. There was no anger in his face. There was not even the supercilious resignation that I thought might be there after the mild and patient way he had sat around waiting. He merely looked at Mac intently; he was deeply thoughtful, and for the first time, I believed, not quite sure what to do.

Lavinia did not explain about Mac. She walked straight up to Conrad as if carrying out a ceremony like presenting credentials and said, " Well, shall we start ? "

Instead of answering Conrad turned to my father who was standing at the back of the group looking in over the heads.

" What do you think, Joe ? Should we go ? " Conrad asked.

My father too, saw only Mac. He was studying him from head to foot, deliberately and silently. He had the same kind of deeply concerned look as Conrad. Mac looked around wildly, like a captive, and all of a sudden clear drops of sweat appeared on his dark sepia forehead.

" Well ? "

As if pulling himself out of a daze, my father said, " It's pointless going now. An utter waste of time."

" I'm not asking your opinion," Lavinia said firmly but not unpleasantly. She was very cool and sure, and I wondered what had happened to change her out of the mood of near hysteria that, according to Marjorie, she had been in before she left the Big House to fetch Mac.

" I don't see the point. We won't get to the Falls much before two, and it's a pretty thin chance that we'll find the spoor. And we'll just about have started when we'll have to come home." My father spoke vaguely as if his mind was not quite on what he was saying.

" I'm not asking your opinion," she repeated, but not looking at my father.

Conrad interrupted, " What's *he* doing here ? " indicating Mac with a jerk of his head.

" I thought we could do with another tracker."

" We've got enough trackers."

" I prefer my own."

" I've got no place for him in this party."

" Then find a place."

" He's not a tracker anyway. He's a chauffeur. What will he do if he sees a lion ? Make a noise like a car horn ? "

" I've employed him for the day—as a tracker."

They were talking softly, outwardly calmly, and not quite to each other. They sounded like two people voicing their thoughts, rather than having an argument. But there was a tension that spread out from the deceptive calm and seized all of us standing around. I looked at Marjorie: she was gazing at Lavinia with something close to admiration. Her look dismayed me, for it told me that she was on Lavinia's side in this, that she hated Conrad. Kiki Pape was also looking at Lavinia, nodding her head and yes-yessing, a look of pure enchantment in her big, doll-like blue eyes. Forsythe looked back and forth between Conrad and Lavinia, his eyes following the exchange like a volley in tennis, and I noticed the hardening, the narrowing into puzzlement or incredulity each time they went to Lavinia. Ruth was looking at Mac, her face a cloud. There was a hard set to her plump features and a grimness that I had not seen when we went to Dale. And when I turned to my father I saw that he was looking at me with a strange desperate tenderness.

Lavinia said, " I'm not going to argue about this. He's coming, and that's all. Now let's get started."

I saw Conrad look at my father again, and now incredibly my father said, " Yes. Let's get started. Let's get it over and done with."

Conrad said nothing. He looked around at the group, trying to assess whether he had any support, but before he could say anything Ruth said in a tough, hostile voice, " Sure, let's go. Let's go and bash lions. Let's go and have a little healthy fun in the bush."

' What about you, Ronnie ? What do you think ? " Lavinia asked Forsythe in a tone that mocked the way Conrad had appealed to my father.

" Sure. Why not ? " Forsythe said, with a wide shrug.

"And you, Gene?" She gave me a brilliant hot smile. She didn't want me, but she wanted Conrad to know she was raiding right inside his camp.

"No," I said.

Conrad said suddenly, "All right, get into your cars and follow me. I'll lead the way to Crampton Falls. There we'll divide the picnickers from the hunters. . . ." He said it with a hint of sarcasm, but at the same time like a school-teacher hustling children into a bus on the way to camp. "I'll give you the hunting plan when we reach the Falls."

He was brisk, energetic and very good-natured about it. I got into the Land-Rover next to Ruth and we followed Conrad's truck out of the ravine, the two station wagons coming up behind us.

Marjorie was in Lavinia's station wagon: I could see her from time to time as we zigzagged along the road. I thought she looked bored. Forsythe was in the same vehicle in the front seat next to Lavinia. My father rode with Conrad in the truck, and the three trackers, together with Mac, crouched in the back.

I could see Mac clearly in the vehicle ahead. I had always thought of him as a curiosity, a riddle, but his oddness had been something I was inclined to laugh at. Trying to lose himself in the bush, he seemed only to bring into sharp relief the differences between himself and the slow simple cousins he came to live amongst, and somehow the effect had always struck me as comic. But now I began to understand what was later to become a precept with me—that oddness has its sinister side. The strange life of this man, the coincidence of his coming to live as our neighbour now seemed uncanny and in some way evil. Mac's arrival seemed to add a whole new dimension of uncertainty and mystery to the hunt. Looking at him, I once more gained the impression that he had been captured.

15

WHEN WE REACHED the Retreat Conrad stopped the truck suddenly, as if on an afterthought. My father got out and went behind the house, and a little later came back driving the jeep. He called Matchbox and the two drove over to the stables where they collected our three hunting dogs. The dogs were tawny ridgebacks from the same litter, and they stood in a row in the back of the jeep, panting and dripping saliva from their floppy red tongues.

Conrad had changed his mind about the dogs. The reason, I thought, was that he decided that finesse and artistry would be wasted on this hunt which had degenerated into a public spectacle like a bullfight, and that in view of the late start, he would try to get the whole business over as quickly as possible.

The jeep came back and manoeuvered into position between us and the station wagon. Conrad started the truck and we all followed.

I sat back and allowed myself to relax into that special kind of loose-jointed slump that enabled one to take the bouncing and jolting with the minimum amount of punishment. I kept looking at Ruth, but she avoided looking at me. She drove in silence, with her eyes glued to the twisting sand track. I wanted her to talk to me, and not just because I was curious to know what was troubling her. I wanted to help her if I could. She seemed so lonely in her distress, and so devastated, and I wanted her to know that she could call on my friendship and sympathy if she needed it. But there was something in the atmosphere between us that made it difficult for me to raise the subject. I thought of asking about Bill but something inhibited me. I let it go, and decided to leave it to her whether to bring up the subject or not. I believed she would. It was too near the top of her mind, too big to hold down, and I was sure that she would do it some time during the ride to the Falls.

The road, which was fairly well marked for the first few miles, gradually lost all definition and became merely a series of negotiable patches through the bush. Driving over this kind of country was a special art and technique, and amply deserved the name we gave it—bush-bashing. We sloshed through miles of mud, slithered over surfaces of wet, loose stones, lurched into potholes, bumped in and out of cat-backs, veered and slid past fallen trees, boulders and overgrown bushes, crunched over dead branches and anthills. Springy thorn branches slapped against the side screen and screeched against the canvas tent as we passed. Conrad set a cracking pace. When the road was reasonably good he put on speed, and when it was difficult he swerved and sliced his way through, not wasting a move-ment or a second. He would pull out far ahead of us then suddenly swing into a skid and veer off at a right angle, and we would lose sight of him for the next five or ten minutes, until an engine roar out ahead told us that he was climbing a steep bank and that we were still on his track. He would dis-appear into a dip, bumping and plummeting down, and come out the other side fifty yards from the expected point of emergence. Every few hundred yards we crossed a stream or donga, climbing gingerly down the steep side, churning in low gear across the rock-strewn bed, hurtling up the other side. Conrad always drove in a hurry, but now he seemed to have some crazy plan to shake us off. But we, and my father behind us, kept up, because we knew the route and our vehicles were made for that kind of work. It was gruelling for the station wagons. They kept falling behind and every few miles we had to stop and wait for them to catch up. For all their sporty look, these cars were not meant for this kind of treatment. They were good for driving to the golf course or meeting friends at the station—not having their brakes and springs tortured on primitive bush tracks, their paintwork scratched by thorn bush, their sumps scraped on protruding roots and rocks. We would stop for them, and they would come limping up, one close behind the other and without quite waiting for them to reach us Conrad would drive off again, setting the same impossible pace. Once, just before moving off he leant out of the window and gave me a jaunty thumbs-up salute, and I gathered that he was doing it purposely to nettle Lavinia.

I looked out for game. The last few miles before Turgeni Drift were usually thickly populated with animals, especially impala and zebra. I missed these now. The drought had ravaged the area. We passed a wide natural meadow, half a mile from end to end, where I had seen a herd of wildebeest holding a sports meeting. They had formed into line, one behind the other, and with their tight muscle-packed bodies gleaming black like locomotives, charged full speed across the meadow, stopped, regrouped, and charged back again—for no other reason than that it was spring and there was a tang in the air. We always saw giraffe here. They would peep at us from the side of the road, the gentle effeminate faces with fur-covered horns appearing first on one side, then on the other of a tree, so that we never knew if one giraffe or two were watching us with that soft gaze. Often a hyena crossed the track, walking with that bent-legged, narrow-hipped hypocritical limp, darting furtive criminal looks at us over its shoulder. Or a wild ostrich would chase us, lifting up its skirt and striding after us with naked muscular thighs ; then stop, shudder its frilly useless wings, open its beak wide and swear at us with a tiny "caw."

But the bush looked empty now. I wondered how long the bitter season of drought, starvation and chaos would linger on. How did life start again after this disaster ? How did the delicate equilibrium of rain and grass and birth and killing and scavenging establish itself again ?

The bush, though apparently empty of wild life was lush and gleaming after the recent rains, washed clean of dust and suddenly full of colours. It had miraculous powers of recovery, responding with exuberant life to the first favourable change of conditions. After a time I saw signs of the first contingents of returning game. Far away, across a green clearing and against a grove of fever trees, I saw a reddish smudge, and with astonishing clearness considering the distance, the nervous black-and-white agitation of flicking tails. These were impala. A small herd, about eight in all, but they were grazing peacefully in the old way. A little later I saw in the distance the fat rump of a zebra protruding from a rock and then the silver dazzle of other zebra running behind some trees. And just as we began the long descent down to the Turgeni Drift, a giraffe and her foal ran out of the bush and galloped along the road in front of us. The engine noise terrified them, but some hypnotic compulsion kept them running in a straight line directly in front of us. We slackened speed to let them run off the road, but they merely slowed down without getting out of the way: we sped up to frighten them—they ran faster but still kept in our path, moving with that peculiar stilt action like camera tripods running. Even though the mother was slowed down by her rubber-legged foal, they went very fast, for giraffe despite their gentle and delicate appearance are both strong and swift. The mother never once looked back ; she thudded along with her muscles undulating in a complicated set of movements caused by her awkward gait. But the foal, staggering and tottering after her, threw us appealing looks, with its face spattered with mud tossed up by the pounding hooves in front. At last sanity returned, the mother allowed the foal to catch up, and straddling it between her front legs, bundled it off the road. They looked at us reproachfully across the top of an acacia tree as we passed.

I saw Ruth smiling. " Things are beginning to get the old look again," she said. She started to say something else, but hesitated, then concentrated on the driving. After a while she said, " I must be an awful strain on you. Behaving like this." And she repeated what she had said at Dale, " You must think I'm a hysterical old woman." She placed her hand over mine, her warm perspiring hand, and squeezed it affectionately. I thought she was on the point of confiding in me then, but she said, " I'm glad we're going hunting to-day. I feel like getting out into the bush again."

I asked, " When did you last shoot any lion ? "

She said, " Last year—we got two over at Chilundwe. And we poisoned one near the tea plantation." She wiped some cigarette ash off her jacket with an impatient gesture. She had been smoking cigarettes all the way from Malinda. " A brute, that one. He'd been living on choice Grade A beef."

" Is that really why you're coming to-day ? To bump off some mangy cat ? "

" To get into the bush again. I've been missing it lately. We've been too busy at Dale, and I never seem to get out of the office any more. I felt I needed it."

I wasn't sure whether to believe her. Somehow it didn't sound very convincing. " I want to think," she said. " I think best when I'm hunting."

That didn't seem the truth either, and I wondered why she was so reluctant to approach the subject. I could tell that she wanted to talk to me but she seemed nervous of starting, as if putting it into words would make the trouble bigger, or more real. She became silent again, and after about fifty yards I asked her outright, " Where's Bill to-day ? "

She started another cigarette, driving with one hand and squinting at the point where the new cigarette was being lit by the old one. " Bill ? Oh, Bill's not feeling well." She flicked the stub out of the window, sending it spiralling over her shoulder. " His sinuses are troubling him. He decided to spend the day at home."

" Conrad said he had some business in town."

She glanced at me, then looking straight ahead, said, " Bill's left me, Gene."

She said it so quietly and undramatically that it took a moment to make its impact. " Left you ? " I asked; my voice must have sounded excited and incredulous, for she swung round to look at me. " I can't believe it. When did it happen ? "

" Yesterday morning. At eleven-forty, to be precise," she said in a matter-of-fact voice that was obviously feigned.

" But you were together last night at the Big House."

" We weren't *together*. I went there to look for him—to ask him to come home. He's left me, Gene, ditched me, deserted me or whatever they say in the divorce courts." She spoke all in a rush now with a note of panic discernible in her voice. "Our marriage is *pfft*. He asked me to be a sport and give him a divorce. Be a *sport*—that's what he said. Can you beat it ? "

" Didn't he give you any reasons? "

" You bet he did. He's found himself a girl-friend. He's in lo-ove." She dragged out and distorted the word to make it sound ridiculous. " Poor boy—madly in love—with—that bloody trashy gutter-snipe."

For some reason I thought she meant Kiki.

" Oh, come on. He can't be serious," I said. " He's just flirting. He makes a play for all the girls at the Big House. It's a joke, that's all."

" No," Ruth said. I saw her close her eyes tightly and bite her lips in a sudden spasm of distress. " They want to get married. In a hurry too."

A moment later she said more calmly, " So that's the score, Gene. Bill Secker and Lavinia Whittaker are swooning with love for each other." She paused, then added with a dry laugh, " Write *that* up in the stud book."

Lavinia !

I was too flabbergasted to say anything. I looked at her, on the wild chance that she might be joking, but when I saw her strained unhappy face I knew that it was true. I couldn't think of a thing to say. All sorts of remarks came to mind, but I kept them to myself because any comment was utterly banal and superfluous. I just sat and tried to grope with the amazing thought of Lavinia Whittaker being swept off her feet by this tedious, ageing ex-policeman.

We could see the Turgeni River now, a broad reach of muddy water with white sand beaches on either side. It was rippling along briskly, the sunlight sparkling all over it, and I noticed with a twinge of disappointment that it would probably be easy to cross. I had hoped that it would be flooded and impassable after the rains, and so put an end to the hunt.

As we came down the last rock-strewn slope to the water's edge, I found myself wondering why Ruth was so keen to go on this hunt, and I began to ask myself the same questions about her as I had done earlier about my father. I had the curious idea that it was going to develop into a four-sided contest of some kind—between Conrad, Lavinia my father and Ruth—and that in some odd way Bill, who was appropriately absent, would be the prize. Perhaps even five-sided, if Forsythe had a part in this too.

" Where *is* Bill this morning ? Has he really got business in town ? " I asked,

Ruth shot me a look. " That's what I'd like to know," she said, wrenching the steering-wheel round and swinging the Land-Rover into a narrow passage between two boulders.

The crossing was two miles from the point where the Turgeni fed into the great muddy surge of the Sabie River. The Turgeni spread out flat and wide here, the ford two hundred yards across with a level floor that was partly stone. The drift was very temperamental ; you never knew what problems it would present. In the dry season, when you could cross without getting your tyres wet, you might find the floor collapse like biscuit under you and the car up to its fenders in soft gluey mud. Yet a few weeks later the same path could be followed in safety. In the rainy season, after weeks of storms that should have made it impassable, you might find the water flowing smoothly along at a uniform depth of two or three feet ; or it might be spilling its banks and making even the approaches impassable. It worked rather like city traffic. If the Sabie was flowing evenly and absorbing the water of the Turgeni, the crossing was feasible in any weather. But if it had too much volume of its own to cope with, it would hold back the flow of its tributary, or delay it with silt deposit, or even plug it off completely by jamming a floating island of uprooted trees, reeds and dislodged earth into the point of confluence. Sometimes the Turgeni changed dramatically in a matter of minutes from a placid shallow lagoon into a raging torrent when heavy rains in the hills fed in through hundreds of tributary streams and hurtled down the empty watercourse in a nine-foot high tidal wave. Several times in past years people walking or pushing bicycles across the shallow ford were overwhelmed and drowned.

We climbed down the side, found a footing on the submerged rock floor and started to cross. Conrad was about fifty yards in front, going slowly in low gear. We followed in his wake knowing that as long as we took the same course, we were safe. My father followed us, about twenty yards behind. The two station wagons were not yet in sight. We went carefully, keeping a fixed distance behind Conrad. Suddenly Conrad's truck lurched forward, throwing the back wheels clean out of the water. The truck righted itself then stopped, held precariously on a rock ledge by its brakes ; then it slowly backed on to solid ground. Conrad leaned out of the window and made wide sweeping movements with his arm, warning us to keep clear of the danger spot. He turned the truck round and completed the crossing with swerving and zigzagging. We swung off too, waltzed over the last fifty yards of shifting sand and climbed on to the opposite shore. Conrad waited for us, then moved on again, up the rock-strewn track out of the river bed, to stop on the high land overlooking the river. We followed and pulled up behind him, and a moment later the jeep roared up the side and stopped next to us. Conrad climbed out of the cabin and came towards us pulling off his motoring gloves.

Just as he reached us Lavinia's station wagon emerged from the trees across the river and started to make the descent to the water's edge.

We got out and stood on the bank. None of us spoke. We all had the same thought. We saw the bright-blue station wagon splash into the water and begin to churn across. It went cautiously at first and then, incredibly, put on speed. I saw the water furl out on both sides of the front wheels, and the wake boil up behind as the idiotic dash gathered momentum. I looked at Conrad, Ruth and my father—they were all smiling. The dogs had got out of the jeep, and following our gaze and sensing that something was wrong, they started barking.

Conrad turned to me with one raised, faintly surprised eyebrow. His hand rested on his hip, his smile was supercilious, and his whole attitude was one of superior amusement. Obviously he was going to do nothing to warn her.

" For Christ's sake stop her ! " I yelled, not caring a damn about Lavinia and her friends, but thinking of Marjorie whose face I saw dimly behind the windscreen. Nobody listened to me. I waved and gesticulated but Lavinia wasn't looking my way, and I watched helplessly as she drove straight towards the danger spot. As she reached the point the station wagon left the stone floor and pancaked into the mud. At the same moment Ruth, who was standing next to me, said, " The silly bitch."

There was an angry wasp-like sound of wheels spinning in mud and water. I put my hands to my mouth and yelled out, " *Don't rev the bloody thing—you won't get out that way!* " But she couldn't hear me, and the useless whizzing of the wheels continued. I saw the station wagon sink into the mud and find a resting point with the water lapping up against the doors. At last the threshing stopped. I noticed the other station wagon now, stopped halfway between Lavinia's station wagon and the other bank. They were not in trouble, but having seen what had happened to Lavinia they were afraid to go on.

Conrad watched the stranded vehicle for a few moments then turned and strolled back to the truck, and with a jaunty leap got back into the cabin. I thought he would have the gall to drive off, to continue to Crampton Falls without them, but he took a magazine out of the glove compartment and started to read. It seemed stupid beyond words. It was the kind of prank that dim-witted schoolboys went in for. He had refused to warn Lavinia and now he was not going to do anything to help her. They were not in any danger, though in plenty of discomfort, for I could tell from the yells and noise coming from the river that the water was flooding into the car. Sooner or later someone would have to rescue them, and this was going to waste at least half an hour.

I looked back at the station wagon and saw Lavinia's long white arm come out of the window and wave to us. Not frantically or appealingly; just wave, as if she had only then noticed us and was asking us to be dears and come and get her out.

Ruth waved back airily, as if exchanging a greeting, then deliberately sat down on a rock. The arm in the window wilted, straightened out and waved again, more urgently now. Ruth answered with a perky little "good morning" salute.

I went over to Conrad and said, " The joke's over now. Let's go and get them out." He looked at me with a perfectly straight face, and said, "Joke? This isn't a joke. I'm going to make it so damned uncomfortable for her that she'll *beg* to go home. Let them sit there for a while."

I came back to the bank again, and now I saw that Forsythe and Hoffman had got out and were wading round the car examining the wheels. Both had their trousers rolled above their knees, but Forsythe also had his bush-jacket off, revealing his powerful hairy-black chest. The sleeves of Hoffman's fawn silk shirt were rolled up and he still wore the gorgeous paisley cravat. They inspected all four wheels, then went behind and tried to pull the station wagon back by its bumper. Forsythe said something through the window, and the next moment Jackson the cook jumped out of the door and landed with a splash without bothering to roll back his snow-white trousers. For several minutes the three men tried, by puny human strength, to move the car-load of ladies, and then gave up and stood panting, resting their arms on the roof, and looking at us.

" Hey, you bastards," Forsythe shouted, " What's the big idea ? "

Ruth gave him a wiggly little greeting with her fingers.

I decided that this was enough. I went to the Land-Rover, looked into the back to make sure the hauling cable was there, started the engine and reversed to go back down to the river. As I moved off, Conrad came up, jumped in beside me and turned off the switch. " Let *me* do this," he said. He got out again, called Cigarettes, Boots and Matchbox, and they all got into the truck. He told me he would need me, and I climbed up the step and sat next to him. He took the truck down the narrow twisting defile to the water's edge.

The river was hidden from us as we came down, but when we reached the beach I saw that the whole party had abandoned the station wagon and was wading ashore. Ed Scobie was walking in his briefs, his trousers knotted around his neck. Kiki Pape was being carried by Forsythe. Marjorie walked holding her skirt bunched up around her middle, her shoes hanging by the laces around her shoulders. Lavinia led the way and just sloshed through the water in those beautiful jodhpurs.

Conrad waited for them to come ashore but avoided looking at them. I felt miserable sitting next to him ; it made me look like an accomplice in this puerile joke, and I was already worrying about explaining it to Marjorie. They came up one by one : Lavinia simply ignored us, but Ed Scobie stood in his dripping underpants and snarled, " You bloody dirty swine, you'll hear more about this ! " I wondered if he was going to get his lawyers to write to us, or fix us in a bear squeeze or some other Stock Exchange finangle. When Marjorie came past I smiled at her, but she glared black fury at me, and walked on. I leaned out of the window and called after her, " Listen, I'll talk to you later," but she didn't even look back. I felt quite sick. I hated Conrad for putting me in this position.

At last Conrad started the engine and took the truck into the water, making a wide encircling journey out to the stranded station wagon. He overplayed it a little, taking a much longer course than necessary, but I thought he did it to point up Lavinia's stupidity in trying to barge the station wagon straight over that tricky crossing.

On the way I spoke to him. " Do you know that Bill's left Ruth ? "

" Of course I know," he answered testily.

" Is that what you were getting at over in the ravine ? " I asked, irritated by his reply.

" Partly." He let the futile word drown in silence. After a moment he asked, " How is she taking it now ? "

" Badly. But she's trying to fight it down. Trying to be tough, but finding it difficult."

"Now you know why I want you to stay close to Ruth to-day. I'm making you a policeman."

" With powers of arrest ? "

" With powers of restraint. It's been a terrible shock to her. Stay with her and try to calm her down. Don't let her do anything impulsive."

He said it very matter-of-factly. I noted it, and then tried to get the conversation back on the original track. " Lavinia and Bill ! It floors me. It's hilarious. She thinks him a big joke. And a bore."

" He's no worse than old Jordan was," Conrad said. " In fact, a damn' sight better in some ways—younger, for one thing, and not viciously unpleasant. If she could endure Jordan she could endure Bill. The attraction's the same—money."

I hadn't thought of that.

By then we had reached the stranded station wagon, and I got in by lowering myself straight into the open door, stepping on the seat to avoid getting my boots wet. The floor was submerged to a depth of about nine inches, so I took off my boots and stockings and found the pedals with my feet under water. I looked around while Cigarettes and Boots fixed the tow cable on the back bumper. Gloves, shoes, jerseys, sun-glasses, cameras, towels, lay strewn over the seats : sodden cigarette boxes and used cleansing tissues drifted around my ankles. In the back an aluminium saucepan covered with a white napkin had become waterborne and floated gently across the flooded floor. Baskets and other saucepans were stacked on top of one another in the back compartment, and the water round them was discoloured with oozing mustard, tomato sauce and mayonnaise.

I felt the tow cable stretch taut, and with the three trackers bouncing and heaving the back wheels over the ledge, Conrad pulled the car back on to firm ground. It was effortless : the whole operation took hardly two minutes. That, too, must have annoyed Lavinia. The cable was unhooked and wound back on to the windlass, and I drove the station wagon over to the shore.

As I pulled up on the beach, Lavinia came over. She looked around the inside of the car before looking at me. " Thanks, Gene," she said quietly. I thought she was grateful to me for bringing the station wagon back and helping to end the non-sensical prank. She looked at me reproachfully and said, shaking her head slowly, " I'll reserve comment."

" Shall I drive it out of here ? " I asked, indicating with my head the steep path up to the place where the other vehicles were standing.

" If you don't mind." She opened the door and slipped into the seat next to me. She seemed subdued. She was barefoot and I noticed that the water which had left one muddy tide mark above her knees had seeped up and left another across the wide flare of jodhpurs at her hips. I started the car, crossed the beach and roared up the almost perpendicular climb out of the river bed. As I did so she cleaned her feet with a towel that was lying on the seat. There was no atmosphere between us. I should have felt like strangling her for what she did to Ruth. She was at war not only with Ruth, but with us too, and by breaking up Dale she was wrecking something that we were a part of. But I could not summon up any emotion about her. It was uncanny. If anything there was a rather friendly feeling between us. There was something disarming in the way she sat next to me cleaning the mud from between her toes. It was as though we were two old friends coming home after a swim.

She said, " I want to see you when we get home this evening. I've got something important to tell you. Come to my room, will you ? "

I nodded. It would be some elaborate defence of her actions. Having seen me ride with Ruth she would realise that Ruth had told me. The trouble was that she liked me, and this wouldn't be the first time she would try to win me over, as a prelude to appeasing other people she had antagonised.

I said nothing, but let her think that I had agreed.

When we reached the top she said, " You won't forget to come to-night ? It's important."

She called Jackson and Mac and told them to swab the water out of the car. Conrad was watching her from a distance ; he said something to Cigarettes and Boots and a few minutes later they came over with cleaning rags and a tin of window cleanser and first helped and then took over the cleaning from Jackson and Mac. It was very subtle, this scheme of Conrad's, first getting her into trouble, then ostentatiously helping her get out of it. Lavinia stood watching them, refusing to notice Conrad. The second station wagon arrived and a few moments later the rest of Lavinia's party came trudging up the hill. Kiki Pape was walking now, barefoot and wincing with every step. They looked sour and dismal, all except Forsythe who, to my surprise, was grinning. He slopped up the hill, full of mirth, like a great happy sheep dog in charge of a dispirited flock.

I thought Conrad would take advantage of Lavinia's discomfort and embarrassment after the river incident and try to get her to change her mind about the hunt. He might have succeeded at that moment. I was sure that there was a good chance of persuading her to turn back if she was approached tactfully and given a way out that would not hurt her pride. I knew that her friends would have been delighted to go home. But Conrad had other plans. He waved the trackers back into the truck, leapt up the step into the cabin and simply drove off. My father, Matchbox and the dogs were already sitting in the jeep and they followed. I got into the Land-Rover next to Ruth : the engine was running and we moved off. As Conrad turned the truck and made for the road, I saw that Forsythe was sitting next to him. There seemed to be some curious competition for Forsythe going on between Conrad and Lavinia, and now he had scored in that too.

I thought about these tactics of Conrad's and decided that

they were probably correct after all. If he had approached her
with any kind of suggestion to call off the hunt, she would have
seen it as a trap and have turned the suggestion against him. He
was waiting for *her* to ask to go home.

After about a hundred yards I looked back and saw the crowd
still standing about near the station wagons. They seemed to
be arguing among themselves. Lavinia had the choice now of
taking them back or following us. But it was not really a
choice, for to have turned back when Conrad had left her
standing like that, would have been ignominious. After a few
minutes they took their seats in the cars and came on after us.
I watched them until they reached the road, then settled into
the seat for the drive to the Falls.

When I looked ahead, I saw Conrad's truck far out in front
doing a queer, back-bouncing jig on a particularly bad stretch
of road. At one point the back of the truck shot up like a
bucking horse, and the three trackers and Mac were bounced
into the air like pieces of furniture. Then the truck swung into
a skid, veered off at a sharp angle and disappeared, bumping
and swerving, over a ridge. It was hard even for us to keep up.
Ruth smoked cigarette after cigarette. Ash kept dropping on
to her clothing and every few minutes she would dust it off
impatiently as if she could not bear such untidiness. I was
struck once again by the contrast between her fine gold rings
and the blotched, unkempt hands. The rings were too big and
kept slipping round so that the diamond and ruby settings
would lie between her fingers or inside her hand—proof that
they had been bought in her absence and without concern for
size. But the hands were women's hands, weathered by the sun
and exposure not to hardness, but to the thin satin of an
underskin. Indeed, there was much that was feminine about
her despite her apparent campaign to stamp out all signs of
glamour in herself. Her small shoes were dainty, even though
scuffed and muddy, and they contradicted the male note in her
clothing. Nobody would call her beautiful, but there was a
pleasant, spontaneous warmth about her that was attractive in
its own way. Her figure was good for a woman of her age.

Her eyes were wonderful. I tried to imagine her in the kind of clothes she could afford instead of in that worn-out leather jacket with its unstuck lining and broken zipper, those shapeless trousers—Lavinia's clothes, say—trim, flattering dresses, smart bright-coloured sportswear, chic, clever hats. But the picture would not form. Instead I remembered how she looked when she came back from Europe in clothes she had bought on her travels—tailored suits each costing the price of a good bull, but which put her waist in the wrong place, and made her walk as if hobbled, and seemed possessed of a will of their own to writhe themselves out of position ; her hair done in a metallic tint, set in stiff paralysed waves and heaped into some inconceivable frivolity of hairdressing style. She seemed all corseted, hot and breathless, and when she sat down, her clothes creaked. She looked awful and she felt it too. It was a relief not only to herself, but to her foremen and ranch hands and herdsmen when she got out of those oppressive clothes and into her comfortable ranch outfit. No, it wouldn't have helped to put Ruth into Lavinia's clothes—in less than half an hour the clothes would have lost their shape, their buttons and morale. I used to hear it said that clothes did something to a woman, but with Ruth it was the other way round. She did something to clothes.

Yet there was a setting in which I could imagine her being desirable in any man's eyes. And I had no difficulty in understanding how Bill Secker, a playboy with an eye for shape and style, whether in a cow, a car or a woman, had come to marry her. In a starched white nurse's uniform she must have looked cool and attractive, with an air of authority that made her seem a little unattainable, and she must have caused a flutter in many a male ward in the hospital. People who knew her when she was young, said she really was beautiful, and although it was usually said as if this were something to wonder at, I had no difficulty at all in believing it. Her hair must have been soft and flaxen, her complexion creamy and clear—before the baking sun and a long succession of punishing summers had coarsened and ruined them. Probably she was never beautiful in the dramatic, spectacular way that Lavinia was, but she must have been more than ordinarily pretty. Her smile was still warm and exciting, and it was not hard to see those eyes filled with the gaiety that must have appealed to Bill. I could understand how she forgot to look pretty and womanly as the years went by. At first everything had to be sacrificed in order to save Dale; and afterwards, when ranch work had become a habit, the most important thing in her life was to make Dale into a big business. What was the sense in manicuring her hands to go out right afterwards to mix the day's ration of sour bran and bone meal? Or wearing cosmetics and putting on crisp cool frocks to tramp about in the mud and dung of the stockades? It would have been different if Bill had done the ranch work. She might have become a lady, a rich rancher's wife attending sales of antique furniture, sitting on church and welfare committees, running an elegant home and entertaining the social set of Bulawayo and Salisbury to house parties. But Bill left the running of Dale to her, so it was Bill who had the leisure to visit tailors, to go to the races, to try out sports cars, to travel and mix in the social set. And afterwards, when she had made Dale into a great ranch, it was too late. All her youth and beauty had been drained out of her: she had lost the woman Bill had married, and had probably more than half-way lost Bill himself.

Those rings! She wore them as a token of a marriage to a man who preferred amusement to work, but just as they lay forgotten on her fingers, so she forgot about the true facts of her marriage. She never understood what Bill meant when he took her to fashionable stores in Europe to be appraised and clucked over by coutouriers. She never saw the irony of those expensive perfumes, those handbags that cost such exorbitant duty to bring into Rhodesia, those boxes of fancy lingerie, those very rings! She thought it touching and tender that he should want to give her such presents and loved him all the more for it. She did not see that the cupboards full of unused clothes, the unopened flasks of perfume, the necklaces and watches lying in the untidy drawers with worm pills and stock show catalogues, were not the proof of Bill's love, but of his despair.

So much escaped me that should have been obvious. If only we heeded the plain evidence of our eyes, instead of colouring and distorting it with judgments and preconceived opinions. Of course Bill had been making a play for Lavinia. He had been doing it for years. Those laboured compliments that he sent lassooing at her from all over the room, that heavy gallantry, had looked to me like middle-aged buffoonery. But now I remembered that no matter where Bill was, he always came back to Dale in time for Lavinia's house-parties. And there was his peculiar behaviour whenever he was in the same room with her, talking too much and too loudly, attempting jokes which normally he avoided because he was no good at it and knew it, beating people over the head with his opinions on politics, or the atom bomb, or the native question, or lung cancer. There was his high mood, and there was his careful, cagey, Squire of Dale mood, when he would be very expansive and advisory on matters affecting the servants, or the ranch, or dogs, or guns, or tsetse fly. His Charles Boyer mood when he made such an occasion of lighting her cigarette or filling her glass or heaping a plate with her favourite salads and meats at the buffet. It was all so clumsy and inept, and I could not believe that a man of the world, as I imagined Bill to be, would try to win a lady in that fashion.

Ruth never went to the Big House, but Bill would spend whole days and evenings there. Nobody got that much attention from Bill Secker, and I should have known. But I thought he went there because he had nothing to do at Dale, and was merely attracted by the presence of a crowd of visitors in the district. What confused me was the fact that Lavinia obviously found him so tiresome. No bore could survive as Lavinia's friend, but I had forgotten the agonies of boredom she had suffered with old Jordan, and had overlooked the fact that to her tiresomeness, although a fatal defect in a friend, was not one in a husband.

Other things misled me. When the quarrel started with

Lavinia we turned, naturally, to the Seckers. Ruth needed no persuading to become our ally—she hated Lavinia for numerous reasons, and seemed almost glad of the opportunity to give her feelings practical expression. But Bill also acted and spoke as if he were on our side. He used his influence to get my father released from cattle buying contracts he could not go on with, and he even saw his attorneys on our behalf. He would say of Lavinia, " That woman ? She's just not my cup of tea," which, coming from Bill, simply wiped her out of existence. She required too much effort, and Bill was a lazy man.

But it had been going on under our noses all the time ; because it was so obvious nobody took it seriously. And now the impossible had happened—Bill's crude and comical wooing had succeeded in winning Lavinia.

Poor Ruth !

I asked, " Had you no idea this was coming ? "

" No," she said. She went on driving and I thought she didn't want to discuss it further. But she suddenly started talking in a tense, bewildered voice. " I had *no* idea. As a matter of fact he made love to me the night before. And the next morning—this ! " Her voice changed, going into a slow, quieter range. " I'm sorry, Gene. Why am I telling you this ? I must sound awful ! "

I protested, " No, please . . ." But as I spoke she was speaking too, going straight on. " That's the funny thing. It was the first time in four months. We don't have much of this sort of thing, but when we do it's perfectly all right." She stopped again and asked abruptly, " You're surprised ? "

I shook my head.

" Do you mind me talking like this ? If you do, say so now."

I told her, " No, not if you want to." But I was beginning to see that she was talking too impetuously for me to have much control over the conversation.

" I can't get it out of my mind, that's why. How can he make love to me one night and do this the next morning ? And he was so sweet and kind to me—paying me compliments

—'You're all right, Chim.' 'My God, for a woman of your age!' Oh, sweet Jesus, make me shut up."

I took a deep breath.

She said, "Surely I can talk freely with you? This part's *important*—if you want to hear what happened, you must let me tell it my own way. I can't pick and choose."

"All right Ruth, just tell it. Anyway you like." I said it sympathetically, knowing that I would not be able to stop her anyway. Now that she had started, the urge to talk, to relieve the pressure inside her, was overwhelming. She was much more distraught and hysterical than I had thought.

"Well, he's only got to make love to me—it can be once a year—and no matter what I've been thinking about him, it starts up all over again, and I know that our marriage hasn't been a mistake. What the hell's the difference if he wants to go frigging off to Europe for the racing season, or buy himself a new Jag every six months? We can afford it, and if that's how he wants to live, it suits me. It suits us both, and as far as I'm concerned, ours is a happy marriage—or was until that jazzed-up sow came into the picture. And the other night I thought 'Bill, you big handsome bugger, if there's anything you want, just ask and you can have it, and if there's anything you want me to do, just ask me and I'll do it.' That's how it was only two nights ago, Gene."

She paused, smoking hard without inhaling, causing the cigarette to glow bright with every draw. She negotiated a steep, nose-dipping climb down into a stream, crossed the water-smoothed stone bed, and made the fast rush up the other side. As we reached level ground she said in a strangely mild way, "Oh, Bill, you big stupid clot, what the hell's gone wrong with you?" She continued in a changed voice, now tender and incredulous at the same time, "Anyway, before we went to sleep, he said, 'Chim, why don't we adopt a kid?' And do you know, it was the first time he had ever said that. I didn't think he was serious—knowing him, a good pedigree red setter would have done as well—and it's the sort of thing he says when he's in a good mood, like, 'Chim, why don't we buy a plane ? ' or ' Chim, let's sell up and go and live in Canada.' I didn't think he meant it, but I asked, ' Who'd look after it ?' I wasn't really thinking. That was the first thing that came to my mind, who'd wash it and feed it. I mean, I was so surprised. He said, ' Why, *you*, of course,' and then he said quickly, ' We could employ a white nurse.' Then he laughed and said, ' Forget it. I'm only kidding. Who the hell wants a squalling brat underfoot ? ' "

" Wait a minute," I interrupted, my astonishment growing with every word. " Are you telling me he's left you because he wants kids all of a sudden ? I can't believe that."

" I don't know. I'm so confused. I don't know what to think. That's what happened and I'm telling you. A thing like this happens, and you go over every little point asking yourself —could it be this ? Could it be that ? Maybe he's been hankering after kids all these years."

" It doesn't make sense. Bill's never shown interest in kids. I can't see him starting now."

" That's what I'd have thought." She held my hand, curling her thumb and small finger into my palm, and giving a little squeeze. " It can't be that, can it, Gene ? " she asked anxiously. I told her I was sure it couldn't be, and she said with real relief, " I'm so glad you think that."

We came past some boulders and saw Conrad's truck drawn up about two hundred yards ahead, waiting for the rest of us to assemble before taking the tricky, last few miles to Crampton Falls. She said no more while we approached : she pulled up behind the truck, leaving the engine running. A minute later my father skidded to a stop behind us. I looked back and saw Matchbox asleep, the dogs still standing up and still all in a row, but now facing the other way, looking out of the back. I caught my father's eye through the buckled plastic rear window, and the distortion imposed a queer drooping look on his face. He smiled at me, in a woebegone way.

While we waited for the station wagons to catch up, Ruth went on, " Next day he was up bright and early to go to the Big House. We had breakfast together, and everything seemed grand between us. He said, 'Chim, that was a pretty outstanding performance you put up last night. I hereby award you the gold cup and certificate of best in the over forty class,' and he gave me one of his big wet kisses. I said, 'Get away, you silly slob.' He told me he'd be back for dinner, and asked if we could have kidneys. They're his favourite—we can't give him enough of them—and I said I'd try to see if I could razzle up some, then I added, ' If you come home with Lavinia's lipstick on your handkerchief, I'll brain you.' It was all a joke. That's how it was, a joke. He said, ' Tell you something—I wouldn't say no to a tumble in bed with that doll. She makes my hormones sit up and bark.' I gave him a clout and pushed him outside the door. I didn't think he was serious. He couldn't have been serious. Does this sound like a man planning to do a flit on his wife ? "

" No," I said, convinced that at breakfast time yesterday Bill had no idea of the whirlwind romance that was about to sweep into his life.

Ruth exhaled a thin stream of smoke and said, speaking now in a tight terse voice, " But a few hours later he was back. I was in the office and I watched him from the window as he came into the yard. I thought he was drunk, the way he drove —careering round the gate on two wheels, nearly smacking into a donkey, biffing the petrol pump with his fender. He jumped out of the car, leaving the door open, and went to his room. I followed him inside to ask what the hell he thought he was doing . . . and . . . and . . . and . . . oh, Gene, I can't believe it—oh, it was terrible ! "

I would never have believed it could happen with Ruth, but she started crying. Not dryly and silently, but whimpering like a child with tears streaming down her face. She turned towards me, with one hand on the steering-wheel and the other on her lap, and made no effort to stop, but just sat sobbing uncontrollably. There was nothing I could do to help her. Once or twice I raised my hand to hold hers, to show my sympathy, but I let it drop again. These gestures were wrong for me. I could not comfort her.

At last she calmed down, took a deep breath, then spoke with her eyes closed, in a soft, barely audible voice. " He had all the drawers and cupboards open, his clothes were all over the bed, and he was searching for something in the black tin box where he keeps his papers. I said, ' Bill, what the hell's going on ? What are you doing ? ' And the next moment he was on top of me, shoving and jostling me. For a moment I was too shocked to speak, but then I got angry and said, ' Take your big paws off me.' And before I knew it he'd hit me. Look at this." She pulled back her hair to show me a milky bruise above her ear. " I said, ' Bill, for God's sake, have you gone mad ? ' But he said, ' Get out of here ; go on, get out, you filthy beast. Why don't you take a bath sometimes ? ' And then he shoved me out of the room so violently I fell on the floor. I lay there sprawled across the passage ; he gave me one look then slammed the door closed. I heard him rattling about inside. It was horrible. At last I got up and went back to the office. It was terrible. That's one thing we've never done, raised a hand to each other. . . ." She shook her head, as if shaking her thoughts into order, and said, " He stomped out of the house and drove away."

The two station wagons caught up with us, but we did not move off at once. Forsythe got out of the truck and walked over to us. " Orders from the borse," he said, poking his head into the window on my side. " We gonna let her ladyship come up front a bit. I know you'd like to see her get lost and eaten by hyenas, but we better keep an eye on her this last stretch. So let her get in here, in front of you. The other car can get in between you and your old man. Okay ? " He saw Ruth suddenly, and pulled his head out of the window with a jerk. " Sorry, madam," he said. He shot her another glance, than walked on to give the instruction to my father.

Ruth moved the Land-Rover off the track to let Lavinia pass, and as she came up I looked inside the station wagon. People were sitting in rows, like bus passengers, staring straight ahead looking bored and disgruntled. Everybody was hating it now. I saw Marjorie at the window and waved to attract her attention.

She gave me a long, slow look, then smiled a little. We rode on, Conrad driving slowly now, and keeping us bunched together.

In the car ahead I caught glimpses of Lavinia. She was talking, raising her hand in gestures, her watch and rings flashing in the sunlight. She was wearing the butterfly-shaped sun-glasses again and they projected as black triangles on either side of her reddish curly hair. There was something maddeningly unassailable about her. She must have realised that Conrad's driving was intended to unsettle her and had made up her mind not to be provoked. She drove in a disciplined way, without showing impatience at the unnecessary crawling pace Conrad was now imposing on us.

It was odd to see her so close, so unruffled and unconcerned, and not notice any signs of villainy about her. She should have had horns or a green complexion or smoke rising out of her hair. Her appearance should have borne some evidence of the vicious thing she had done. But she just looked cool and groomed and self-assured and rather beautiful.

Looking at her, I found it impossible to believe that she could ever want to *marry* Bill Secker. It occurred to me that it might be a stunt to get Bill on her side so as to turn the tables on us. I congratulated myself on having the foresight to ask Ruth for that letter. It put a stop to *that* possibility.

Ruth was speaking. ". . . I saw that he'd taken a change of clothes and his shaving things, though most of his clothes were strewn over the bed. I looked in the black tin box and saw that the money was gone—he usually kept a couple of hundred pounds there—and so was the wallet in which he kept his passport and travel papers. I was dazed, flummoxed. I spent most of the afternoon sitting on the veranda, trying not so much to think, as to get my brain to work again. For some reason it never occurred to me that it might be a woman. I thought he must have got into a scrape—gambling, maybe, or some stupid deal—and that he'd biffed me because I'd barged in on him when he came to get money to pay somebody or bribe somebody—something like that. I couldn't understand why he'd taken his clothes—that floored me—or his passport. But he didn't have much money, nor many clothes, and I reckoned he'd be back in a few days' time. He can't get very far without me—he runs his own bank account, that's true—but I operate the Dale account, and that's where the money is. Not that I don't trust him with a Dale cheque-book—don't get me wrong, Gene. It's just that he's away so often, and I run the business, so it's more convenient for me to have charge of the bank account. Well, I sat. Then, about half past four, who comes driving up to Dale in *that* car . . ."—she indicated the station wagon ahead—" but That Creature."

That Creature was Kiki Pape. More pungent epithets were reserved for Lavinia. That Creature was the name Ruth gave Kiki the first time she saw her, and it was not so much an expression of dislike as a comment on Kiki's insipid boneless appearance and mild, insidious manner. I didn't think Ruth knew Kiki's real name.

" She came traipsing up the steps to where I was sitting . . ." Her voice trailed away and I saw her shoulders making mincing, twitching movements in a slight but startlingly accurate caricature of Kiki's fussy bird-like walk. She obviously enjoyed taking Kiki off, for she continued doing it for a while, adding an inane touch of coquetry by pulling her face into Kiki's sugary, innocent expression. It was neat and funny, but savage. The burlesque died out and she went on : " She came up to me and said, ' Mrs. Secker ? ' I didn't answer—I was scared of her, I knew this had something to do with Bill. She sat down and I ordered tea for her, and while we waited she talked a lot of drivel about what a beautiful place Dale was. She made me edgy—I was waiting for her to talk about Bill— but all she did was blather away about the scenery and the bougainvillæa. She finished her tea, wiped her mouth on her handkerchief. . . ." Ruth mimicked her again, pulling her mouth into a fatuous little simper and fussily dabbing at the corners. ". . . and then she came out with it. ' I met your husband at Umtali to-day,' she said. ' And he asked me to give you a message. He must see you urgently. He's staying at the

Hotel Cecil; he'll wait in for you to-night.' I asked her,
' Was he alone ? ' Yes, he was. I asked, ' What's he doing in
Umtali ? ' and she said, ' I don't know. I thought you would
know. I only saw him for a minute, by accident naturally, and
he gave me this message to pass on to you.' Then she started
up that claptrap about what a gorgeous place we had, and
poured herself some more tea, and looked like staying the rest
of the afternoon. I began to get suspicious. I don't know why
—it's just that there's something so snaky and underhand about
her. At last I stood up and said, ' Thanks for the message. But
it's too late to go to Umtali now. I'll take a run over to-
morrow.' She got quite excited then. She said, 'Oh, no, you
shouldn't do that. He said specifically you must come to-night
—he seemed most anxious that it should be to-night. Of course,
I don't know what this is all about—I'm just passing on the
message—but I got the impression he'd be *very* disappointed
if you didn't go.' That satisfied me. It was a trick of some
kind. To fool her I said, ' Very well, in that case I'll leave
immediately.' So she got up and left.

" I didn't believe a word of it. But do you know what I did?
I *went* to Umtali—or, at any rate, I started out for Umtali. I
thought maybe it *was* true, and there was Bill sitting in the hotel
waiting for me, perhaps in trouble, perhaps ill—anyway,
needing me. So like the dumb, blind baboon that I am, I got
into the Land-Rover and started out for Umtali. On the way
I stopped at the Bell Hotel—nobody had seen Bill there, but I
thought maybe he'd driven straight through . . ."

" Unlikely."

" Of course. I asked the man at the petrol pump, and he
said definitely Bill's car had not passed on the road. But I still
wasn't satisfied and I drove on another ten miles, until I
realised I was on a wild-goose chase ; then I turned round and
drove hell-for-leather back to Dale. I thought now that I'd
find Bill back home. I don't know why—I just did, and I drove
like a bat out of hell, absolutely certain that I'd find Bill at
Dale. But when I got there—nothing. Oh, Gene, I felt so
sick."

She slumped her arms on the wheel, while I tried to think of something to say. It was easy to imagine how bleak and desolate the house must have looked after that long ride home. It had the same kind of look this morning.

" Then one of the milk boys came out of his hut," she said. " He told me that the baas had been there about an hour earlier —and he added 'with a missus.' And you know, I was so damn' gormless, I still never suspected who it was. I asked, ' Which missus ? ' and then he told me. ' The missus from the glass kraal.' And only then did I realise I was being ditched for this trashy tart. Oh, God . . ."

She made a curious sound—a kind of stifled sob. Realising that she was under great strain, I offered to take the wheel. She said, " No, it's quite all right, it's better if I drive." I told her to stop talking now and tell me the rest of the story some other time, but she said, " No, Gene, you don't understand. It's horrible, and I hate off-loading it on to you like this. But if I keep it bottled up much longer, I'll go off my nut ! " She lit a new cigarette, flicked the old one over her shoulder and inhaled deeply : that settled her a bit, and she continued :

" I'm ashamed to tell you what I did next. It was so stupid, so childish. When I think of it I begin to wonder if this thing hasn't sent me off my rocker. I made up my mind to go over to the Big House, so I went inside to put on a dress. And then, somehow, I started putting on one of those flouncy, frilly things Bill bought me in Paris last year. And nylon stockings and fancy shoes with little bows. And I got out some of that perfume and sprayed it on me. I even made up my face with cream and powder and lipstick and eye-shadow. Then I put on a big flowery garden hat I found in the top of the wardrobe, and stood in front of the mirror. I looked like an idiot. I actually laughed at myself. God knows why I got dolled up like that. Oh, I suppose I thought Bill would like to see me in something he had bought me. I was trying to win him back— and compete, I suppose . . . Oh, but I looked a scream, and I ripped the dress off, and the hat, and scraped the muck off my face, and dressed in something simpler. But just as I was ready to leave I had another look at myself and put back the make-up. . . ."

I smiled at this, and felt a wave of foolishness come over me as I realised that those cigarette ends which I saw in Conrad's truck in the early morning were Ruth's after all. I interrupted her :

" If I'm not mistaken, you visited Conrad in his truck last night ? "

" That's right—but later. He came out of the house, and parked down there in the ravine, and I went to ask his advice. But it was *much* later. He was a great help and comfort . . ."

In my mind I apologised to Conrad for thinking he had had a woman in his bed last night, and for thinking him a liar when he told me his visitor was Ruth. I felt, all over again, how far out of my depth I was in this involved situation.

Ruth said, " But I'll come to that. I drove over to the Big House—and sure enough, there was Bill's car outside. And, honestly, Gene, if I'd seen either Bill or her at that moment, I'd have shot them stone dead. I always carry a pistol in the car." She patted the closed glove compartment. " And I'd have used it without any hesitation . . ."

" Ruth ! "

" Playing that dirty trick on me. Sending me off to Umtali to get me out of the way. I think I could have forgiven him everything except that. That was low and slimy—I never thought Bill was like that. It made me sick, and honest to God, if I'd seen him at that moment I'd have plugged him."

" Ruth ! "

She wasn't listening. Her eyes were burning, and it was the road, not me, which at the moment distracted her. The driving now was excruciating. We were lurching and slithering over marshy ground, searching, every yard of the way, for grassy tufts and stone outcrops to give the wheels something to grip on. The station wagon ahead was dipping and ditching like a fishing boat in a rough sea. There was no merit in this route, except that it was intended to infuriate Lavinia. But Lavinia was driving as coolly and expertly as the difficult terrain would allow. And uncomplainingly too—she didn't stop to protest, or sound the horn. The plan wasn't working now. Ahead we could see Mamisa's Rock, a huge ball of granite standing on a stone platform, looking like a gigantic egg in an egg-cup and saucer. That meant we were nearing the Falls.

I said, " Ruth, you might as well know this. Conrad has put me on your tail to-day."

" That car is going to bust an axle. It's too overloaded anyway," Ruth said.

" Ruth—Conrad doesn't trust you to-day. Do you know that ? He's asked me to keep an eye on you."

" Tell Conrad to go and drown himself." But a moment later she said with sudden intensity, as if the idea of settling scores with Lavinia during the hunt had only at that moment occurred to her, and then only because I had put it into her mind. " Don't be crazy, Gene. I wouldn't do that. Much as I'd like to see her a corpse, I'm damned if I'd swing for her. I'm telling you how I felt *last night*."

Suddenly the back wheels slithered round, the engine stalled, and we found ourselves foolishly facing the way we had come. Ruth restarted the engine, swung the wheel, and found the track again. She went on, hardly noticing the interruption. " But I feel different now—and the main difference is that I hate them both. Yes, Bill too—and shooting would be merciful . . ." She was incoherent now, talking in jerks, caused not by her feelings but by the bouncing car. " Because, let them have each other. Let them enjoy each other, and it would . . . that would be . . . the best . . ."

She suddenly found a good firm length of track, and as the car began to ride smoothly so did her sentences. ". . . punishment for both of them that anyone could think of. I can't think of two people more certain to make each other's life a hell. Gene, let me tell you the rest. Maybe this is going to make you sick, but I've gone so far, and you might as well know the rest of this filthy story. I want you to know this, Gene, and I don't care a damn who else knows it, because I don't see that I've got any obligation to keep quiet about it.

What for ? To protect *their* feelings ? Not a chance, not after this. This is what happened, Gene. I went up on the veranda but couldn't see him there. He wasn't in the lounge either, so I came outside and walked around the house. Then I heard his voice. It came from her bedroom—as you know it opens on to the lawn at the side. A moment later I heard her voice too. The curtains were drawn, but not properly, and I went over and looked in. I know what you're thinking—snooping. But that's a privilege allowed to ditched spouses—it's one of their few rights. If only I'd had a camera with me . . ."

She was laughing, rocking in the seat and laughing to herself, in a dry, mirthless way that made me nervous. Her eyes had a hard glint, a cruel fire I had never seen in her before. I felt myself tense as she went on. " She had just come out of the bath—she had her bathrobe in her hand, and one foot in one of those fluffy slippers—and he was standing behind her, my Romeo, holding her breasts in his hands, while she had her arm up holding his head and kissing him over her shoulder. It looked very artistic up there, but lower down she was rubbing her backside against him, and my God, even from where I stood, I could see that bastard of mine almost bursting out of his pants."

" Ruth, please . . ." I said, placing my hand on hers, trying to restrain her. She brushed my hand away impatiently.

" My Bill, my romantic tom-cat—I never knew he had it in him. He picked her up in his arms . . ." There was no stopping her. Dismay flooded through me as she went on, speaking not to me, not even to herself, just letting the intolerable story burst out. " Picked her up, like a little itty baby and carried her round the room, and she kicked her feet just like they do in the pictures. They stopped in front of the mirror and had a good look at themselves and laughed. Laughed like robins. Then she coiled her legs around his waist and hung down backwards, while he held her hands. She looked at herself upside down like that and they laughed again. Oh, it was *such* fun. I've never known my Bill laugh so much in all his life. Then he threw her on the bed and sprinkled talcum powder on her and she laughed and laughed and kicked her legs. It was a riot, Gene, such joy and laughter as I've never seen before—not with my Bill, anyway. Why didn't I ever think of that? Why didn't I make him powder me after my bath? Think of the fun we've been missing."

I closed my eyes and tensed my jaws, trying to stop the gloom from spreading inside me.

" Then he dressed her, my bullfighter. That's where I could have used that camera. I really learnt something about bed-room shenanigans then. You see, you don't just let him put things on you. You wriggle and squirm and make sure he's got plenty of work to do. When he tries to put on your stockings, you pull your foot away so he's got to keep diving all over the bed for it. And you keep sticking all your different parts in his face, just to make sure you get thoroughly kissed all over. Even if he does get powder all over his face and looks like a circus clown. That's the new way, Gene—that's what they must be teaching them in these new-fangled charm schools. I'm just old-fashioned. Just a frump. When *I* get dressed, I just yank on my things and walk out of the bedroom buttoning up my shirt. But I'll know in future. My next husband . . ."

" Ruth, please stop," I implored her.

" Anyway, it finished then. He must have hurt her or some-thing, because suddenly she kicked him off and finished dressing by herself."

" Ruth, listen to me. I know how you feel. It must have been terrible seeing a thing like that—your own husband. . . . But please stop now. This isn't doing you any good."

" Terrible ? " She laughed again in the same merciless way. " Not at all. It was an education. We've been married twenty-three years and we never once tried any fancy hoopla of that sort. But I'll know better for next time. I'll tell you now—I'm going to get myself a lover-boy. Oh, *Jesus Christ* ! "

She stopped then. She gave me a quick glance, frightened and aghast, as if she only then realised the horror of what she had been telling me. But the look was fleeting and by the time she gave her attention back to the driving, a fixed wooden expression had settled on her face. She did not speak for a while. We passed Mamisa's Rock in a silence that dinned with her words, that swam with the scenes she had described.

She said, " What beats me is why I didn't go in and bust up their little party."

Yes, why hadn't she ? Wasn't that the sort of thing one did in these situations—kick open the door, stand there looking outraged, hurl threats and accusations, shoot, if one had a gun. Wasn't that the stock reaction ? But I saw that it would have been futile. Ruth would never have coped with the situation ; she would have ended by humiliating herself.

" I didn't break it up. And I didn't go home. I just hung around. I was completely witless. I strolled about in the garden, then went into the lounge. A little later Bill and Lavinia came in—through different doors. Bill nearly dropped dead when he saw me. But Lavinia sailed right over and said, ' How nice of you to drop in, Mrs. Secker. I was telling Mr. Secker only this afternoon that he should simply haul you out of your office and force you to come and see us. You'll stay for dinner of course ? ' I said yes—I was so foozled I would have said yes to anything. That dinner ! What a joke. Bill never spoke to me, not a word, and Lavinia didn't speak to Bill and That Creature dripped friendship all over me without once mentioning her trip to Dale in the afternoon, or her stunt to get me to go to Umtali. Nobody could have guessed what was going on—all the undercurrents, I mean. What dishonest people they are, Gene—and so clever at it. Anyway, we finished dinner and all trooped into the lounge. And there I saw you and Joe. The next part you know—they started arguing about the hunt."

" Which you thought a good idea ? "

" I didn't."

" But you were in favour of it. You seemed very keen, in fact."

" I wasn't going to let them spend a day in the woods together, that's all. When I saw Bill backing Lavinia against

Conrad, I said to myself, ' Oh, no, you don't—this is too cosy.'
I had a plan—I was going to stick to Bill like glue, not let him
out of my sight. So when Bill said, ' Sure, let's go and pot
them,' I said, ' I'm coming too.' "

" What you said was, ' I'm ready any time, to go and bump
off any stinking pigs that come marauding into the district.'
Something like that. That's a funny remark. I mean it's funny
now. Last night I didn't know all this about Lavinia and Bill,
and I thought you were talking about those lion."

" That's right—I meant it," she said a little vacantly, leaving
me with the feeling that she had missed the point of my
question. I didn't press it. I asked, " And this morning—now
that Bill's not here ? "

" I couldn't stay home to-day, Gene. I couldn't just stay
there jumping to the window at every sound in case it might
be Bill coming down the road. Trying to get the programme
started, giving the men their orders, doing paper work—I
couldn't. Besides, I want to be near *her* to-day. I haven't
finished with her yet."

I looked hard at her before asking, " Ruth, you're not going
to try any rough stuff, are you ? Because if that's in your mind
I'll take the gun away from you."

She got angry at that. " What are you suggesting ? " she
asked hotly. " I told you before I wouldn't swing for *her*. You
don't understand—I've *got* to stick with her. I've *got* to. She's—
well, she was the last person who was with Bill, and—oh, you
don't understand."

But I did understand. She meant that Lavinia was the link
with Bill, that as long as she kept Lavinia in sight she kept Bill
from disappearing over the horizon and out of her life. But
she spoke vaguely, and altogether there wasn't much sense in
what she was saying. Although she made suggestions, they
were obscure, as though she herself didn't know what she
meant. I was glad of the diversion that arose at that moment.
The vehicles in front of us stopped, and we drew up about ten
yards behind the station wagon. I saw the doors of the truck
open, and Conrad and Forsythe come down and walk over to a

termite hill a little way off the road. Conrad climbed to the top and surveyed the area with binoculars. He did it carefully and deliberately, taking in the whole countryside with a slow sweep round. He actually made a full circle, then reversed and just as deliberately swept round the opposite way. He came down and handed the binoculars to Forsythe, who climbed up the mound and made his own survey, but concentrating on a few particular spots.

" Very stagey to-day, aren't they ? " Ruth commented.

" It's a big audience." I watched Forsythe for a moment, then said, " Very impressive. Any minute from now they'll blow a bugle, and give us orders to capture that hill."

" There *are* lion about, you know."

" They haven't got a chance against those master strategists. Anyway, unless they're stone deaf, they must have heard our cars and cleared off by now.

" So you think it's an act ? " Ruth asked.

" I don't know. I can't make Conrad out to-day. Somehow, I think this is a stunt."

" Maybe they're right not to take anything for granted," Ruth said. " Lion are tricky bastards. Particularly now, after the drought. And with all this crowd to look after . . ."

" Maybe . . ."

We watched Conrad and Forsythe climb back into the truck and the column moved off again. After a few moments I asked, " What were you doing chasing all over the country in your Land-Rover last night ? "

" How do you know about this ? Conrad seems to have told you everything."

" No, he refuses to talk. He's guarding your secret like a gaoler."

" Then how do you know so much about it ? "

" Because your Land-Rover left its footprints all over the road. And because one of my intelligence agents reported to me that someone visited Conrad in the early hours. And because you left a saucerful of half-smoked cigarettes in the truck. I must say, though, the last item flummoxed me at first.

The cigarettes had lipstick on them, and I thought Conrad had got himself a call-girl last night."

She laughed. " That's a joke. As a matter of interest how do you call a call-girl out here in the wild blue bundu ? "

" Easy. Just sit in a sports car, rustle some money and give the mating call—Hon*eee*, here-I-am, Honk, Honk, Honk. That will flush one out of the Big House in a matter of minutes."

She became serious again. " I wanted to talk to Bill—I *had* to. I was even prepared to forgive him if he came back home with me. But he kept avoiding me. I gave up trying, and then quite late, he came to me and said, 'Chim, come outside. I've got something to tell you.' We went out and sat in his car and he said, ' I don't know how to say this, but I've had the feeling for some time that things haven't been going well with us. I'm unhappy and if I'm not mistaken, so are you.' I said nothing so he chucked me under the chin and said, 'Come on, admit it—you're unhappy.' Can you imagine anything more slimy ?—putting it on to me like that. I still said nothing, and he took that to mean that I agreed with him. He said, ' You see ? It's mutual. Look, Chim, what's the use of dragging things out ? Let's shake hands and call it a day and be good friends about it.' I was still feeling the nice friendly bruises he'd given me in the morning, but I didn't mention that. I asked, ' What do you want ? ' and he said, 'A divorce, Chim. Be a sport and give me a divorce.' I nearly burst out laughing —he said it as though he were asking me for money to buy a speedboat. I mean, he just took it for granted that because he'd asked for it, I'd give it. He went on, ' You see, Lavinia Whittaker and I have fallen in love, and—well, this is a tricky thing to talk about, but we need each other desperately. We can't fight it any more. So be a sport—sue me for divorce, and we'll stand the rap financially. Give me a chance, Chim ; a chance to have a few years of happiness in my life.' I could *smell* his happiness—the stink of that floozie was all over him, and it made me want to spew up. I asked, ' What will happen to me ? ' That knocked him back a bit—he hadn't thought about that aspect. He said, ' Don't worry, Chim, we'll look after you.' That did it, that *we*. I screamed at him, ' You can go to hell, Bill Secker, and you can take that cheap, lousy, stinking whore with you. You're not getting a divorce and you're not getting a penny of Dale's money either. You can live in sin with her. But you're not getting any money from me. You can get your old job back in the police and support her on that. Good luck, bon voyage and tons of happiness. Now bugger off.' That shook him. ' What do you want me to do ? ' he asked. I told him to come home with me. He said, 'All right, that's fair—I'll do that and we can discuss the whole thing more calmly.' So trust me—I fell. I was so relieved, I kissed him. He said, 'Okay, Chim, you go back home now. I've got a couple of things to see to here, but I'll follow you in a few minutes. Go home and wait for me.'

" He drove me over to the Land-Rover, and I started for Dale. But suddenly I had a feeling, and after a few hundred yards I stopped. I just had the feeling there was something phoney about this. I pulled the car into the bushes, switched off the engine and lights. It was a long wait—more than an hour, but then I saw him come down from the house, start his car, and drive down the road in my direction. I got into a panic. I couldn't start going now, because he'd see me and know I'd been sitting there. And I didn't want him to go back home and not find me there. Then a queer thing happened. He stopped too—about a hundred yards before reaching me. He switched off his lights and engine, and sat waiting for something. He didn't know I was there of course ; it was raining by then and we couldn't see each other. But I tell you, it was damn' queer sitting there in the rain and knowing that he too was waiting only a short distance away. I saw you go home on that bicycle. And a little later Conrad came out of the house and drove off in his truck. But just when he got down into the ravine, I'm damned if *he* didn't stop, and switch off his lights and engine. It was the weirdest thing—three of us, sitting there in the rain, out of sight of each other, all waiting for something. I hadn't the vaguest idea what to expect—but I sat, because I was certain *something* was going to happen."

The story had run into familiar surroundings now, for as she spoke I recalled what Marjorie told me about the comings and goings and disturbances in the Big House last night. Now, as Ruth went on speaking I had the feeling of following her story with a map or score in my hand.

" Then there was a signal from Lavinia's room. It was definitely a signal, the curtains were pulled aside, letting the light shine out for a few seconds, then drawn back again. And like a bullet out of a gun, Bill started the car and tore up to the Big House. He didn't stop in the driveway, but went straight on across the lawn and flower-beds and stopped outside her room ; then he went in. After about half an hour he came out again, started the car, switching on that big yellow fog-lamp ; then he came screeching round the driveway down into the road and right in front of me. As the car passed I saw *her* inside. She was dressed like now, and talking, talking. Then——"

" Yes ? "

" I did another stupid thing. I tried to chase them. They spotted me of course, and tried to shake me off. We had a real hectic chase right across the valley. In all that rain too. It was crazy—we drove like maniacs—I saw I'd never catch them unless they bust a spring or had a blow out, but I kept on and kept them in sight because the dirt road limited their speed. But when they reached the tar road, Bill just opened out and left me standing. I didn't have a chance against that big souped-up Jag of his. I lost them but went on as far as the cross-roads, then not knowing which fork they had taken, I turned back."

" And saw Conrad ? "

" Yes, I decided to ask his advice. He said he'd been expecting developments, as he put it, and he went down there to keep watch. We had a long talk—a proper legal consultation, in fact, and—well, the picture's pretty grim. For one thing, Bill can chuck me out of Dale any time he wants to. The place is his legally. He started it, the land's registered in his name, and even though I've worked it up——"

" There would have been no Dale without you. He'd have been back in the police force years ago."

" Maybe, but the fact is he can pitch me out, and all I'd be entitled to is compensation for my services. *Services*—that's a nice whack in the eye. I built this place up from scrubland ; I made Bill what he is. And that comes under the heading of services. Of course, in return for giving him a divorce, I could probably swing a settlement in which Dale would be made over to me. Conrad thinks that would be possible. He believes Bill would settle on that basis."

" And they'd live on *her* money ? "

" No, she hasn't got any money."

" Then it can't possibly work. Bill without his trips and cars and horse-racing ? Lavinia living in a small flat ? They can't be *that* much in love."

" Oh, Gene, wake up. They'll live like fighting cocks on the dividends of Malinda Copper Estates Limited, or whatever they decide to call this copper mining racket of theirs."

" Just a minute," I said with a nervous panic, " there's an agreement between you and my father about this. You were going to buy the place from the liquidator and sell it back to him. We came over to Dale that day, remember ? You agreed then."

" If it rested with me, there'd be no trouble. You know that."

" But you put it in writing. You gave us that letter confirming the deal—you must remember that ? Surely they can't get past that letter ? "

" According to Conrad it's worthless. As I told you, Dale belongs to Bill, not me. I've been no more than a glorified employee there all these years. I had no legal right to give that letter. Just as I have no legal right to sell Dale or give it to the Cats' Home. It doesn't belong to me. The trouble is I'd forgotten that : running the place by myself all these years, signing cheques, buying and selling cattle, paying wages—I naturally thought I could give you that letter. But it was a mistake. I'm just a clerk there. I was clean off bounds making that promise to Joe."

" But Bill also promised. He never once objected to it. I could be a witness to that."

" Bill only gave his word. These things have to be done in writing. Besides, Bill wasn't even in the room when I wrote that letter. No, Gene, what I'm telling you is the law." She gave a bitter laugh. " I learnt quite a lot of law last night, out there in the truck in all that rain."

" Well, I don't know," I persisted, but with a sinking heart now because I knew that my arguments were growing more and more feeble. " Bill's an honest man basically. As far as I'm concerned he's still our friend. I just can't believe he'd break his word to my dad."

She laughed, a shrill peal of derision. " You don't ? He's prepared to ditch *me* for her. What makes you think he wouldn't ditch Joe Latham ? Come off it, Gene."

I had to accept it then. Lavinia had outwitted and out-manœuvred us—beautifully, brilliantly. All of us—my father, Ruth, even old Jordan Whittaker. By stealing Bill from Ruth she had stolen Malinda from us, and had stolen the vegeance out of Jordan's will. I tried to go back over the events of the last twenty-four hours and understand how it had all happened, but listlessly and dispiritedly, because nothing mattered now. I saw how Ruth's life had been smashed and our work and striving at Malinda reduced to ashes because of a few minutes of inattention by my father. Bill had no idea that he was going to be involved in a runaway romance with Lavinia when he left Dale after breakfast yesterday. Yet only a few hours later— "at twelve-forty to be precise"—he was back to fetch his pass-port and money, and was attacking Ruth as if demented. I remembered the conversation with my father as we walked to keep the rendezvous with Conrad at dawn this morning, and his worry at having left the file of papers on the table while he went to attend the injured herdsman. He knew the moment he came back that they had seen Ruth's letter and had learnt about the deal. The meeting broke up then—they simply gathered their papers and left. After that Lavinia couldn't have wasted a minute. It was swift, ruthless, audacious. It couldn't have taken her more than half an hour to snare Bill. He was ripe for plucking and she knew it. And that small mistake of my father's was swooped on and turned into this immense, devastating defeat. How did we ever come to underestimate her so badly?

I remembered my father's anxiety about the incident and my own complacency and how I managed to talk him round to my view. How naïve, how idiotic this airy dismissal of the incident seemed now. Yet could he be blamed? The deal with the Seckers was his trump card—the last trump in the game. How could that minor lapse have upset a situation so firmly secured in our favour? Who could have foreseen that Lavinia would make this smash and grab raid on Bill? Or that Bill, our friend and neighbour and fellow settler, our partner and companion in so many enterprises in the valley, would callously break his word to us? Could anyone be blamed?

But Conrad *had* blamed him. To Conrad it was weakness, flabby deficiency of character to leave yourself exposed to your enemies. There was no *need* to leave the papers on the table when he went out of the room. One simply didn't make mistakes of this kind. Negligence was just as criminal as any deliberate action, and knowing the kind of people he was dealing with, my father had no right to take even the smallest chances with them. I was sure Conrad had spoken to him in this fashion when I went to fetch water for the truck. I could understand now why he was so furious with my father this morning. Now I understood the reason for my father's sudden plunge into paralysing gloom when I returned from attending to the truck. Conrad had told him about Bill and Lavinia in my absence, had done it without sparing him, had lashed him with it. That was Conrad's way—he never forgave you even the mistakes you paid for.

A feeling of vast futility came over me. I thought of all our wasted years at Malinda and of the utter hopelessness of trying to make any impression on that sullen, hostile valley. No matter how hard you tried, or how much you put aside, or how high you built the walls, it always found a way to come back and destroy you. It always had the last word. I thought of those hard early days and the later happier days, of the good times and the bad times, and saw them now as a heap of dried leaves, useless, meaningless, lifeless ; existing only in the brief space of time between death and total disappearance. Nothing had been of any value. We had been merely passing time, waiting for the inevitable end. I remembered times when friends had tried to persuade us to get out of Malinda, because we were killing ourselves and didn't have a hope of making it pay, and my father saying, " Not on your life. I'm going to show Jordan and all the boys back in the office what kind of a job can be done with this place." And later, when things were better, telling my mother, " Agnes, we can sit back and enjoy life now." Once when he received his bank statement and for the first time saw a credit balance of a few hundred pounds instead of the usual red overdraft figures, saying to me, " I feel like a cripple who has started to walk again." And all the times and all the people to whom he said, " I knew it would come right one day." I felt sick at the thought of how we had deluded ourselves, of how thin and vulnerable our security had been. We had naïvely imagined that we built a life at Malinda on a foundation of hard work, integrity, courage, sacrifice and family love, when in truth it was teetering on stilts—on the fickle character of a country playboy named Bill Secker, on a slipshod contract made ten years before by Jordan, on a malevolent will.

The hunt had become important and serious to me now. I had been taking it lightly, talking of it as a nuisance or a joke. treating it with derision. But now I had the kind of bitter, reckless loathing for Lavinia that made murder possible. I knew that if I saw her through the bushes, and I was alone with a gun at my shoulder, I should easily be tempted to make a slight, infinitesimal change of aim and shoot her. I felt ironical amusement at the idea of Conrad appointing me to look after Ruth, when now I needed looking after myself. Now I understood perfectly Conrad's precautions concerning Ruth. She too would be under a temptation to solve her problems, to rescue her shattered life, with one effortless twitch of her finger. I knew, too, what the other reason was for calling off the hunt. It was my father, who, having poured his life into Malinda, had no further life to lose now that the ranch was taken away, and whose stunned despair spoke of a desperation worse than Ruth's or mine. I knew that however much we hated Lavinia now, our feelings would be inflamed and exacerbated even more in the tension and strain of hunting, in the hot sun and tingling silence and enticing solitude of the bush.

About half a mile ahead we could see the rain forest that surrounded Crampton Falls and rising behind it a cloud of spray holding a rainbow. There was bustle and activity all around us, as if we were entering a city. Hares leapt across the track, squirrels scurried up trees and hung by their claws as we passed, monkeys flung themselves about in the branches, and the air was so full of birds that several crashed drunkenly into the vehicles. The vegetation began suddenly to have a rich tropical look, and as we trampled down ferns and liana vines with our tyres I had the feeling that we were actually riding into a net. Crampton Falls was a famous beauty-spot, and I always enjoyed visiting it, but now I approached it with fear and suspicion, as if it had collaborated with Lavinia in trapping us into this situation.

Ruth said, " I don't believe it, Gene. I keep feeling that I'll wake up any minute and find it's all a dream. It doesn't make sense—I've put so much into Dale, I've sweated and slogged, it's been hard physical labour." She held up one of her roughened hands and shuddered. " We've got a hundred and seventy-five thousand acres, and the business has been valued in the books at over a quarter of a million. And in one day I lose the whole bang shoot to a bit of paint and lipstick, and a cute little bum-waggle."

" Unless you agree to give Bill his divorce."

" Yes . . ." Her voice tailed off.

" What are you going to do ? "

" I don't know." She waited again, then said in a mild

resigned voice, " Maybe I'll give him his divorce. At least, I'll save Dale for myself." But her voice sounded doubtful, and a few moments later she said, " I don't know. It won't be the same, of course. Without Bill it will be rather pointless, and I don't know if I wouldn't prefer him simply to chuck me out. I don't want to grow old all by myself in that place. I'll end up like the cattle. I'm nearly like that already."

" Oh, come on."

" I shouldn't be talking like this. You've got enough of your own to worry about. I've thought about this, but I can't see any way out for your family. It's your mother I'm most worried about. It's going to be a terrible blow for her."

" I think she's been expecting something like this. Not Bill running away with Lavinia—I don't mean that. But losing Malinda. I've had the feeling for some time that she had given up hope of keeping Malinda."

We said no more for a while. Just before we reached the edge of the rain forest, I asked, " What made you go up to the Big House this morning ? "

" I wanted to find out where they went last night. I thought somebody there might tell me. I got the surprise of my life when I saw Lavinia there. I arrived just as she was getting into her car, and when she saw me she seemed to get into a panic and drove off in a hurry. She seemed to think I'd follow her. I was sure then that Bill would be around somewhere. I searched everywhere—even in her room—but I couldn't find him. He's definitely not at the Big House this morning."

" It's the screwiest elopement I've ever heard of," I said. " Breaking off in the middle to go and bump off some cats that aren't bothering anybody."

" Yes, everybody's gone completely mad. By the way, I found this in her room. Does it mean anything to you ? "

She fished in her pocket and pulled out a piece of blue scented notepaper. It contained some hastily scribbled notes in pencil and as soon as I saw it I recognised it as one of Lavinia's lists. She drew up lists for everything—supplies to buy in town, repairs to be done to the house, lists of guests, lists of complaints—she was a list addict. This one was made up of items that didn't seem to belong to any category. " Papers—hand over to Frank H." " Power of Attorney." " Phone Wallace—letter of credit." " Surveyor—plans." " Shoes and winter overcoat." " Alter Deed." " See Eddie Scobie and instruct." Underneath them all, written heavily with a ballpoint pen and underlined, as if added as an afterthought, " MTETWA ! ! ! "

As I read it, Ruth asked, " Who's Mtetwa ? "

" That customer in the back of Conrad's truck. The one she spent most of the morning going to fetch. Only we call him Mac."

" Of course. I remember him now."

BOOK FOUR

16

THE ROAR of the waterfall was beautiful. . . . We could not see the Falls from where we stood, for we were level with the upper reach of the river and they were obscured by the dense growth of the rain forest. But they made an exciting sound. From the hollow cistern roar and the hissing and gurgling that seemed to reach us through the ground at our feet I could tell that the water was spouting clear over the top like the stream from a teapot. The Falls were a hundred and thirty feet high and in normal times a thin silvery cascade fluttered down the sheer cliff, splashed on to a sloping rock shelf at the bottom and slipped into the narrow scooped channel below. But now it was shooting, with perfect aim, straight into the dark chasm that had been scoured out of the rock. Crampton Falls lay on the Rezandi River, which although also a tributary of the Sabie belonged to a different river system from our Shindze. The satisfying *boom*, magnified like sound in a tunnel, told me that the rain had fallen plentifully and over a wide area.

We stood in two groups, Conrad's and Lavinia's, and nobody seemed willing to make the first move to reconciliation. There was an air of feud separating us and we all seemed to be waiting for a gong to sound or a flag to drop. The American couple, Mr. and Mrs. Bertram Taylor, looked embarrassed ; they stood apart from the rest and from the way they kept glancing at us I could tell that they wanted to put an end to this nonsense and come and join us. But the others just stood glaring at us and hating us for what we did to them at Turgeni Drift.

Conrad gave the trackers the signal to make a reconnaissance in the bush nearby, and Cigarettes and Boots jumped out of the truck. But instead of going into the bushes they started scanning the ground, sniffing the air and peering into the sky where we were standing. They were looking for spoor right under the wheels of the cars. It was a joke, a leg-pull at the expense of this citified audience. Matchbox, holding the ridgebacks on taut leads, like a charioteer, stalked behind the other two, ready instantly to deal with anything that might spring out of the ground.

" Sic 'em. Go on, sic 'em," Hoffman called out.

They caught Conrad's eye and stopped fooling. He gave them a signal and they loped off into the bush to make the first search for spoor. They would take a circular route about half a mile around, hoping to cross the lions' tracks.

While we waited, Conrad and Forsythe began taking the rifles down from the rack. I saw Marjorie in the crowd near the second station wagon. Somebody handed her a cigarette, and Peter Wickham appeared suddenly and flipped a lighter in front of her. Hoffman made a joke and four or five people laughed, but the laughter died out quickly, and they stood talking, with Marjorie in the centre of the group. She held the cigarette elegantly on a level with her shoulder, her palm upwards and the cigarette dangling down between her fingers ; a man said something and she smiled, blowing out a puff of smoke, and the smile was so devastating and beautiful I felt a deep pang of grief, and a sudden crude childish jealousy. She seemed a thousand miles away from me at that moment. I wondered how it was possible for two people to make love and so soon afterwards be like complete strangers to each other. In every way the day was becoming a disaster for me.

I was watching her from the distance, when I heard Forsythe's voice and saw him standing up in the back of the truck calling the crowd together. The fact that Conrad was using him to announce the arrangements meant that they weren't going to be popular. Forsythe shouted, " Hey, there, everybody, let's have your attention, please. We got work to do, so gather round and listen to teacher." He spoke with forced cheerfulness, and I could sense that he was uncomfortable. When the crowd collected round him he said, " Now, there's a pretty little picnic spot down there through the trees, and I suggest you all go and have yourselves a good time while Mr. Webber, Mr. Latham and I go and spray those simbas. Keep tea warm for us because——"

" *Who* are going ? " Lavinia asked angrily.

" Mr. Webber," he indicated Conrad with a flat palm, like a conductor introducing his leading violinist. " Mr. Latham," pointing to my father, and noticing me, he added, " Senior. And yours truly, Fearsome Forsythe."

His humour didn't go down at all ; so, like a stage comedian with a flat joke, he tried turning it against himself. " All right, all right, throw stones at me. Three's all it will take. More'n that's a crowd and somebody's liable to come home with ugly tooth marks all over them."

" Stop being an ass, Ronnie," Lavinia said. " What kind of bloody nonsense *is* this ? *I'm* coming—and *Mister* Latham can sit this one out if we're too many." She almost hissed the *mister*.

" What about me ? " Ruth demanded in a tough loud voice. " Do you think I came all this way to sit on the river bank and eat tomato sandwiches ? "

" Steady on, steady on," Forsythe said, holding up his palms and playfully hiding behind them. " This is going to look like the march past of the Grenadier Guards. Somebody's got to drop out. What about you, Mr. Latham ? "

" No, thank you," my father said, with a dull look at Lavinia.

Conrad came forward and said in a calm, pleasant voice, " It's up to you, Lavinia, but I suggest you leave it as we've planned—Forsythe, Joe Latham and myself. It's not only the *size* of the party. You didn't get much sleep last night, and I think you'd be well advised to take it easy to-day." He said it very deliberately, nodding in a way that dropped a prim little smile on her. He turned to Ruth, and said in exactly the same tone of voice, " And that goes for you too."

" Thanks for your solicitude," Lavinia said. " Let me have my gun."

" Mr. Webber's right," Forsythe said.

" WILL YOU KINDLY SHUT UP ! " she burst out at Forsythe. " What's got into you ? What kind of a game are you playing?" She was glaring at him and very tense, but she quickly curbed herself, and asked in a controlled voice, " My rifle, please."

While Forsythe hesitated, Conrad peeled it out of its sheath and with ironic courtesy handed it down to her. He then reached behind him for a box of cartridges and passed that too. Lavinia stood holding the rifle and cartridges, suddenly embarrassed at her outburst. She looked around her at her friends and the next moment spoke to Forsythe with a bright smile. " Why are we all getting so excited ? We've come out here to enjoy ourselves, so let's stop this bickering." Very nonchalantly she aimed the rifle at something in the trees, and said, without lifting her cheek off the carved wooden stock, " I've got no quarrel with anybody. I don't bear any enmity."

The effrontery took my breath away. She didn't bear any enmity. Having just collared two ranches and a copper mine for herself, she was big enough not to be cross with anybody. I looked at Ruth, saw her eyes narrow, and a curl of contempt form on her lips.

" Of course you don't," Forsythe said encouragingly.

" No, of course not," Conrad said in a different tone that echoed my own thought—how big of her.

" So why don't we stop this silly quarrelling and make friends ? " But she realised that her hypocritical overtures were angering us, and she said with hardly a pause, " At least let's behave with normal good manners to each other. Seeing we're going to spend the rest of the day together let's try and do it with a minimum of unpleasantness." She lowered the rifle and turned to Conrad. " Is there any particular reason why six of us shouldn't go—you, Ronnie Forsythe, the two Lathams,

Ruth Secker and myself? After all, that's what we decided last night. Let's all go, and what the hell if we don't find any lion, that will be just too bad."

" I don't mind staying behind," I said.

" As you like, but let's call back the trackers and make a start. We came out here for a hunt. I can't see why there's all this difficulty."

Conrad said, " Well, it's up to you." He handed my father his rifle, then gave me my Greener, at the same time passing me a close private look that I understood to mean that I was to come on the hunt, and keep my mouth shut. Standing up again, he said, " Well, that's settled. Now, will all you good people make your way down to the river and wait there until we return. Jackson will show you the way." He indicated the white-clad cook who was sitting on a log eating an apple. " It's past lunch-time now, and you must all be hungry, so the sooner you get down there, the sooner you'll get some food into you. I don't know how long we'll be away, but you can expect us back before nightfall. Be careful if you go swimming. The river's dangerously high. If you get bored, you're at liberty, of course, to go back home. In that case take such vehicles as you need but leave us the truck. We'll return to the Falls by not later than nightfall. It might be earlier. Jackson! "

" Yes, sir," Jackson said, standing up.

" Show them the way to the waterfall."

We saw the crowd collect their food, beach bags, umbrellas and picnic equipment and follow Jackson into the trees.

When they were out of sight Conrad said to the six of us who remained, " Now the order will be first Lavinia, then Gene Latham, then Ruth: that will make up a front party, with Cigarettes and Boots as trackers. The rest of us, myself, Mr. Forsythe and Joe Latham in that order, will make up a second party—with Mac as the tracker. We'll be about two minutes behind you. *Don't double back*—even if the spoor turns back. If that happens, just stand and wait for us. We don't want to go shooting at each other. Now, are you ready? "

" Yes," Lavinia said.

As we started off behind Cigarettes and Boots I wondered again, and with my former amazement, at this extraordinary hunting order. The two women in front with me, out of practice and unenthusiastic, in between but with the two best trackers. Again I believed that Conrad was making a burlesque of it, yet it bothered me that he seemed so sure we would not come across any lion.

The mist in the rain forest was like a cool sponge on our faces, and wet ferns and gleaming dripping leaves slapped against our clothing. In a few minutes we were drenched, but the cool feeling was delicious. We saw rainbows wherever the sky showed through the tangled overgrowth, and the sound of the Falls reached us with a curious muffled effect, like rain on a thatched roof. I wished Marjorie were alongside me. We would have enjoyed exploring this forest with its mahogany and ebony trees growing almost out of each other's roots, knotted all together by liana vines, its orchids peeping over the branches on which they had taken root, its mosses and feathery ferns and great bottle-green palms with stems covered in brown bark like loosely wrapped sacking. There were monkeys in the trees, swinging on fantastically long skinny arms, and great, fluffy white spiders, and parakeets that flashed across patches of sunlight like exploding fireworks, and widow-birds flying slowly and laboriously, dragged down by their foot-long, waterlogged, jet-black tails. Lizards in gleaming metallic colours—magenta, tarnished copper, dull steel, clung to trees like scared pedestrians. We saw a gorgeously coloured snake striped like a candy pencil, swinging head down from a branch. Tortoises, wet and clean and shining like new toys. And porcupines, and fat, vividly coloured caterpillars. There was a special kind of animal and plant life in the hothouse climate of the rain forest; I was sorry that we were spending only a few minutes here.

Cigarettes led the way without looking for spoor and it was that which first aroused my suspicion. He was going too fast, too sure of his direction. I looked at Ruth who was about ten yards behind me and something told me she too was puzzled.

Once she stopped and stood with her hands on her hips, peering around ; then she turned to me and jabbed her finger in the direction of Lavinia whom I glimpsed among the trees ahead. What she tried to tell me I didn't catch exactly, but she seemed to convey that something odd was going on, something at Lavinia's expense. I walked on convinced now that we were soon to become victims of some new trick of Conrad's.

I was right. Cigarettes led us out of the forest right to the spot near the waterfall where the picnic crowd had assembled. They must have arrived just ahead of us for Jackson was still setting up his kitchen, kneeling beside a tree pumping the pressure stove ; the hampers were still unpacked. Somebody was spreading rugs on the flat rock beside the river, somebody was struggling with a sun umbrella. The rest were standing about. Lavinia saw them, then swung round angrily and looked back into the rain forest. I knew by now that the second party had not followed us, and this was confirmed a moment later by the sound of the truck starting up. My first thought was that Conrad was going to drive down to join us, but I realised that there was no road through the forest, or around it. No, he had given us the slip—to my vast, thankful, joyous relief. I heard the sound of the truck turning round and driving away, taking Conrad, Forsythe, my father, Mac, Matchbox and the dogs to hunt on their own. Where they were making for I had no idea. Perhaps they had private information of the lions' whereabouts.

I was so happy I wanted to dance. Happy that the hunt was off, happy that Conrad had so neatly solved the problem of handling a hunting party that seemed more bent on destroying its members than any animals, happy that the hunting order which I had thought preposterous, and a sign of Conrad's insanity, had turned out to be a stroke of such brilliant strategy. Happy, too, that Lavinia had been so beautifully cheated out of her hunt, and in full view of her friends, and in a way that made her look so ridiculous.

She was dumbfounded. She stood gazing into the sky above the forest, a smouldering look in her face—as if seeing rather than hearing the sound of the departing truck. A sound that to me was like the wild ironic laughter of bush-crows flying away from a cornfield.

She swung round. " You slimy, loathsome, lying little trickster ! "

I realised suddenly that she was screaming at me, but I didn't care or protest. There was a big silly grin on my face, and I remember only being impressed by the fine alliteration of her unfair accusation. Cigarettes and Boots were standing behind her, and over her shoulder I caught the sly look in their eyes.

17

IT HAPPENED, incredibly, in the next second. Her words were still dinning in my ears, when a shadow, streaking across the stone floor on which the picnic was being laid out, struck dumb horror into us. I was the first to see it for it was directly in my line of sight, and some of the others saw it a fraction of time later; but the rest had no need to see it, for it appeared not so much as a material shape, but as a paralysing chill emanating from a tall flat-topped boulder about ten yards away. A movement in the buffalo grass, a glimpse of the fat, paint-brush tuft of tail, and it sprang with effortless strength to the top of the boulder. There was a sound of claws scraping on the rock for foothold, of loosened stones rattling down the side and splashing into the water; then it rose, lean and terrible, looking over our heads into the distance. It was huge—gaunt, filthy and mean-looking with a bitter, sunk mouth and a glint of madness in its shallow, pale-yellow eyes. Its famished body had shrunk on its frame, and festering sores slid with ghastly fluidity about the thick knobs of its protruding bones. Its haunches were thin and bony, with a high, narrow look that made its testicles seem monstrously huge. What must once have been a fine black mane was dry and ragged with dirty reddish streaks bleached into it, and matted hard around clusters of thorns and burrs. It was loathsome and sick and hungry and degraded and ugly. It might once have been the king of beasts but the last hideous season had turned it into a vicious, depraved felon.

For a time I could not estimate—it might have been minutes or seconds—it did not see us. I was astonished. There were fifteen of us, dressed in all colours, standing in the sunlight a few yards away from the rock, but it gazed over our heads, swaying a little and turning its shadow, clear as a paper cut-out, on the stone floor at our feet. Then I realised that the din of the waterfall had drowned our voices, that the spray and freak breezes created by the turbulent water in the chasm had confused its sense of smell—and I tried to think of a plan that would put this to advantage.

I looked around—with my eyes only—keeping dead still. I saw only eyes—livid, frozen, terrified, stunned, shocked, shrieking eyes. Nobody seemed to breathe, but I imagined I heard a panic of beating hearts like a roomful of clocks. I prayed for the terror to last a little while and keep everybody still, until we had a plan. Three of us had rifles, and the lion was a perfect target, propped up on the rock before us with no cover in front and the silver curtain of the waterfall behind. But we could not raise a gun—any movement would startle him, bring him crashing down on us, ripping and flailing into the soft-fleshed helpless crowd. It was a perfect shot—except that our cartridges were in our pockets and we couldn't lift a gun to aim. He had surprised us, not we him. *We* were cornered.

Then he saw us. His eyes found us by accident, narrowing and hardening in alarm. His jaws parted a little, his shoulders went taut, his heavy ragged head lowered and aimed a clouded, fear-laden look at us, his tail began a vicious low-slung back and forth sweep.

I caught looks from Cigarettes and Ruth, and by hunters' telepathy we began to communicate with one another. We understood certain things—we had to kill with the first shot; wounding would be a disaster, worse than not firing at all, for it would provoke him to attack us from his advantageous position; even killing entailed problems for there were sure to be other lion in the tall grass behind the rock. Cigarettes lowered his eyelids; his shaded eyes said we must shoot now. They said he was in charge, that the plan was to let Ruth shoot, that I was to cover the grass at the side, but if Ruth failed, shoot too. Ruth caught the message and confirmed it with her eyes. Cigarettes nodded his head fractionally, almost imperceptibly, towards Boots who was standing at the back of the crowd. The nod referred to the ground. We were ready.

A stone lobbed by Boots sailed over our heads and landed on the rock behind the lion. He swung round, taking his eyes off us, and simultaneously Ruth and I slid in the cartridges. The click of the bolts made him swing back with a spitting snarl. We waited while he glowered at us, the snarl becoming a slow resonant growl. Then Boots lobbed up another stone; it landed too far back, but the lion turned again, and in that split second Cigarettes dropped on his knee, picked up a stone and sent it whistling past me to land with a crack at the back of the boulder. The lion leapt round to look, bringing his whole body into view. Ruth and I raised our rifles, and I saw Ruth get steady, plant her feet firmly, aim, lowering the muzzle tip to allow for the short distance. It was easy, the whole lion pinned out in front of her like a chart in a butcher's shop, with the lethal spots ringed off. She took her time, making sure. But a shot rang out from the other side of me, and the lion dropped. The sound rocketed into the silent sky, disappearing in a series of rapid thudding echoes. It set off a riot in the forest, screeching monkeys, squawking flapping birds, yelping bushdogs, swishing branches; the forest shrieked and shivered but a moment later the noise was obliterated by the sudden hysterical pandemonium that broke loose in the crowd around me. I was not sure if the lion had been killed, and was worried because Ruth had not fired, so I kept my eyes and rifle trained on the tuft of brown mane, the inch of forehead, and the two peaked ears that showed over the edge of the boulder. But my senses were distracted by the screaming and yelling all around me, and the voices of Cigarettes and Boots telling everybody, in curious pidgin English, to keep quiet and not run away because the lion was not dead. The uproar sorted itself into individual sounds and meanings—a woman wailing, somebody saying, " Oh, my God! Oh, my God! " Somebody laughing hysterically, a whole agglomeration of shouts and excitement about the fact that someone had fainted, Ed Scobie screaming in a high, panicky voice, " Let's get the hell out of here ! " Meanwhile I saw the ears flick, the head raise a little to bring the pale murderous eyes into view, the thick paws crawl to the edge of the rock and then, like a declaration of war, the tail sweep up and swish angrily back and forth.

I heard the biting contempt with which Ruth said to Lavinia, " You stupid bitch. You *had* to shoot, didn't you ? I hope you missed. God, how I hope you missed." She spoke without shifting her aim from the tiny impossible target, without moving her eyes.

The noise around us dropped and once again we were standing in petrified silence, now made more achingly sharp by the knowledge that three guns had so far failed to cope with the danger, had in fact, increased it. I longed to have Conrad, my father and Forsythe with us at that moment. I could not guess what they would do, but it would be three more rifles and an extra fund of resourcefulness. I thought bitterly of Conrad's terrible mistake in luring us down to the waterfall, of his arrant misjudgment that the lion would be in some other part of the bush. The worst possible thing had happened—this picnic party, inexperienced, undisciplined, unarmed, had wandered into a lion's lair. I hated the responsibility, which I shared with Ruth and the trackers, of rescuing this panic-struck crowd from the consequences of Conrad's blunder.

Nothing except the tail moved on the rock. The eyes stared at us, unblinking, the tail swung back and forth, whip-like, counting. The lion had sunk down lower, pressing his belly flat on to the rock, and I began to think he might have been wounded in a way that paralysed his legs, that perhaps he was actually dying before our eyes—silently, uncomplainingly. But I rejected the idea—lion don't die like that.

I saw the tail lash in a new, angrier rhythm, and I tensed, expecting him to spring. My gun still covered the side of the rock, and I was tempted to shift aim and be ready to shoot if he leapt over the side ; but something restrained me.

It must have been an instinctive reaction to imperceptible

signs in the tall grass, for the next moment the grass parted and a lioness stepped out. I heard a shriek behind me, and at the edge of my consciousness was aware that somebody else had fainted, that Boots was holding his arms out to prevent the crowd stampeding. I knew, too, that the lion had crept nearer to the edge of the rock, that Ruth's rifle was level with my eyes, very steady, very straight, waiting for the precise instant when there would be enough of the target to make a shot possible— and that something was going on between Cigarettes and Lavinia. A whole lot of things were going on at the same time. But my attention was concentrated on the lioness. It, too, for the moment, was unaware of us. It crouched, bounded up the side of the rock, smoothly, easily, lifting itself to the top with a push of its hind leg on a projection half-way. As the body stretched out, the ribs defined clearly against the verminous skin, the black, flaccid teats swung against the shrunken belly. My rifle followed the ascending figure. I sighted on the heart-lung area and as the bunched, tight-muscled body paused at the top for balance, I fired. But I was too tense, and lifted my cheek off the butt a moment too soon ; I had flinched and my shot pulled up and back. I had two shells threaded between my fingers and I reloaded at once, but before I was ready, another shot rang out, and I caught sight of the smoking rifle at Cigarettes' shoulder—Lavinia's beautiful hand-chased Martini-Henry that he had grabbed out of her hand. The lioness rose on her hind legs, clawing the air and frantically shaking her head like a dog with an insect in its ear. Strangely, she made no noise—just went into a paroxysm of silent agony. The lion jerked up, but not to attack us ; he hurled himself on his pain-racked wife, snarling viciously and ripping at her with razor-sharp claws. I had not seen this happen before. I had heard about it—how a lion at the taut, nerve-strung peak of tension when cornered or wounded, will insanely attack anything that surprises it, even a member of its own family—but this was the first time I had witnessed it. It was a rare thing, and for us a miracle.

As he rose, Ruth's gun rose too, and with a beautiful fluid

motion she aimed, eased rather than squeezed the trigger, and
fired. But the lion had twisted out of sight behind the body
of the female, and her shot ripped into the female's shoulder.
The two animals rose up together, paws touching, gently,
almost as if in a minuet ; the female's back was towards us, and
I tried to fire past her into the chest of the male which I could
just glimpse. My brain and heart steadied and I did it right this
time. But the moment I fired they leapt at each other in a
snarling, spitting fury of grappling bodies, and I hit the female
again, now low in the back. She lurched upwards, twisting
violently, and I saw blood burble out of a small hole in the neck
where Cigarettes' shot had struck. A moment later I saw the
silver-wet glint of the wound made by my second shot, and
I knew she would not live.

Ruth was still waiting for a proper shot at the lion. Cigarettes
had lowered the rifle, for he had no more ammunition. The
frenzied, spitfire tussle went on a moment longer, then both
animals lost their foothold and went slithering and bumping
down the farther side of the rock, a helpless, flailing, ton-heavy
tangle of dinge-yellow bodies. They were obscured by the rock
so we could not fire, but somewhere on the way down the
lioness died. We saw her land upside down, crash her head on
the ground, crumple up and flop on to her back, then roll over
and lie on her side with her front paws crossed. The lion
struggled free from his dead mate and stood behind the rock
with his back towards us. All we saw was his tail swinging
back and forth into view from behind the rock. He just stood
there bewildered and desolate, slowly swinging that tragic tail.
Then he let out a roar—violent and shuddering, but breaking
off in a queer strangled cough—and suddenly he was gone. I
saw the high grass shiver as he ran through, heard twigs crack
in the distance, saw birds whirl up and then once more heard
the hard, forced, throat-wrenching cough that told us he was
probably wounded. After that, silence.

Suddenly I heard Jackson working on the pressure stove,
pumping fast as if to make up for the delay. It was a welcome
sound, for my only emotion now was hunger, and it was a good

way to bring the tension down. But I made him stop. The
danger was not yet over. I saw the crowd sitting close together
on the ground, with Boots standing behind them grinning over
their heads at Cigarettes. The crowd looked stunned and
vaguely ashamed of itself, like a gang of schoolboys that had
been rounded up raiding an orchard. They were very subdued
and manageable now; dazed and shaken, but the panic had left
them. Cigarettes returned Boots's look with an expressionless
face, solemn, dignified and beautiful as an archbishop. I saw
Marjorie looking at me keenly. She said "phew" very loudly
and raised both hands to me in a boxer's victory salute. My
shooting had been terrible, but to have started protesting would
have looked like heroic modesty, so I pretended to wring the
sweat off my forehead, and suddenly, from embarrassment,
pointed dramatically at my heart and did a nonsensical imitation
of a staggering, expiring lion. For some reason everybody was
looking at me, and that made me play the goat, but I caught
a cold look from Ruth who still had her rifle poised, and I took
control of myself, and motioned to the crowd to stay where
they were, indicating that there might be other lion in the
grass.

Cigarettes still considered the situation serious. He asked
Lavinia in sign language for some cartridges, and reloaded with
the rifle hanging from the strap in front of his chest. Then he
slid it round to his back, and climbed the boulder, gripping
both hands firmly on projecting rock and hoisting himself up
with a kind of scrambling baboon motion. Once on top of the
boulder he looked around carefully, then bent down and
pressed his palm against the spot where the lion had lain. He
held up his hand to show us that it was wet with blood. Now
we knew for certain that he was wounded. I asked Cigarettes
" Where ? " and he pointed to his stomach—a conclusion
reached both from observation of the shot, and from the
position of the pool of blood. He stood up again, with the
rifle held at his hip and shading his eyes with his hand,
began a careful scrutiny of the grass all around him. He did
it minutely and expertly; one could see his eyes cutting up the

area into small squares and ransacking each one thoroughly before tossing it away. At last he lowered himself down the side of the rock, stopped and raised the lioness's paw with his foot, while Boots came over; then they both went into the tall grass. Ruth and I moved back, with our rifles ready to get a wider view of the grass just in case Cigarettes had overlooked a lion or two, but they came out soon afterwards and made a signal that said "All clear."

Boots said that there was the spoor of a third lion in the grass, probably a large cub. It might have run away when the firing started, or perhaps had been waiting farther back in the grass from the beginning, but by now it would have joined the wounded lion, pacing it and nagging to keep it running. I felt sick at the prospect of trailing this gut-wounded horror of a lion; this was the worst and cruellest and bitterest kind of hunting. We did not know how badly he was wounded; he might take a long time dying, with the mounting agony in his bowels driving him insane. We would have to follow him on a clear blood spoor that would not let us lose him, knowing that he had become as single-minded about killing as we ourselves, and twice as cunning and ruthless; every copse of trees or shadow among rocks might be a death trap, and we would walk nervous of every step, our eyes turned inside out for every surprise and peculiarity in the bush, our skin twitching at every sound. It would be in the torpid heat of afternoon when the whole bush was in siesta, and we would have to move fast, with no rests, no let-up, yet ironically we would have to give him a start to let him bleed a little, sicken a little, to let the drain on his stamina counter his desperate death-wish to kill. And that other lion—or lioness—would be working for him, scouting, decoying, covering up and if necessary, fighting. If only we had a little elbow-room—if only we could wait until nightfall and trail them with hunting lamps we might have the advantage, but the lamps were in Conrad's truck, and Conrad was having a fine, carefree time miles away in the bush. Now I saw the whole gruesome idiocy of this hunt, dreamed up like a charity bazaar, or a project in amateur theatricals, in a drawing-

room full of town ladies and country-club gentlemen. This
was what happened when you ignored the basic principle,
when, like Lavinia, the Seckers and my father, you agreed to
hunt for motives that had nothing to do with hunting.

Lavinia was standing a little away from us but within earshot; she looked very pale and subdued. She had taken off
the suède jacket and carried it on her arm, and I could see how
scared she was from the sweat which not only showed in her
armpits but spread through her silk shirt right across her
breasts. I had never seen Lavinia, or any woman, sweat like
that.

She came up to us and said in a flat voice, " I suppose there's
nothing else to it—we'll have to go and finish him off."

Ruth said, " That's right, honey. He's your baby. That's
what comes from being careless with firearms."

Lavinia ignored her. She said to Jackson, " Do you know
the way home from here ? " When he answered, " No, missus,"
she stood biting her lower lip.

" You'd like to go home ? " Ruth asked. " I don't blame
you. It's going to be a messy business from now on, and I
quite understand that you don't want to get all dirtied up."
And she added in a sugary tone, " Go home and get some
beauty sleep. You must feel like a rag after last night."

" Oh, stow it," Hoffman said.

Lavinia spoke to me. " I'm not thinking about myself. What
are we going to do with all these people ? We can't leave them
here."

Somebody suggested, " Why don't we go back there and
wait in the cars ? We could turn on the radio or something."

" What—all afternoon ? " Ed Thornton said irritably.

" Perhaps all night too," I said. " Until we dispose of that
abdominal case. We owe it to him to put him out of his misery.
And we owe it to the local citizenry not to inflict this error of
judgment on unsuspecting wayfarers." I don't know why I
spoke in this stilted and vaguely sarcastic way. I suppose it was
because Ed Thornton was a much older man and I couldn't
be forthright, and because I was annoyed at how quickly the

Big House attitude was revived—impatience, selfishness and the demand to be amused all the time.

Lavinia was looking around. " Surely somebody knows the way home ? " she asked. She seemed to search among the faces around her, and finally her eyes settled on Cigarettes.

" No," I said, shaking my head. " We're going to need him. And Boots too."

" It's going to be an awful piddling bind just footling around in the jungle all day," Pamela Forster said.

I heard Ruth talking to Cigarettes in a mixture of Shona, and Fanagalo, sprinkled with English. " This female bush pig is asking if anybody knows the way home. But she wants them to say no so she can take them. She's too scared to go bulala that lion, so now she's walking backwards but trying to make us think it's forwards. First, she makes a buggerlo up by hitting him in the stomach and now she wants to let him go around and kill children and wives all over the district, while she goes home and drinks whisky and plays her glamofolo. Now, watch this."

She turned to Lavinia and said with a sweet smile, " I don't know what all the bother's about. Anybody here can find the way home. There are five sets of tyre marks showing the way as clear as a painted yellow line."

Lavinia said, " Thanks," without enthusiasm, and turning to Hoffman said, " I hadn't thought of that. That's right of course, that solves it. Let's have lunch first, then you can all go back home in the station wagons. I'll leave you to look after everybody, Frank."

" You don't have to come with us, really," Ruth said brutally. " We'll finish him off for you. Go back home and curl up your toes and have a good sleep. I'm sure you'd prefer to be with your friends." And she added as an afterthought, "Oh, but leave us your rifle. I'd like Cigarettes to use it. He's pretty good with it, isn't he ? "

" I agree with that," Hoffman said. " Look, Winnie—this isn't exactly your line of country, hunting lions. These people are *used* to this kind of thing, they're doing it in season and out, so why don't you simply leave it to the experts and come home with us ? " Angela Forster said, " I don't know—isn't there some sort of form about this ? Aren't you supposed to go after your wounded lion like the mounties hunt down their man ? " Kiki Pape said, " Oh, what rubbish. As long as he gets killed off, that's all. It doesn't matter who does it. You've wounded him and he'll probably die anyway, and that's a pretty good contribution if you ask me. Come on, Ducks, let's call it a day and get back home."

While they were speaking I heard Ruth telling Cigarettes, " Her friends are trying to get her to come home. But they are like friends who, while trying to save a drowning man, poke his eye out with a stick. She can't come home after this. She'll come with us, but she'll be like a crocodile with a broken back and will try and do everything to stop us reaching that lion. But she'll come."

Ruth was making me nervous. There was so much seething enmity in her that I wondered if it wouldn't be better to call off the hunt and let the lion roam. But I knew that it would be impossible to suggest it, that I should sound like Lavinia's friends and make it more difficult for her to refuse.

I knew that Lavinia had understood enough of what Ruth told Cigarettes to know that she was being mocked. But she did not react. She was very quiet and preoccupied. There was a subdued look in her eyes, and her arm hung limp at her side with her agitated hand twisting her rings round and round on her fingers. I had never seen her so shaken, not even when she first encountered a lion in those far-off novice days. But I saw that her fear was not merely the fear of trailing the wounded lion. Many things contributed to it—the shock of missing such an easy shot, the scare at exposing her friends to this experience, the dismay at seeing her plans go wrong, the irritation caused by Conrad's constant goading and teasing, the tension and tiredness caused by the crisis she had stirred up—her fear was built up in layers of various substance and thickness.

She said with sudden firmness, " It's no good arguing. I'm going to help finish off that lion. It just can't be helped. Let's eat and then we'll start. Or should we start right away ? " The question was addressed to me.

" No," I said. " Let him stiffen up a bit. Give him about three-quarters of an hour, then go. I'm hungry."

She said, " Well, as you say." And I realised that somehow I was taking charge of this hunt.

18

We did not go through the buffalo grass—it could have been dangerous with the grass over our heads and vision restricted to a few feet—so we looked for the spoor where the grass ended and found it on the beach five hundred yards downstream from the waterfall. Cigarettes and Boots knew instinctively that the lion would go that way, and they found the spoor without difficulty. There it was—loud as a clanging bell—two sets of paw prints impressed in the sand, scuffed from running, with a perceptible wobble about the larger tracks, and every forty or fifty yards, like a name tag tied round it, a spot of blood. I had expected to see more blood, but even this small amount did not necessarily mean that the lion was lightly hurt. The heat of a striking bullet often cauterises a wound, and gut-wounds tend to close up, anyway. The route was drawn for us on the soft white sand, and Cigarettes and Boots loped ahead on either side of the spoor, looking vaguely like two men paying out a rope. Each carried a twig and every time there was a blood mark they turned and pointed to it, then loped on. They were too fast for us but I kept our pace down to a steady walk, both to avoid getting winded too early and to allow our nervousness to settle. They would go out far ahead, often out of sight behind a curve of the river bank, then sit down and pelt stones into the water until we came up.

I had taken first place behind the trackers, with Lavinia second and Ruth last. We had not discussed it; we simply started walking that way. I thought that Conrad's order no longer applied, that, anyway, it was merely part of the ruse to detach Lavinia and Ruth from the hunting party. I had also decided to ignore the instruction to stay behind Ruth all the time. Everything was different now. I knew that I had to have authority in this hunt. It would have been impossible to give it either to Lavinia or Ruth—and I was going to have too much on my mind to play watchdog to Ruth.

As we walked on the hot sand I felt old hunting sensations revive.

I began to slip into familiar habits and attitudes, and into the mood of those early hunting days with Conrad, when every twist and turn of the spoor taught me something new about the bush. I had shot badly during the scare at the waterfall, but the shock and excitement had jerked me back into hunting ; I had the feel of the rifle again, the automatic knowledge of its weight and capacities, and I knew that I would be able to rely on my responses when the time came. My senses had burst out of a dull confinement of lethargy, and I felt alive, alert, receptive. I was hearing things again—distant sounds that came on the wind, minute sounds in the forest above the river bank, the sounds of insects, the river and the wind. I was smelling things too—a whiff of perfume from a flowering shrub, the faint tang of pollens in the air, the reek that hung about a cave where wild dogs had been, the faint fetid sourness at the roots of a fever tree where a crocodile had lain.

The spoor followed the river for nearly a mile, then turned off into marshy ground. As we squelched through the marsh a grey lourie screamed, " Go-away. Go-away"—not to us, but to the inhabitants of the marsh for whom he had appointed himself sentry. Weaver birds came pouring out of their communal nests, flying in swarms like midges. I saw bee-eater parrots lined up in rows on the branches and that eccentric Bohemian of the bush, the hammerhead, solemnly pushing his foot in front of him to dredge frogs out of the mud, while his wife lay down like a cat on some grass to watch him. Their nest was wedged between rocks nearby—a huge untidy cartload of sticks, mud, grass, papers, rags and tins, a shanty-town slum that took them six months to build. Marjorie had been delighted with the hammerheads at Malinda. What a waste this was !

The spoor left the marsh and came out on to stony scrubland, still dense with trees, but more like the country we had ridden through on our way to the waterfall. The spoor was thinning out now. For long distances the ground did not show paw marks and we followed a trail of dislodged pebbles, bent blades of grass and blood splashed on stones or grass. The trackers would come to a sign, examine it with no more than a glance, then change direction and go unerringly to a torn spider's web, a snapped twig, or a spot of blood on a stone forty or fifty yards away. Sometimes there seemed to be no spoor at all, but they went on without slackening pace and without hesitation, relying on the strange gift of animal mind-reading that told them how the lion would have behaved under the particular conditions of the terrain. They worked with all their senses and extra senses, threading through the bush like weasels, noiselessly, swiftly, finding a kind of camouflage in a nerveless economy of movement. It was uncanny, magical almost, and it brought back the picture of Cigarettes's gibbering trance and violent exorcism of spirit in the village that morning. The trackers gave a new dimension of mystery to the hunt. We hunted by mechanics and by the crude instruments of eye and ear. They employed instinct and intuition bred in them by an ancient hunting ancestry. I noticed how, as usual, they were taking the hunt away from us. We imagined that by giving them a few shillings we were employing them, that by giving orders we were directing the hunt. But they were the hunters, and we merely their baggage. They would manipulate us without our knowing it.

My mind was on the hunt and I was hardly thinking of Malinda and its feuds, when I heard from behind me, like the voice of an unwelcome visitor outside a window, " I think you ought to go up front, honey. That's how Conrad wanted it. You first—now go on."

There was a pause, then Lavinia said, " To hell with Conrad." "GET OUT FRONT ! "

I swung round to see Ruth holding her rifle at her hip, pointing it at Lavinia's back. Lavinia had stopped, half-turned

and was staring incredulously at Ruth. Her own rifle hung
from a strap over her shoulder. She stared at Ruth, then
suddenly wrenched it off and pointed it at Ruth.

With a white face Lavinia said, " If you do that again, I'll
drill you with both barrels."

I pushed myself between them and grabbed each of them by
an arm. " Stop this, both of you ! " I yelled. I snapped at
Lavinia, " Get up front." And to Ruth, " You stay here."
With a murderous look at Ruth, Lavinia walked away. I let
her go ahead then followed her, making it quite clear to Ruth
that I was going to stay between them. I caught up with
Lavinia and told her, " You'll be safe here." Then I fell back
again and as Ruth came up I said, " What the hell got into you
just now, pointing your gun at her ? Are you crazy ? "

She said, " I'm sorry, Gene. I didn't mean to point the gun,
it was by accident. But I thought she ought to go up front and
sweat a little, seeing she put us in this mess." She seemed
genuinely sorry, and for a moment I believed her.

But the second I left her I felt my heart thundering. Ruth
was an old hand and knew that you *never* pointed a gun at
anybody while hunting. You never did it even by accident,
for every novice knew how to carry a gun without endangering
others. I began to feel convinced that she *had* threatened
Lavinia, and that she had told me a lie. Once or twice on the
ride out I had gained the impression that she had become
unbalanced ; the same thought occurred to me now. I had
never seen her like this, so angry, bitter and cruel. Yes, cruel.
It was the last thing one would have thought about Ruth, but
there was cruelty in her face when she stood pointing that gun
at Lavinia. I didn't blame her—it was natural for her to loathe
Lavinia—but how was I going to handle this ? Were these two
women actually going to turn this hunt into an armed brawl ?
I knew that Ruth would have been overjoyed to see Lavinia
dead, and that it was the easiest matter to bring it about. But
my mind balked at such an extreme possibility. I simply could
not imagine her raising that rifle, aiming—and murdering.
Perhaps it *was* an accident. She too was upset—maybe I should

have made allowances. I walked on full of conflict and misgivings.

As we strung out in the easier country, I watched Lavinia about twenty yards ahead of me. She was walking badly, kicking up stones and twigs and she kept shifting her rifle from shoulder to shoulder as if it had grown too heavy. She had always walked better than this, even in her earliest novice days. But now she was walking mindlessly, like a sleep-walker. Ruth had definitely frightened her.

She was wearing the fawn suède jacket again; it shone dull gold in the sunlight, making a nice contrast with her golden-red hair. Those wide-flaring near-white jodhpurs were too conspicuous, but they gave her the right sporty look. She looked perfect for this hunt, or any hunt, like a magazine illustration. But her look was misleading, and I could see that she would soon tire and become a beautiful, ornamental nuisance.

I saw the new problem now. It would be madness to allow her the first shot. I made up my mind to keep right behind her and when the time came take the shot myself. There would be problems involved in this—among them keeping her out of trouble, for she would be exposed—but I did not try to work them out now, I just knew that in this hunt the usual courtesies were going to be suspended.

I saw the trackers waiting for us about a hundred yards ahead, pointing to something on the ground. As I came up I studied the spoor and saw that the blood spots were closer together, although no bigger, and that the prints meandered. The lion had started to get sick here. I found the trackers looking at a mess of greyish vomit, very thin and gruelly, with chewed leaves and grass and a blob of dark blood in it. A few yards away was a patch of flattened grass where he had lain down. He was weakening and slowing up. Normally, I would have been pleased with these signs, but as we walked on I found myself wishing that the lion would not be as sick as he appeared to be. Or that he was sicker. I was beginning to want him to do one of two things—to get away, or to die before we reached him.

This hunt was full of twists and ironies. A short while ago I has been enjoying it, but now I was hating it, and even trying to avoid it. I thought how odd it was that I, who had wanted the hunt least of all, who besides Conrad had been the only one to stand out against it, should find myself up to my eyes in it, taking charge, making decisions—and trying to cope with the utterly bizarre side problem of keeping two grown women from hunting each other instead of the wounded lion.

I marvelled too at the irony of becoming Lavinia's protector —Lavinia who had caused such heart-break in our family and had ended by ruining us, whose life meant misfortune and poverty to us, and whose death meant the return of Malinda. I thought of all the times I had wished for her death, and of all the methods I had devised for it—pushing her over the cliff at Monk's Castle, putting a snake in her bed, running her down with the tractor. I told myself that this was the chance, here was the hour for which I had waited for years, that I did not have to do anything deliberate, merely not extend myself to protect her. But I knew I was no more serious in wanting her dead now than I was when I basked in those fantasies. I would do what I could to keep her out of trouble, to guard her from the normal as well as abnormal dangers of this hunt, from the animal as well as human perils. Yet I hated her and would not have minded if she were killed.

The trackers were out far ahead. I watched them pulling away like eager hunting dogs until they went behind a clump of trees and disappeared out of sight. The spoor had become more erratic now, the blood spots bigger and closer together. I tried to imagine what kind of surroundings the lion would be in when we found them. I had not hunted in this area for many years, but one takes sharp, lasting impressions when hunting, and I remembered the country well. We were heading for a stony, treeless hill ; I liked that and hoped we should run him down there. It would avoid our having to approach him through thick bush. But I remembered that there was a cave there and possibly he was making for that. If he holed up in it, it would mean a siege. No, on second thoughts I hoped now that he would find some other place. Being sick, he would get desperately thirsty, and that would drive him over to the river ... but there were numerous possibilities and I gave up trying to theorise.

There was something in the bush ahead, something large and yellow and incongruous, and as I saw it I stiffened. But a few minutes later the stench told me what it was. A dead giraffe, not merely scavenged in the ordinary way so that its bones lay strewn about, but eaten out completely from the inside, leaving its thick, yellow-patterned skin spread out like a tent. Its long neck drooped forward, its head resting on top of a bush, its thin knobbed legs spread-eagled under it, acting as props that raised the hollow skin several feet above the ground. It looked just like a spectacularly coloured tent and was big enough to house a troop of Boy Scouts.

In fact, it housed a pack of wild dogs. As we passed they came streaming out, yapping and yelping in jittery uncontrolled excitement. They leapt up above the grass to look at us, springing straight up on all four legs, twitching their circular ears ; then yipping and twittering in a sudden scramble, they ran into the bushes. I was tempted to kill a few, just to show my disgust at these ferocious, hysterical pests who had infested the bush that year like a deadly virus.

As we walked on we saw the bones of antelope they had slaughtered, and then a bush-buck recently killed and devoured. I saw the unmistakable signs of killing by wild dogs, the loose broken tendons of the hind legs. I knew from this that we were not far behind the lion. The dogs had been disturbed in their meal as he came past, and had not yet summoned up the courage to return.

We came upon the trackers suddenly. As we passed a clump of trees we found them squatting in the shadow of a rock, wearing that serious, alert look that meant that the time for action had come. Cigarettes made a patting down movement with his hand, and as we knelt next to him, he pointed to some trees about a quarter of a mile away. There were shapes moving in the branches and a sense of agitation about the area that told me there was an intruder present. I peered at the trees through my telescopic sight. Great grey shapes of vultures moved in the branches and I could discern movements in the under-growth. A vulture glided up, flying sideways, then dropped like a stone back into the trees. High in the sky were tiny black specks—other vultures, recognisable by their slow, almost stationary flight.

In my excitement I slapped Cigarettes on the shoulder. I said to Ruth and Lavinia, " He's passed out. Isn't that decent of him ? " But Cigarettes shook his head gravely. I realised then that he might not have died. There could be some other corpse in the trees.

We approached the trees cautiously, taking cover behind the bushes and anthills. The trackers walked wide apart in order to watch the trees from different angles. As they wormed forward I kept up with them, and in so doing I overtook Lavinia. We walked level for a few minutes, then I left her behind. I watched the trees, but at the same time kept my eyes on the trackers, as one watches the conductor of an orchestra. I would act on signs from them, and at the right moment, take over. I had surrendered thinking to instinct, and I felt wonderfully calm.

The spoor led straight to the trees. It was clear and fresh now. Boots pointed to a bush and as I came up I saw a tuft of hair from the lion's mane stuck to a thorn. The fact that it had not blown away meant that he had passed there very recently. A few moments later the trackers came together and stood looking at something on the ground. When I reached them I saw that it was a heap of excrement, wet and flecked with blood, not half an hour old. There was no doubt now that the lion were in the trees ahead, but whether the one we had wounded was dead or alive I could not say. Judging by the excrement he had been very sick a short time before ; he might have died, but until the moment of death he would draw desperate strength from his pain and would kill blindly and viciously.

We were close to the trees when I heard a tense whisper

behind me. " Honey, I think you'd better give Cigarettes that gun."

" Keep quiet, damn you."

" Give it to Cigarettes. He knows how to use it. We can't take chances now."

" Will you shut up ! "

Ruth and Lavinia were about ten yards behind me. I dared not look round. They kept their voices down, but every sound make my flesh creep, and even that whispered altercation reached me with unnerving sharpness. Suddenly I heard, no longer in a whisper, "GENE, KEEP THAT WOMAN AWAY FROM ME ! " And the next moment Lavinia had broken cover and was running towards me, kicking up stones and trampling twigs with a sound like fireworks bursting, her near-white jodhpurs flashing like a flag in the sunlight. She reached me screaming, " *If she does that again I'll shoot her, I'll shoot her. So help me, I will.*" At the same time I saw the clump of trees gently explode in front of me. Birds flurried into the air, animals darted through the undergrowth, five or six vultures flapped up with a tearing and shuddering of branches and glided heavily and clumsily away, like damp newspapers caught in a gale. And then we heard him, his sick, strangled roar, rasping and screaming through the trees, and a moment later the firm young roar of his companion. The trackers looked at each other, then turned to us, their bodies sagging in despair.

I pulled Lavinia down behind the bush, and kept my gun trained in the trees, hoping and praying that the lion would not come out this way. Lavinia was shivering and clutching my arm. I pushed her hand away, then her thigh that was pressing against my leg, and concentrated on the commotion in the trees. I saw Ruth kneeling behind a bush about five yards to my right, calmly, deliberately getting ready to shoot. She was very steady, nerveless and self-controlled. Lavinia was crouched beside me, her eyes closed, her breath coming in short chopped gasps. She was hysterical and I thought, "Oh, God, don't let them come out this way, please don't let them come this way," because I knew that she would crack completely if they did, and perhaps run out, or scream, or do any demented thing. I patted her shoulder soothingly and whispered, " Don't worry, we've got this under control. Just keep calm." She took a deep breath and forced out a little smile, and after that seemed better. We sat and waited and at last heard the sound that told me my prayer had been answered—a shuddering passionate roar coming from the other side of the trees.

The trackers came back and I had a quick conference with them. They were disappointed and very disgusted. I pretended to agree with them, but in truth I was relieved : I was convinced now that we would have to stop this hunt, that the usual bush chivalry of killing off wounded game would have to be ignored. The trackers wanted to go straight on. It was a hot spoor and they were excited and thought we could catch him in the next fifteen minutes. They were hunters and wanted to kill him, not merely find his corpse. I said, " Wait a minute," and went back to Lavinia.

I asked her, " Do you want to go on ? We can turn back and call the whole thing off, if you like."

She said, " I don't know." Her eyes darted momentarily towards Ruth.

Ruth was standing a few yards away, watching with her hands crossed over the top of her rifle. There was a faint smile on her face, half amused, half contemptuous.

I said to Lavinia, " What happened ? "

She did not answer, so I turned to ask Ruth. But Lavinia suddenly burst out in a high, shrill voice, " That woman's mad —stark raving mad. I'll kill her, Gene. I can also use a gun. Don't let her try that business with me. I'm not frightened of her." Suddenly she grabbed her rifle and held it trembling towards Ruth. " You fat ugly cow," she screamed, " leave me alone ! "

Ruth did not move. I pushed the rifle aside with the palm of my hand and asked Ruth, "For God's sake—*what's happened?*"

" That's what I'd like to know," Ruth answered.

" I'll tell you what happened," Lavinia said, making an effort to control herself. " She tried to shoot me. She had her gun trained on me. I saw it—she was waiting for you to fire, and at the same moment she was going to let me have it. She's been planning this all afternoon ! "

I said angrily to Ruth, " I'm going to tie you up. I'm going to take your gun away and get the trackers to help me truss you up until all this is over. And then we'll hand you over to the police."

" Oh, shut up, Gene," Ruth said. " I never did anything of the kind. She's imagining things. She got in my way for a moment, that's all. She wasn't looking where she was going—it was her fault. As soon as I saw her I dropped aim. Let's get moving. We're wasting time." She started laughing, not ironically or affectedly, but out of plain amusement.

I was not sure who to believe, but I said to Lavinia, " I think it was a mistake for you to come with us. But you can go back now if you want to. We can call the whole thing off. If that's what you want just say it. It's all the same to me—just say it, one way or the other. You're not in the mood for hunting to-day, that's all there is to it."

" I don't know," she said. She seemed a little rueful and embarrassed as though realising that she had been mistaken. She stood up and said, " Perhaps we'd better finish the job. But don't put me first."

" You can go last," Ruth said. " That should make you happy. Only don't plug *me* in the back."

" Okay, let's get cracking," I said.

I walked on feeling better about the new arrangement, and relieved at what I thought was Ruth's change of attitude. It did seem like a mistake, and Lavinia herself seemed to have admitted it. It had frightened Ruth too, and I hoped that for the rest of the hunt she would drop her hostility to Lavinia.

But as we came to the trees she said, from close behind me,

" I still think she ought to give Cigarettes that rifle. I'm going to insist."

I said angrily over my shoulder, " Ruth, get this straight— *I'm* giving the orders to-day. Now, once and for all, shut up ! "

" You're getting very big for your boots," she said.

" Maybe. Now, just pipe down."

19

THE TREES were silent as a tomb when we entered but by the time we reached the spot where the lion had rested the first vultures had begun to return. They glided in silently through the leaves, casting huge shadows over the dappled shade and sat hunched on the branches waiting for us to go. I saw that neither of the lion had killed here—they had stopped to eat off a bush-buck that had been killed by wild dogs. The loose dangling hooves, the gnawed tendons and lacerations on the backs of the legs left no doubt that this was the dogs' prey, and that the lion had frightened them off. Only the younger lion had eaten. The other had tried but had become violently sick and had lain down to rest under a bush nearby. There were several pools of vomit around the flattened grass, and this time he had spat up flesh as well as blood. The bush was lacerated and still wet with his saliva : in his agony he had chewed on leaves and branches. The whole place stank not only from the carcass but from the smell of death that the lion carried with him. I could not make up my mind about him. He was a huge lion, probably a buffalo killer, and seemed to have built up a desperate stamina in his grim struggle for life during the drought. From the signs around us he should have been near death, but he had got away fast and his wild passionate roar had made it clear that there was still much life in him. I stood shaking my head sadly, thinking, " Why did we have to start conclusions with *this* one ? " Cigarettes looked at me and nodded, the same thought in his eyes. We left the clump of trees to the vultures and to the second pack of wild dogs that we could hear yipping in the distance.

We came out into scrub country again. Now straight ahead was the hill that I remembered from years before, and the spoor still headed towards it. The hill was a geological freak, like many in the area—a huge granite sphere completely bald, standing on a flat platform of rock with smaller, perfectly rounded boulders strewn about like an abandoned game of giant marbles. The cave, as I remembered it, was on the other side, and I trained my telescope on the rock platform for signs of life. But I saw nothing.

We were on higher ground here and could see the spray of Crampton Falls about four miles away to our right; it made a pearl-grey cloud filled with rainbow colours swirling above the craggy skyline. The air above was specked with vultures coming in to feast on the dead lioness. It was a good day for the vultures.

I looked at my watch—it was four-fifteen. We had taken an hour and a half from the waterfall, and there were still about two and a half hours of sunlight left. I made a number of decisions. We would hunt for another hour, then turn back whether we found the lion or not. If they were in the cave I would leave them there and come back with Conrad to-morrow morning to finish them off. I would not go too fast nor try too hard, and would avoid taking risks. If we found them in circumstances that made it safe and easy to shoot we would finish the job that afternoon: otherwise, call it off and come back to-morrow. I was prepared to be a thorough-going coward if the circumstances required it. And at the first sign of fresh trouble between Ruth and Lavinia I would turn back immediately.

I called the trackers and told them what I had decided. They nodded, with that look of bland, unsmiling assent which meant that they acknowledged the instructions without agreeing with them. They would try to carry them out, but would find it difficult to put a curb on themselves, to hunt with reservations. I knew that I would have to watch them carefully if I was not going to be lured by them into changing my plans.

We walked on.

Mechanically we followed a blood spoor that had been laid down hardly fifteen minutes before. It behaved peculiarly—aiming for the hill, turning off suddenly, meandering and swinging back, over and over in a recognisable pattern. The trackers ambled ahead, stopping to examine bloodstained leaves as if each were a major discovery, collecting feathers and sticking them in their hair, tracking very intensely when the spoor was as wide as a city street, pretending to lose it and making a showy display of finding it again, fanning out in a wide circle and picking it up eventually at the point they had left off. I let them play the fool, and I kept looking at my watch.

Everything was quiet, the hunt became placid, and I walked with the feeling that at last I had the situation under control. I weighed up the various aspects of the hunt as if they were factors in an equation, balancing dangers against precautions, fears against facts, and the answer seemed to be that this nightmare hunt would fizzle out without anybody coming to harm. The terrain, on the whole, suited us, being wooded enough to provide cover for approach, but not so much so as to require a close, groping, dangerous approach. If they took cover in the region of the hill it would be easy to corner them, unless they holed up in the cave. In that case we would suspend operations until next morning. We had a first-class shot in Ruth, who despite her uncertain mood would forget everything except killing the lion when the time came—as she had done at the waterfall. We had two of the best trackers in the business. True, they would want to take the hunt to its limits, and might have to be held back ; but in an emergency they would be cool and resourceful and worth a platoon of hunters. The lion himself was violently dangerous, was fighting death with impossible obstinacy and if provoked could be expected to explode like a land-mine up to the last second of his life. But he was sick, his strength was draining out, and time was on our side. The other lion was just a lion. We had all hunted lion before, and he presented no special problems. Lavinia had gone to pieces, might do any stupid hysterical thing in a new crisis, as she had done in the last two. But she was cared for by the

decision not to run risks, not to hunt in difficult terrain, and by
the fact that she was last in the line. I had that rare good feeling
of confidence that comes to one, for no explicable reason, on
certain hunting days, and I felt comfortable in the knowledge
that the others had accepted my leadership and that I had plans
for any contingencies.

But half an hour after leaving the trees my carefully contrived
system of self-assurance went skidding away from under me.
I saw the trackers stop fooling and examine the ground with a
tenseness that made me hurry to them. Cigarettes pointed to a
mark. I recognised the print of the rope-soled boots that I had
studied only that morning as I walked behind my father from
the Retreat to the Big House. A few yards farther Boots found
the deep-cut pattern of Mac's new brown shoes. Then we saw
the signs everywhere, the paw marks of the dogs, a discarded
shell carton, Conrad's dapper footprints, and finally at a point
where they must have rested, several butts of cigarettes, among
them one of the squat Turkish kind smoked by Forsythe. We
had walked into the tracks of Conrad's hunting party. The trail
cut in from the left, from the direction of the river, and
appeared to be making for the hill, just as we, and the lion, were.
But they had been there a good time before us : it was difficult
to say how old the tracks were, but they were already covered
with dust and dry grass, and at one point the lion print was
pressed neatly in the middle of Mac's fancy patterned footprint.
The spoor told the curious tale of the lion stalking the hunters.

Cigarettes and I climbed into a tree and we surveyed the
countryside with my telescope. I could not see the party, but
away in the distance I made out Conrad's truck half-hidden
behind some trees near the river. I judged that it must have
taken them about half an hour to reach this point, and by that
means fixed the age of the tracks at about an hour. Conrad's
party were therefore three or four miles away at the most,
assuming they went in a straight line. If they took a round
course, or had turned back, they would be nearer. They might
be anywhere in the vicinity.

As we walked on I saw that it was not by accident that

Conrad's group had come this way. Under their tracks, and under those of the lion, was another older lion spoor. I sorted it out as we walked, and saw that the old spoor was that of three lion; a heap of dried dung told me that it was about two days old; and the general direction, back to Crampton Falls, convinced me that it was the path of the lion family on their doomed expedition to the waterfall.

For some reason I felt acutely uneasy. I could find no place for this in my scheme of thinking; there were now so many possibilities that I had the unnerving sensation of blundering blindly through the bush. I *ought* to have been glad at the news —at the knowledge that we had allies, at the possibility that they might run the lion down and kill him themselves. But I had never been in a situation like this, I had no experience to draw on, and hence couldn't think how to deal with it. The fact that they were walking away from the lion disturbed me. And, generally, I was upset by the idea that they were stalking in the bush without knowing about us, and that any plans I might make could be upset by some unexpected action of theirs. Everything was back in the realm of chance, risk and uncertainty.

Ruth came up to me and said with a serious face, " Couldn't we flag them or something ? "

" I don't know where they are. We can't just walk with a flag flying. Besides, the cat would see and it might tempt them to jump us."

" We'd better go careful now," she said, falling back and taking her position in the line.

I looked over my shoulder at Lavinia. Strangely, she seemed more composed now. I told myself that it must be because she had stopped worrying about Ruth. And I reflected that she might end by getting her hunt after all—the outsize carnival hunt with Forsythe, my father, Mac—even Conrad—all thrown in together with ourselves. For there was a chance that we might meet up with them, reorganise and finish the day in a grand joint effort. Maybe that pleased her. She was walking normally now, and seemed rather jaunty, and I had the thought that she might even become a useful member of the party. The main thing was that she was not hysterical now and Ruth was leaving her alone. I was glad to have that problem off my hands.

The lion did not go up to the hill. At the last moment the spoor turned off and went back down to the river, parting from that of Conrad's group which veered off the other way around the base of the hill. I had allowed for this. A wounded lion would thirst desperately, and although the cave might have had its appeal as a safe hiding place, the need to be near water would be the deciding consideration. I realised that this dilemma had been evident in the spoor all the way from the trees.

We followed the lion spoor.

There was no particular point at which the terrain became difficult, or the conditions dangerous. As we approached the river the trees got bigger, the bush denser, the grass higher— that was all. Before noticing it, we were pushing our way through tall reeds that limited our vision to a few feet. And suddenly we were on the lion. There was no point at which we could have pulled back, because the situation did not develop in stages ; it grew insidiously around us, while the spoor hypnotised us and our legs kept walking. And suddenly there were the lion, and the issue was joined and there was no retreat.

We did not see them. There was some dense bush growing around a heap of boulders, with an old acacia tree rising out of the middle, and a fringe of seven-foot-high buffalo grass. Farther back there were other boulders piled up by some clumsy natural masonry into the vague shape of a wall, and beyond that a strung-out line of trees. That was all we could see above the tall grass. We were near the river and the trees farther away were full of birds. But the acacia was deserted and a tense silence clung to the area around it. Then suddenly we heard them—a growl that was really a groan, and the short anxious rumble of a second throat. The two sounds merged into one then stopped at the same moment and dropped into the silence.

Cigarettes and Boots froze then sunk to the ground ; I was crouched down with my rifle over my knees. Ruth and Lavina were behind me in the reeds, but out of sight. There was no noise or movement behind me ; they too must have heard the sound and taken cover. Near me was a rock that rose above the reeds. One side was a gradual slope that ended almost at my feet ; the top was covered by the leaves of a tree that grew close up against the sheer side. I saw Cigarettes looking at the rock, then at me, then at the rock again, his eyes moving from bottom to top. I understood the message, which corresponded with my own idea, and got ready to climb to the top. I slipped out of my rucksack and lowered it quietly to the ground, took off my belt, cut some branches off a bush and stuck them around my hat, slipped some shells into my hand and pressed up the safety-catch on my rifle. I climbed very slowly and carefully, moving loose stones out of the way before crawling up, stopping every few inches and edging the rifle up ahead of me.

When I reached the top I peered cautiously over the edge, down through the leaves, into the bushes around the acacia tree. The lion were not there. I examined the rough wall of boulders farther back, but there was no movement and no sign of them. Carefully I searched the reeds and buffalo grass all around me, but without success. I conducted a second examination, dividing the area up into small sections and studying each one separately, as I had seen Cigarettes do at the waterfall, but saw nothing, and decided that we must have been mistaken.

I was about to climb down when I heard a sound below me, a soft but nevertheless tense purr. I wormed my way forward until I was able to peer down the side of the rock. Then I saw them, almost directly under me, on a rock ledge with a small cave behind, and a ridge of rock and bushes in front. It was a perfect hiding place ; they could never have been seen except from on top of the rock. The wounded lion was lying stretched out with his head on his paws, breathing heavily. The other stood over him, glancing back and forth between his sick charge and the hedge of bushes in front of him. He was a good lion, this second one, about two years old, strapping and wiry, with the huge, narrow look of the older one. They must have been father and son. I saw the wounded lion raise his head heavily off his paws, look round with glazed eyes, then let it slump back. I edged back, and the tiny sound of a button dragging on the rock caused the son to whip around and stand facing the rock, viciously swishing his tail.

It was impossible to get a shot from the ground on our side of the rock. And to have leaned out to aim from above would have alerted them and sent them back close to the wall, or into the cave. I was thinking what to do. Possibly we would have to creep round and try and get them from the front. And suddenly the hunt was over.

I saw it all from above, a sudden whirlwind of happenings rushing with ghastly blind certainty to a foredoomed climax. I heard tense voices below me, and looking down saw Lavinia run out of the reeds. I heard Ruth's angry whisper, *"Come back—you'll get killed—oh, you bloody stupid fool . . ."* and glimpsed the brown leather of her sleeves falling helplessly out of sight into the reeds. I saw Lavinia run past the ledge, below the lion, but hidden from them by rocks, bushes and reeds, into a patch of buffalo grass about fifteen yards the other side—and the grass open to reveal Mac, crouching with a rifle. I saw the whites of his startled eyes, and some frantic frightened movement of his hands and gun, then Lavinia turn back in wild terror and stumble up on to the ledge. The next moment, all at one time, the dogs were whippeting through the grass, a shot roared out, and then two more, and a shriek—all so close together that they made one booming screaming sound that rocketed into the air and tore the world apart and Lavinia lay dead with blood seeping through her golden suède jacket, and the lion, both of whom had reared up at the instant of the first shot, toppled back and lay dead on top of one another—all before the dogs could reach the ridge.

Looking where the shots had come from, I saw Conrad standing behind the wall lowering the rifle and peering into the reeds with his keen, clever hunter's eyes—a smile of smug triumph on his face. Next to him, Forsythe grinning, and a few yards away to their left, my father, wearing his first smile of the day. It had been magnificent shooting.

I knew, because his had been the first shot, that Conrad had killed Lavinia.

And that Forsythe and my father had between them killed the two lion. It was clever, skilled, lovely opportunist hunting. Only superb hunters, taking instant advantage of a fleeting glimpse of three golden-brown bodies, could have achieved such a feat of perfect shooting.

20

ON THE WAY BACK from Crampton Falls I sat next to Conrad, looking at him hard and weighing him up mercilessly, as he always did with other people. Lavinia's death was an accident, of course. Nobody could blame Conrad. There *must* have been three lion hidden behind the rocks and bushes on that ledge. Hadn't they spoored three lion all the way from the river, past the freak hill, half-way back to Crampton Falls before deciding it was too late and turning back to the truck? So when they heard those unmistakable grunts and coughs near the acacia tree, how could they know that one of the lion had been shot at the waterfall? They had heard our shots, naturally, but that was only those idiotic picnickers fooling around—shooting birds, perhaps, or firing at trees—with the guns of the three dupes who had been so neatly dropped out of the hunt. Who could have guessed that those shots killed one of the lion and wounded another? Normally you have to hunt a long time before coming across a lion—sometimes for weeks : lion don't just amble up to a crowd of picnickers and insist on being shot. There had been three spoor and that meant three lion, and it was as good as a certificate by a notary. Who was to know that Lavinia, Ruth and I were hunting a gut-wounded lion right there, under their noses? We were out of the hunt, having a lazy afternoon among the scenic wonders of the waterfall. Hadn't Conrad fixed it that way? And when that fawn-coloured jacket moved fleetingly through the reeds, who could blame him for mistaking it for a lion and getting in that splendid, lightning-quick, difficult shot? How was he to know that Lavinia, convinced that Ruth wanted to kill her, would crack under the strain, panic at being left alone with Ruth, and do such a damn' fool thing as run from cover when there were lion hiding in the reeds a few yards away. You couldn't blame him, or the others, for anything, except drawing reasonable conclusions from straightforward facts, for not expecting the utterly unforeseeable, and for being such wonderfully keen-eyed hunters.

Yet I did blame him. He had taken it on himself to master-mind everything, to order events to behave as *he* wanted them to, and I saw that this arose from an overblown conceit that was as dangerous as any more obviously evil fault. I had been distressed when Marjorie called him an "opinionated old fool," but I agreed with her now. I accepted the judgment that the day passed on him. It made an absurdity of his plans, rejected his claim to impose his will on people and events, and belittled him as a hunter, the role in which he thought himself infallable. All his elaborate precautions and manœuvres had become sign-posts leading to the very tragedy he had tried to avoid. As a final ironic joke, fate turned his own trickery on him and made him shoot Lavinia. For the first time in my life I saw him as vulnerable and overrated and rather ridiculous.

Of course he had done it only for our protection. He had acted as usual with great perception and skill. He was quite right to be nervous of a hunting party so laden with animosities; and to be suspicious about the way the hunt was suggested at the Big House. He reacted like all of us in thinking there was something sinister in Lavinia going to fetch Mac. It was a clever move winning Forsythe away from Lavinia when there was the strong suspicion that she must have had some special motive in bringing a professional hunter out to Malinda. It was good strategy to unsettle her on the ride out in the hope that she would call off the hunt ; and he solved the problem brilliantly with that odd hunting order which enabled him to get rid of those who might cause, or be the cause of trouble. That was a masterstroke. He was right, all the way, except that things didn't work out as he expected them to. How could anybody be so right and yet so wrong ? Who was to know that the lion wouldn't follow the script, but would take it into their heads to put on a show of their own and lead us right into the guns of Conrad's party? Or that Mac would get carried away by being given a rifle and would creep too far out to steal a shot for himself? Conrad had expected trouble from Ruth, not that Lavinia would lose her wits at precisely the wrong moment. Things didn't pan out as expected, that was all: he was unlucky. But Conrad himself was the last man to accept an excuse like that. He made no allowance for luck or accident in other people. And however you viewed it, it would not have happened at all if Conrad had not taken it on himself to do the thinking for everybody. You couldn't criticise him on any particular point, except that the result was wrong. Yes, there was a flaw in it, a flaw in him, that made all his actions mistakes.

Cigarettes would never have made these mistakes. Cigarettes was a figure out of a boys' comic with his horns and skins and phials of medicines and terrifying bush magic. In all his life he had never read a book or written a line. I had never heard him speak a sentence of more than ten words. But he had a philosophy that was superior to Conrad's. He understood his world better than we could ever hope to do. Better even than we understood our own. He knew that in Africa at any rate, Nature still controlled life, that it had not changed its way in deference to the small groups of white settlers who had come to live briefly in some scattered areas. He did not expect the laws of the bush to submit to human thinking and planning; life was a swirl of erratic forces, a turbulent surge of growth against the boulders of death—violent, unpredictable, headstrong. So he refused to be precise or to place faith in plots and plans. He lived from minute to minute and reacted to dangers or emergencies as they arose, and did so with the whole of his body and nerves and instincts, and not just with his head. For all his mysticism and superstition, he was a realist. Conrad, although he would violently deny it, was the romantic.

It was hard to read Conrad's emotions as we drove back to Malinda. It was dark then and he drove carefully with a battery

of headlamps scouring a tunnel of light through the encircle-
ment of trees. The lights seemed to etch a diagram of his
moods on the road ahead, dipping slowly as if cautiously
exploring a line of thought, jerking up as if suddenly saying
" No," feeling and probing into the trees as if seeking a way
out of a dilemma. He did not show signs of distress, but he
was very quiet and there was an ominous anger about him.
There was no indication of regret in his expression or in anything that he had said. All the rest of us had felt that we were
responsible in some way, and had said so. But Conrad who
had fired the shot, and had unwittingly planned the whole
disaster, said nothing in self-reproach. I wondered what he
was thinking. Maybe he was angry at the bush for daring to
do this to him, maybe he was coldly and methodically analysing
the collapse of his plans in the same way he would hold a post-
mortem on a case he had lost. I could not say if his thoughts
were concerned with Lavinia.

There were only Conrad and myself in the front, and Lavinia
alone, and lonely, covered with a blanket and strapped to the
bed behind. At Crampton Falls, Ruth and Forsythe had
changed over to the Land-Rover, and my father to the jeep.
Cigarettes, Boots and the other Africans, who had refused to
travel with the body, were divided between my father and Ruth.
It seemed strange to see Lavinia now, so deserted, when all
her life she had been surrounded by friends. And lying on
Conrad's bed, with the rifles neatly arranged in the rack
beside her, the stainless steel washbasin at her head, and all the
tidy, space-saving gadgets in their proper places around her.
It was all too peaceful and unsensational, a painstakingly
arranged tableau, rather like the interior of one of those show
caravans. I imagined the scene at the Big House at that
moment : everybody sitting around looking at their watches.
waiting for Lavinia to come back and wake up the evening.
By now the events at the waterfall would have been cut up
and parcelled out among them. Each would have his own
version and his own way of telling it, with characteristic
trimmings and wisecracks, all ready to take home from Malinda,

like picture postcards. All would agree that the day at Crampton Falls had been the making of the holiday. But they would wait for Lavinia to come back and tell the sequel to complete the experience.

Conrad was incredible. Only he would have had the presence of mind to act as he did after the shooting. Since it was an accident—and everybody could see that—he took all the proper steps to get the facts on record. He fetched his truck which was only a few hundred yards away, and unpacked his Leica, a reel tape-measure, and his leather-bound loose-leaf journal. He took numerous photographs from different angles, showing the scene from the spot where he fired, from either side of the ledge, illustrating how Lavinia lay, how the lion were found. In his note-book he wrote a description of her jacket, made observations on the height of the grass and reeds, the condition of the light. He measured everything—the distance between Lavinia and the lion, between Lavinia and the wall from where he fired, the height and length of the ridge, the distance between the point where she crouched with Ruth and where she was killed. He drew a diagram of the scene showing all the points and distances, with an explanatory key underneath. When he finished, he asked us all to sign the pages of the note-book as being "true and correct."

He was a methodical man, and a lawyer. Perhaps another man would have been too distraught to think about preserving the evidence for a possible court case, but there was no doubt that this was the correct thing to do. This was known as having a cool head, and Conrad was noted for his icy calm in a crisis. When he finished I tipped my hat to him. I was most impressed and made a mental note to do the same if ever I accidentally shot a lady.

He refused to speak to me on the way back. Once or twice I tried to get him to talk, but he ignored me. He wouldn't even talk about things like the Seckers, or the future of Malinda. He was very angry about something.

The first person we saw on our return was Bill Secker, who had

x

driven out to meet us. We found him parked on the road about
three miles from Malinda. Conrad pulled up and Bill got out
of his car and climbed on the step of the truck. " I thought you
people had got lost, or got gobbled up by that cat," he said,
with a big smile of relief. Obviously he had heard about the
incident at the waterfall from the picnickers. He asked, " Tell
me, did you get that son-of-a-bitch in the end ? What happened ? " While talking he looked round inside the truck ; his
face fell then brightened again. " I suppose she's back there ?
Lavinia, I mean." The other vehicles had drawn up a little way
behind us, and he leaned back and peered into the lights, but
I saw his face fall as he realised that she could not be in Ruth's
Land-Rover or my father's jeep. He asked in a puzzled voice,
" Where *is* Lavinia ? "

Conrad said very precisely, " You'd better steady yourself,
Bill. Lavinia's dead."

I saw Bill close his eyes and sway, hanging on to the door-
handle, as if he were going to faint.

Conrad went on, " She's been shot. It's most distressing,
but it was an accident, of course."

Bill acted as if he hadn't heard properly. He stuck his head
inside the window, then wrenched the door open and slumped
into the seat next to me. I felt him shivering all over, and he
kept opening and closing his mouth as if trying to speak.
Eventually a silly distorted grin came into his face, and he
asked, " Are you kidding ? Go on, I don't believe it. You're
kidding."

" I'm not kidding," Conrad said, nodding his head towards
the back of the truck. Bill swung round violently, and as he
stared at the form on the bed, Conrad said, " Unfortunately it's
true. I had no warning she was there ; I saw a movement in
the grass and mistook it for a lion."

" You ? "

" Yes. It was unavoidable in the circumstances."

Bill looked back and forth between Conrad and the bed with
the same strained incredulous look, as if still wanting to be
told that Conrad was kidding. But suddenly he got into a

clumsy rage and lunged in front of me to give Conrad a loose
slicing blow on the chin. Conrad caught his arm by the wrist,
and said, " Stop this, Bill. Control yourself."

" Ah, get to hell," Bill said, wrenching his arm away. He
glared at Conrad in wild disbelief, then flung the door open
and climbed out of the truck. He slammed the door then
climbed the step again and said through the window, " You
dirty bastard," then jumped off and walked like a drunk man
to his car. As he did so I heard Ruth sound the horn behind
us. Bill took no notice ; he started the car and drove slowly
for about twenty yards, then suddenly accelerated and drove like
a dervish to the Big House. As he drew out in front of us I
heard Ruth frantically and pathetically blaring the horn to
attract his attention.

By the time we reached the Big House everybody had heard
the news from Bill. The whole crowd was waiting for us on
the veranda steps. I could tell from their faces that nobody
believed it was an accident. At first they refused to speak to us.
They came round to the back and stared into the truck and
then at us, clearly suggesting that we were murderers. But
nobody said a word. Then Kiki Pape climbed inside and
pulled the blanket down, and as she saw Lavinia's face she gave
a wild terrible wail and collapsed over her, sobbing and kissing
her eyes and cheeks. We stayed in the cabin, and after a few
minutes Hoffman and Ed Scobie came round and spoke to us.
Hoffman told Conrad in a tense, choked voice, " You'll hear
more about this, don't worry. We're going to see that this
little affair is very thoroughly investigated."

Conrad said, " Quite right. I don't blame you. And if it
puts your mind at rest, I'm going to report the matter myself
and give the police a full statement, supported by photographs,
diagrams and measurements. You may accompany me if you
wish."

Forsythe had been standing in the dark a few yards away,
listening with his hands on his hips. Suddenly he stalked up.
" Listen, mister," he said to Scobie, " you got any complaints,
take them to the police, see ? Against him or me." He jabbed

his thumb against his chest. " Don't stand there beefing about
things you know nothing about. Is that clear ? Anything you
wanna say save it for the police." Then he turned round and
spoke with unexpected gentleness to the crowd. " Now, please,
folks, don't all stand around like this. Go inside while the body
is moved. It will only upset you to watch. Now, please go
inside." They drifted away.

I noticed my father standing near the truck on Conrad's side.
He was very upset. Even in the faint light that filtered down
from the veranda I could see the lifeless pallor in his face. He
seemed to be in the same mood of helpless despair that I had
mistaken for illness when I interrupted the argument between
him and Conrad early that morning. It reminded me, too, of
that ride in the jeep from Umtali to the Bell Hotel when I
caught my first glimpse of the ominous sickness of spirit that
had recently afflicted him.

Hoffman, Scobie and two other men moved the body off the
bed, but I did not turn round to look at them. Instead I
watched the crowd move slowly, in a stunned bewildered way,
up the veranda steps. Marjorie lagged behind them, the tallest
of the group, walking dejectedly with her hands in her pockets
and dragging her feet. She had not come near me nor looked
at me while I sat in the truck. Lavinia's death had come down
like a wall of ice between us.

Conrad and I must have looked cold and unsympathetic
sitting in the truck, but I knew it would be a mistake to offer
to help the men behind. I had never felt so hated and despised
in my life, and I sensed that it would only provoke an insult
if I joined them. Nevertheless, I got out of the truck and stood
watching them from a few yards' distance, then I strolled away
into the garden.

I was still near the truck when I heard a hubbub on the
veranda, Kiki's voice raised angrily and people trying to
restrain her. I saw them lead her into the house, but a moment
later she came running out again, sobbing and shouting. Her
friends followed, trying to hold her back, but she pulled away,
ran down the steps and across the lawn to the truck. I thought

she was going to throw herself over the body in a scene of hysterical grief, but she came instead to the front of the truck, stumbling into the rays of the headlights. Forsythe was in her way, but she pushed him aside and walked, with wild groping movements of her hands, up to Conrad.

For a moment she said nothing. She just stood glaring at him with demented eyes, her mouth trembling, her breath shuddering through her tense, frail-boned body. She started to say something but it choked in her throat, and suddenly she jerked round to face my father. " You . . ." she sobbed. " Why didn't somebody shoot *you* ? " My father said nothing; he looked at her dully, then closed his eyes and turned away.

Then she swung round again and screamed at Conrad, "And you—you, Conrad Webber. Oh, you smug swine. I know you killed her deliberately. You've been wanting to do it for years. Oh, you dirty murderer ! Don't stare at me like that—I know all about you. Yes, you've been hounding her for years. You pursued her and humiliated her and finally to-day was your big chance and you shot her."

" Just a minute. Ju-ust a minute," Forsythe was saying, holding her by the shoulder and turning her round. " Calm down and let me talk to you. I was there when it happened and I can tell you you're making a big mistake, honey."

" I'M NOT MAKING A MISTAKE ! " she yelled, wrenching herself away. " And he knows it. Go on, Conrad Webber, is this the truth or isn't it ? You've been her enemy for years, you got her tied up to this stinking cattle swill of a farm, and to-day, to help out your dear phoney friend here, you killed her. Is that the truth or isn't it ? "

" Nonsense," Conrad said, but so mildly that I turned to him in surprise. " It was an accident."

" An accident ? " She spat straight into the air. " Accident ? Who'll believe that ? You can rig it anyway you like, but you won't get away with *that*. I'm going to the police too. I'll tell them everything I know."

She started to laugh, gently but insanely, a queer, mirthless, empty laugh, with tears streaming down her cheeks.

" Come on now, Kiki," Forsythe said, putting his arm round her and trying to lead her away. " You've had a bad shock. Come back to the house and we'll get you a drink and put you to bed."

" A drink ? " she giggled.

" Yes, and get you to sleep. Come now, honey." He started to lead her back to the house.

" *I'm not finished*," she said, pulling herself violently away, the laughter abruptly gone. " I've got a few things to say to *him*." She stared accusingly at my father.

" Kiki . . ." my father said sharply.

" Yes, you, Jeremy Joe Latham ; you phoney lying fraud. You've also got a hand in this. She was too smart for you, she tripped you up beautifully over that copper deal, so you worked out an answer—kill. I think it's time people knew the truth about you, Jeremy Joe Latham. Sleeping with her . . ."

"SHUT UP ! " my father shouted.

" Sleeping with her for years—all that time in Johannesburg, and here at Malinda too, right under your wife's nose."

" She's out of her mind," my father said excitedly, turning to me. " She's raving."

" Oh, no, I'm not, you philandering hypocrite. You double-crossing jerk. Double-crossing your wife *and* her. Yes it's time people knew about you—especially your family. Especially your son here."

" I'll kill you, Kiki ! "

" Kill me ? Please do. I'd love you to kill me. That will make your score two in one day. That will make *certain* you'll swing. Gene, do you remember—— ? "

" Please, Kiki, don't ! " my father begged desperately.

" Do you remember when you were living in Johannesburg, in that nice house up on the hill ? Well, you're a big boy now and you're old enough to face the truth. Your daddy was having a tender love affair with his boss's wife all that time in Johannesburg . . ."

In a daze I heard my father, " Kiki, stop this, stop this ! " and Conrad who had come out of the truck saying, " This isn't fair," and Kiki snarling, " Stop snivelling, both of you." She went on, " Do you want to know why you came to Rhodesia ? Because Jordan found out and punished your dear daddy by sending him here. Unfortunately all of you had to be punished —your mum, your sister, and you—because you belonged to his darling family. Yes, Gene, that's why you've grown up as a country lad, to pay for your daddy's unfaithfulness to your mummy."

" Kiki "—my father was standing in front of her with his fist raised—" if you say one more word I'll smash you. I mean it."

" Please smash me," she said, raising her chin towards his fist. " I'd love that. Hit me, cave man. I'm waiting."

" Oh, my God," my father groaned, dropping his hands. He gave me a look of desolate misery. Suddenly he squeezed up his eyes and walked stumbling across the garden.

" And you remember that time after Jordan died, and Lavinia used to come and visit you every few weeks ? Well, that was *it* again. Love . . ."

" Go to bloody hell," I said, swinging round and starting to walk away. She grabbed my arm and held me with a tense strength that I never thought could exist in those thin hands.

" And then he let her down. He suddenly discovered that he loved his family. His family—*pooh*. You make me want to vomit. Do you wonder why Lavinia hated him. He smashed up her life. That's your daddy for you."

I wrenched my arm out of her grip and hurried away.

" What do you think of your dear daddy now, Gene ? " she called after me.

" You WHORE ! " I yelled back.

I walked about in the garden not knowing where I was going, and with a feeling that I had never experienced before. I felt lost and totally confused, in the frantic desperate way of people who lose their bearings in the bush at night. It seemed as if in some nightmare transformation the whole landscape around me had changed out of recognition. No situations, no people, were the same as those I knew before. I was utterly alone. Kiki's voice, the things she had said, my father's desperate pleading, Conrad's ominous lack of protest—these I hardly thought about, for my brain reverberated with the sound of Conrad's shot from behind the stone wall—the sudden instantaneous uproar, ripping a wide shrieking hole in the silent air, and destroying not only Lavinia but my whole world.

I saw Kiki walk from the truck to the house. She went briskly with firm steps. The hysteria had subsided after her outburst, but I could sense the determined fury in her walk. She started to go up the steps but changed her mind and went across to Lavinia's station wagon instead. She got in, started the engine and turned the car around, and as the lights dipped into the ravine I knew that our torture had only started. She was driving to the Retreat to tell my mother.

My first impulse was to get into the jeep and follow her, but I knew in the next instant that I could not be there to witness my mother's humiliation.

For the next fifteen minutes I wandered about the garden trying to marshal my thoughts. I was still convinced that it was an accident. That part of her outburst I did not believe, for I had been at the scene, and knew that the evidence was overwhelming that it was not a deliberate killing. But the rest was true—nobody had denied it. Besides, it fitted in with everything I knew about Malinda. Doubts and enigmas that had haunted me for more than half my life could be explained now. We had lived with this secret putrefying in the ground under our feet, yet without knowing its true nature I had always suspected it was there. Kiki had not invented this. I refused to think of my father, or how I ought to feel about him now. I could not think of the future, in the sense of something that grew out of the past, for there was not one. That one shot of Conrad's had blasted the past out of existence and the future was unchartered and incalculable. I felt alone in a way I had never known before. Deserted, like a man marooned on an island.

Yet I wanted to talk to somebody. The loneliness that had

come over me was terrifying, and I wanted to reach back into the ruins of the past, to try and salvage for myself something of the last two weeks that had been the happiest of my life.

I thought of looking for Marjorie, to explain, excuse, just to talk in order to break down this intolerable loneliness. I went up to the house and down the passage to her room. I could hear her inside—going from the wardrobe to the bed, folding things in tissue paper, opening drawers. But I could not raise my hand to knock on the door. I would not know what to say to her. Our love affair had ended in the greenish gloom of the hut—destroyed by both of us out of terror that it would grow too possessive, monstrous and destructive. I could not ask anything of Marjorie now—no favours, privileges or consideration. Nor could I offer her any.

Dimly I sensed that she had helped me through a crisis that was part of the general crisis of Malinda. Vaguely I knew that my love for her might revive one day in a new setting and atmosphere, like an ember in a heap of ashes starting a new fire with fresh fuel. I was full of conflicting emotions about her. I hated her for tricking me. I felt a bitter regret that the affair had started, but was desolate and lonely now that it was over. I felt a chilling coldness towards her, yet a gnawing fear that I would miss her and be plagued by this forlorn affliction for years to come. I longed for one more day to make the affair end differently, but realised that it could not have ended in any other way. I was too confused and uncertain about what would happen if I knocked on the door and faced, in this mood, the ordeal of trying to say good-bye.

I listened for a few moments as she packed her things to leave Malinda in the morning. Then I turned and went down the passage out of the house.

Outside I found Bill Secker and Forsythe talking on the lawn just below the veranda. They seemed unaware of Conrad who was listening to them from a short distance away. Behind Conrad, standing in the shadow, was Ruth ; and my father was standing near Conrad's truck, his hand on the door-handle, facing Bill and Forsythe and also listening to the conversation.

Bill was in a different mood now. The blundering anger had left him and he seemed merely bewildered. He was very talkative and his slow croaking voice appeared to come from all over the lawn. He sounded desperately anxious to convince Forsythe of his innocence in the affair.

" God, I had no idea," he was saying. " Honest to God, if I'd known what you were thinking I'd have come right out to Crampton after you. What a stupid bloody all-round balls-up." He kept pulling a yellow silk handkerchief out of his breast pocket to mop the sweat on his high pink forehead and mash between his beefy fingers. " What a ridiculous bloody balls-up."

" So that was the stunt—a survey ? " Forsythe asked in an astonished voice.

" Precisely. Not a full-scale job, naturally. There wasn't time for that. All we did was lay down some markers and show them in a plan. But we needed the surveyor out here. And the lawyer chap too, naturally." Looking around blankly, he carefully folded the handkerchief and tucked it back into his pocket.

" So *that's* why everybody was yanked off to Crampton Falls ? " Forsythe asked.

" Exactly—to get them out of the way. You see this place was never properly surveyed before. We simply never got round to it, that's all, because between us and the Lathams there was never any bull about boundaries and what have you. We just let it ride. But this attorney chap said there would have to be a proper contract with a proper diagram showing exactly what portion she was to get. You see, some of the copper lies on the Dale side, and some on the Malinda side . . ." He stopped breathless.

" Bill," Forsythe asked, puzzled, " when did you have time to see a lawyer ? "

" Yesterday afternoon. I took a run over to Umtali to make the arrangements—buy air tickets, luggage, and so on, and have a word with this lawyer."

" So *that's* where you went when you did a flip out of Dale yesterday ? " Ruth said aggressively from the shadows.

" Oh, pipe down," Bill said, making a little swatting movement with his hand in her direction. " Keep out of this." He turned to Forsythe again. " That's the whole lark—honestly. The lawyer said we needed a diagram and when it was ready I was to bring Lavinia into town and sign the deal. But when I got back here she didn't like the idea. She was jittery over something and didn't want to wait. So late last night we took a run over to Umtali to get the deal signed, meaning to do the diagram stunt later."

" Do you mean to say that when I was chasing you across the bundu in all that stinking rain last night you were going to see a *lawyer* ? " Ruth asked incredulously.

Bill glowered at her, but looked exasperated rather than menacing. " Oh, go home," he said. " This is none of your business."

" Bill Secker, I could slit your throat ! " Ruth said, coming out of the dark and standing next to Forsythe. " You try to ditch me for a flossy jazzed-up tart and it's none of my business ? "

" Oh, save it for later, you two," Forsythe said. Then to Bill, " You mean you actually drove all that way back just to sign a contract ? "

" Yes. We woke up this attorney chap and he typed out something—a sort of interim thing—which we signed there and then. But he still wanted a diagram, so he said he'd come out with the full contract in the morning, and at the same time bring out a surveyor. That was the plan. I was to meet them at the Bell to show them the way into the bush. So I drove Lavinia back here and left straight away for the Bell to wait for them. That's all there was to it. The stunt was to get everybody off the place. We didn't want any noscy Joes asking questions and trying to interfere."

" Trying to talk you out of it, you mean," Ruth said, with a snorting laugh. " She had you taped all right. She knew damn' well that if Conrad or Joe or I got at you while you were busy on this phoney survey you wouldn't have had the bare-faced nerve to go through with it. Maybe too, we might have shown you what a gibbering baboon you were making of yourself. Or that you were buying yourself a packet of trouble big enough to bury you. That woman was going to twist you —the whore."

" CHIM—SHUT UP ! If you don't stop that fat mouth of yours I'll slam you, so help me. The woman's dead. If you say one more word like that I'll let you have it ! "

" Not this time, you won't. I'd plug you before you could lift a hand." She was talking in a hard, cutting voice but standing casually with her hand in her trouser pocket. Maybe she had a pistol there ; I couldn't tell.

" Not here," Forsythe said, coming between them and holding them apart with open palms, like a referee separating boxers. " No shootin' allowed on the lawn. It's agin the bye-laws. Keep it till you get him home."

" She's always got to throw the whole bucketful," Bill said sullenly.

" Don't tell me," Forsythe said. " But that's dames . . . So you were saying you went back to the Bell to wait for this surveyor and law merchant and show them the way through ? "

" Precisely. I met them later in the morning and brought them out here. By then everybody had left for Crampton. They did the job and went away just before the crowd came back. All according to plan. So, as I was telling you, it was nothing, really—a storm in a teacup." Nobody gasped at this most breathtaking understatement of all time. Bill looked around with a where-am-I-and-what's-happened expression, then flipped out the handkerchief and had another ceremonial mop up.

" And that's the whole story ? "

" Yes, except that we were going to fly to London in the morning. Sort of a——"

" Honeymoon ? " Ruth suggested.

" Sort of a holiday until things quietened down here.

Only "—his hand went to his pocket and pulled out a travel agent's wallet—" what am I going to do with these?" he asked, easing two air tickets out with his thumb.

"Get a refund," Forsythe said airily.

"Yes, maybe if I explain . . ." Bill mused, tapping the wallet against his thumb.

"What *will* you explain?" Ruth asked mercilessly.

Bill looked at her defiantly. She held his look and he dropped his eyes, embarrassed. But suddenly he stared at her again, this time with the sheepish expression of a guilty schoolboy.

Conrad had joined them now. Speaking very seriously, he said, "Do you happen to have a copy of the contract you signed last night at Umtali?"

"Sure," Bill said, fishing in his pocket and pulling out a wad of typewritten papers. "You mean the one we actually signed?"

"Yes."

Bill picked out a single sheet of paper and passed it over. Conrad glanced at it. "And the diagram?" he asked, holding out his hand.

"Sure." Bill gave him that too.

Conrad perched his glasses on his nose, moved into the light and studied the two documents carefully. He peered at the green and pink wash drawing of the diagram, then held it behind the typewritten contract and read the sparse and hastily typed clauses.

"Dead loss," Bill said, watching him. "Might as well chuck them away now."

Conrad glanced up but said nothing. He studied the diagram again, then the signatures to the document very carefully, tilting it into the light and adjusting his spectacles, and holding it at arm's length in that long-sighted way of his. At last he handed both papers back to Bill. "Thanks," he said, then added, "You'd better hang on to these. This is a binding contract."

"What?" Bill said at the same moment as Ruth asked, "Between who?"

" Between Bill and Mrs. Whittaker's estate. Her executor will be obliged to enforce this."

" Just a minute," Ruth said angrily. " You mean even though she's dead . . ."

" The benefits of this contract fall into her estate," Conrad interrupted her.

" So Malinda's gone anyway ? Oh, come off it, you're joking. You can't mean it," Ruth said, gazing at him with the strained smiling expression of one whose credulity has been stretched beyond its limit.

" I do mean it. I've never been more serious in my life."

" Are you trying to say that some bloody little twerp of an heir who's probably never been within two miles of a live steer is going to get a present of Malinda ? "

" Very likely," Conrad told her dryly. " All her relatives are in England, and I doubt if any of them are farmers."

" Give me that thing," Ruth demanded, holding out her hand to Bill. Bill, without taking his amazed eyes off Conrad, handed her the contract.

" To hell with her executor," Ruth said, tearing the document into shreds and tossing them over her shoulder.

Conrad watched her without a smile. " I'm afraid that won't help," he said. " There must be copies of that document."

" That's correct," Bill said glumly. " The attorney's got them—one for his office files and the other for Lavinia."

" For her executor," Conrad corrected, walking away.

I stood rooted to the ground, feeling the numb shame of total defeat. Bill's one wild aberrant day of romance had cost us Malinda. The long feud had ended, with both sides vanquished.

I heard Bill say, " I'd better take a run into Umtali and try to get a refund on these tickets."

And Ruth, " I'm going to make a proposal, Bill. Cash in one and keep the other. Take that trip—you'll still make it in time for the English racing season—and if you want any money just cable me. Then when you return, perhaps we can talk things over."

I saw Bill replace the tickets in his pocket, his hand moving absent-mindedly because he was turning over the suggestion and beginning to bite on it. One could see his thoughts roaming all over his big bewildered face.

" I'll think about it," he said, and I knew then that their troubles were over for it was obvious that he had done all the thinking he ever would. " Yes, I'll consider that."

I had heard Ruth say in that bossy, assertive yet kindly way that I knew so well from countless hours spent in their company. " But when you come back, don't bring me any flipping French perfume, or chorus girl's underwear, or fiddly little bits of jewellery. If you want to buy me a present, make it a good English saddle ; or a decent shotgun. I'll treat it the same way as a new wedding ring. If not . . ." She shrugged. " Well, save the money."

Bill didn't answer. He looked vague but not unhappy. But one could hardly expect more in the circumstances. Lucky Bill —saved by the gong once again. He was one of those whose luck ran in a clear unbroken streak right through their lives.

21

I COULD NOT GO HOME while Kiki was there. I told myself
that my mother would prefer me not to be there, that my
presence would only make it more agonising for her, but it was
probably only my cowardice that kept me from going home.
I was flooded with shame, a profound wretchedness that ex-
tinguished all decent feelings in me. I hated everybody who had
anything to do with this loathsome affair—even my mother.
I wanted to turn away from it, to hide in a dark room, to blot
it out of my memory. I had no desire to help anybody, to
sympathise, to find explanations, or express regret. I felt my
father's shame impressed on my skin like a cattle brand. I used
to think that it was Lavinia's mark that we all carried at
Malinda, but now I saw that it was a different kind of stigma.

I was in an anguish of conflicting feelings. I was desperately
sorry for my father, yet felt a hard, icy contempt that made it
impossible for me to go near him. I avoided looking at him
and just mooned about in the garden pondering over what I
was going to say to my mother when I eventually summoned
the courage to go home. I tried to work out sentences, but
rejected them one after the other, because they sounded so
melodramatic, or phoney, or precious or hypocritical.

At last I saw Kiki come back from the Retreat, swinging the
station wagon wildly through the gates and pulling up with a
skid below the veranda. She got out leaving the door open,
but she turned back and bumped it closed with a playful jerk
of her behind. She was happy now, in a skittish, light-headed
fashion. She came up the steps walking fussily and humming
something. As she passed I caught a glimpse of the savage glee

336

in her eyes and the sick, simpering grin on her face. She had done her last favour for Lavinia, and done it well.

I saw my father sitting inside the jeep, his rifle propped on the seat beside him, his hunting-hat pushed back off his head and on to his shoulders, held that way by the strap around his neck. He made a move as if to start the engine, but changed his mind and just sat still, hesitating, as I thought, before driving home to the Retreat for his cruellest ordeal.

But suddenly the door swung open and he got out, carrying his rifle. He stood looking around, as if not quite sure what to do, then abruptly started walking towards Bill's long grey Jaguar. He peered inside, opened the door and placed the rifle on the passenger seat. He looked around again, quickly this time—I could see the live flash in his eyes—then slipped in under the steering-wheel and drove away. Bill swung round as the car moved off. " Hey, where are you going ? " he shouted. " Hey, Joe ! " Then his hands sunk to his sides. " Well, what the hell ! "

My father did not stop at the Retreat. He went right past, the big yellow fog-lamps carving a tunnel into the night along the crude road that led out of Malinda to the main road, the Bell Hotel . . . Umtali . . .

" Gene ! "

I looked around to see where the voice came from.

" *Gene!* "—urgently now. It was Conrad. I saw him standing with his foot on the step of the truck, his hand holding the rung above his head. I hurried down. " Get in—quick," he said, swinging himself up into the cabin. I ran to the other side and lurched into the seat just as the truck pulled away.

" What's the matter ? "

" Everything's the matter. We've got to stop him."

" Why ? Where's he going ? "

" I don't know. But this is serious. We mustn't let him get away."

" For God's sake tell me what's the matter."

" I shall in a moment. Let's get on to some good road first."

We whooshed down into the ravine, swerved and bounced

around the snake bends, roared out on to the road at the top
and sped after the crimson tail light now flittering away into
the distance. The wind had come up, thrashing the trees
around us, whirling dust and leaves across the track and
spattering the window with the first heavy drops of the coming
storm. We hurtled along the loose sandy track, hanging on to
the bobbing spot of light that seemed to scribble a tangled red
design on the glass, but after a while we could see the light
only intermittently, when he was on higher ground, or when
sparse bush separated us. He was driving dangerously.

I was frightened. I wanted Conrad to tell me what it was
all about but he kept stubbornly absorbed with the driving,
his eyes fixed on the ground ahead, his sturdy gingery elbows
working like a boxer's to control the agitated steering-wheel.

" Aren't you going to tell me ? "

" I said I would." We came to a stream, plunged down the
bank at a slant and used the momentum to hurtle up the other
side. He righted the truck, picked up speed, drove on a little
farther and then said, " I'm going to tell you everything. Please
try to take it calmly." He spoke testily, as if I had been making
a nuisance of myself by persisting with the question. Raising
his voice, he said, " What hap . . . happened . . . That Pape
woman . . . was raving . . . some of it was ridiculous . . . but
it's true that . . . he . . . thrown out of the . . . Wait a minute."

It was impossible. The track was so bad I could hardly hear
him. He drove on until the jolting subsided, then said suddenly,
in a harsh voice that for some reason I found preferable to any
sweet sympathy at that moment, " What happened to-day is a
disaster for him. He'll probably go to gaol."

" What ? " I gasped. I didn't understand him at first. I was
thinking primitively, grappling with one thing at a time and
the nearest thing first. " You mean because of this shooting
affair ? "

" No." He waited for a shudder to die out of the steering-
wheel. " Because of that affair in Johannesburg. He's in
trouble. *Serious* trouble."

" Trouble ? " I repeated glumly and then to myself I said,

" My God," and suddenly remembered that awful night at the Bell Hotel when Una Cameron told him of the rumours that were going the rounds—that he was in trouble or heading for trouble or trouble was heading for him. Now we were right back in that fevered atmosphere.

" Yes, trouble," Conrad said. " *Old* trouble that's been locked away in a bank vault for ten years. Now, because of the contract . . ." A crunch and lurch as the wheel cracked a log lying in our path. " Between Bill . . . and her . . ." A violent scraping.

" It comes out of the safe," I suggested.

" Yes."

He said nothing for a moment. His eyes flicked round to catch my reaction. Then he said, " As long . . . as he . . . st-stayed . . ."—a fresh bout of violent jolting—"stayed on Malinda . . ." Further conversation was impossible. He gave up trying to talk and attended to the driving until we reached a spot where the track from Malinda forked into the more frequently used one from Dale. From here on the going was easier.

Now the speed of both vehicles increased, and as we settled down to the steady, gruelling chase he relaxed his shoulders and told me the rest. But he spoke in a terse level voice that tried to keep his remarks as impersonal as possible. " That trouble in Johannesburg was more than just a love affair. It involved a crime. I know about it because I was briefed by the Whittaker Organisation to straighten out the confusion afterwards. I should mention too that I knew both Jordan and Lavinia even before that. I knew them, in fact, before they knew each other."

He leaned forward and pulled the knob to start the windshield wipers. The last remark seemed to hover in the air, waiting, to the noisy rhythm of the wipers. There seemed to be something hidden behind the remark but when he went on he did not elaborate.

" You might remember that Lavinia became a figure in the Whittaker Organisation. Jordan drew her into his business

activities, used her as a front for deals, even had her appointed
to the boards of some of his companies . . ."

Yes, I remembered. Even as a child I knew this from all
those newspaper pictures. Mrs. Lavinia Whittaker in a
summery frock and wide garden hat, looking attractively
startled as she smashed a bottle of champagne against the steel
girders of a new mine head-gear. Mrs. Lavinia Whittaker with
a gorgeous welcoming smile shaking hands with visiting
industrialists at the airport. Mrs. Lavinia Whittaker sparkling
with diamonds at a banquet for the Minister of Mines—bringing the kind of glamour to the affairs of the Whittaker Organisation that the Royal Family did to public occasions.

" It was *his* way of showing affection—yes, he doted on her.
But for all that he kept her short of funds. He gave her a life
of luxury but paid all her bills himself. Well . . . I won't
dwell on this. . . . She met your father and they fell in love.
Hopelessly in love. Foolish as it was, it was a touching
romance." I glanced at him to try and detect some sign of
mockery in his face for there was none in his voice. But I saw
no evidence of it, and heard him go on. " They planned to
run away, to get married if they could arrange divorces . . ."

" Do you have to tell me all this ? " I asked, finding it
intolerable. I did not want to hear this rigmarole. I knew
enough without it, and what I knew I wanted to forget.

" Sooner or later this story is going to catch up with you."

" Then can't we leave it until another time ? "

" No."

I listened with a mixture of prickly discomfort and
apprehension as he went on, " Lavinia had been poor once,
and was determined not to let it happen again. So she began
thinking of ways to use her position in the Organisation to get
her hands on some money. Real money. Her opportunity
came when Jordan went overseas for a business trip."

I thought I heard the engine of the Jag—a brief choked-off
roar and a series of sharp bursts.

" Let's hope he gets stuck," I said, glad to be able to talk
of something else.

" Our best chance."

I rolled the window down and listened for the engine but didn't hear it again. Probably some minor trouble crossing a stream; the car was on its way again. Now it was a pleasure to hear the regular swish of the wipers and the sloshing of the tyres, instead of Conrad's voice.

But he went on. " Her chance came when Jordan left for that overseas trip. Using his scrip and his credit with the brokers she started dealing in the stock market. Nobody questioned it; she was Mrs. Lavinia Whittaker. At first it looked as if she would be spectacularly successful. She concentrated on one particular group of shares—those of a new gold-mining company in which your father had supervised the bore-hole drilling. There was a phenomenal assay result and the shares boomed. She was all set for a killing—and then Jordan returned unexpectedly. Alerted by these unusual share dealings, he soon found out about the love affair itself. But he didn't confront them. He didn't force a showdown that would have made him look ridiculous as an aged cuckolded husband. And naturally he couldn't hand Lavinia over to the police for raiding his assets to finance this little romp. Instead, like the wily fox he was, he started playing the market against her. As soon as she tried to unload her shares, he released his own, forcing her to buy them in to protect the price. She tried again and again, and each time he simply deluged the market with shares. The shares crashed, the company was ruined. It was extraordinary—a financier deliberately engineering the bankruptcy of his own wife—but it was a brilliant stroke. As it turned out he caught both of them in the same net. Not only had he safely rounded in Lavinia, but your father was in special difficulties that were only discovered afterwards. That assay result was fraudulent. The samples had been tampered with."

" Do you mean he salted a gold mine ? " I asked, really astonished now, although I had told myself that nothing would ever surprise me again.

" No. He signed a confession saying he did, but I have never believed it. As you can imagine, with so many important names involved, many things were suppressed. But I studied the case exhaustively and formed my own conclusions. Lavinia used to visit him at the mine. It stood on the open veld a few hundred miles out of Johannesburg. She would come out, driven by Mac . . ."

" Mac ? "

" Yes, he was her chauffeur. He knew everything—about all the times and places where they met—and about the salting. They found a bottle containing a few grains of powdered gold —the kind used to doctor the samples—in the glove cabinet of the car. Only *he* used the front section."

His voice died away. He was leaning forward for a better view through the window, his foot stroking the accelerator to coax out a little more speed.

" Yes ? "

He didn't answer. Then I, too, looked out, peering past the rain streaking into our lights, and saw the Jag near the top of a long hill rising before us. It had stopped. The lights were not moving, and I could tell from the fact that I saw both front and back lights that it was straddled across the road.

But just as our lights spread up over the long grey torpedo shape, it pulled out of trouble. I saw the tyres get a grip on the road, the car reverse, swing into position and shoot off with mud spraying out under the leather flaps on the mudguards.

We plunged after it, mile on mile, over the foul pulped-up mess of a road, hanging on to that red tail light, keeping it the same size and hence the same distance in front, skidding and slithering with controlled recklessness in a nerve-jangling race in which neither car could gain or lose a yard. We just churned endlessly and agonisingly after that twisting, teasing red light pinned like a firework on the black cloth of the night.

Then suddenly it disappeared. It blacked out—simply that —but a few moments later we caught a brief flash of lights through the trees on our right. It had swung off the track. Moments later we reached the same spot. I recognised it as the junction of a detour over a strip of exposed rock that cut a narrow corridor five miles long through the bush. I knew the detour well. We never used it in good weather for it was torture to the springs and tyres, but in rain that long mud-free surface was a blessing.

Conrad saw it too, but a moment too late. He tried to swing off but he pulled the truck into a skid. We spun round wildly, three full circles, then skated backwards and crashed into a bank.

We got out and saw the truck lying with its belly resting on a mound of sand, its wheels spinning slowly and idiotically in the air. We stood in the rain, saying nothing, but feeling sick with frustration at the sight both of the stranded truck and the red light disappearing with a sudden new turn of speed along the narrow stone avenue through the bush.

We jacked it up, jammed branches under the wheels and at last got the truck back on to the road. But when we moved off the Jag was gone. We followed the same route, straining for every ounce of speed over the punishing, bone-jolting rock surface, but we never saw it again. At last we came out at the main road. There we stopped and got out to look for the tracks —there were none.

Puzzled, we got into the truck and drove slowly back along the same route, scanning the ground to find the point where he turned off. But it was hopeless. We searched for over an hour, but the last sign of the tracks was at the beginning of the detour. Somewhere along that five-mile stretch he had swung off into the bush. We tried driving back and forth with the searchlight aimed into the trees and sounding the horn. But we couldn't find him, and at last we simply had to give it up.

Most of the time we didn't speak. I tried not to think about my father. The idea that had formed was too awful to contemplate and I tried to push it back into the black shadows of my mind. I had little doubt now what the chase was about.

We drove home slowly, and at last Conrad took up the story again. I listened with the strange feeling of knowing it all in advance. For, although the facts were new to me I had lived with this story for years, and every aspect of it had made an impression of some kind on our lives at Malinda. All Conrad did was strip off the disguises that had enabled this aged old scandal to migrate with us to Rhodesia, and stalk unrecognised through the years there.

"Mac had something to do with the salting. But it was unlikely that he would have done it alone, or have had access to the samples without help. Besides, he had nothing to gain. Your father confessed—but if *he* did it what need did he have of Mac? And why did Jordan send Mac to Rhodesia? You can guess who was behind it. . . ."

He gave me a sidelong look, with a half-smile that rammed home the point more effectively than the mention of a name could have done. I nodded, reflecting on the bitter fruits of this once gallant act of love.

"With that document, Jordan had power over your father for the rest of his life. He used it to send him here—to exile and punishment—and to keep him here. For he undertook to lock it away in a bank vault and not use it as long as your father remained at Malinda. It became the weapon of revenge. . . ."

He went on to explain, but he needn't have. I saw it all for myself—why nothing could persuade my father to get out and try something better even in the most hopeless and desperate times, why Jordan could make him squirm for that money he promised but never intended to pay, why he could keep Malinda just short of bankruptcy and make my father work to no purpose and sweat and writhe and suffer for years on end. He had made Malinda into a prison, and at the same time a scene for the sadistic pleasure he got out of seeing my father's humiliation—and Lavinia's too. Yes, I saw that. This was the reason he was unable to resist bringing her out for those holidays which seemed so pointless and miserable for everybody. But for Jordan these were *real* holidays. He got the keenest delight out of the tensions and hidden agonies it caused Lavinia and my father to be thrown together for weeks at a time on a lonely ranch, under the constant stare of those oily gloating septuagenarian eyes. At last I understood why he had been so frantic with worry when he got the court decree. He *dared* not lose Malinda. And why he had been so childishly and exuberantly happy over the deal with the Seckers—it had saved his life. Or so he thought.

" When Jordan died there was still no escape. In fact, his death made the position worse than ever for both of them. After the crisis he made a new will that practically disinherited Lavinia ; all it did was tie her down to Malinda too. That will added a new twist—it was subtle and cunning. By making Lavinia's income dependent on how much your father earned at Malinda, he created a situation that was certain to degenerate into quarrelling and hatred. He made it impossible for them to escape from each other or from Malinda. The will kept them tied up together like a cat and a snake in a sack."

Some of these subtleties were beyond me, especially as I remembered the time immediately after Jordan's death when Lavinia had been only kind and generous towards our family. The " Friendship Years," as I called that period, when she paid us all those visits and gave us presents and left her money in the ranch, and did everything possible to help Malinda get on its feet. I reminded Conrad of this.

" It was because she expected the affair to resume after Conrad's death. She was still in love with your father ; in fact, this was the one real love in her life of many affairs and adventures. She had gone back to Jordan waiting only for the day he died so that she could take up the affair again. But by then too many things had changed. Your parents had found a new life out here, in spite of the hardships ; your father discovered a sense of responsibility he had lacked before, your mother a new strength that gave a totally different meaning to your home and family. So eventually your father decided to end the affair. That was why she turned so bitter and vengeful. She had ruined her life over him ; that Pape woman was right. Now Lavinia had to accept defeat at the hands of your mother —it was a bitter humiliation. Her hatred of him grew until it became violent and reckless. But she could never escape from him. Jordan seemed to have foreseen it all."

" Yes," I said. " He seems to have taken care of everything." I remembered a previous occasion when I had made the same observation—that ominous ride back from the Bell Hotel, with my father sitting in torment beside me and the drought-stricken country unfolding before us. " He's taken care of me, all right," he had replied, and of course I had no way of know-ing the depths of defeat that the remark implied. All it did was remind me of Lavinia's words when shown the samples of copper ore—" Now I'm going to get out of the noose that Jordan tried to throttle me with." That, too, I did not under-stand fully, but I saw now how apt it was to link the two remarks.

" Just why did she bring Mac into the hunt ? " I asked as we were nearing home.

" Nobody will know for certain. She must have had a reason, but whatever it was it has died with her. I have a feeling, however, that old Mac's lucky to be alive right now. It's obvious that she had forgotten about him until the last moment. It must have struck her only this morning that having got Malinda into her hands she was flying to England with Bill and leaving behind a witness who could wreck all her plans. Mac could incriminate her, if that confession was used in a prosecution against your father. I think she was planning to get rid of him. Early this morning she had a quarrel with Forsythe. He told me about it. Just before leaving she wanted to borrow his rifle. He told her that he had already delivered it to me. She then started looking around for her own rifle, but Forsythe told her that it, too, had been sent down to me. She got into a violent uncontrollable temper ; quite obviously this last unforeseen complication rattled her badly. I think she was reckless and desperate enough to think of getting him away from his kraal and disposing of him on the way back. That seems to have been in her mind when she decided to go and fetch him early this morning. It would not necessarily have been such a far-fetched idea. If she had said he attacked her in the car, tried to rape her perhaps, she might easily have got away with it. In any case, she couldn't simply leave him there, so she went to get him anyway. Perhaps her idea was to wait for the chance of a shot at him during the hunt. That, at any rate, was my theory. That's why I took the precaution of . . . well, detaching him from the rest of you at Crampton Falls. I did the same with your father and Forsythe—simply for good measure."

He said nothing for a while. We could see the lights of the Big House now—clearly nobody there thought of going to bed. The Retreat was in darkness.

22

THE NEXT DAY my father killed himself. There was no beautiful madness, no eruption of tragic passion to cloud his mind and relieve him of the harsh knowledge of what he was doing. Not even the Coroner could bring in the rider 'while of unsound mind "—although he wanted to, perhaps to ease our feeling, and had tried to find ground for it in my father's black moods of the previous few weeks. It was all too sane, and perhaps he had no choice. Perhaps in some circumstances committing suicide is the sanest and bravest and most dignified thing a man can do. I don't know. Even now, five years later, I'm still confused about this aspect. I have never been able to find the emotional detachment to judge properly.

He had given us the slip the previous night. He had waited in the bushes until we gave up the search, then had driven on to the Bell Hotel. But he did not sleep. The light was on all night ; and near dawn he decided what to do.

Police in a patrol van found him at the roadside about three miles from the Bell. The Jag was smashed—he had run it full tilt into a baobab—but he hadn't managed to kill himself that way, so he shot himself through the breast with his rifle, working it with his left arm because his right was broken. It was a curious mixed-up kind of death. It seemed as if he had wanted to make it look like an accident, but hadn't bothered to plan it very carefully. There were no skid marks showing that he had tried to avoid hitting the tree, and altogether no reason why he should have left the road in broad daylight at that point. He ended by shooting himself, anyway. And there was that suicide note.

The troopers came out to Malinda to break the news. They asked to see my mother, but I told them she had gone into town early that morning, not wanting to admit to anyone that she had packed up and left Malinda the previous night. So they broke it to me. I was alone in the house, for Conrad had gone back to the Big House to change his clothes. I did not want him in on this. The troopers knew my father, and while one of them told me about it the other stood at the window squeezing up his face to keep back the tears. It was a real tribute to my father, coming from policemen to whom death and bad news were routine matters. They took it worse than I did at first. I was still angry and bitter and resentful towards my father, and still too dazed by Lavinia's death and the events that had followed it so remorselessly. I heard the words in a kind of dry, exhausted painless dream.

But when I saw him I broke down. The troopers drove me out to the scene and I saw him—smashed, bloodied, finished—my father—a lifeless heap sprawled in the mud beside the smashed car. Bill's fancy luggage that he bought for his trip with Lavinia had spilled out of the car and lay strewn all around him. A great wave of grief overwhelmed me and I cried like a child. The troopers tactfully left me with him and went back and waited in the patrol van. As I looked at him all the love and tenderness that I had found so hard to express while he was alive poured out, too late, and I felt the first pangs of that desperate regret that was to torment me for years afterwards. The rifle was still in his hand, the handsome heavy Winchester that he had brought with him to Malinda ten years before. I took it from him, opening the tight fingers one by one. Then in a sudden rage I whirled it round my head and sent it flying far into the bushes. I listened for the crash, which was like shattering glass, and somehow felt a little better after it. I kneeled beside him, took his head on my lap and cleaned off the blood and mud with my handkerchief. He looked handsome in death and years, years younger. He looked relieved too. I thought then that I understood the argument for his suicide, for all the pain and strain and illness and sorrow had miraculously disappeared from his face. I straightened his eyebrows with my fingers and tidied his hair, then buttoned up the shirt that he had undone all the way down before turning the gun on himself. I noticed his right arm lying limp and crooked at his side. I went round and cut away the sleeve and probed the flesh with my thumbs, gently, as if he were alive. It was a double fracture and I had a sudden impulse to do one last thing for him. I set the bones very carefully, easing and manipulating the fractured ends into position, tied on a splint and bandage from the first-aid box that Bill kept in the car. After that I called the troopers and we carried him to the van and laid him in the back with a sail over him. I went back for one last look round and only then saw the letter stuck in the small flap window.

Dearest Gene,

I have pondered all night and now with bitter reluctance I have reached a decision. I detest having to do this. My life is still burning strongly within me. I loathe having to turn on myself, to make the last act of my life my own obliteration. But there is no other way.

Some people can outlive their mistakes. Others, like maimed animals, bear them permanently on their bodies and succumb to them in the end. I am like that. That has been my fate.

I cannot endure the future that faces me now. To stand shamed before my family, to lose my home and the ranch I strove so hard to establish, to face trial for an act I did not commit—these make up a burden too crushing to bear at this time of life. At this point I must, however reluctantly, accept defeat.

Please try to understand and if possible to forgive—for what I'm about to do and for the events of the past which I hope to take with me out of the world of living things. I will say only this in mitigation—I tried to make amends, to bring happiness to my family and find it for myself here at Malinda. But it was too late. My past hung like a millstone around my neck and made happiness impossible.

There will be much in this letter that you will not understand, but I am in no mind to go into details. I prefer, at this moment, not to think of my past actions that have suddenly reaped such a grim harvest. If at some future time you should wish to know more, ask Conrad. He knows what happened. He has been a splendid friend to me. Thank him.

I have addressed this note to you because I feel that what I have said here would only hurt your mother more if addressed to her. But I beg you to try and comfort her as best you can. I cannot frame any tender messages. I choke on my feelings as I write this. With all my heart I am sorry for what I did to her—I loved her and desperately regret that much of the love due to her was squandered so senselessly on another.

Peggy's life is opening out now. I wish her all the happiness that eluded me. Try to help her too, to get over this.

I see the dawn coming up over the hills. I must set a time and a manner for this, otherwise it won't be done.

Good-bye. . . .

But he hadn't signed it.

I climbed into the van next to the troopers and we set out for Umtali to report the death and make arrangements for the funeral.

I looked back several times at the shrouded shape behind me. It was impossible to believe that this was my father in the back, that he was dead, or that anything unusual had happened. Nothing was real.

Last night was a lie. So was yesterday, all of it, from the time I walked with my father into the dawn and heard him say that Lavinia had found out the secret of his deal with the Seckers, to the frantic chase in the mud last night and Conrad's relentless unfolding of the ten-year-old chronical of betrayal and misfortune that had snared our lives like a steel trap. It was a dream, and what proved it was that only last night I had sat through a long, slow drive with another wrapped-up body behind me. Such freakish things only happened in dreams. There was no such day as yesterday; no such time as now. It was an hallucination—something conjured by Cigarettes out of fever and demons, omens and black curses.

Exhausted I sank back and resigned myself to the drive. I did not want to look round now—neither at the shape beneath the canvas, nor at the past receding from me like the shore from the stern of a ship. There was much to be done. I would find my mother, get in touch with Peggy in Salisbury, and break the news to them. Together we would bury the long years in my father's grave. I would see that he had a proper funeral. Settlers would come from all over in their dusty trucks and Land-Rovers. And storekeepers, patrolmen, road engineers— country people of all kinds. Kamba would bring a truckload of people from the village, all in their stiff Sunday best. His friends would not hold it against him how he died. His credit was still good in the district.

After that I would return to Malinda and make arrangements to hand over to the new owner. But first I would perform an act of ritual cleansing. It would not make sense at the University, but it would be what Cigarettes would have advised. I would take my rifle, climb up to the Finger, and lie in wait for that leopard.